AND THEN SHE SAW THE SPECTER . . .

On the pathway stood a charger as white as milk, even to its eyes and the linings of its ears and nostrils. Astride it sat a man just as devoid of color. His trim hair and forked beard, styled in a cut fashionable some generations before, were deep, solid ivory. His limbs and clothing were shaped of lighter shades of pale. Even his lively and laughing eyes were pearl touched with cream and snow.

Removing his hat from his head, he bowed deeply, saluting Rabble with the fluttering plume before returning the hat to its jaunty pearch atop his head.

"My lady," he said, "a pleasant, if somewhat damp evening, is it not?"

"It is wet," Rabble said, cheerfully, "though not as wet as earlier. In any case, the rain seems to have little effect on you."

"No." The rider stroked the horse along the curve of its elegant neck. "We are rather beyond wet since we have become . . . this way."

"'T[...]e?" Rabble aske[...]

"Th[...]Dead."

Avon Books are available at special quantity discounts for bulk purchases for sales promotions, premiums, fund raising or educational use. Special books, or book excerpts, can also be created to fit specific needs.

For details write or telephone the office of the Director of Special Markets, Avon Books, Dept. FP, 1350 Avenue of the Americas, New York, New York 10019, 1-800-238-0658.

WHEN THE GODS ARE SILENT

JANE LINDSKOLD

AVON BOOKS • NEW YORK

This is a work of fiction. Names, characters, places and incidents either are the product of the author's imagination or are used fictitiously. Any resemblance to actual events, locales, organizations, or persons, living or dead, is entirely coincidental and beyond the intent of either the author or the publisher.

AVON BOOKS
A division of
The Hearst Corporation
1350 Avenue of the Americas
New York, New York 10019

Copyright © 1997 by Jane Lindskold
Cover art by Gary Ruddell
Published by arrangement with the author
Visit our website at **http://AvonBooks.com**
Library of Congress Catalog Card Number: 96-95168
ISBN: 0-380-78848-9

First Avon Books Printing: June 1997

AVON TRADEMARK REG. U.S. PAT. OFF. AND IN OTHER COUNTRIES, MARCA REGISTRADA, HECHO EN U.S.A.

Printed in the U.S.A.

WCD   10 9 8 7 6 5 4 3 2 1

For David Weber—a good friend despite the miles.

Thanks to Susan for the loan of hair, eyes, and freckles.
And special thanks to Nuada for introducing me to Gimp.

1

'Ware the gaze of a one-eyed man,
'Ware the skip of a one-legged lass,
'Ware all things too good to be true,
A Power may be watching.

Downs proverb

BLOOD BEADED from the slash cut in the red-haired warrior's cheekbone. Sun glinting off his sword, the blond warrior's attacker spun about. Then the redhead dove clear, rolling, her own sword rising to parry. A roar rose from the crowd leaning into the ropes around the sand-pit as they urged their champion in for the win.

"Bryax! Bryax! Bryax!"

Tombstone-square teeth bared, blond Bryax slashed out again, heartened by the crowd's feral cheers. But off to one side of the sand-pit arena, seated high in the driver's box of a brightly painted wagon, two fat and oily men looked at each other and exchanged luck signs.

"Bryax is done for, Tambor," said the fatter, an olive-skinned man named Rylus. He stroked the stylish curls of his chestnut-brown hair.

"I fear so," agreed Tambor, a plump man with skin the color of old ivory, silver-shot ebony hair, and dark, slanting eyes. "Not one who has drawn our Rabble's blood has stood after to boast of it. Good thing news travels slowly these days—before the Loss you would have been hard put to get decent odds for the betting."

"True," Rylus said cheerfully. "Now, dear Tambor, would you care to wager on how many blows before Bryax falls?"

"No," Tambor chuckled dryly, toying with an earring in the shape of a tiny gold monkey that swung from his earlobe. "Our Rabble is like a hero from the days before magic vanished from the world. The only thing that I would predict is that burly blond Bryax will fall."

Below, the crowd's roar was fading to astonishment as an enraged Rabble beat at their favorite. The woman eschewed all but the flat of her copper-colored blade, most of her blows coming from pummelling hands and slight, bare feet.

Burly Bryax's confident composure vanished. His sweat mixed with the thin rivulets of blood that streamed from his nose, the corner of his mouth, the knuckles of one hand. Weakly, he waved his sword in an ineffectual parry, but his skill no more stopped his opponent than a stick waved through a fire stops the flames.

Solidly, Rabble's leg flew out, her foot hitting just below Bryax's kneecap. As he crumpled, she spun and brought her blade's flat around, knocking him to fall on his back. He did not rise. As one, the crowd stepped back from the arena, eyeing the lightly panting woman with ugly fear.

"Quickly, Tambor! Bring back your bears and monkeys before we have a riot," Rylus ordered.

"Aye," Tambor leapt down. "I'll distract them. You pay Bryax his silver. See what Angie can do for his wounds."

Sparing one last glance for the sand-pit, Rylus made his ponderous way down from the wagon box. The crowd now milled near fallen Bryax. Rabble had vanished, waiting neither for the crowd's praise nor its censure.

"Angie! Angie!" Rylus bellowed.

"I'm here!" came the answer from a tent erected a short distance from the wagons as Angie popped out.

She was slim, petite, with skin several shades darker than Rylus' own. Her hair was currently dyed the bright gold of spring daffodils. She wore a patchwork, many-pocketed robe over a flower-embroidered tunic and clasped in her hands was a heavy case of medical supplies.

Like all Far Shore's Healers, she wore decorative face paint. Today, a white rose bloomed on her round cheek.

"Fight's over with and Rabble has flattened another, aye, Rylus?" she chirped. "I'll look to the loser. How badly hurt does he seem to be?"

"Not too bad," Rylus replied. "She's learning our ways, getting more cautious. She barely even used her sword this time."

"Good, good!" Angie said. "She's understanding that we want to win bets, not slay enemies. Easier for me, too."

Angie's chattering was interrupted when a lean, grey-bearded man hurried up to them, kicking the hem of his ankle-length robe with each long-legged stride. His pale blue eyes were intense and his visage equal parts windburnt and dour.

"Are you the owner of this Spectacular?" he demanded of Rylus in a voice that seemed too deep to come from such a thin chest.

"I own it, with my partner, Tambor," Rylus replied.

"I would speak business with you," the grey beard said.

"One moment," Rylus turned to Angie. "Can you find Bryax on your own, Angie? Treat him and then pay him?"

He tossed her a small sack of jingling silver.

"Aye, patch and pay. I can." Angie glanced curiously at the stranger, hefted her case, and scurried off.

"What may I help you with, sir?" Rylus said smoothly.

"I want to buy her."

"Who? Angie?" Rylus sucked in his gut and stood taller. "Sir, I don't know what type of business that you suppose we run, but let me remind you that trade in healers is expressly forbidden in the Downs."

"No, no, not the healer!" the stranger snapped. "The warrior, the red-haired woman who was fighting just now."

"Rabble?" Rylus eyed the man critically. "She's not a slave—she's a free woman. Nor is she likely to take kindly to hearing that someone wants to buy her as a toy. Take my advice and leave quietly, friend."

"I am no friend of yours, fat man. You may call me

Hulhc.'' Hulhc scowled. ''Nor do I want this 'Rabble' as a bed-toy. I simply assumed that she was a slave because I could think of no other reason that such a skilled warrior would be working for a cheap travelling show.''

Cheap travelling show! Rylus burned with barely contained fury. The Travelling Spectacular was his pride and glory, his ticket—if not to respectability, at least out of the gutters.

Barely restraining a flood of profanities that would have done credit to his origins, Rylus smoothed his scented brown locks, then breathed to fill the vast pit of his stomach. When he spoke, his words were clipped but civil.

''Well, Hulhc, you'll need to ask Rabble herself why she stays with us, as she has since my partner found her unconscious by the roadside with naught but a tattered tunic and her sword.''

''She was alone?'' Hulhc's disbelief was evident in his voice.

''Not a human in sight,'' Rylus drawled, his natural good humor returning as he anticipated Rabble's meeting with this grey-beard. ''Not even a sign of one.''

''Hrumph,'' Hulhc scowled again. ''How did you train her to become such a warrior?''

Rylus belly-laughed, his eyes brightening with tears, his chins shaking. Hulhc shuffled his feet uncomfortably at the noise.

''Us make her a warrior? Us?'' Rylus wiped his streaming eyes. ''That is Rabble's doing and hers alone. Rabble may have had little more than the clothes on her back when Tam found her, but her fingers were wrapped around that odd blade she favors. Tambor was honestly afraid to approach her for her eyes were so fierce. And Tambor's no coward, thin man. He works with bears and great cats like they're kinfolk. But Rabble scared him.''

Hulhc paused, gnarled fingers tugging at his beard as he digested the information. Reaching into his purse, he tossed Rylus a small coin.

"For your time. Where can I find this Rabble? Has she no other name?"

Rylus considered tossing the coin back, then pocketed it. The monkeys still had to be fed, no matter what he thought of Hulhc's manners.

"Rabble's what she told us to call her and we weren't arguing. Usually after a show she goes to her tent—the small black one. If she's not there, check the pasture for her horse." He chuckled. "It's the large grey one—you'll know it if you see it. If you don't see either, you'll have to wait. We don't keep tabs on her—it's not like we need to worry about *Rabble* getting hurt."

Hulhc nodded and started toward where the black tent was pitched some distance from the wagons. Then he turned back.

"You don't resent my trying to take her away? I estimated what your take was when she won the fight. Your bets on Rabble must bring you and your partner a fair amount of money."

Rylus sighed theatrically. "Speak with Rabble. If she chooses to go with you, we won't try to stop her. Wouldn't even think of it, actually. She's like an elemental force of nature, that one. I'd no more try to stop her than I'd try to stop the wind."

With a satisfied grunt, Hulhc departed. Rylus looked after him thoughtfully. He turned at the sound of Tambor's footsteps.

"What did he want?" Tambor asked, putting a hand on Rylus' arm. He smelled of bear and the monkeys had been tying knots in his hair. "You're growling."

"As if you weren't eavesdropping." Rylus punched Tambor gently. "He wants to hire Rabble away from us. I've been trying to decide how I feel about it."

"Relieved," Tambor suggested. "Rabble's welcome with us as long as she wants to stay, but that one's a storm waiting to break. I don't fancy being around when it does."

2

Cats roll in catnip,
Wanders cross seas or climb mountains.
Their reasons are equally unknowable.

Tambor

HULHC STRODE in the direction of the black tent, still unsettled by his encounter with the fat showman.

When he arrived, Rabble was nowhere to be seen, nor was there any sign of a grey horse. The only inhabitant of the campsite was a very lean grey-striped tabby cat sleeping sprawled in a patch of sunlight near the fire circle.

Opening baleful yellow-green eyes, the cat blinked insults at Hulhc for disturbing its nap. Then it rose and stretched languorously. Slightly shocked, Hulhc realized that the cat lacked its right leg, clean to the shoulder.

Ostentatiously ignoring the man, the cat flipped to sleep on its right side, apparently reveling that no awkward shoulder impeded its comfort.

Watching the cat drowse, Hulhc decided that it had made a virtue of its impediment. He wondered, though, why a warrior would keep a maimed animal. Sentiment? A reminder of mortality or of the fortunes of war? Pity?

He dismissed speculation and was about to check the pasture for Rabble's horse when a promising drumming of hooves halted him. From the west, back-lit by the setting sun, came the object of his search.

Rabble rode up to her camp on a steel-dust grey stallion with scarred knees. Other scars, thin and puckered, threaded the horse's rippling coat. Loping along at the horse's left side came a mottled brown and tan cur, its ears shredded from fighting, the eyelid limp over its right eye.

Rabble herself was clad in a leather jerkin and trousers, her copper sword sheathed at her back. A knife peeped from each boot-top and she held a bow lightly in one hand. A brace of fresh-killed rabbits bounced on the horse's flank.

"Whoa, Dog Meat!" she commanded, reining in a few yards from the tent.

She inspected Hulhc suspiciously. The dog flattened its battered ears and growled. Even the horse seemed wary, stomping an iron-shod hoof in warning.

Hulhc studied her in turn; the crowd at her recent fight had been too thick for him to form more than a general impression. The first things he noticed, other than the flame-red hair she wore in an elaborate braid down her back, were her enormous brown eyes, so dark as to be almost black and flecked incongruously with gold. Her features were sharp— almost angular—an impression intensified by her hairline's widow's peak. Her skin was fair, though weathered, with a dusting of freckles, like laughter, across her nose.

She swung down from the saddle, to stand next to the still growling cur.

"Hush, Scrapper," she ordered, her voice fluid with a trace of some alien accent. "What do you want, old man? You're making my dog edgy."

Hulhc found himself unaccountably nervous. Silently, he reminded himself of all of his years of study, privation, and mockery . . . of why he had started on this journey. Surely, he was not to be put off his stride by some sword-wielding chit? He cleared his throat.

"My name is Hulhc," he said, "of Grey Hills Farm. I saw you fight today and I have a business proposition for you."

"Hmm, sounds like this could take a while," she said, unhooking the rabbits from the saddle. "Let me settle Dog Meat here and then I'll listen—that is, if you don't mind my making my dinner. I've promised Scrapper and Gimp rabbit and they don't understand waiting."

"Of course." Hulhc managed a polite bow. "Please tend to your needs."

When he and Rabble faced each other across a freshly kindled fire, Hulhc warmed to his pitch as the warrior gutted rabbits, tossing the offal to her eager pets.

"I want to hire you as a sword-arm for a small expedition that I'm mounting," he said. "I have reason to believe that the trip will be dangerous and you especially interested me since you can apparently fight either with or without a weapon."

"Ah, so you don't want me just as a sword-arm," she said, thrusting a skewer through the first rabbit and rubbing the bloody meat with salt, then setting the whole over the fire. "You want me to fight hand-to-hand as well. What else might you want?"

"Well, all of your weapons talents, of course," Hulhc said wondering if this mad woman would insist that he contract for each separately, "and any related talents you might want to suggest—hunting, guard duty, perhaps scouting or lending a hand with the livestock."

Rabble thoughtfully beheaded the second rabbit and flipped the head to Scrapper, who snapped it from the air. The cat mewed piteously and she sliced it a gobbet of flesh.

"Fighter, hunter, guard, scout, even drover." She raised an ironic eyebrow. "I can do all of those things, Hulhc, but you expect quite a bit. One thing, right up front, I'm not interested in being anyone's leman."

Hulhc flushed. "Of course not. I am a contentedly married man."

"Just so we have that straight," Rabble said calmly. "Now, tell me, where is this excursion of yours headed?"

"Into the Storm Shroud Mountains," Hulhc answered defiantly, waiting for the inevitable cringe, the look of horror, the "Are you mad, man?" But Rabble only studied him calmly, turning the rabbit on its spit.

"Those are up north, aren't they?" she said. "Old mountains, some say going down to an older ocean in the far north. Yes, I've heard of them. Folks don't go to them so often now. What do you seek there?''

Hulhc frowned, wondering if she was truly so brave or merely so young as to be ignorant of the legends of the Storm Shroud Mountains and what dwelled within them. Rabble didn't seem young. There were lines between her eyes and bordering her smile. Yet she hardly seemed stupid, either. Perhaps she was as fearless as her combat abilities would suggest. He put his musings from him, aware that Rabble was patiently awaiting his answer.

"I seek the magic," he said firmly.

"The magic?" Her eyebrows did not quite mock him.

"The magic that was as real in my parents' day as wagon wheels, roof shingles, or oat porridge.''

He took a deep breath. Rabble was still waiting, her head tilted to one side as if this old tale was the freshest news.

"Then one day," he continued, when Rabble said nothing, "the magic vanished. All in a day spells simply stopped working. Magical ships ceased to sail the air, stranding diverse peoples half a world from their homelands. Spirits that had hastened across space carrying messages vanished. Amulets and talismans became mere pieces of jewelry. The exotic beasts of magical nature grew scarce and then faded away. The last confirmed dragon sighting was when I was a youth. Even the Deities stopped answering prayers and miracles became like unicorns and pixies—things of legends and bedtime stories.''

In ripe embarrassment, Hulhc realized that yet again his passion had run away with his tongue. He glanced shyly at the warrior, but Rabble's dark brown eyes held only curiosity, not the contempt he dreaded. She lifted the first rabbit from the fire and set the second in its place.

"Will you eat, Hulhc?" she asked. "The meat may be a bit rare, but I am famished.''

"No, thank you, but please go ahead," Hulhc answered. "Perhaps I shall have a piece when the second is cooked.''

"Suit yourself," she replied as she sliced off a haunch.

"Go on with your tale while I eat. I still don't understand how you could be after something as intangible as magic, especially if it all vanished in a day."

"My father," Hulhc explained, "was a wizard. A great one, some still say. I don't rightly recall. He died when I was young, when I was small enough that all magic seemed wonderful to my eyes—a common light globe or an amethyst talisman charmed to ward away drunkenness were all parts of one marvelous whole. I don't doubt that it was much the same for most people then, though my father's household may have had more charms and marvels than many."

"I wouldn't know," Rabble said, "but this still doesn't tell me how you plan to find the lost magic."

Hulhc nodded. She was right. He'd gone off on another tangent, but the path that had led him thus far was so intertwined with his goal that he could not separate them.

"My father's holdings were divided after his death. My mother was guardian to my share since, as I have said, I was but a boy. She did well enough by us, but times were hard, especially for a family that had relied on resources that had vanished. Our once-great estates were split apart. Some land was sold, more was turned into a farm with cattle grazing in the ornamental gardens and chickens roosting in what had been guest houses. We survived, but by my mother's death only a small part of my inheritance remained: the farm and my father's library."

He paused. Rabble chewed the end of a rabbit bone before tossing it to the dog. She cut off another haunch, leaning back to fish a leather bottle from her tent. Almost as an afterthought, she sloshed some of the contents over the roasting rabbit. The fire burned blue for a moment and the scent of brandy sharpened the darkening air.

Accepting a horn cup of brandy, Hulhc continued.

"My life has not been easy, but I have kept up the farm and even made it prosperous. In what time I have had in these later years, I have pored over my father's books— books I suspect remain to me because of their utter uselessness in our changed world. And concealed within an ornate

Bestiary so heavy that its book box has its own wheels, I found one of my father's personal journals.'' Hulhc's pale eyes burned with fanaticism. ''And from these most personal writings I have found clues that I hope will lead me to the magic.''

''In the Storm Shroud Mountains,'' Rabble said.

Hulhc chose not to hear the doubt in her voice.

''That's right. I've tested my father's writings against other lore and in case after case, the magic seems to have lingered longest in the vicinity of the Storm Shrouds. Moreover, in the days before the Loss, lightnings without storm, winds of changeable humor, and other portents were seen, though their significance was not understood at the time.''

''So you plan to go and test your theories,'' Rabble said. ''You and who else?''

''Well, I had hoped to hire you and a few other skilled warriors. I also plan to hire a local guide when we get to the Storm Shrouds.''

Rabble wiped greasy fingers on her trouser leg. ''Scrapper, fetch my map case.''

The cur looked longingly at the rabbit, but obediently dove into the tent. There were a few thuds, then the dog emerged, tail wagging, a bone map case in its teeth.

''I had been wondering why you kept such an ugly mutt,'' Hulhc said in surprise. ''I can see why now. She's very smart.''

Rabble grunted, occupied with unrolling a map and weighting the corners with stones. Despite her silence, Hulhc got the impression that she was annoyed at him for criticizing her pet.

''We're here, just at the Downs above the Great Salt Sea.'' She walked her handspan across the map, stretching her long fingers to the limit. ''The Storm Shrouds are a good distance away, past the Salt Lakes, above the Sweet Lakes, through the foothills, and then into the mountains themselves.''

Hulhc could have sworn that Rabble shuddered as she

indicated the various lakes. He dismissed the thought as unworthy of her obvious courage.

Rabble leaned over the map, muttering place names under her breath and tracing possible routes. Gimp, the three-legged cat, hopped up and plopped himself in the middle of the map. She patted him absently, but did not move him.

"All right," she said. "I'll go."

"Don't you want to know what I'm paying?"

"Sure." Rabble grinned at him. "Sure I do, but nothing you could pay could convince me to travel all that distance just for money. You've hooked my curiosity with your strange tale, woken a fancy in me. However, I do have a few suggestions."

Hulhc nodded, eager to keep Rabble happy.

"You're planning on hiring other warriors and perhaps a guide. Have you considered a healer? Cook? Quarter-master?"

"Uh, no, I hadn't really," Hulhc said. "I thought we could fend for ourselves. I'll have some coin."

"I'm not sure that's a good plan," Rabble said bluntly. "Hiring fighters for a trip that long and into such territory will be rough. Good chow can go a long way toward convincing people to take a job."

"Oh," Hulhc looked worried. "I thought warriors were different from ordinary workers. I could take some of my staff from the farm, but I was planning on them running things while I am away. My wife is frail and my children have their own concerns."

"They think that you're crazy, chasing phantoms, and things." Rabble nodded, not quite compassionately. "I see. I have a suggestion."

"Yes?"

"What you should do," Rabble grinned again, "is hire Rylus and Tambor. They have the gear and the knowledge to get you across the more civilized lands where a gang of warriors could actually be a problem. They are also flexible enough to go into the Storm Shrouds. Angie will come along if you hire them first. She has a wandering foot, that one, and Far Shores Healers are hard to find these days.''

''But Rylus and Tambor? The fat man I was talking with before and his animal handler?'' Hulhc frowned, biting the end of his beard.

''They're both very talented—there's no other way that they could make such a good living with an itty-bitty show like this if they weren't. Tambor's very good with animals and Rylus . . .'' Rabble winked. ''There's more to Rylus than fat.''

Hulhc nodded curtly. ''I will consider your suggestion, Rabble. Will you still be taking the job even if I don't hire them?''

''I think so, but I'll do only what I'm hired for—not cook or quartermaster. I *might* hunt, if the impulse moves me.''

''You still haven't asked what I'm paying.''

''Well,'' Rabble split the rest of the rabbit meat between the dog and the cat. ''You'll cover care and food for me and my beasts. Pay me coin as well and give me my fair share of any loot. You'd be fool not to, not if you expect me to stay around and save your hide when trouble comes. You don't seem like a fool, Hulhc.''

He studied her. Rabble had the largest eyes of anyone he had ever met. The dark brown pools threatened to swallow him.

''I'm not a fool, Rabble,'' he said, shaking himself. ''You, however, are the strangest negotiator I've ever met.''

''You'll meet stranger,'' she predicted. ''Now, I'm for a scrub and then to my bedroll. The Travelling Spectacular moves on in the morning and one way or another, I'll be moving, too.''

Hulhc rose stiffly and handed her the brandy cup.

''Thank you for your time and hospitality, Rabble, and for accepting my proposal. I need to return home for a few days and finish getting my business in order. Then I will collect you.''

''Think over what I've suggested,'' she said, banking the

coals of her fire. "Chow may serve you as well as blade or bow."

"I will consider your advice," he said, turning away.

"Do."

Her tone was not quite a command, but when he turned to question her, Rabble had vanished into the darkness.

3

An enemy is only a friend you haven't met yet—or do I have that backwards?

                                                          Bryax

WHEN HULHC came for Rabble some days later, he was accompanied by a familiar figure. Bryax, the blond warrior whom Rabble had bested, rode a deep-chested dun gelding with darker points and a thoughtful expression. Hulhc's mount was a dapple grey mare as thin and dour as himself.

Bryax dismounted immediately upon seeing Rabble, favoring his injured leg far less than might have been expected. He extended his open hand and limped toward her with a warm smile.

"Hello, Rabble. Remember me?"

"Of course." She gave him a firm handshake. "Knee hurt much?"

"Not as much as I thought it would." Bryax beamed. "That Angie is a treasure. She gave me some herbs and told me how to wrap the knee with them and warm cloths. I've kept off it pretty much, too."

"No hard feelings?" Rabble asked, her enormous brown eyes challenging him to lie.

"None," he assured her. "It's all part of the game."

"Good," Rabble nodded now to Hulhc, who had been quietly fuming at not being acknowledged. "Good afternoon, Hulhc."

"Good afternoon, Rabble." Hulhc dismounted and handed the reins of his horse to Bryax. "Bryax is to be another member of our company."

Bryax shrugged. "I had to get away from town."

"Not because of our duel?" Rabble said.

"Not the duel, the losing of the duel." Bryax bared his square teeth at her. "You made beating me look too easy. I'd have been hard-pressed to get work even as a laborer once my knee had healed. Hulhc's offer came at a very good time. Besides, I've always wanted to travel. I don't think I've been much further than the Lake of Charm."

Hulhc folded his hands within his robe's long sleeves.

"Rabble, where would I find the masters of the Travelling Spectacular?"

"Rylus and Tambor?" Rabble gestured with a toss of her red mane. "Check first at the wagon with the blue trim. If they're not there, just roam the grounds. They'll show up soon enough."

"What was that about?" Bryax asked after Hulhc had walked away. "Old Pickle Puss actually looked nervous."

"I suspect he has decided to take my suggestion and try to hire the owners of the Travelling Spectacular to manage this trip." Rabble sparkled with suppressed laughter. "The problem is that he rather insulted Rylus the first time they met."

"I see," Bryax said. "Might be interesting to hear how they work it out—if they do."

"I think they will," Rabble said. "I broached the idea to the gents a few days ago and they've slowly come around to the realization that it could be an interesting and profitable venture." Rabble's smile vanished. "I'm not sure that Hulhc has thought very much about what he's undertaken."

"You sound as if you fear trouble from more than the wilds and traveller's ills, Rabble," Bryax replied.

"I do," Rabble touched his arm lightly. "Come. We can

pasture your horses with ours and I'll offer you some brandy while we talk.''

Bryax brightened, his naturally good spirits resurfacing from the gloom her ominous hints had brought.

"Lead on, Rabble," he said, clapping her on the shoulder. "The day I turn down a drink when no work is expected from me is an evil one for us all."

Once they were comfortably slouched by Rabble's fire, horn cups of brandy in hand, Rabble returned to the subject of their impending journey.

"Let us leave to philosophers the arguing of why and in what fashion such a potent intangible as magic can flee a world. I do not doubt that if Hulhc's quest—or some one like it—fails, that by the time your beard is grey, magic and miracle will be dismissed as dotard's fancy. Even now, going about with the Travelling Spectacular, I have heard some cry out that Rylus' sleight of hand is magic or that Tambor commands his beasts through enchantment."

Bryax grunted. "I know of a temple—I won't say where—wherein clever mechanical devices are used to create effects that the priests pass off as miracles. But what does such mummery have to do with us? We will travel with crazy Hulhc, protect him, and when he has wearied of poking in the Storm Shrouds—or perhaps found what he seeks—we will return him to civilized lands."

"What if the magic didn't go away?" Rabble asked, the gold flecks in her dark eyes catching the firelight's dance. "What if it was *made* to go away? Might not those who made it vanish have ways to make vanish those fools who would meddle with their work?"

Bryax swallowed hard, obviously not pleased with the implications of Rabble's musing. He scratched his head with one broad, muscular hand as if to encourage thought.

"Have you any plans on how we can guard ourselves against discovery?" he said, the idea of retreating never troubling his direct soul. "We have a long journey ahead."

"Hopes," Rabble said with a half smile. "Most of which center around Hulhc making a deal with Rylus and Tambor.

I've ridden with those two long enough to appreciate their cleverness. Moreover, none will question a travelling show crossing between holdings and domains and whatever other names people give to their governments. We should be safe from curiosity until we have passed through the most populous areas.''

"Yes, I see your point . . ."

Bryax's words were interrupted by angry shouts. Rabble was on her feet, her sword in hand almost before Bryax could set down his cup. Then she relaxed, a finger to her lips.

"Shhh, listen," she whispered. "I believe that they negotiate, even now."

"Make us partners in your venture, not hirelings," Tambor said, his voice clear as the three men strolled near Rabble's camp. "That is our final offer. We will supply gear and our road knowledge. You can hire mercenaries and scouts."

"Though I advise you to hold off on that until we are at least across the Salt Lakes," Rylus added. "Sooner would be unnecessary in familiar lands."

Hulhc sputtered. "Partners?"

"In risk and gain," Tambor agreed. "We will keep the Travelling Spectacular going to the very foot of the Storm Shrouds, easing you through border guards and greedy speculators alike. In return, we get equal shares of whatever treasures you find."

"Treasures?" Hulhc shrilled. "Knowledge is what I seek."

Rylus grinned. "But I recall my grandsire's tales of jeweled talismans and golden swords and armor. There should be something for every taste. What say you?"

The voices faded as the trio withdrew to the blue wagon, presumably to work out their agreement.

"That's settled then," Bryax said. "To sleep for me. I've travelled with a half score of armies and guards, but I've never been part of a Travelling Spectacular before."

"Well," Rabble said, tossing the last of her brandy into

the fire and watching the blue flame, "think of ourselves as a army of two and the enemy as yet unknown."

Lakeside, the town that the newly augmented Travelling Spectacular stopped in a few days later, was quite a bit larger than the Downs farming village in which they had met up with Hulhc and Bryax.

After the evening had become too dark for the spectacles and gambling games to continue, Rabble and Bryax released themselves from duty to see the sights and possibly find a tavern or two.

They strode through the broad, cobbled streets, well pleased with themselves, drinking in the sights and sounds of a metropolis large enough to live after nightfall. Cheerful laughter and drumful music poured out of open doors.

"Looks promising," Bryax said. "I heard today that the local ruler's army is rotating field and garrison about now— must be why the town is so lively."

"I know a good tavern," Rabble offered, "if you want to catch soldier's road gossip as well as a drink or three."

"The Horned Moon, perchance?"

"That's it."

Bryax slapped her shoulder. "I'll stand you the first round."

The Horned Moon was built largely of stone, paneled within with dark wood that drank the light. The tables were solid two-inch-thick planks nailed to trestles and the food and drink were equally unpretentious. Bryax was served beer in a tankard large enough to need two hands to raise it. Rabble's neat whiskey came in a smaller, but still substantial glass.

As they sat watching the crowd and listening to the fragments of conversation that came their way, Bryax's head nearly swiveled off of his shoulders as a particularly well-built barmaid went sauntering by, her heavy tray of beer mugs not slowing her a whit. When he saw Rabble's amused gaze following his, Bryax blushed.

"Bryax, you're far too old to be shy around the ladies. What's wrong?" she asked in a tone that made quite clear that she did know. "I could swear you were blushing."

Bryax gratefully grabbed the basket of salt pretzels that the barmaid set down as she passed their table.

"Good service," he commented, then blushed again. "Damn, Rabble, I didn't want to be rude to you."

"To me?" Rabble sipped from her whiskey. "Rude? Oh, you thought that I'd be upset . . . Look, if you aren't against it, I'd like to swear Ferman's Oath with you. You know, so you can think of me as a *comrade* not as a woman."

Bryax visibly relaxed. "Sounds good—not that I don't think you're pretty, but I want to avoid trouble. Tonight will be too late for it. The temples will be closed."

"So, we go tomorrow, before the Spectacular gets started. I know Rylus and Tambor well enough to know that we won't start until they've drummed up a crowd."

"Great," Bryax sipped his beer. "Wait. We don't have a company! Who will be our witness?"

"Well, we can ask Rylus or Tambor," Rabble swirled the liquor in her glass, "or even Hulhc."

Bryax's guffaw turned heads at nearby tables. "Yes, let's ask him!"

"Now that that's settled," Rabble grinned. "What are you going to do about that fulsome lady with the tray?"

4

A promise given to be kept is as great a gamble as any roll of the dice.

Rylus

THE NEXT morning, Rabble was up with the birds. She made certain that Bryax was too, handing him a cup of strong tea through the doorway of his tent. The blond warrior accepted it with a theatrical moan, sitting up in his bedroll and rubbing his eyes with the heel of his free hand.

"Did I have a good night last night?" he asked. "I sure better have for my head to feel this way."

"Drink up," Rabble said. "It has rosemary, valerian, peppermint, and some other stuff. One of Angie's remedies—Rylus swears by it when he has too much. Gulp it down now because . . ."

Bryax followed orders, swallowing the contents of the cup in a single gulp. His face twisted. Rabble caught the cup as he flung it at her.

"It's a bit strong," Rabble finished, "but it will make you feel better."

"If it's one of Angie's concoctions, it probably will," Bryax agreed, "but, oh, my head!"

"I'll leave you to get ready," Rabble said, "are you still up to going to Swear? I checked the location of the Temple District last night while playing darts with some mercs."

"Of course. I've fought battles in worse shape than this," Bryax rubbed his head, "but give me a chance to clear my head."

"Fine. Hulhc will be awake soon if he's not already. I've

noticed that he keeps farmer's hours. I'll go and ask him to witness for us, fill in Rylus and Tambor, and burn some breakfast. You want anything to eat?''

Bryax grabbed his belly. ''No offense, but no thanks.''

''I don't understand what you're doing,'' Hulhc protested as Rabble and Bryax hurried him through the streets. ''What is Ferman's Oath? And why do you need me as witness?''

The two warriors were resplendent in their best gear. Bryax wore a chain shirt and heavy leather trousers that met heavier boots. A peaked helmet covered his flaxen locks. His sword was scabbarded at his side, a matching long knife opposite, both barely concealed by his flowing royal blue cloak. He carried a horse-bow in his hands, the quiver over his shoulder.

Rabble wore dark brown armor of hardened leather, reinforced at elbows, knees, and shoulders. Her red hair was braided and her head protected by a leather cap with wavelike cheek guards. The copper sword was sheathed at her side and a regiment of knives concealed on her person. She carried a long bow and a back-slung quiver of red-fletched arrows. Her black cloak had a scarlet lining. Scrapper trotted at her side, the cur's enjoyment of the town's smells not diminishing her caution.

Between the towering warriors, Hulhc looked like a skinny winter-killed tree.

''Ferman's Oath is fairly common in the Downs and Salt Sea areas, where men and women often serve together,'' Rabble said. ''Legend tells that it was created by an isolated mercenary team that nearly destroyed itself through in-fighting.''

''They must have had a very weak commander,'' Hulhc snorted.

''No,'' Bryax retorted. ''There's not been a commander born who has control over how his or her people chose to link up after hours. And nothing's more deadly than having spatting lovers in the same place during a crisis. And the Deities being as they are, this does happen. What Ferman's

Oath does is to bind the company as brothers and sisters for the duration of the oath.''

"Normally, the company stands as witness to the Oath," Rabble said, "but Bryax and I have no company but you.''

"But who do you swear before?" Hulhc asked.

"Before the Deities, especially those who concern themselves with war," Bryax said. "You are the Witness, the Deities enforce.''

"Deities!" Hulhc didn't quite snort. "Do you really believe that Deities care to enforce piddling human concerns?''

"They do send miracles," Bryax said coolly.

"They did, before the magic vanished," Hulhc said. "Haven't you ever wondered if the Deities ever cared? What if the miracles came from the priests and priestesses who used their own magic to create effects that they then credited to Deities?''

"You're saying that there might not be Deities?" Bryax said, his voice too soft.

Hulhc drew himself up. "Of course not, just that beings like the Elements, who are said to be the source of all the Deities, really couldn't have interest in human concerns on the personal scale. Their priests and priestesses deal with that.''

"And who do they answer to?" Bryax said angrily. "Do the Deities even answer them?''

Bryax's agitation was attracting stares from the worshippers they passed in the early morning streets. Rabble put a hand on his arm.

"Easy, friend. The grey-beard isn't thinking." She turned to Hulhc, the gold flecks in her eyes strangely bright. "Hulhc, you are a fool to reshape the cosmos to fit your private obsessions. The Deities take note of human affairs, never doubt it.''

Hulhc looked away with an uncomfortable mutter, "Of course, of course.'' Conversation diminished to the jangle of Bryax's armor and Scrapper's growl at an elegant pair of silky-haired flop dogs towing a frilly young matron in their wake.

The buildings had become subtly more elaborate now, upward arching cornices melding seamlessly into rooftops, painted roofs vaulting into bell towers or needle-tipped steeples. Walls were shaped from cyclopean blocks of marble or from single slabs somehow brought here entire and fitted into buildings as a child builds with wooden blocks.

Before the Loss, in some of the most important cities, the temples had thrust their gem-encrusted towers hundreds of feet into the air. Their gold and silver-plated arabesques had been visible for miles and the sound of their peeling bells had been the chimes of heaven. Architectural styles had differed from region to region, but one and all had vied to honor the Elements with the best of the earth's treasures.

Yet, when the magic had vanished, so had the power to maintain those sylph-sculpted structures. Heroic measures kept only a few of those wondrous buildings accessible. In an ironic turn that the young philosophers were quick to note, the only places where the Deities were worshiped in something like their accustomed pomp were in those structures that owed as much to human craft as to miracles.

"There's our destination." Rabble pointed to a grey granite building. "The Temple of War and Chance."

They paused before the building both to admire and to get their bearings. Broad steps hacked from grainy granite blocks rose to a broad portico. The portico itself was roofed, the supports well-made sculptures of stern warriors, each three times as tall as life. Though the height of each was the same, each face was different and each bore a slightly different array of weaponry.

"I've heard," Bryax said with pride, "that each of these is a portrait of a man or woman who died with especial fitness—showing the honor of the Warrior's Way."

"Portraits these may be," Hulhc said, thin hands inspecting a robust dame in the silk and wood armor of the lands far away across the Spindrift Seas, "but they were sculpted by human hands, not by magical art. See where the chisel slipped here? It's been cleverly done, but it's not by magic."

"And why should it have been?" a new voice said.

The three turned. The querant was a tall woman clad in the splendid embroidered garments of a priestess of War and Chance. Her robes were cut to flaunt, rather than conceal, the sword-cut scar that ran from shoulder blade between her breasts, then puckered across her belly. She leaned heavily on an intricately carved staff and moved gracefully despite lacking three toes on her left foot.

She nodded to Bryax and Rabble, but her cool gaze remained on Hulhc.

"These statues are tributes to heroes whose valor and nobility may inspire those who are yet to come. Why would magical art be preferable to human sweat in their crafting?"

Hulhc flung his hands out to mold the air, "Magic could have made perfect portraits, could have shaped your figures from exotic stones rather than common granite, could have done anything you wanted without human limitations."

"This," the priestess said, "is what we wanted. Human limitation is what the warrior must daily face."

She turned to Rabble and Bryax, inspecting their attire with the hawklike acuity of one who has held command. Satisfied, she gave a sharp nod.

"You two look like seasoned warriors. Something tells me that you have come to swear Ferman's Oath." Her grin was impish, playful. "No magic tells me this, either. A few members of the local guard came by this morning before leaving for a new posting. One of them mentioned that an outland woman with red hair had been asking about where the Oath was administered."

The priestess became solemn again. "If you and your Witness would follow me . . ."

They followed her to the center of the portico, to where a nearly smokeless fire burned in a broad, shallow brazier of beaten bronze. The enameled tracery about the edges reflected the flickers of the coals. Motioning them to places about the brazier's rim, the priestess tossed a spicy powder over the coals and breathed deeply of the scented smoke that immediately rose.

"Join hands," the priestess commanded, "all three. Have you explained the Oath to your Witness?"

Rabble and Bryax nodded.

"They have," Hulhc volunteered, his tone respectful.

"Then you watch while they swear."

She raised her arms so that the sleeves fell back, baring her arms to the elbows. In a clear voice she drew from the warriors their solemn promise that henceforth they would be as brother and sister to each other, held by the same bonds and banes as children of the same blood.

After Rabble and Bryax had accepted this binding, the priestess turned to Hulhc, admonishing him that he was to stand Witness to this oath "until the need for Arms has passed."

Bryax turned and embraced Rabble, chastely kissing her on one cheek. She returned his embrace with equal solemnity.

"Shield Brother!"

"Sword Sister!"

Hulhc offered a stiff, apologetic bow to the priestess.

"Thank you for your teaching. I promise to think on it."

"Don't just think," she admonished gently. "Pray. We have hearts as well as minds. You should no more guide yourself by one or the other alone than you should go through life with one eye closed. Go now. War and Chance watch over you all on your journey."

"Thank you," Rabble said, as the men bowed.

Scrapper led the way from the temple, a thoughtful and more silent Hulhc trailing the warriors.

When they returned to the Travelling Spectacular, Rylus welcomed them back by handing Bryax a bag of tools and shoving Rabble over to where Tambor was hammering in posts for an arena.

"Bryax, please help Angie set up her fortune tent. Rabble, Tambor needs help." Rylus threw his pudgy hands in the air. "The local hirelings have not yet arrived and already we've had people by to try our events."

"The battle's won," Rabble promised. Setting fine cloak and weapons on the ground, she added to her dog, "Scrapper, watch over these."

The dog plopped down, her forepaws on Rabble's sword sheath.

"Good idea," Bryax said. "Sister?"

"Of course," Rabble said as she hurried off to help Tambor.

"Sister?" Rylus said.

"Ferman's Oath," Bryax explained, hefting the tool bag. "We'll stow our gear properly once the Spectacular is set."

Rylus nodded. "That's right! I remember—Rabble spoke with me this morning."

When Bryax left, Rylus stared at the muddle around him. "Now what needs to be done?" he said, half to himself. He jumped as Hulhc cleared his throat.

"May I be of assistance?" the farmer asked awkwardly. "I know nothing of fortune-telling or wild beasts, but I could do something small."

"You can read and write, can't you?" Rylus said excitedly, for those skills were far from universal. "Can you run a game of chance—dice or a numbers wheel?"

"I can." Hulhc hid a smile in his hand. "I am even quite good with cards."

Rylus beamed. "We must talk on that later. For now, we have some simple games of chance and skill—all honest, I swear. I need someone to oversee their running."

"All honest?" Hulhc said in surprise.

"Aye." Rylus parted his fingers in an oath sign. "I swear. Are you interested in the job? I can show you how the games are run and scrawl a few notes to remind you."

"Lead on," Hulhc said.

When dusk fell even the most determined players left for brighter places. The weary Company, assisted by local help, set out lanterns and packed away the Spectacular. The solemn courtesy that had followed Rabble, Bryax, and Hulhc home from the Temple remained despite the long day's labor.

Angie grasped Tambor by his sleeve as he emerged from bedding down the bears.

"I just heard Hulhc asking Bryax for help with a table that was too large for him to move alone. Asking—not ordering—and he even thanked him with a smile!"

"They've all been exceptionally peaceful today," Tambor agreed. "Miracles may have vanished from the world, but the Deities still touch our lives, especially when they inspire us to live up to more than ourselves."

"Excuse me, sir," a musical female voice asked, "but can you tell me where I might find Hulhc of Grey Hills Farm?"

The speaker was a round-faced, round-bodied Downs woman with glossy dark brown hair piled in a simple twist on her head. The dress she wore was dyed pale blue and stamped with dark purple flowers, the neckline embroidered with silky violets. Only her worn hands gave away that she was not a gentlewoman of leisure. A little boy in neat overalls clung to her hand, eyes the shade of his mother's violets trying to get a better look at the golden monkey who sat grooming herself on Tambor's shoulder.

"Hulhc," Tambor said, wondering if the old man had acquired an admirer while working Rylus' gambling concession, "has probably retired to his tent by now. We've closed for the night, ma'am."

"Could you show me where he is?" the woman pleaded. "He must have mentioned me. I'm his daughter, Adona. This is my little boy, Rue."

Angie and Tambor looked at each other in puzzlement. Hulhc had mentioned practically nothing about his family or his farm. The rest of the travelling company had concluded that those who remained at Grey Hills Farm had been glad to see the crotchety senior go. Adona, however, was visibly distressed.

"I'll show you to your papa's tent, Adona," Angie said. "It's late for a lady like you to be out alone."

Adona dimpled at the compliment.

"The boat got in late and then I had to get a room at a respectable inn. Then Rue had to be fed. Besides," Adona lowered her voice as if embarrassed, "I was a bit afraid when the Spectacular was all a-lit and a-bustle. Coming when it was quieter was easier."

Angie nodded her understanding, then led the way past the animal pens and the gaming tents to the stretch of Common where four small tents had been pitched. Bryax and Rabble's were dark—no surprise as the two had gone into town for a quick drink to celebrate their Oath swearing.

Hulhc's tent was lit from within, the flicker of lamplight illuminating an irregular shadow bent over a book or some papers.

"That's your papa's tent," Angie said. "Want me to announce you, Adona?"

"No, this is plenty," Adona thanked her. "I can see that he's awake."

"Fine, then, fine." With a toothy smile, Angie swept a flower from her sleeve and handed it to Rue. "Be a good boy, Rue. Maybe tomorrow you come back and I'll get Tambor to show you the llama and the bears and the bird that talks."

Rue gave her a shy smile. "I am a good boy, even on the boat."

"Tomorrow, then." Angie excused herself to return to her own tent.

Adona drew herself up and straightened her hair. She could see her father busily at work by lamplight, his bent posture so typical that she felt a pang.

"Father," she called, tapping on the canvas. "It's me, Adona."

She heard the thump of a book being dropped. Then Hulhc's hand lifted the flap and his weathered face peered out.

"Adona—and little Rue! I thought I had fallen asleep and was dreaming! Let me come out and sit with you—my tent is rather close. I can stir up the fire, put on tea. Angie—Have you met her?—Angie blends a wonderful raspberry tea." Hulhc set the beaten copper kettle over the coals and added kindling. "What brings you here? Is Napen with you?"

Adona took the camp stool that her father shook open for her and set Rue on her knee. She couldn't help but be flattered by Hulhc's attentions. At home he was so serious and sour that the farmhands called him "Bitters" behind his back.

"No, Father, Napen isn't with me. It's planting time at Grey Hills, you know."

Hulhc only grunted.

"I came to Lakeside," she hesitated, her grip tightening on Rue so that the little boy squirmed, "I came to ask you to come home to Grey Hills. We need you."

Hulhc stared into the fire, his work-knotted hands feeding twigs into the flames. He sat that way for so long that Adona wondered if he had somehow fallen asleep with his eyes open.

"Father?"

"Grey Hills doesn't need me, 'Dona. Not if I raised you and your brothers right. I left you a good-sized farm. I left your mother to rest against her illness."

He paused and crumbled leaves from a little pouch into boiling water and set the kettle aside to seep. Leaning into the tent he brought out a compact mess kit and found two mugs.

"Rue, you still like sweet things?"

"Yes, Grandfather," Rue held out his flower. "The gold-haired lady with the flower face gave me a poesy."

"You *have* met Angie, then." Hulhc handed Rue a bit of sugar-lace. "Try this Rue. Adona, here's your tea."

She took the cup gingerly. "Thank you, Father."

Hulhc sipped from his own mug. "I'm not coming back to Grey Hills, yet. I've promised myself since I was a boy that I'd make this trip. I'm going to make it now, before I'm too old—before it's too late and I'm like Cooper Pier sitting on my porch and muttering about might-have-beens.''

"Father . . ."

"No, I'm set."

"Father . . ." Adona's voice broke. "Mama's not well. I mean, she's worse."

Hulhc scowled into the shadows beyond his firelight. For a moment, tears glittered. Then he shook his head angrily.

"No, I can't let that stop me. Not that especially. I'll speak with Angie. She's a Far Shore's Healer and the best I've seen—it's not just festival games with her." Hulhc reached and awkwardly patted his daughter's hand. "Come back in the morning and I'll have something for you to take to your mother. We can talk more then."

Adona squeezed his hand. "As you wish, Father. Perhaps I should go to my inn. Rue has fallen asleep on my lap."

Hulhc's reply was interrupted as an off-key warbling in alto and baritone howled across the meadow. "Old Man Moon has bright, bright eyes . . ."

"Home and Hearth!" Adona cried. "What is that!"

"That," Hulhc actually grinned, "is my two employees—Rabble and Bryax back from celebrating Ferman's Oath, which they swore this morning. With *me* as Witness, if you can believe that. Let me call them over, they can give you an escort to your inn."

"Two drunken warriors?" Adona's eyes widened. "Home and Hearth, Father! What are you thinking?"

"Don't worry, Adona. They are exemplary people."

"Home and Hearth," was all Adona could murmur.

Adona stayed with the Travelling Spectacular for the next several days, trying persistently to convince Hulhc to give up his journey. The rest of her time was split between speaking with Angie about her mother's illness and chasing after Rue, who was quite ready to emulate his grandfather and run away with the Travelling Spectacular.

When a reliable riverboat with a stop not far from Grey

Hills Farm departed for the Downs, Hulhc put Adona and Rue firmly aboard. Adona carried a leather packet of Angie's cures and a thick letter from Hulhc to his wife.

Rue clutched in both arms a floppy-eared brown and white spotted puppy—a present from Tambor. His tears ran over the pink and yellow daisies that Angie had painted on his chubby cheeks in farewell.

Hulhc insisted on going alone to see them off. He stood on the quay until the riverboat was far out of sight. Then he scrubbed the tears from his wrinkled cheeks and turned his face once again towards the distant, yet unseen, specter of the Storm Shroud Mountains.

5

The vixen does not weep for the rabbit, nor the rabbit for the starveling fox pup.

Downs proverb

WHEN THE Travelling Spectacular left Lakeside some days later, a throng of children of that delightful age too small for serious work and yet too large to need supervision ran alongside the departing caravan until the edge of town. Among the members of the Company, the fragile accord that had been forged during the swearing of Ferman's Oath had become the beginnings of camaraderie.

Rabble and Bryax rode first, Gimp curled asleep on the bedroll behind Rabble's saddle, seemingly indifferent to the commotion the spectacle caused. Scrapper ranged in front of the horses, clearing the way.

Then came the two boxy wagons. The first carried

supplies and a compact compartment that served Tambor and Rylus as a home. Its sides were hung with all manner of furled tarpaulins, awnings, ropes, the lot painted and dyed in gaudy hues so that the wagon rather resembled the nest of a color-blind pack rat.

The second wagon was far less elaborately bedecked, but even more fascinating. The majority of it was given over to straw-padded comfort for Tambor's two dancing bears. A vaulted area above the bears was reserved for the three long-armed, golden-furred monkeys that were Tambor's inheritance from his sky-sailing father. Smaller cases held an array of serpents, a purple bird that could mimic human speech, and other small creatures collected by Tambor.

Both wagons were drawn by heavyset, glossy-coated plow horses. All of these were past their best farming days and might have found themselves transformed into sausage or dog feed without Tambor's intervention. The old horses throve on the easy schedule of the caravan and, consequently, the Travelling Spectacular actually made good time from place to place.

Today Tambor and Hulhc rode on the box of the first wagon, discussing the logistics involved in running the Spectacular. Although Rylus was the Spectacular's day-to-day road manager, Tambor contributed more than his menagerie. As the son of a sky sailor (in the days before the Loss), Tambor had odd insights that frequently contributed to the Spectacular's success.

Rylus sat in the driver's box of the second wagon, less driving than reassuring the horses that there was a human agent who appreciated their efforts. The majority of his attention was centered on repainting the Wheel of Chance, one of the Spectacular's most popular adult attractions.

Above it all, Angie sat atop the animal wagon's roof, singing old country ditties as she sorted and packaged herbal cures and teas to sell at their next stop. One of Tambor's golden monkeys sat on her shoulder, pulling at her hair. Occasionally, she would look across the sprawling farmlands and the blue of the Lakes both near and distant, an expression of intense satisfaction on her flower-painted face.

Last in the parade was Hulhc's horse, tied to the rear of the wagon along with Tambor's latest project, a brown and tan llama. The sailor Tambor had purchased it from had claimed that the beast was descended from creatures that had come halfway across the world in the days when magic winds lofted ships through the clouds.

Tambor believed him, citing tales his own mother had told him of voyages to now inaccessible places that had lasted less time than it now took to drive a wagon between two of the Lakes.

"But mind you," Tambor usually ended the stories he told to wide-eyed boys and girls, "my mother also told me of being attacked by creatures made of storm clouds and chased by birds larger than their entire ship. At least these days all we need to worry about is weather, toll collectors, and earning enough to pay for our keep."

"The soldiers in Lakeside," Rylus said, "told me that bandit activity has been growing more fierce of late. Some suspect that there's a new leader and others say that times have been harder, forcing more people from their farms and shops to earn a living as they can. We must take care, at least until we reach the Sapphire Lake. Saltport should be safe enough."

The surrounding terrain seemed to support those claims that times had been harder. Even the lushness of early spring growth could not conceal the winter's damage; cracked ground showed clay rather than fertile soil.

Although the trees still stood tall, much of the smaller growth was twisted and stunted. The farms they passed after the first day's travel looked less than prosperous. Even the children were too tired to show much interest in the prospect of a show. The adults were not rude, but neither were they welcoming.

"We'll not make much until we reach Saltport," Rylus predicted. "These farms look worse than they did last year and we had bare enough welcome then."

"What ails them?" Bryax asked. "Is the soil just poor here?"

"No," Hulhc spoke out before Rylus could answer. "Where I live, the farmers tell tales of this place and shudder. Crosswinds from the two salt lakes compete over this region, seeding enough salt to poison the area and stripping off what good soil there is. Legends say that in the old days the farmers would make offerings to the Elements and in return the winds would turn aside and sweet rain would fall to refresh the soil. Without miracles, the land is dying, but the people are reluctant to leave their homes."

"It is hard to be a stranger," Angie said, "and harder still to be a poor stranger or a beggar."

Ever compassionate, Tambor frowned. "We're a day short of Saltport and I'll need fresh water for the beasts. Given what these people put up with, I am loath to simply camp tonight in someone's field."

Rylus squinted, picking out landmarks. "Tambor, do you remember how last year we had an invitation to stop from a farm just a ways ahead?"

"Let me ride ahead and ask them if we can stay this year," Bryax suggested. "They may be shy about offering, since they know they can't pay for our amusements. I know something of how poor farmers can still have their pride."

"Good thought," Rylus said. "As I recall, the Grandame could read. I'll set our proposal down in writing since you'll be a stranger to them."

"Ride carefully, Sword Brother," Rabble added. "If there has been bandit trouble the farmers may not take well to strangers. I'll send Scrapper along to keep you safe. I would ride with you but I don't want to leave the Spectacular without a guard."

"I'm not going far." Bryax gestured. "I can see the tracery of hearth smoke just over the rise."

Shortly after he rode out, Bryax returned to report that he had not only secured camping privileges, but even a welcome of sorts.

"As I left," he said, "they were sending a boy out on a

scrubby pony to tell their neighbors of our arrival. I saw a bonfire being stoked up.''

By the time the Travelling Spectacular's wagons rumbled down the rutted dirt road to the farmhouse, a kettle had been slung across an outdoor fire-pit and water was being heated.

"We can't offer much," said the bent old lady who everyone called The Grand, "but you're welcome to water and wood. I even have a flitch of bacon we can spare you.''

Tambor grinned. "I hope you don't mind if we put the beasts through their paces—perhaps in that empty corral. I don't want them to forget their lessons.''

"And I wanted to test out this wheel I've been fixing," Rylus added. "Would that trouble you?''

"Not at all," The Grand replied, her faded eyes nearly disappearing into the wrinkles of her smile. "May we watch?''

"I hoped you would," Rylus said. "Perhaps we can place some bets—just for fun—no cash. Chance might forget to watch if we aren't betting.''

In very little time, a scaled down version of the Travelling Spectacular was underway. The farmers entered the charade with pleasure and though they couldn't pay for the entertainments, somehow The Grand's flitch of bacon found potatoes, salt butter, and early greens. As they settled into the picnic supper, the Company cautiously asked about the rumors of bandits—well aware that these were the very people the city folk of Lakeside suspected.

"Oh, the stories are true enough," The Grand said, "all but the hint that the bandits are our people turned to robbery. Most of us wouldn't know what to do with swords and armor. These ruffians know both well.''

"There've been other changes," a wiry fellow called Sonny added. "Trade out of Saltport has cut way back. There's still a market for foodstuffs, when we get a load together, but they're not shipping out as much, neither by water or by land. Rumor says that a new government has taken over there. Changes are happening, that's sure enough.''

Early the next morning before the Spectacular left, The Grand hurried out with a bundle of messages to friends in Saltport.

"Not as easy to keep up with people as it was when I was a girl, no spells to whip the words across the miles—not anymore." She sighed, giving the packet a parting pat. "Still, I like to believe we're not completely lost from civilization. Be careful, hear? And stop in when you come back. Spring is a lean time, but come Autumn and we'll feed you 'til you look like one of Tambor's bears."

"I'll hold you to your promise," Rylus said, patting his triple chins. "I keep telling Tambor that I'm underfed."

Rabble, already mounted on Dog Meat, trotted up.

"Hate to leave so quick," she apologized, shooing the two men to their wagons, "but even with lots of daylight ahead I'm worried about trouble on the road."

The land grew gradually more desolate as the morning passed. The few trees that had put forth blossoms looked as out of place as a juggler at a funeral. Tree trunks were bent from resisting the steady winds—some saplings looked as if they had been twisted between invisible hands that sought to wring out the sap as a laundry press wrings water from clothes.

Farmhouses stood boarded up, their people gone to neighbors or to kinder lands. Occasionally, the Company would pass a lone family struggling on despite the evidence around them of inevitable failure.

When the denser growth of the swamp forest loomed against the distance, worrying about bandits was a welcome relief from contemplating the ruin around them.

"How could this be allowed to happen?" Bryax muttered angrily to Rabble. "Could Hulhc be right and all the Deities' miracles be nothing more than human magic?"

"I don't know," she replied, her lips tight, "but we will find the magic. We must, for these poor farmers if for no one else."

Some hours later the trees of the forest completely surrounded them. Curtains of vine flowering over the decrepit trees they buried, dimmed the daylight. Only infrequent glimpses of the sky reminded them that beyond the forest a spring afternoon stretched lazily on. The same riot of growth made a clear view away from the roadway difficult and often impossible.

Bryax and Rabble frequently dismounted to move deadfalls and slash through curtains of vines. Although the swamp was muggy, both wore their armor—not only in anticipation of bandits but also as protection from various plants that Angie agitatedly warned them were caustic to human skin.

"There are an awful lot of these fallen trees, Sister," Bryax grunted as he flung a hunk of oak into a brackish pool.

"Aye, Brother," Rabble replied. "Could be the winter winds, but I've been wondering if they might have been placed to slow travellers. Scrapper's been edgy for a while now—I'd give much to know what her nose has told her."

Rylus had been clambering on the wagon tops since before they entered the swamp forest. Now, greasy with sweat, he waddled up to the warriors.

"Before we move on," he said proudly, "let me show you what I've done."

"Quickly, man," Bryax urged. "Only the length of the day gives me any hope that we'll reach open ground before dark."

Rylus pointed to where heavy crossbows were now mounted on the wagon tops. A screen of canvas and wood protected each.

"The bows are mounted on pivots and have special quarrels of my own design that can be loaded six shots in advance. The perch is dangerous, yes, but far better than waiting for bandits to close. I will man one, Tambor the other. Angie plans tricks of her own and Hulhc has agreed to act as driver."

"Good," Bryax said, a rustling in the bushes making his suspicion that they would be attacked becoming a certainty. "Keep ready."

Rabble hurried Rylus to his wagon. Her quiver was ready

in its harness and she had secreted Gimp in an empty saddle-bag.

"I saw a bit of movement ahead," she whispered to Bryax. "Too large to be anything but human. A scout, I'd wager."

"Aye, I saw something, too." Bryax pulled out his sword. "I'm ready for a fight. I'm tired of this skulking."

Rabble grinned, something feral seeming to brighten the golden flecks in her large, brown eyes.

"Scrapper! Let's oblige my brother," she ordered softly. "Flush 'em, girl!"

The ugly mutt slunk off into the scrub. Even the marsh peepers fell silent and the only sound was the hoof-falls of the horses and the creaking of the wagon wheels as the Spectacular made its cautious progress.

Then, with a volley of barking, Scrapper burst from the underbrush. A lean, balding man with a short sword in hand stumbled in front of the bitch, his hand groping at his calf.

There was a yell. "What's Har doing?"

"Attack!" shouted a second voice.

The command was followed by a volley of arrows from the underbrush. Most flew wild, but a few thudded into the wagon sides. One sliced a thin furrow in Dog Meat's flank. He bellowed in pain.

"Elements take you!" Rabble yelled. "That's *my* horse!"

She urged Dog Meat directly into where the hail of arrows had originated, loosing two wild shots of her own before swinging down and diving into the scrub. She backed out almost as rapidly, crossing blades with two confident ruffians who believed that they were forcing her into retreat. They learned otherwise as Dog Meat reared, neighing with what seemed like rational fury.

One of the bandits dropped his sword in an instinctive move to cover his head from the flailing iron-shod hooves. The second waved his blade wildly, undecided whether Rabble or her steed posed the greater threat. Rabble decided the point by knocking the bandit flat with a solid kick to the groin.

Across the road, Bryax had slain his first bandit easily. Dismounted now, he furiously fought against an opponent who, while certainly no better, had the advantage of reach granted by her barbed spear. Ducking a thrust that holed his riding cloak, Bryax brought his blade up and through the seasoned wood of the spear's shaft.

The bandit spun the shaft in her hands and came at him again, using the wood as a staff. Who would have won the odd contest was left undecided, for Scrapper—having treed her man—darted through Bryax's opponent's legs. The woman lost her balance, though not her hold on her staff, and Bryax pressed his sword into the hollow of her throat. Instantly, she threw the wood away in surrender.

Meanwhile, several well-placed bolts from Rylus and Tambor's crossbows had spooked the rest of the bandits. Preferring to attack the wagon—which logically must hold the loot—they ran forward, inside the top-mounted bows' range where only Hulhc and Angie stood on defense, apparently weaponless.

Before they were in sword range, Angie raised her hand to her lips and blew. The bandits reeled back, choking and rubbing their eyes.

"Hold these, Dog Meat!" Rabble ordered, abandoning her first two opponents to help the healer and the farmer with their opponents.

Brutally, the red-haired woman dispatched two more bandits, beheading one and then knocking his partner out with her sword's pommel on the return stroke. Leaving Scrapper, with her paws planted firmly on the chest of the spear woman, Bryax hurried to help Rabble.

As the blond man came pounding up, the remaining bandits threw down their weapons.

"We surrender!" pleaded a man, his voice clearly the same that had so confidently given the order to attack. "Mercy!"

Bryax accepted the man's surrender, cheerfully collecting the swords and spears the bandits had tossed down in defeat.

Hulhc steadied the draft horses, while Rylus and Tambor kept their crossbows ready for treachery.

Rabble strode over to disarm the two bandits that Dog Meat still guarded. The woman remained unconscious, but the man—perhaps in panicked contemplation of what penalty might be exacted for his crimes—leapt for the warhorse's saddle.

Dog Meat snapped at him, narrowly missing. Before the horse could even begin to throw his intruder from the saddle, Gimp's long grey forepaw struck out of the saddlebag. The cat's claws imbedded solidly into the bare flesh of the bandit's arm.

Popping half out of the bag, the cat repeated the blow, striking with the speed of a venomous snake, glaring at the man with evil green eyes.

The bandit slumped forward, weeping about demon spirits as he clutched his bloody arm. Rabble hauled him roughly from the saddle and marched him to join his compatriots.

"Is this all of you?" Bryax demanded.

"Yes, sir," the spokesman replied nervously. "All of us, except for Tai, who you ran through, and Omei, who the lady beheaded. This is all of us."

"What manner of folk are you?" asked the spearwoman. "We outnumbered you more than two to one—even if you count the oldster and the fat men. How did you beat us?"

"Witchcraft," muttered lean Har, whom Scrapper had treed. "They command the beasts to fight with them."

"There is no magic left in the world," the spokesman retorted, but he seemed far from certain. "What will you do with us, gentles?"

"We've heard," Rylus said, "there is a price on your heads in Saltport. I suppose we'll turn you over to justice there."

"Justice!" the spearwoman spat. "There's no justice for such as us in Saltport. The rulers there usurped our homes and property, forcing us into this wasteland banditry."

Tambor had been studying the captives intently. Now he

stepped forward and lifted the leather cap from the woman's head. Her close-cropped hair was ashy blonde and her grey eyes widened in astonishment.

"I know you!" Tambor said. "Aren't you Valma?"

"I am," she replied. "How do you know me?"

"Your new attire confused me at first," the beastmaster said, his soft voice holding malice, "but when last we came to Saltport I did business with you. You were collecting merchant's tax then and explained your town's new tax on imports so carefully that I vowed never to forget you. What are you doing here?"

Valma flushed red with embarrassment. "We all have been forced out by those who now rule in Saltport. You have their look—you with your golden skin and slanting eyes."

"Their look?" Tambor asked, puzzlement replacing some of his anger.

"Aye! Outlanders," Valma said. "Exiles to whom our town gave welcome when the Loss stranded their magic vessels in our lands. Now the outland elders have gathered a cabal of their own people in union with some of Saltport's traitorous types. Together they have made us exiles from our own city."

"You see why we doubt that we will find 'justice' there," the spokesman said, interrupting Valma with a weary sigh. "I am Altus and I was head of the Merchant's Guild until the outland coup. I decided that if they had my town at least they would not have easy access to the lands around it. With like-minded allies, I founded this band and we have been fighting against the usurpers since."

"I wonder how the 'outlanders' would tell the tale," Tambor said, his face lined with old memories.

"We should learn more, I suppose." Rylus blew his breath out in a hearty gust. "Still, we are clear victors today. We owe War and Chance thanks. However, I am ill-disposed to show courtesy to those who have attacked me and mine."

"Hobble the captives hand and ankle," Rabble suggested, "and I'll set Scrapper to keep them in line."

"Good." Rylus turned to the captives. "Altus, delegate four to bury your dead and quickly. Valma, you show Bryax and Rabble where your loot is cached. I wager it isn't far."

When found, the bandits' loot proved poor enough and substantiated their claim that they had been living hand to mouth.

"If we move fast, we'll get clear of this cursed wood before nightfall," Rylus stated when the various tasks were done. "In the morning, a few of us will go ahead to Saltport and learn how much truth there is in these scoundrels' tale of woe."

"Fair enough," Tambor agreed, though his gaze was hard when he looked at the captives. "Perhaps this victory is a good omen for the rest of our journey."

"Perhaps, old friend," Rylus said with a worried frown. "Perhaps."

6

Rebellion or revolution? As I see it, they're just different words for saying that someone new will be collecting the taxes.

> The Grand

As SUNRISE touched the skies with pink and yellow, Rabble and Rylus prepared to ride into Saltport.

"Hey, Rylus! Where's your mount?" Rabble called, leading Dog Meat to the first wagon.

The battered grey stallion's wound, once cleaned and treated with a salve Angie had compounded from calendula flowers, plantain leaves, wormwood, and comfrey leaves, merged into the general disreputable tapestry of Dog Meat's hide. Gimp rode pillion, arrogantly grooming himself like a knight preparing for battle.

"Here," Rylus patted a baldface draft horse on one brown flank. "I had Tambor give me one of his beauties. The wagons won't be moving until we come back. Anyhow, I need something Bet's size to carry me."

"We'll be back by mid-day, latest," Rabble promised the stay-behinds, swinging astride Dog Meat and whistling for Scrapper.

"Take care," Hulhc cautioned her. "I've been listening to our captives and they have very low opinions of the ethics of the new rulership of Saltport."

"Don't worry about us," Rylus said. "I value my hide and I'm sure that Rabble values hers."

Once they were underway, Rylus asked his companion, "Have you ever been to Saltport, Rabble?"

"No, I don't think I have been," Rabble answered, her brow wrinkling momentarily, "though I've heard of it, of course. Anything special I should know?"

Rylus shrugged. "Saltport is not a large town—not these days—but when the magic was still vital, it was one of the most thriving ports in the Fresh Lakes. It was a free trade zone—not like Lakeside, or most towns, which pay taxes to a ruler. Somewhere in the dim reaches of the past the port was given its freedom and it fought to keep it, even when it had become a jewel that many would have liked to claim."

"Ah, yes, I remember," Rabble said. "Saltport—yes— it requires mandatory military tours by all its citizens, doesn't it? No wonder our 'bandits' were so well-trained."

"Makes you wonder about those who threw them out," Rylus agreed, "but there'll be no need to wonder soon. There are the gates before us. Closed, I note."

"And guarded," Rabble commented. "What business do we give for our visit? Do we tell them about the bandits?"

"Our business is the Spectacular," Rylus answered. "Let's learn a bit more before we tell them anything else."

The guards at the gate permitted them to enter as far as a solid one-story cobblestone building. The sign swinging out front identified it as the Office of the Commissioner of Revenue. For the illiterate, a sketch of an outstretched hand, a pile of coins on its palm, told the story.

"Blunt, but honest," Rylus said. "Typical of the Saltport I remember."

They tied Dog Meat and Bet to a hitching post and left Scrapper to guard. The door opened into a neat office, with a solid desk on one side, a series of windowed cubbies on the other. A clerk looked up from the desk as their bootsteps echoed off the shiny board floor.

He was a skinny bird of a fellow with a sharp nose and a thin line of purple running from the corner of his mouth— caused by the bad habit of sucking on his pen while filling out documents.

"May I assist you?" he asked, setting down a gull-quill pen.

"Yes, I believe so," Rylus said. "I am Rylus, part owner of the Travelling Spectacular."

While Rylus and the clerk discussed taxes and operating expenses, Rabble ambled about the waiting area. The three cashiers looked at her with friendly curiosity. She nodded politely, but her attention was for the boldly lettered news items hung on the walls. One caught her particular notice and while the clerk was fetching a permit, she poked Rylus.

"Read this and look at the sketch," she whispered. "Those are our prisoners!"

" 'Bandits!' " Rylus read aloud. " 'Reward offered for the bandits who have been harrying travellers on the landside of Saltport.' "

The clerk returned and Rylus pointed to the poster.

"I don't recall bandit trouble last year," he said.

"There has been a shift in government," the clerk replied. "Some who did not care for the changes have become outlaws."

"What? That's a bit extreme!"

"I think so," the clerk agreed, "but you might say that the outlaws created their own troubles."

"I don't understand," Rylus admitted. "Bandits don't usually see themselves as trouble for anyone except for those they prey on."

"Did you meet with the bandits on your way in?" the clerk asked eagerly. "I had forgotten that you had come in on the land road."

"We did," Rylus said, allowing a slow grin to tease the corners of his mouth.

He had everyone's attention now.

Silently decrying Rylus' desire to create a sensation, Rabble shifted so that she was covering their escape route. The cashiers were leaning out of their windows and a tang of excitement filled the closed room.

"Was anyone killed or injured?" the clerk asked.

"Two killed," Rylus answered, "and some cuts and bruises."

"Well, that will settle it," the clerk gave a short jerk of his head. "The Council has been debating over whether to raise the reward or maybe to sanction bounty hunters. They've been reluctant, since the troubles were political rather than simply economic. This will settle the question. Come, you must tell your tale directly to the Commissioner . . ."

"Wait!" Rylus fought not to laugh. "You misunderstood me, friend. The dead were bandits—the wounded as well."

"You escaped?" a cashier chirped breathlessly.

"Not precisely . . ."

At the clerk's insistence, Rylus told their story to the Commissioner and then again to the Council. Rabble was given an escort and sent to bring both the Travelling Spectacular and the bandits into Saltport.

"It seems that we're to be heroes," Rabble told Bryax as they trotted toward Saltport. "They're not quite ready to hand over the Key to the treasury, but they are granting remittance of fees and a prime spot to set up the Spectacular. Business should be good."

"Hulhc won't like it," Bryax commented. "He begrudges anything that slows him on his quest. I wonder why? After all the years that have gone by, I'm surprised that he's in such a hurry. The seasons will be with us, too. Spring comes later in the mountains and here planting time has barely begun.''

"Odd, isn't it," Rabble commented, "that a farmer would leave before the crops are in."

"Maybe that's his rush," Bryax replied. "Perhaps he hopes to be home before the harvest."

When the Spectacular arrived in Saltport, the bandits were immediately taken into custody. The promised reward came just as quickly.

"Well, this is a good turn of events," Rylus said, spilling out the coins. "Any thoughts on how to use it?"

"This is a port," Tambor replied. "We've already set money by for passage across the Sapphire Lake. I say divvy the reward into six even shares and split the remainder between Rabble and Bryax since they took the big risks."

"All I want is drinking money," Rabble said. "Tambor, take mine and find us another lost beasty for your menagerie."

Tambor accepted her offering readily. "Keep enough to get yourself some of the local liqueurs, Rabble. Some are world famous."

"Too sweet for me," she said, dropping most of the coins in his hand. "I like a drink that burns."

The next day, the Travelling Spectacular began performances. Business was indeed very promising. The local Council had sent along talented assistants, most of whom Rylus delegated to Hulhc, who had taken over the games of chance which he ran with stern efficiency. Angie vanished into her tent and only the long line snaking through it gave evidence that she existed at all.

"I don't like it, I tell you," Bryax said, late one afternoon several days after their arrival. "There's been a hum in the air and I keep overhearing debate about the bandits' trial. Things could get ugly—Altus and Valma did have partisans here in the city."

"All we can do is warn the others," Rabble said with a shrug. "We have only a few more hours before the final sparring match of the day. Rylus tells me that I'll have a fairly good partner this time around."

"Nervous?" Bryax asked. "They make trained warriors here."

Rabble spat. "Nervous? No, I need a workout."

Rylus hurried up then. "Rabble, we have a problem. The elimination matches are down to two and they refuse to fight each other—at least not by tournament rules. It's this political thing. They both insist that they would be honor bound to kill the other."

"So," Rabble grinned, "I'll fight both, together or separately. Just remind them that in the final round I'll try to leave them alive, but I don't promise to leave them walking."

Rylus shook his head. "Rabble, you sound positively bloodthirsty, but your solution works."

News that judgment had been passed against the bandits came as Tambor's two bears were dancing with ponderous stateliness to drumbeat and trumpet supplied by Hulhc's erstwhile croupiers. The games of chance had been closed for the duration of the performance and even Angie had emerged from her tent.

"The word that the bandits are condemned ripples from mouth to mouth like waves on the Great Salt Sea," Angie said. "Some smile, some scowl. I have listened to much today. Saltport is a drawn bow—will this decision fire the arrow or snap the string?"

"Pretty words," Rabble said as she checked the straps on her armor, then glanced to where Bryax was briefing the first of her opponents on the rules, "and sadly true. We can only hope that the Spectacular will distract those who are here."

Stately despite his rolls of fat and garish clothing, Rylus stepped to the center of the area to announce the local opponent.

"Our first challenger tonight says that his father and mother came to Saltport on the sky ship *Swallow*. He has chosen to begin fighting with spear and shield, secondary weapon long sword. I ask you to welcome M'theny!''

The challenger stepped out, a fair-skinned man in his thirties with brown hair that frizzed to his shoulders and thick brows over brown eyes. He bowed to Rylus and waved to the crowd in the tiered bleachers.

Wild cheers answered his gesture, but only from some clumps. Other areas remained stolidly silent. A few anonymous voices shouted, ''Outlander! Go home!''

''Well,'' Rabble said, ''I'd better beat them both. We're not the enemy, here but we could become one if anyone decides that we're taking sides and after that bit with the bandits . . .''

''Go!'' Angie gave her a soft shove. ''Rylus has nearly finished introducing you. Good luck!''

Rabble saluted and strode onto the field. The ground was firm and grassy underfoot, but she'd practiced here earlier with Bryax and knew it could turn treacherous. She tuned out both Rylus' hyperbole and the crowd noise to focus on M'theny. He lowered his spear and studied her through eyes so narrowed that eye and brow made two dark parallel lines.

Slowly, tauntingly, Rabble smiled, wrinkling up her freckled nose. She shifted her grip on her sword, took a step back. As she expected, the temptation became too much for her opponent.

M'theny might be good—in fact, as he lunged at her she was certain that he was very good—but the arena differs from the battlefield. The first move chooses the strategy, and Rabble had seen so many openings in the ancient game of honor that she was well prepared to answer any.

M'theny charged, leveling his spear at her mid-section. Rabble spun to one side, her braid trailing like a comet's fiery tail. When the spearhead passed her, she grabbed the shaft and jerked it from his grip.

''Did you see that!'' Hulhc cheered. ''Rabble's incredibly fast—incredibly strong! She's making a fool of her opponent.''

"That may not be a good idea." Bryax came over to join the farmer. "The crowd is getting ugly."

As Bryax spoke, M'theny went down. Rabble hit him as he tried to rise.

"Foul! Foul!" came shouts from the stands.

Rabble pivoted and slowly scanned the crowd.

"She don't need to cheat," a new voice yelled, "not to beat an Outlander. My ancient grandame could beat an Outlander."

"Foul!" the voices insisted.

The arena conflict was now forgotten as the stands erupted into dozens of brawls. Rocks, fruit, and raw vegetables flew. The westering sun glinted from metal as a variety of bladed weapons were drawn.

"War and Chance!" Bryax cursed. "Riot!"

Unwilling to leave him to the mob, Rabble stood guard over her erstwhile opponent.

Tambor and Rylus had backed to the wagons and were readying their crossbows to defend their livelihood. Bryax, Hulhc, and Angie were edging to join them when a wildly thrown stone smashed Rabble in the side of her mouth.

The blood welled out, dripping onto M'theny. Rabble's enormous brown eyes widened further and the copper sword was not so much drawn as it blossomed in her hand. M'theny forgotten, Rabble charged the stands. She leapt from riser to riser apparently precisely certain who had cast the stone that had wounded her.

"Rabble!" Bryax hollered. "Sword Sister!"

A streak of mottled brown and tan burst by him as Scrapper bolted after her mistress. Screaming, a woman fell as the dog bumped into her.

"Bryax! Come away!" Angie tugged at his arm. "Rabble is blood mad now. There's no stopping her."

"No." Bryax scowled. "You and Hulhc get to safety. Help Rylus and Tambor protect the wagons. Rabble is my oath sister."

Even in the maelstrom of the riot, finding Rabble was

easy; near her was the only place that any order existed and it was the order of a wild and steady retreat. The setting sun bathed her in red-gold light so that to Bryax she seemed to be afire. Scrapper crouched at her back, keeping away any who came too close.

Charging into the stands, Bryax bellowed, grabbed the first person who got in his way and threw him to the ground. As the Saltporter fell with a satisfying crunch, Bryax was charged by another, this one armed with one of the long thrusting spears the Saltporters favored.

Bryax solved this difficulty by backing up as if in retreat. Then, when he was just out of the spear's range, Bryax bent and grasped the plank on which the Saltporter was standing. His corded muscles bulging with the effort, he tore the plank free from its moorings and the man toppled.

In the lower reaches of the arena, the Saltport militia was efficiently quelling the riot. The unconscious and severely wounded were put on wagons commandeered from the festival-goers. Those who persisted in fighting were entangled in heavy fishing nets and then led away.

Only Rabble seemed unaware that the riot was under control. Her brown eyes were wide and yet somehow unseeing, the gold flecks pronounced. The bleeding at the corner of her mouth had slowed, but the clotting blood left an ugly trail against her fair skin.

From her perch atop the highest tier of the stands, she stood poised, sword in hand. A heap of the fallen lay about her or dangled grotesquely from the wooded risers. Some still breathed.

When Bryax moved closer, she swung her head and that unseeing, all-seeing gaze transfixed him. Even Scrapper growled. Bryax could hear the murmurs of the militia behind him and the words "bow and arrow" stole his breath from his chest.

"Rabble," he said steadily. "Sword Sister. Don't you know me? It's Bryax, your Shield Brother."

Scrapper's tail wagged hesitantly, but Rabble gave no sign

of recognition. Still, neither did she lunge toward him so he took another cautious step into that dark gaze, then a third until Rabble shifted her grip on her blade.

Bryax halted. " 'Tis Bryax, Rabble. The battle is over, the enemy is vanquished. Come back to the wagons and let Angie take care of that cut."

Rabble's free hand drifted to the corner of her mouth. The tips of her fingers brushed the swollen and bruised flesh.

"They dare harm me!" she hissed, her voice so soft that Bryax doubted any but he heard the mad pronouncement.

"They are all vanquished, Rabble," Bryax repeated, a note of desperation sharpening his voice. "Come away with me and Scrapper."

The cur thumped her tail against the boards at the sound of her name. Rabble started, her gaze flickering to the dog. She blinked then, her shoulders loosened. For the first time, she seemed to see the fallen at her feet. When again she looked at Bryax, her eyes had lost their mad, passionate depth.

"It is over," she said, the words not quite a question.

"It is," he answered. "Come away. I'm for a mug of dark ale. Fighting is thirsty work."

"None of that goat's piss for me," she smiled, her tone normal. "I want a hit or two of that clear stuff that smells of juniper. Angie has a bottle or so somewhere."

Bryax was aware that a few members of the Saltport militia were climbing to retrieve the wounded and slain. He put out his hand to Rabble and she sheathed her sword and stepped over the heap of bodies. Scrapper trotted happily beside them as they descended past the awed Saltporters.

"No foul," Rabble said, suddenly fixing one with a shadow of that disconcerting gaze.

"No foul." The man paled beneath his sailor's tan.

"Tell them," Rabble said, her voice echoing oddly. "Tell them all."

7

*Old Man Moon has bright, bright eyes,
Sweet Mother Earth has warm, soft thighs . . .*

Traditional

"WE CERTAINLY don't blame you or your Company for the riot," the Saltport council chief explained nervously, "but we do believe that your immediate departure would be best for all involved. We have arranged for a reliable ship and paid your passage and freight to White Foam Sound."

Rylus hesitated, pulling at the curl at the tip of his goatee. He didn't think it was necessary to tell the Councilor that the Spectacular had already decided to leave Saltport on the first available ship. The wagons had escaped all but minor damage and Rabble's initial wound had been the only one that any of their number had taken, but they no longer felt that Saltport would be receptive to their entertainments—or that they would be so lucky in the event of a second uprising.

The councilor chief cleared her throat. "Rylus, please understand, we are not ungrateful for your help with the bandits. The rest of your reward money will be waiting at the docks."

The rest? Rylus knew a bribe when he heard one. The reward had already been paid in full. This money was for the Company's lost business and to keep them pleasant-tongued toward Saltport. In these days of slower communications, a traveller's word carried much weight.

"I certainly appreciate your gracious offer," Rylus said in his best courtly tones. "I must, of course, consult with my partners, but unless they offer some major argument against

52

your proposal, I believe we can depart as you wish. What is our ship called and when does she sail?''

''The ship is *Bolla's Ninth*,'' the Councilor replied, ''and she sails with the tide in about four hours.''

Rylus summoned Tambor for a private conference in their wagon. The beastmaster arrived promptly, a long, multicolored snake coiled about his neck.

''Lovely, isn't it?'' Tambor said. ''I bought it with my share of the reward money.''

''It is attractive,'' Rylus answered, though to be honest he hoped that Tambor wasn't planning on making it an indoor pet. The monkeys were just about his limit. ''Speaking of the reward money, we've been offered a bonus if we agree to leave on a ship that the city council has found for us.''

Tambor's hands restlessly stroked his new pet. He pulled up the corner of his mouth in an unconvincing smile.

''We will leave, of course,'' he said. ''We had decided to already, but Ry . . .''

Rylus let Tambor fume for a few moments. During the years of their partnership he had learned to accept that Tambor's eloquence came in fits and spurts. Honestly, the beastmaster would prefer the company of a rabid dog to that of most people—which didn't keep him from being the most loyal of friends to those he had given his trust.

''Ah, Ry!'' Tambor said. ''It's small of me but part of me wants to stay here and rub these bigots' faces in their smallness. I want . . . I want . . .''

''The bigots are out of favor,'' Rylus reminded him.

''Out of power, not out of favor.'' Tambor's bitterness seemed to transmit itself to the snake which raised its head and hissed.

''Out of power then,'' Rylus said, ''and with what happened to Valma and her cohort, they may be out of favor as well. This really stung, didn't it?''

Tambor nodded. ''It brought back memories of when I was small, after Father's . . . death. We were harried from town to town then, you know. There are lots of places that don't want you if you weren't born to them.''

"There are places," Rylus said softly, "that don't want you even if you *are* born to them. I've seen the dark side of the city, Tambor. Saltport has its bigots, but it has its citizens and laws, too. I've lived in places where that was far from the case. In Saltport, when the bigots got too tough on the 'outlanders'—remember how they were about taxes last time we were through?—they were out."

"I remember," Tambor said, "and I remember what you dealt with growing up—the thieves band, the prostitution, the . . ."

Ignoring the snake, Rylus leaned to embrace his partner.

"Enough now, Tam," he said. "The past is past. We've made a virtue of homelessness and there's not many who can claim that. Time to tell the rest that we have scant four hours to get the Spectacular aboard a ship called *Bolla's Ninth*."

Tambor leapt to his feet, nearly hitting his head on the low ceiling. "Four hours! That's barely time to get the horses aboard! Rylus!"

Rylus chuckled as he watched Tambor flee. He knew Tambor would manage what needed to be done. He always did. Always.

Bolla's Ninth proved to be a magnificent tripled-masted vessel, amply equipped for passengers, cargo, and livestock. Alba Bolla, the captain, was a dark-skinned, androgynous woman with broad features and close-cropped hair like the finest wool. She welcomed them aboard with minimal fuss.

"The Saltport Council has paid for my best available cabins for you all. The horses—Indigo Lake love you, you have enough of them!—are to be berthed below. It will be difficult getting the wagons into the hold. Do you have any problems with lashing them to the deck?"

"None," Rylus said. "We've made this crossing before, though never on such a fine ship. I can remove the wheels and lash the boxes so they won't shift."

"Good!" Bolla grinned, giving them a clear view of the brilliant rubies set in her front teeth. "Welcome aboard *Bolla's Ninth*."

"Excuse me, Captain," Rabble said nervously, "but why *Bolla's Ninth*? What happened to the other eight ships?"

"Why they're all still in service—as are ships ten through fifteen," Alba Bolla replied. "My family has wet sailing in its blood since generations before the Loss. We've ships on this salt lake and on four of the sweet lakes as well."

"Ah," Rabble nodded. "I am pleased to hear it."

Under Captain Bolla's casual direction, the Company loaded livestock and gear. Afterward, Bryax and Rabble volunteered to load the slings that brought aboard the bales of hay, bushels of oats, and other more interesting cargo that were being fit into the *Ninth*'s already crammed holds by Bolla's skilled crew.

"I'm for a brandy or three before we get underway," Rabble sighed when the last crate and bundle had been shifted aboard. "There's a tavern just over the way. What say you, Sword Brother?"

Bryax looked at the sun and the rising tide with concern. "Don't think we'll have the time, Rabble. The tide's nearly in and the Captain will want every moment of high water she can get with the ship loaded so heavily."

"Ah," Rabble stood, undecided. "Then wait aboard and yell for me. I want a keg of something to take aboard."

"But, Rabble, you saw what we loaded as galley supplies . . ."

Bryax's protest trailed off and he cursed, for the red-haired warrior had already pelted away. Barking excitedly, Scrapper loped after.

Bryax walked slowly up the gangplank, and once aboard leaned onto a land-facing railing with an aggravated groan.

"She's afraid of water, you know," Angie said, appearing silently beside him.

In honor of the impending sea voyage the Far Shore's Healer had painted a wavy fronded sea anemone about each eye, which gave her an expression rather like a startled owl. Her bright gold hair was brushed into two broad wings, completing the effect.

Bryax glowered at her, despite her perky cuteness. "Rabble afraid of water! Nonsense! Rabble's the bravest person I've ever met."

"I didn't say she wasn't brave," Angie corrected. "Far from. She's going on the ship, you see. But she's afraid of water, look and see you. She only drinks it when she must, never swims, bathes in little cat baths with cloth and bowl. She's afraid, all right. I've watched her over the time since we found her off of Old Shrine Road in the Downs and she near died of fright when I brought a tub for her to have a hot bath."

"Afraid of water? Even that little bit?"

Bryax fell silent, watching the road, wondering what he'd do if Rabble failed to return in time. He sighed in relief when he heard barking and saw a flash of coppery hair.

"Here comes Rabble, Angie. War and Chance! She's got a brandy cask under each arm. How does she still run so fast?"

"Odd one, our Rabble," Angie began.

Her words were cut short by the clanging of a great brass bell.

"All aboard!" The cabin boy crowed. "All aboard for White Foam Sound!"

"Rabble! Hurry!" Bryax yelled, heading down the gangplank toward her.

"Get out of my way!" she called. "These casks aren't light!"

Bryax backed off, putting a restraining hand on the sailor who was about to pull in the gangplank. "Just one more passenger to come aboard, friend."

Rabble bounded up onto the deck, Scrapper preceding her, still barking loudly.

"All aboard," she gasped, collapsing to the deck, one arm still around each of her casks. "All aboard. Elements all! I hate sailing."

She grinned at Angie and Bryax. "This one's a several day crossing, isn't it? Well, I'm for my hammock. Ask

Tambor to mind my beasties for me, will you? Gimp likes being down with the horses. He's murder on rats. Don't let him bring me any, please. He did once and I got sick.''

She paused, considering.

"Sicker."

Bryax stood gaping. Rabble had grown so pale that her freckles stood out like pox on an ill child. When she stood, she could barely heft the casks she had been running with before. Even her thick red hair seemed to have lost its luster.

"I hate sailing," she repeated, watching the sails belling out.

"Let me help you to your cabin," Bryax said. He took one of the brandy casks and tucked it under his arm.

"Come along with your brother, Rabble. I'll even make your bunk."

She followed docilely, not without one more look of loathing for the water.

Rabble spent a miserable crossing. She vomited up anything that she tried to eat. After Angie brewed a potion of cinnamon, cardamom, nutmeg, and cloves—and insisted that she drink it—Rabble recovered enough to get sodding drunk. For the next three days, she lay on her bunk, rising only when she must and alternatingly drinking, sipping small doses of Angie's potion, and sleeping.

The last was a relief to passengers and crew alike; when she was drunk Rabble sang soldier's songs loudly and tunelessly. Her creatively off-color versions of songs that largely had been lewd to begin with were so artistically perverse that the listener's ears usually burnt from involuntary blushes.

"I've never seen her so far gone," Bryax commented in awe to the rest of the Company one evening during dinner, "and we've gone drinking plenty of times."

"The Council in Saltport did us a favor when they arranged for private cabins," Rylus admitted. "We'd be in trouble if she had ended up slinging a hammock below decks."

"We've one more water crossing," Tambor reminded him, "if we're to carry out Hulhc's journey before the weather becomes too cold to dare the mountains. Going around the Slate Lake would add months to our journey."

"If she can't make the voyage, we'll have to pay her off," Hulhc said reluctantly. "Deities know, I'll never find anyone else like her, but I have no wish to spend years rather than months on this journey."

"She'll be all right," Angie said. "I'm sure of it."

The passage—except for Rabble—was as calm as a voyage could be. Spring squalls occasionally splashed the *Ninth*, but the weather's rage seemed reserved for other areas of the lake. Captain Bolla ran a taut ship. Her crew came from all over the Seven Lakes region, though most were lake sailors rather than veterans of the Great Salt Sea.

"There's nothing out there worth the time and trouble," Captain Bolla explained. "Takes weeks or months to get anywhere interesting and the poky fishing villages don't have any of the treasures you still find inland. The Seven Lakes were called the Gemstones of the Deities, you know. Up farther north, they call 'em the Gemstones of the Elements, but what it all comes down to is that the Lake regions were special, especially before the Loss."

"I've read about how it was," Hulhc said, his voice husky with wonder. "There were colleges to teach the magical arts, libraries for its lore, and cities crafted to show off what the sorcerous arts could achieve."

"I've seen some of these places," Captain Bolla said. "Sad places now, but there's always scavenging and that makes for good cargoes. My grandchildren may find that crossing the Great Salt Sea is what they'll need to do to find treasures, but me and mine are stringing a shipping network that will rival the airships. You just wait and see."

Hulhc frowned, as if something she had said made him uncomfortable, and pointedly turned the discussion to whether Captain Bolla thought that there was any truth to the persistent rumors of sea dragons.

*   *   *

White Foam Sound was an attractive town, clean and populous. However, some of the same political factionalism that was tearing up Saltport was active here as well and, after discussion, Tambor and Rylus decided that moving onward would be wiser than remaining.

Rabble recovered quickly once she was ashore. After a day of eating, she regained her strength and sense of humor.

"Look at Gimp," she demanded. The cat was asleep on his accustomed perch on Dog Meat's rump, his usually sleek, almost whip-thin body visibly plumper. "I should have charged the captain for Gimp's services. If there is a rat on board, it won't be for his not trying."

"The horses and the llama did have a better trip than usual," Tambor noted. "I guess Gimp kept the rats and mice from their feed. The bears are doing well, too. I wonder if Gimp shared his catch?"

Gimp licked his front paw with a satisfied expression, catlike, refusing to give anything away.

"We're heading into the fringes of the territory the Spectacular usually frequents," Rylus said. "Normally we would spend time in White Foam Sound, then go up and down the coast, and inland a few miles before heading back."

"Actually," Tambor added. "Our usual route is even more aimless. I hope that there are no disappointed children waiting for us in the smaller towns."

This last was in response to a panicked look from Hulhc, who clearly had been steeling himself to once again remind them that they needed to waste as little time as possible.

"We'll take the northerly road." Rylus patted his new map case. "According to the maps Captain Bolla sold us, the route is direct while still offering opportunities for us to perform. I have maps that will take us all the way to the foothills of the Storm Shrouds."

Angie unrolled one map and traced a slim finger down the drawn roadway, humming happily.

"I love maps!" she chirped. "From here we will pass through Collinsville and then past several small holdings—

that's what these little x's must be—then through Falconersville. Then the paper is shaded differently. Is that another country?''

Rylus nodded. ''See the big letters across the area? It's called the Domain of Roses.''

''Pretty name,'' Tambor said. ''I've always fancied going there.''

''At the border of the Domain of Roses,'' Rylus continued, ''we'll take a boat across the Slate Lake. From there on, we'll travel overland, mostly through the Domain of Dragons.''

''And then we'll find where the magic went,'' Hulhc said, so softly that he might have been thinking aloud. ''And maybe we'll be able to bring magic into the world again!''

''And maybe we should decide where to stop tonight,'' Bryax interrupted practically.

Rylus studied the map. ''If we can make Falconersville by dark, I'd like to rest there—maybe play a few shows, learn the local gossip.''

Hulhc scowled. Rylus shook his head, silencing the rebuke before the farmer could speak.

''Hulhc, different territories have different rules. Falconersville is a border town. Our questions will be expected. Further on, ignorance could get us hurt or delayed— questions could mark us as potential targets for bandits. We haven't had to be so careful before this because Tambor and I knew the area. Even so, look what happened in Saltport.''

''I know.'' Hulhc's scowl remained. ''Forgive me, but I am impatient to realize the dream of my life.''

He stalked off. Rylus rolled up and cased the map. Tambor reached out and patted his companion's hand.

''Frustrating, isn't he?'' the beastmaster said softly. ''The trouble is, I feel almost sorry for the old fellow. Then he gets sharp with someone and I want to lock him in with the bears so that they can teach him some manners.''

Rylus forced a chuckle. ''Don't do it, Tam. It wouldn't be fair to the bears.''

* * *

Falconersville, they discovered upon arriving, was technically two towns separated by a river. One town belonged to the Domain of Roses, the other to the Domain of Sapphire Sound. In practice, it was a trade city, the borders and rules of the Domain of Roses not coming into practice until after a traveller departed Falconersville. This, as the company rapidly concurred, was all to the good of Falconersville, for the Domain of Roses was a military dictatorship of the strictest type.

Rylus returned from the town registry with his arms weighed down with paperwork, grumbling about regulations.

"Passports, cargo manifests, licenses for all the animals—each to be filled out with complete descriptions in case of theft! Their ruler must own a paper-mill!"

"He does," Hulhc said, looking up from a copy of the elegantly printed weekly news-bill that each shop in town carried, "at least in one sense. Apparently, taxes are prohibitively high and any new business larger than a family shop tithes a portion of its profits to the Duke. I wonder why anyone lives here."

"The same reason that people live on farms ruined by salt winds," Angie suggested. "They don't have anywhere else to go."

"Let me buy you a drink or three," Rabble muttered to Bryax, "or they'll give us a heap of these forms to fill out."

"Wouldn't do them much good—at least with me," Bryax shrugged. "I can make my mark and puzzle out a few simple trade signs, but that's it. What languages can you read and write?"

Rabble's expression went completely blank for a moment. "Languages? Most of them, I think, though I might need to think about the ones I haven't heard recently."

Bryax looked impressed. "A military career can be good for that kind of thing, but I never managed it. Now, where shall we go drinking?"

"Let's find a place near a river crossing," Rabble answered. "I want to learn about the Domain of Roses."

The tavern they settled on advertised itself with a simple painted sign of a river barge loaded with beer barrels and wine casks. Although dark clouds threatened rain, the cut-glass windows were open and loud chatter spilled out. Inside, a central bar staffed by three men and a burly woman was doing steady business.

They headed toward the bar. Bryax shouldered them a path through the crowd without much difficulty. One of the bartenders, a thick-set man with a mustache like two gull wings that nearly concealed his mouth, came over immediately.

"Yer pleasure?" he asked in a guttural accent.

"A dark ale, easy on the foam, for my brother," Rabble said, "and a *pfneur breit* for me, double."

The bartender raised an eyebrow only slightly less impressive than his mustache, but he drew Bryax's ale. Then he poured a pale green liquid with an acrid minty scent into a widemouthed goblet. He slid it over to Rabble, who inhaled appreciatively.

"The garnish, please," Rabble said, as the bartender turned away.

The bartender puffed with artistic pride and appreciation for Rabble's sensibilities.

"Ah, you know how to drink a *pfneur breit*."

From a drawer built into the side of the bar he pulled a little bottle and a flat wooden box.

"Peppermint oil," he explained, rubbing a fine coating on the rim of the glass, then pouring a dollop into the *pfneur breit,* where it rose to coat the liqueur.

From the box he withdrew a flat, spear-shaped mint leaf, so perfectly dried that it had kept a memory of its green color. This last, he placed carefully on the lip of the glass. Taking a spill from the base of one of the lanterns that illuminated the bar, he carried a tiny flame over and set the mint leaf alight. The dry herb caught rapidly and then the oil and lastly the *pfneur breit* itself.

Rabble lifted the goblet by its stem, gave an expert swirl

of her wrist, and extinguished the fire. Then she drank deeply from the smokey liqueur.

"Lovely," she saluted the bartender. "Beautifully done."

He patted her hand paternally. "I hadn't realized that the lady was so well versed in the customs of my homeland. Please, call again if you want another."

He bustled off to draw another ale and Rabble sipped her drink with a contented sigh.

Bryax elbowed her. "Rab, I think your little show attracted some attention. I don't like how that group across the room has been looking at us."

"The ones in the dark green with the crimson trim?" she asked dreamily.

"Those."

"Domain of Roses, cavalry," she said softly. "These are mostly from the mainland. *Pfneur breit* is made as a specialty in an archipelago of islands in the Slate Lake that the Domain of Roses claims, but which has maintained some independence. I believe the Duke of Roses finds difficulty enforcing claims on islands that are somewhat self-sufficient and are willing to relinquish profitable trade in return for virtual independence. The problem has become acute since the Loss, since the magical airships are no longer available to transport troops quickly."

"So you did that on purpose," Bryax asked incredulously, "just to stir up trouble?"

Rabble grinned, her brown eyes snapping with mischief. "We haven't been in a bar fight in ages. Anyhow, I wanted to see if the Domain of Roses' internal politics were as testy as I thought."

"Well, they are," Bryax growled. "Here comes trouble—two fellows. You do the talking, since you know so much."

As they spoke, a couple of junior officers in the Domain of Roses cavalry sauntered up to the bar as if they rather fancied themselves and took seats, one on the side of Rabble, the other next to Bryax.

The one next to Rabble, a lanky fellow with a high-bridged nose and brown hair that had been stylishly oiled, shouted, "Bartender, ale here. And can't you do something about this terrible odor? Smells like a compost heap."

He guffawed, a nasal sound that resembled the whinny of a horse. His buddy, a stockier man with dark, bristly hair, and jug-handle ears, chortled approval.

"I suppose that you would know," Rabble said, a dangerous fire in her eyes. "Isn't that compost you've smeared in your hair?"

The man gaped, then swung wildly at her. Rabble easily blocked and sent him flying with a low punch to the gut. When the other would have come to his buddy's rescue, Bryax grabbed him by the front of his uniform jacket.

"I don't think that's wise, friend. My sister is bad-tempered. I've got to save her from herself."

Meanwhile, the agitated bar owner came running around the bar, waving his hands.

"Please! Please! No fighting. Remember Regulation 37A, sub-C."

Amazingly, his cryptic plea worked. The other Domain of Roses' soldiers who had been rising to their feet froze in place.

"Regulation 37A, sub-C?" Rabble asked, disappointment that she wasn't going to get to fight showing in every line of her fine-boned face.

"Yes," Bryax's captive growled. " 'Any officer caught fighting within the limits of Falconersville will be fined and expected to cover damages at twice the cost of replacement of goods.' "

"It doesn't prevent contests outside of Falconersville," the man Rabble had punched said as he got to his feet. "I, Durez of the Guard, challenge you redheaded bit of an islander to a duel, tomorrow, at dawn, outside of the western side of Falconersville."

"Make it the east side and it's a deal," Rabble said. "What are the terms? To the death? First blood? Honor satisfied?"

Durez blinked. "Why the east side?"

"Because I don't want to be late to help with the Travelling Spectacular and because the western side is purely Domain of Roses' territory. I don't want to run afoul of some regulation or other."

"I see," Durez said. "Very careful of you."

"Now, Durez, what are the terms?" Rabble said briskly. "Do you want to die or is bleeding enough for you? Or do you want to go halfway and allow yourself the option of surrender?"

"I am an officer of the Domain of Roses cavalry!" Durez bellowed. "I am not afraid of dying!"

"You should be," Rabble said. "Most mortals are—it tends to be rather permanent. Terms?"

Durez looked prepared to shout, "To the death!" when one of the officers across the room called out, "Remember Regulation 12C, sir."

"Oh, right!" Durez glowered at Rabble. "To first blood, then."

"What is Regulation 12C?" Bryax asked.

"'Officers on active duty may not engage in duels with deliberate intent of causing death,'" Durez replied. "Too many good officers were killed that way. Duels until 'Honor is satisfied' are forbidden under subsection A. Too many maimings."

"War and Chance!" Rabble swore. "They really hog-tie you. I believe that choice of weapons goes to the party challenged?"

"That is so."

"Well, you're a cavalry type, so to make things easier for you, let's duel with lances from horseback."

"Very good!" Durez agreed. "Lances and first blood—delightful."

"Then my second and I will await you on the field of honor," Rabble said. "Until dawn, Durez."

"Wait! What are you called, woman, so that the heralds can record our duel?"

"I'm Rabble."

"Rabble? That is all?" Durez looked indignant. "No family name? No military company?"

"No, just Rabble. I'll get back to you on my second."

"Tomorrow will be soon enough," Durez said. "My second will be Iron, also of the Cavalry of the Domain of Roses."

"Delighted," Rabble said, with a nod at Bryax's captive.

Still nonplussed, Durez scowled and strode from the bar, Iron skittering after him.

Bryax frowned worriedly. "Rabble, lances and first blood is quite likely to be fatal for someone."

"Durez doesn't seem worried," Rabble shrugged. "Do you want to be my second?"

Bryax straightened. "Of course! What is a Shield Brother for?"

"I didn't want to draw you into a private quarrel, especially since you didn't seem to approve." Rabble cheerfully finished her drink. "Now, want to help me buy a lance?"

8

Any violation of any published Regulation is punishable by the penalty published in said Regulations.

Regulations—Domain of Roses

"OF ALL the stupid, irresponsible behavior!" Hulhc stormed when he learned of the proposed duel. "You could very well be maimed or killed."

Rabble ignored him and glanced over at Bryax. "Think they'll wear armor?"

"Don't know," Bryax answered, "but there's probably a regulation for it."

"Well, I won't bother with more than a shield. I've got a chest guard for Dog Meat, though."

"Why are you doing this?" Hulhc continued angrily. "You said you were going out to find information, not to get into a fight. Were you drunk?"

"I only get drunk at sea," Rabble said with dignity. "Anyway, ask Bryax. I only had one drink. Listen, Hulhc, I wish you'd realize that we've already learned a great deal. The law is the real ruler in the Domain of Roses. If we could get a copy of their code—especially regarding their military—we would have a much easier trip."

"I'm working on that," Rylus said, joining them, his arms filled with forms. "Oh, Rabble, do you think that you could find a way to mention the Spectacular and the towns that we're planning on passing through during your introduction?"

Now Bryax became indignant. "Rabble is going to fight a duel—maybe be killed—and you are worrying about advertising?"

"No, be peaceful, blond man," Angie said, looking up from restocking the medical kit she was taking to the duel. "Rylus is a thinking man, beneath the belly. Tell us what you're thinking now, belly man."

Rylus squared the pile of forms. "Simple. Rabble has gotten us in a scrap with a member of the Domain of Roses military, right? And we probably won't be very popular with them, especially if she wins. Right?"

"Right!" Bryax and Hulhc agreed fervently.

Rylus' chins wiggled as he nodded with them. "Now, in a nation like the Domain of Roses, it would be rather easy for the military to make us disappear—or at least to delay us. They could pull all sorts of games—charge us with improper paint on the wagons or some obscure tax we haven't paid or not having enough paperwork on the livestock."

This last drew a hearty groan from Tambor, who had been silently scratching in details on forms, even as the argument raged around him.

"So," Rylus continued, "we make certain that everyone knows who we are and where we're going. From what I've heard, the Domain of Roses' current plethora of regulations is far from having complete support, especially among the merchants. By making our route and our stops *very* public, we will increase our safety."

"I like it," Bryax said.

Rabble nodded, looking up from her inspection of the lance she'd purchased earlier that day.

Hulhc shook his head in amazement. "Your thinking has more curves and wrinkles than a walnut's shell, Rylus, but there's real wisdom there. If you ever get tired of the road, I'll make you foreman of my farms."

Rylus grinned.

The next dawn was grey and damp, but a cool, quick breeze chased away the mist even before they had the horses saddled. Rabble, Bryax, and Angie left with plenty of time to spare.

"We'll be back for the Spectacular," Rabble promised.

"Good luck, you idiot!" Hulhc scolded.

She leaned from Dog Meat's saddle and kissed him on his thinning hair. "It's awfully nice to know that you care."

Hulhc blushed purple.

"What a lovely morning for a fight!" Rabble said as they road to the open field where the duel was to be held. "Scrapper! Come back here! There are probably regulations against chasing rabbits."

The cur came over, panting slightly, burrs in her fur.

"Rabble," Bryax turned toward her, a serious expression on his face. "Don't kill that young fool if you can help it. Don't let him kill you, but don't kill him."

"Why? He's a bigot and a troublemaker," Rabble said. "He did challenge me, you know."

"Well, he's an arrogant son of a bitch, I'll admit it, but I feel sorry for him," Bryax shrugged. "I feel sorry for him, that's all."

"I," Rabble said, her words clipped, "feel sorry for the people of the Archipelago of Truth, like that bartender. He's in exile because he agitated for freedom from the Domain of Roses for his people. However, since you are my Sword Brother, I will spare Durez."

They rode on in silence for a while more. When the field was visible, Bryax cleared his throat.

"Rabble, how did you know that about the bartender? I would swear you had never seen him before. He certainly didn't know you."

Rabble's slight smile vanished. "I just know. That's all."

With a drumming of hooves, a herald on a white horse draped in crimson and green trappings rode up to meet them.

"Please, take your places on the northern side of the field," she said formally. "You are Rabble, the Islander, my lady?"

"Rabble," the red-haired warrior said. "Just Rabble. I'm currently with the Travelling Spectacular, going into the Domain of Roses with stops at Floribunda and Grandiosa."

"You are not from the Archipelago? the herald said curiously. "Then why did you get into this conflict?"

"I chose to," Rabble said. "Let's get on with this. I want to try my new lance."

Across the field, mounted on a handsome black war horse, Durez readied an obviously custom-made lance. A pennant with a five-petaled rose fluttered from its end.

"The bastard has armor on!" Bryax said. "Do you want me to tell him to take it off?"

"No need," Rabble said lazily. "Where does he have skin showing?"

"Not much of anywhere," Bryax answered. "Nice armor. Our Durez is nobody's poor kid."

"Doesn't matter," Rabble said. "The herald is gesturing for us to come forth."

Rabble and Durez met in the center of the field, Bryax and Iron taking their places as seconds. The herald shook out a satin-draped trumpet, blew a ringing call for silence, and then cleared her throat.

"Here these two devotees of War and Chance meet on the field of personal combat. In order that Honor's requirements be satisfied, I must first ask you if you will put aside your differences."

Durez shook his head, a self-satisfied smirk on his face as he tossed back his cloak so that Rabble would be certain to see his armor.

Rabble grinned. "I think not, Madame Herald. Pretty armor, Durez, guess you must be pretty scared to bundle up so well."

Durez sputtered indignantly. Iron grabbed him before he could retort.

"Forget her, Durez, and get in position," Iron hissed. "Settling questions of honor is what this duel is for. Don't let the mercenary annoy you."

"Listen to him, Durez," Rabble said and she winked at him.

"Please take your positions," the herald said. "I will announce you as soon as you are in place."

"You can be a real bitch, Rabble," Bryax chuckled as they rode to the starting post. "Even if he wins, Durez will never live down that he came to a duel in fancy armor and you just wandered in wearing riding clothes."

"That's the idea, Shield Brother. Give me a kiss for luck." She straightened in the saddle and set her lance. "Scrapper, stay. Stay with Bryax."

"Good luck, Rabble," Angie called.

Angie was the only observer on Rabble's side of the field. Durez' entire company had apparently turned out to watch him; they stood silently, a unified flank of green and crimson cloaks turned up against the morning's chill.

Her voice thinned by distance, the herald announced them—politely including the Travelling Spectacular's planned itinerary in her spiel.

Rabble did not appear to hear a word, her gold-flecked gaze fixed on the crimson and green scarf in the herald's hand, poised for it to drop. When it fluttered to the ground, Dog Meat leapt forth, apparently without a signal from his rider.

From their side of the field, the members of Durez' company shouted encouragement, shouts that faded into incredulous silence as the riders met.

Effortlessly, Rabble caught Durez' lance point solidly against her shield. It hit with a loud crack, splintering a segment of her shield. Her own lance shattered Durez' rose-adorned shield to flinders but was itself split by the impact.

Durez, his weapon intact, did not wait for Rabble to get a second lance. He bent over his steed, using the animal's neck to replace his destroyed shield. Rabble yelled encouragement to Dog Meat and the battered stallion put on a burst of speed.

Unprepared for Rabble's sudden shift in velocity, Durez did not adjust his angle swiftly enough and his blow only grazed her shield. Rabble's splintered lance tore through the softer leather at the inner elbow of his right arm. He screamed and dropped his lance, clutching where blood fountained forth.

The herald pelted onto the field. "Blood has been drawn! Honor is satisfied!"

Rabble dropped her lance without slowing Dog Meat and circled over to sweep Angie and her medical supplies onto the saddle and over to where Durez was being helped to the ground by Iron. Durez might have protested charity, but Iron took one look at Angie's painted face—today the motif was a delicate red and white dianthus—and nodded welcome.

"A Far Shore's Healer. Wonderful!"

Rabble rode a polite distance away. Angie was quite safe but some of the members of Durez' group were glowering at her, as if steeling themselves for a challenge of their own. Bryax rode forward to join her, the horse Angie had ridden on a lead.

"I didn't kill him," Rabble said. "I could have. The

leather on his gorget was just as soft and he would have had to stop hiding behind his horse when he braced his lance for impact. He might even keep the arm.''

Bryax shook his head at her. ''You're unfeeling, Rabble.''

''That's unfair, Bryax,'' Rabble replied. ''I just don't approve of people who refuse to think through their actions. Durez was stupid to challenge a stranger. Even after he could have learned something about me, he chose to persist in the duel. I gave him a chance to resign. Remember?''

Bryax sighed. ''I apologize. I understand battle heat. I understand war for a cause. I simply have a problem with 'affairs of honor' that are really just adult temper tantrums.''

''Durez' tantrum,'' Rabble reminded him. ''Not mine.''

''But you set the stage with that *'pfneur breit'*—you wanted a brawl.''

''I wanted to learn,'' Rabble insisted.

''Let's leave it,'' Bryax said, ''or we'll be having a duel of our own.''

''Never,'' Rabble said seriously. ''You are my sworn brother. I will never fight against you.''

Angie rejoined them, patting Scrapper before strapping her bag into place and remounting.

''What's the verdict?'' Bryax asked.

''He'll keep the arm, but he won't be fighting with it for a while,'' Angie said. ''Not now. Not for a long time. Maybe not for ever, though I like to think I patch better than that. You're good with that lance, Rabble. Use one much?''

Rabble shrugged. ''Enough, I guess. Enough.''

They returned to the Travelling Spectacular, Bryax thinking about honor, Angie thinking about the mystery of Rabble, and Rabble thinking about nothing more than what Rylus might have prepared for breakfast.

Hulhc ran up to meet them, his face tense with anticipation and dread.

''You're back,'' he crowed, his grey eyes searching Rabble. ''And Rabble looks well. Are you victorious?''

''Yes,'' she replied laconically. ''Does Tambor need my help with the beasties?''

"Yes!" came a yell from behind the second wagon. "When you're ready, I could use a hand with the bears!"

"Coming!" Rabble removed Dog Meat's gear and slapped the steel-dust grey lightly on the rump. "Go on. You were wonderful. I'll be out to groom you later."

The stallion lipped her hair, then trotted off. Rabble vanished to Tambor's menagerie with a sharp whistle for Scrapper.

"It went well?" Hulhc repeated uncertainly.

"She bloodied her opponent in only two passes," Bryax said, "even with him armored. I wonder where she trained? There aren't many professional units that go for lances. They have become the noble's war toys."

Angie opened her mouth to speak, but at that moment Rylus came thudding around the wagon, bellies a'jiggle in his hurry.

"Peace and Profit!" he beamed. "You're back! Bryax, when you could, would you take over set-up direction? Even the damn urchins are guilded here, but I can get better rates if I provide the foreman.

"Hulhc, the list of regulations for games of chance is as thick as my wrist. Review them, please.

"Angie, they have some odd Physician's Guild here. You're going to need a temporary certification. Technically, you don't need it for Falconersville, but if you get it here— praise all the Deities—it will be good until we leave the Domain of Roses."

Before the force of Rylus' urgency, they scattered like leaves before an autumn wind. Angie paused long enough to put her and Bryax's mounts to pasture. Dog Meat was already grazing. Gimp, with baleful but watchful eyes, stretched out along a fence rail, self-evidently on guard.

"You're a puzzle, all of you," the Healer said to the cat, "a puzzle that wants and don't want solving. You know."

Gimp stretched out his front paw and yawned. Angie could have sworn that the cat was laughing.

9

Regulations, to be fair regulations, must be regulations that regulate all without exceptions.

Duke of Roses

THEY CROSSED into the Domain of Roses several days later to the sound of Rylus grumbling about the taxes. At Falconersville's western gate, soldiers smartly garbed in dark green and crimson glowered as Dog Meat pranced through the gate at the head of the caravan. Rabble wisely ignored them. Bryax was suppressing a sigh of relief when there was a bellow from Rylus.

"What do you mean we need to wear roses?"

"Regulation 47A, sub 4," said the gate captain, an exasperated flush travelling from her tunic collar up to her close-cropped black hair. "A rose must be worn on collar, jacket, vest, or anywhere visible, at all times."

"Slowly," Rylus said, leaning down from the wagon seat, a hand cupped behind one ear. "Please tell me again what you said. Slowly, I'm an old man."

Tambor guffawed. Rylus' hair was as glossy, his round face as unlined as ever. The gate guards gave the beastmaster a dirty look and he pulled his expression into unconvincingly serious lines.

"In order to abide by Regulation 47A, sub 4," the gate captain repeated as if for a stupid child, "each member of your company and each uncaged piece of livestock is required to wear an emblem denoting your status as outlanders. It's for your own protection, sir merchant. The military usually issues warnings to outlanders caught in violation of regulations."

"Usually," Rylus grumped. "I'll note that. Please continue, Captain."

"The emblems are not gifts. You may either purchase one for each member of your company . . ."

"And each piece of livestock," Rylus interrupted. "Yes, Captain, do go on."

"Or you may lease them. Leases are contingent, however, on the emblems being returned undamaged."

"Undamaged," Rylus said. "Yet we are to wear them openly at all times."

"On collar, jacket, vest," the Captain agreed. "Headstalls for horses, collars for dogs."

"What about cats or llamas or bears or monkeys," Tambor asked. "Do you have regulations for those, too?"

"I can refer you to the Hall of Regulations," the Captain said, "but usually we overlook any minor deviation from regulated placement if the intent to display the emblem is obviously intended."

"Peace and Prosperity!" Bryax swore in a whisper. "Rabble, what do you bet that there are regulations—just that our Captain there doesn't know them?"

"No bet," Rabble grinned. "Anyhow, they'd probably tax our winnings."

Still grumbling, Rylus paid the gate captain for a bouquet of cunningly made peacock-blue roses.

"It could be worse," Rabble commented, fastening one to Dog Meat's headstall, another to a length of leather that she turned into an impromptu collar for Scrapper. "They could be white, awfully hard to keep a white rose looking sharp."

"You have something there," Bryax said.

"Chance take you, cat!" Rabble swore, jerking her hand back and sucking on a scratched finger.

"Gimp doesn't want to wear it?" Angie asked.

"Nope. Refuses."

"Put it on his saddlebag," Angie said. "I'll see what I can do with catnip to get him to change his mind."

"Thanks. You're a wizard if you can," Rabble said. "Gimp's one ornery cat."

"I'm not promising," Angie said with a smile. "Just said that I'd try."

"Now," Rylus said, once they were far enough from Falconersville that interruption seemed unlikely, "gather round and let Papa tell you what he has for you."

Bryax and Rabble reined in until their mounts paced the lead wagon side to side. Tambor and Hulhc joined Rylus on the box seat and Angie, her herbs spread in little bundles around her, listened from a perch atop the wagon's roof.

"First," Rylus said, displaying a satchel of papers, "I have been reviewing the Regulations that pertain to the Travelling Spectacular. I've already given Tambor the rundown on showing animals."

"And I'll be able to do my part of the act," Tambor said, "just barely."

"Angie has already been certified into the Physician's Guild."

"But if I am telling fortunes, I must be careful to state this is for amusement only," she chirped. "I'm having Hulhc draw me up a lovely sign, with flowers and purple paint."

"Good." Rylus sighed. "The rest is a mixture of good news and bad. The good news is that because the Domain of Roses is so very careful—and because mandatory public assemblies of various types are common here—we will find full-fledged arenas, complete with tiered seating, ticket stands, and trained support staff in both Floribunda and Grandiosa."

"That will cost us," Hulhc grumped.

"It will, but they do have set rates for such things, so I know we can cover the cost. I already have reserved approximate dates for us." Rylus lifted a pamphlet. "This little booklet I don't have—understand?—is the condensed *Manual of Regulations* dealing with criminal and military matters. I've skimmed it and, sadly, especially given the money we can make on it, I think we need to cancel Rabble's contest."

Rabble glanced at him in surprise. "Too many Regulations, Rylus?"

"More than that. The Regulations state that dueling of any type is restricted except within very tight parameters. I'm concerned that their definition of dueling may extend to contests of skill, especially since at least one branch of their military has a reason to hold a grudge against you."

"I left Durez alive!" Rabble shook her head. "But I see your point. Even without magic, news still could travel ahead of us. We can't outpace a fast horse or carrier pigeon. Very well, I won't fight."

Tambor reached out and patted her. "Don't worry about getting bored, Rabble. With all the restrictions on animals, I'll need your help even more."

"Hulhc," Rylus continued, "I bought extra copies of the Regulations on games of chance. We'll need to put the dice aside completely. They'll also be sending an Inspector in each city to look at the wheels."

Hulhc accepted the stack of papers. "I'll review these right away."

"That's it, then," Rylus stroked his goatee and smiled. "Just remember the Regulations, keep your roses clean, and we'll give them a Spectacular to remember!"

At the entry to Floribunda, a harried-looking guard inspected their paperwork. As Rylus paid him the gate fee, the guard poured hot wax onto a bit of satin ribbon and impressed the city seal—a bundle of rosebuds around a single perfect blossom—onto the papers.

"Number 135 today," the guard said as he stamped the wax with brass numerals.

"Busy?" Rylus asked.

"Very, at least for a day that's not a market day," the guard gestured. "Follow this road straight through. Turn at the fountain shaped like a bouquet of a dozen long-stemmed roses. You'll see the Arena easily from there."

Arriving at the Arena, they were met by a sweet-faced, grey-haired lady clad in a skirt and blouse reminiscent of the military uniform, but adorned with a cluster of yellow rose-buds.

"Greetings," she said, waving Rylus back when he proffered their papers. "No, don't worry about your paperwork yet. You must be tired and dusty from the road. I'll show you where the animals can be released and where to stable the horses. Then we'll go over the paperwork while having some rosehip punch and muffins."

"Why, thank you, ma'am," Rylus stopped himself from gaping at her kindness when he heard Angie giggle. "Please, lead on."

When the animals were settled, she brought them into a comfortable office in an upper tier of the Arena.

"My name is Brytti," the woman introduced herself, pouring them translucent, spicy, red punch. "I will be your liaison while you are in Floribunda and I may travel with you to Grandiosa—that will give me an excuse to see my grandchildren! Twins just born and six older children. Lovely, all of them. Their parents stayed in my home city, but my job took me here."

Brytti bubbled on in this fashion for several minutes, her green-grey gaze efficiently darting over the pile of documents and forms that Rylus had brought in from the wagon.

"These look just wonderful," she said, returning them to their leather carrying case. "Now, when do you plan to start performing?"

"Tomorrow," Rylus said with a glance at the Company, "and the number of days we remain will, of course, have to do with how long business is good."

Brytti's laughter trilled in their ears. "Then you may never leave Floribunda! How do you think I knew to wait for you? We have had questions all day about when you would arrive. Apparently, word of your coming preceded you. We don't get much outside entertainment in the Domain of Roses."

"I'm not surprised, given how difficult your government makes travel," Rylus said hesitantly.

"Yes." Brytti lost her cheer. "Our current Duke believes

that the strength of our Domain lies in knowing everything that we can quantify. It is hard to know who is where when strangers are trooping through.''

She brightened. ''But from tomorrow, we have a Travelling Spectacular—not the same routine assemblies and parades. Before I leave, let me show you where the rooms are.''

''Rooms?'' Hulhc blurted.

''Yes,'' Brytti twinkled at him. ''We have sufficient on-premises quarters for a small group like yours.''

''How nice,'' Rylus said, trying not to seem rude. ''They *are* covered in the arena-use fee, aren't they?''

''Yes, they're covered,'' Brytti assured him, ''part of the Domain of Roses' service to you.''

''Not to mention that it keeps us in one place,'' Bryax muttered.

The Travelling Spectacular burst into shape almost instantly. Brytti carefully directed the Arena's staff, assigning runners to Rylus and Hulhc. She even supplied a pair of animal handlers to assist Tambor.

In addition to the usual tents and arcades, stands for selling refreshments and wooden toys were set up around the Arena's perimeter. There were even pony rides. Everything that could be brightly painted was and what could not be was draped in bunting and the ubiquitous multiblossomed rose from which the city took its name.

Tambor, a golden monkey hanging from each shoulder, exercised the bears and put the llama through its beginner's tricks. Ebullient, he grabbed Rylus when his partner came to observe.

''Isn't this something!'' he said, his waving arms encompassing the bright colors and the fluttering banners. ''It's barely opening time and we're better set up than ever before.''

''I know,'' Rylus said. ''These people may be onto something with all their regulations. Brytti's staff knows its job like an army drill team.''

''Speaking of military,'' Tambor asked, ''where are

Bryax and Rabble? Rabble helped me earlier, but I had almost too much help from the locals, so I sent her to see what else needed doing.''

''She and Bryax are practicing a choreographed weapons demonstration to replace the part of the Spectacular where Rabble normally takes on a local champion,'' Rylus explained. ''We needed something and Brytti couldn't find anything in the Regulations to forbid it. They're working on something with lots of flash and dazzle—more of a playlet than a demo, if I understand them.''

''Wonderful,'' Tambor sighed. ''I can't wait. Maybe, Rylus, the Domain of Roses really is a foreshadowing of how a civilized nation should be run.''

''Maybe,'' Rylus tugged his silver hoop earring, ''but they pay for their order and not just in taxes. No, not just in taxes.''

They opened the Arena gates when the sun was an hour shy of noon. Rylus, standing with Brytti in a special booth constructed just for the purpose, handed out wooden tokens in exchange for coin as quickly as he could.

''Nimble fingers, those,'' Brytti commented during a lull. ''You are the Spectacular's mechanician, as well as its manager?''

Rylus puffed out his chest. ''That's right—carpenter, leather-worker, metalsmith. Nothing fancy, all practical, but all good and solid. I like your people's idea about selling little toys to those who come to see the show. I plan on starting some myself during our next voyage.''

''You plan on crossing the Slate Sea?''

''Yes, that's right. Tambor has a hankering to see what beasties dwell inland.''

''Tambor is certain to find some,'' Brytti pursed her wrinkled lips, ''but if you keep your eyes open, Rylus, I suspect that you will see wonders.''

The flow of customers picked up again and what Brytti might have added was lost in the confusion. When things quieted again, Rylus had a new question.

''Brytti, I've noticed that many of the people coming

through are wearing clusters of roses. At first I thought that they were merely patriotic ornaments, but there seems to be too much regularity in style—a pattern of sorts.''

"Yes, there is a pattern. I'm not surprised that you noticed. Yellow is for city workers, white for military, red for merchants and guild-members. You see?''

"I do,'' Rylus handed a stack of tokens to a young mother. "What is the meaning of pink roses in a bunch? I've seen more and more as the day has gone on.''

Brytti's expression became neutral. "Ah, that denotes the Archipelago of Truth in the Slate Sea. To wear a bunch of pink roses on the mainland, unless you also have a traveller's blue rose, is a bit of a statement.''

Rylus, remembering Rabble's confrontation in the Falconersville tavern, thought it wisest to remain quiet. He did warn Tambor, Angie, and Hulhc that there could be trouble. Knowing Rabble's odd whimsies, ignorance was probably best in her case and as Bryax was training with her, there was nothing that could be done on that part.

When late afternoon brought time for the Spectacular proper, as opposed to the menagerie, gambling games, fortunes, and other such amusements, the crowd was cheerful and noisy. They applauded the dancing bears with enthusiasm, sat in rapt appreciation of Rylus and Tambor's two-part recitation of the story of Tempest of the Downs, and howled with laughter whenever Angie bumbled between the scenes in the persona of a lost visitor searching for the Floribunda Hall of Regulations.

In between, they bought sacks of roasted gourd seeds and called for vendors to fill their wooden mugs with weak beer. By the time Rabble and Bryax's turn came, a less well-disciplined crowd would have been termed rambunctious. Perhaps they kept to their seats because of the white rose-wearing staff members who didn't need the dark green, crimson-trimmed uniforms to proclaim them soldiers.

"Are you ready for me to announce you?'' Rylus asked, glancing at Rabble and Bryax.

The two were beautifully costumed, largely in garb that Brytti had produced from the Arena storage bins. Rabble wore a very feminine gown, white, trimmed with clusters of dark-red roses and lace at the sleeves and neck. Her red tresses were piled high in elaborate curls and tendrils, interwoven with golden ribbon and yellow roses.

Bryax was a rogue from a romance. His broad chest seemed barely contained in a tight-fitting, strategically torn leather shirt. His breeches showed enough muscular leg to delight the ladies. Angie had washed his hair with camomile, then bound it with a dark green rag so that it fell loose and silky past his shoulders. His beard was rakishly trimmed.

"When the Arena staff gets our props out, we'll be ready," Bryax promised. "Do you have the bit Rabble wrote up for you?"

"Right here," Rylus waved the sheet of paper and, taking his megaphone in one hand, he strode onto the field.

"The end of our Spectacular today," he boomed, "is a dramatic representation of a folk tale from the Downs. After the presentation, our other activities will remain open until dusk. Although I will provide some words to fill in the story, we believe that your eyes should be your own bards."

He gestured covertly and Rabble came into view. She was mounted sidesaddle on Dog Meat. The scarred war horse was hardly the ideal choice for a maiden's palfrey, but they needed the stallion's intelligent obedience to Rabble's commands.

To costume the horse, Angie had brewed a stain from walnuts and other plants that did a fair job of hiding the white hairs on the stallion's scarred knees. Rabble had groomed him until he shone and braided into his long mane a cascade of the ubiquitous roses—none pink, Rylus noted with relief.

"Many, many years before the Loss," Rylus narrated, "a lovely maiden rode from her parents' estate. She was searching for her brother, who had been stolen from the family when he was but a lad of ten and never seen again."

Rabble mimed searching, hand over her eyes, looking to

the right and then to the left. Scurrying around her, boys in green carried branches, so that her "progress" was into a dark and increasingly foreboding forest. Off to one side, Tambor beat a solemn measure on his drums.

"The maiden's way took her into a dangerous wood where she was spotted by a desperate bandit. Down to his last crust of bread, his starving dog hulking at his heels, the bandit crept up to the maiden and attacked!"

Bryax, who had been stealthily advancing on Rabble, now sprang from concealment. Barking and growling with quite believable ferocity, Scrapper leapt out with him.

From the audience, someone screamed, "Watch out!"

Dog Meat reared, pawing the air above Bryax's head. From under her pearl satin rose-embroidered cloak, Rabble swept a shiny length of polished whitewood. Bryax met her swing with an artfully painted wooden sword.

On the sidelines, his hands concealed, Tambor provided the muffled crash of metal against wood.

The crowd rose to its feet, screaming in excitement as the maiden and the bandit twirled through the elaborate steps of their choreographed battle. The rearing stallion and the barking dog added to the impressive chaos.

"The maiden had not ventured on her journey unprepared, but the bandit was very powerful," Rylus continued. "Just as it seemed certain that they must slay each other, the maiden made a terrible discovery."

Rabble slipped her staff beneath a prepared tear in Bryax's tunic. The leather ripped away along weakened seams, revealing a gaudy serpentine dragon painted on one brawny shoulder.

"The maiden," Rylus continued, "recognized her family birthmark. Here was the brother she had journeyed so far to find. Knowing that they were equally matched in battle, she made a daring choice."

Rabble dropped her staff. Then she ducked so that the sword swipe meant—apparently—for her heart sliced through the shoulder of her gown. Her cloak and gown fell away in a graceful billow, revealing a slender white shoulder adorned with the same dragon sigil.

Rabble caught the gown before more than her shoulder was bared. Bryax "the bandit" froze in surprised discovery, his sword falling from his hands and to the turf with a satisfying thump (this last supplied by Tambor's drum).

"The bandit had been a lad of ten when he was stolen from his family," Rylus boomed. "Well does he remember that the birthmark on his shoulder is his last tie to his lost family."

Bryax crushed Rabble in his arms.

"Gentle! You'll squash me!" she whispered.

"Sorry," he smiled, lifting her onto Dog Meat's back and vaulting up behind. Scrapper gathered up the dropped sword and staff, holding them clear of the ground, her tail wagging proudly.

"So, reunited, brother and sister journey home to their grateful family," Rylus continued, as the procession road a slow circuit about the Arena. "Thank you for watching our production!"

The crowd roared with applause, foot-stomping and cheering. Bryax and Rabble returned to the center of the Arena to take their bows. As Rabble straightened, her brown eyes snapping with pleased excitement, the timbre of some of the cheering changed, becoming a resonant chant.

"Rabble! Rabble! Rabble! Rabble!"

Before any of the Company could wonder about this surge of enthusiasm, from all points of the Arena a shower of pink roses rained down around the two warriors turned actor.

"Peace and Prosperity!" Rylus groaned.

Rabble bent, scooped up a double handful of roses, bowed again, and taking Bryax's arm made an exit just shy of hasty. The crowd gradually quieted, some dispersing to the exits, others moving toward the games.

Rylus, Hulhc, and Angie hurried to their posts. Tambor, his drums dangling from his hands, congratulated Rabble and Bryax as they stripped out of their costumes.

"Good job," he said, "but our Rabble seems to have a following."

"Yeah, what was that about?" Bryax asked. "I had a distinct feeling that more was going on than admiration for Rabble's feminine charms."

Rabble, thoughtfully feeding Dog Meat rose petals, stuck her tongue out at him.

"Local politics, again," Tambor explained. "Rabble's little duel back in Falconersville apparently has made her a symbol for the resistance of the Slate Archipelago against the Domain of Roses."

He had barely finished speaking when Brytti hurried over to join them, more than ever a hen fussing over her chicks.

"What a stir! What a mess!" she said, extending a ribbon-tied bit of parchment to Rabble. "Let me advise you, lady, don't take any more duels, not if you hope to ship out from Grandiosa!"

Rabble untied the ribbon. "I'll remember that."

She fell silent, reading, slowly a smile quirked the corners of her mouth.

"Rabble!" Bryax pleaded. "What is it?"

"As Brytti suspected, a challenge to a duel, but," Rabble bowed to the round little woman, "as Brytti suggested, one I shall not accept. My honor is proof against refusing a few duels."

Tambor shook his head. "Ry will never believe this. Fiery Rabble backing down from a fight. Well, I must to my beasties—the myna has picked up some rather colorful obscenities. I'd better take care that he doesn't find himself challenged to a duel."

Chuckling at his own wit, Tambor hurried off.

"I will take care that this duel is refused according to Regulations," Brytti offered.

"Thank you," Rabble said. "I would hate to create new reason for offense."

That evening, when the Spectacular was closed, Rylus called a conference.

"We can't ignore that Rabble has unwittingly become a rally point for local unrest," he said. "We're making money, even with the taxes, so I hate to suggest moving on, but I think it would be wise."

"Let's do tomorrow's show," Tambor suggested. "I don't want anyone to think that we can be run of town. That's a bad idea in itself."

The next day was as prosperous as the first. Although pink roses blossomed on a number of breasts, the only brawls were the usual scraps between overindulging fair-goers. Again the stands were filled to capacity for the final Spectacular. Tambor's animals were greeted with applause, but the noise became thunderous when Rylus announced the playlet of the Maiden and the Bandit.

No one would have known how nervous the members of the Travelling Spectacular were for the performance went according to plan. As it ended, again voices cheered Rabble, and again a cascade of pink roses came from the stands.

Just as Rylus and Tambor were trading sighs of relief and Rabble and Bryax prepared to leave the field, there was a commotion from the edge of the Arena.

Two warriors in glinting chain mail and wearing the tabard of the Domain of Roses, a cluster of white roses over their hearts, rode onto the field.

"Regulation 2D, sub 2 and 3," called a piercing soprano voice.

"Rabble, you are in violation of this Regulation," came the deep basso rumbling of her companion. "Accept arrest and we will be merciful!"

"Regulation 2D?" Rabble said to Bryax. "Sounds pretty basic. How did we miss it?"

Rylus came puffing out to them. "Regulation 2 deals with treason! 2D deals with inciting treasonous activity."

"She didn't on purpose," Bryax protested. "They just fastened onto Rabble as some sort of symbol. Maybe we should just go with them and explain."

"No, you don't understand," Rylus said, anxiety making

his voice shrill. "Subsections 2 and 3 deal with penalties and they include death—even for 'incidental collaboration.'"

"You mean," Rabble said, "if I surrender, I'm likely to be executed? War and Chance! Then I'm resisting arrest!"

She leapt onto Dog Meat's back, scooping her white wooden staff from the ground. "Brother, I charge you by our Oath. Remain here and carry out our obligations to the Travelling Spectacular. Wish me luck!"

"Crazy woman," Bryax said. "I'll do as you request— only because I don't want you to surrender meekly."

Rabble saluted her companions, then, wheeling Dog Meat around, she shouted, "I am not going to be dragged off by you white rose-wearing dogfish! If you want me—come for me!"

The female Domain soldier lowered her spear. "Just remember, outlander, this is no duel. It is an execution!"

Her partner also lowered his spear and as a unit they charged Rabble.

Still clad in the torn maiden's costume, her red tresses shimmering in the light, Rabble urged Dog Meat into an answering charge. The crowd screamed in excitement and terror as playacting disintegrated into blood sport. The contest was deadly uneven, two armed and armored warriors assaulting a half-naked woman armed only with a slight staff of polished wood.

The company of the Travelling Spectacular clustered together, watching nervously. Each of them knew that they should be packing up the gear and preparing to head out if things went badly. Yet, as the combatants closed, the company stood riveted, as if their attention alone could change the course of the battle.

Rabble took Dog Meat between the other two horses. The left-hand warrior lost her attack, her spear set on the horse's right side. The left-hand rider frowned confidently and continued his charge.

At the last possible moment, Rabble drove Dog Meat

toward the left-hand warrior, thereby diverting herself from the right-hand spear point and allowing Dog Meat the opportunity to take a solid snap at the left-hand charger's flank.

Then, as the spear's point went by her, she leaned over, grasped the shaft in both hands, and held on. Faced with abandoning his weapon or being wrenched to the ground, the Domain soldier let go.

Rabble then shoved the butt of the spear into its former wielder's gut. Retching, he fell backwards and off of his horse, taking the spear with him.

The crowd cheered and Rabble saluted them as she wheeled Dog Meat around to meet the other soldier. She had somehow kept her hold on the whitewood staff and now she raised it on high.

"By War and Chance," she called to her opponent, "surrender and retract your charges before these witnesses and I will spare you."

The Domain soldier spat and continued to bring her steed around. Rabble shook her hair back from her face and positioned her flimsy staff. When the other horse leapt forward, Dog Meat carried Rabble to meet her opponent. Rabble successfully struck aside the other's lance but the force of the blow blasted the prop to flinders.

When they wheeled for another pass, Rabble was unarmed, but she didn't slow. She raised her arm as if for a sword strike. There was a flicker of brightness and the Domain soldier's spear was sundered. Shocked, the soldier let the spear shaft drop. The shorn length of wood dug into the turf and the soldier was flung from her saddle to crumple in an unconscious heap.

Like a single person, the crowd rose to its feet, a wild cheer rending the air. Still astride Dog Meat, her hair tumbling free from its silken ribbons and flowers, Rabble raised her hands in acknowledgment. The cheering broke off abruptly as a unit of soldiers in the dark green and crimson rode onto the field.

"You cannot fight us all, Rabble," their leader called. "Surrender or we will fill you with arrows."

Rabble straightened haughtily, but was saved from the need to reply as Brytti ran out onto the field.

"Regulation 7B, sub 1," she called breathlessly.

"Remind me of that Regulation," the patrol leader growled.

Brytti squared her shoulders and pulled a battered Regulations manual from the pocket of her dress. "Regulation 7 deals with executions, 7B with field executions. It states that no one may be executed twice for the same crime. When these two charged Rabble, they stated that they were acting as executioners, not duelists. Subsection 1 notes that if a jury-rigged execution fails in such a manner that the criminal is not killed, then the matter is considered settled and the charge is dropped."

Her voice, light and birdlike, carried over the hushed crowd. Then a patter of applause began. The patrol commander saw which way the tide of opinion was headed.

"Very well, but keep these Outlanders in the facility. The city governor will want them kept where they cannot incite further trouble."

The patrol also ordered the Arena emptied. Even with profits draining out the gates, Rylus did not complain. Taking Hulhc and Tambor with him, he hurried to collect the Arena staff and start breaking down the Spectacular.

"I guess I had better change out of this stuff," Rabble said, indication her ruined costume. "I'll pay for its replacement, Brytti."

"Come with me, dear," Brytti said, "and we'll see what's salvageable."

Bryax watched Rabble leave, a fond smile on his lips.

"I can't believe she won again," he said to Angie. "The spear getting snapped off that way was incredible."

"'Incredible!' A very good word," Angie said, running lightly out to retrieve the discarded spearhead. "Look, it's been cut, not broken, cleanly sliced."

"But Rabble didn't have a blade, not even a small one," Bryax protested. "That dress wouldn't conceal one."

"So how did she cut it?" Angie said, staring down at the spear tip. "So how did she cut it off?"

10

Pass the jug around!
Pass the jug around!
Might as well be dead drunk
As dead drowned!

Great Salt Sea Sailing Song

"BRYTTI'S A great coach," Rylus reported the next morning. "We paid a few bribes and now the Travelling Spectacular will be permitted to remain within the Domain of Roses, as long as we travelled to Grandiosa by the shortest route."

Hulhc looked pleased, but Tambor shook his head worriedly.

"How long do we have to stay in Grandiosa? What are we going to do about money if they're hurrying us across the land?"

"Brytti and I convinced them to permit us to remain in Grandiosa until a suitable ship is ready. Even those humorless officials at the Hall of Regulations had to admit that finding a transport capable of moving eleven horses, a llama, two bears, assorted smaller animals, two wagons, and six humans would be difficult. In Grandiosa, the Spectacular will be permitted to run simpler attractions, such as the games, but under no circumstances is Rabble to be permitted to perform in any capacity—even as a guard."

Rabble shrugged. "I always wanted to be a freeloader.

That look on your face says you're holding something else back.''

Rylus nodded. "It's not all bad news. Brytti was commanded to accompany us—much to her delight. However, we're also going to have another escort. A platoon of the Domain of Roses military that 'just happened' to be being transferred to Grandiosa will be riding with us.''

Bryax groaned. "Rabble, please, don't do anything to incite them!''

"As you wish, Shield Brother,'' she said. "I won't even speak to them.''

They rapidly discovered that nothing Rabble could have done would have annoyed their escort more. She delighted in riding in her usual post near the caravan's front, chatting with Bryax about the finer points of some tactical situation or what refinements they might add to their mini-drama. As they rode, she often sipped from a flask of *pfneur breit,* so that its sharp peppermint scent mixed with the odors of road dust and spring flowers.

The only thing that could stir Rabble from her post were the intermittent, but violent thundershowers. Then she dove inside the wagon or took refuge under the canopy Angie had rigged on the top of the lead wagon.

In Grandiosa, they were housed in the Grandiosa Arena, a place very similar to the Floribunda Arena, but decorated with broad-petaled roses. Three days after their arrival, Rylus reported that he had found them a ship.

"The *Bolla Fifteen,*'' Rylus said happily. "It's a bigger ship and has plenty of room for us all. I even made certain that Rabble would have an inside cabin and a supply of good brandy laid in.''

Rabble, the great warrior and fomenter of rebellion, looked up from where she had been dragging a leather thong along the ground for Gimp to chase and stuck out her tongue at him.

"When can we leave?'' Hulhc asked.

"With the morning tide,'' Rylus answered, "if we load up most of the gear tonight.''

The captain of the *Bolla Fifteen* was lounging on the deck when they arrived to load their gear. Rylus shouldered the duffle containing his clothing with a mysteriously self-satisfied smile and strode past the Company to where he could watch them come aboard. Angie skipped two steps after him, then saw the Captain and stopped so suddenly that Hulhc, immediately behind her, nearly spilled off the gangplank and into the Grandiosa Harbor.

"Angie!" the farmer snapped, but she had already bounced to stare up at the Captain.

"Captain! Captain Bolla! How did you get here so quickly?"

"Ah," the Captain chuckled in a voice a shade deeper and richer than the one they recalled. "Like Rylus, you mistake me for my sister, Alba. This happens. No, lovely lady, I am Betram Bolla and I welcome your illustrious—or should I say notorious?—company aboard the *Bolla Fifteen*."

When he smiled, they saw that sapphires, not rubies, were set in his strong, white teeth.

"We shall sail nearly directly north across the Sea of Truth," said Betram Bolla, when all of the Company except for Rabble had gathered on deck and the ship was safely out of the harbor, "as directly as one ever sails, of course. I have charted us a course that will keep us clear of a certain archipelago, as well. In due course, we will be putting into port at Bookhome in the Domain of Dragons."

"Domain of Dragons?" Hulhc said. "That sounds fascinating."

"It is an old, old name, from before the Loss," Betram said.

"Brytti, the lady who was our liaison in the Domain of Roses," Rylus said, "told me that the Domain of Roses and The Domain of Dragons are ruled by brothers."

"Ah, yes, that is the case," the Captain replied. "The Dukes—they are quite different from each other. Not that I have ever had the pleasure of meeting either, of course.

Dukes do not have time for ship's captains, even successful ones like the Bollas.''

"You say that the brothers are different from each other," Tambor said. "I hope this means that the Duke of Dragons is not as interested in—uh—control as his brother."

Captain Bolla's rich laugh rolled out until his crew members turned and stared in curiosity.

"Oh, I didn't say that, Master Tambor," he said, still chuckling. "Control takes many forms. The Duke of Roses believes that his Regulations create a more orderly and more prosperous land. His brother, the Duke of Dragons . . ."

Captain Bolla paused. His rich voice dropped to a whisper, so that the listeners leaned forward to hear his words. In the background, Rabble could be heard tunelessly singing.

"The Duke of Dragons," Captain Bolla continued, "claims that he and he alone in all the world still has the power to work magic!"

"Oh, my!" Angie said, fluttering her eyelashes at the captain. "Has anyone seen this magic?"

"Well, there are those who say they have," Betram Bolla said. "I haven't personally, but there is some call for believing his claims. One of the great magical schools before the Loss was in the Domain of Dragons, one of the finest magical libraries as well. The library was right in the port city to which we sail. That's why it's called Bookhome."

Hulhc pulled at his long grey beard nervously. "Does this library still exist, Captain? Can one use it?"

"Some say it exists, some say it doesn't," Betram shrugged. "Some say in-between, that the books are there, but no one can read them because they are writ in sorcerous script and since the Loss all that remains on the pages is gibberish."

Hulhc grunted his thanks and wandered off to his cabin in thoughtful silence. Peeking in his cabin later, Angie saw him poring over a worn, hand-written book—no doubt the very journal that had started him on his quest.

The early days of sailing went well. The weather was often stormy, but the *Bolla Fifteen* was a large vessel and her crew was skilled. They were delighted to have the Spectacular aboard and convinced Tambor to drum along with their songs.

Bryax, who cheerfully admitted to saltwater soldiering on the Dark Opal and Sapphire Lakes, though never on the Great Salt Sea, kept himself in tone by hauling at the rigging with Bolla's crew. He let his beard grow out and flirted with every woman aboard.

The Captain was so pleased with Bryax's help that he gave the blond warrior a stitched wristband with an elaborate knotwork design burnt into the supple, dark-brown leather.

"Keep this, wear it, whatever," he advised Bryax, "and if you get weary of the soldiering life, you take it to any port where Bolla ships berth and you'll find yourself with a job."

"Captain Alba said that your fleet has fifteen ships," Bryax said accepting the gift. "Do you sail all the Lakes?"

"Not yet, but the fifteen ships only counts those with two masts or more. We have many smaller vessels." Betram smiled proudly. "Most recently, we established a route in the Sea of Strangeness, up to the northwest of here."

Bryax fingered the wristband and then strapped it on his wrist. "Thank you for this. I will remember your offer. I was wondering if you could tell me something that has been nagging at me. Some people refer to the lakes as 'Lakes' and others refer to them as 'Seas.' If I'm going to be a sailor, I'd like to have it right. Which is it?"

"Fair question, Bryax, but there is no simple answer," the Captain replied. "My family has noticed that the terminology varies from region to region, even from culture to culture within a region. A general rule is that the further from the Great Salt Sea that you travel, the more likely you are to hear the Lakes termed 'Seas.'"

"Maybe never having seen how vast the Great Salt Sea is," Bryax guessed, "inlanders think of these inland bodies as being larger than they are."

"Perhaps. Different peoples have different names for the Seas as well," Betram added. "You tend to call them for types of stones, do you not?"

"That's right," Bryax said, ticking them off on his fingers. "Dark Opal, Sapphire, Slate—that's this one—Amethyst, Turquoise, Lapis Lazuli and . . . I always forget the last one . . . Jade! That's it, Jade."

"Another tradition names the Seas for flowers," Betram Bolla added. "Called so, this sea we are sailing on is the Cornflower Sea. Another tradition names the Seas for qualities. This one is the Sea of Truth." Betram rubbed his chin, which after several days at sea was covered with a dark, tight-curled fuzz. "I rather fancy the name. The wizards did, too, so I've heard."

Some days later, Bryax, who was spelling the watch and delighting in the power of the brass telescope that he had been given to carry aloft with him, was the first to see the menacing ships racing toward the *Bolla Fifteen*.

"Hey!" he yelled down. "Somebody! Is that trouble coming from the windward side?"

Betram's first mate, Jeiss, swarmed up the rigging. Jeiss was a thin woman with long hair like polished onyx that she wore in single plait down past the middle of her back. Bryax thought that she was rather attractive, but after losing to her in a knife-throwing contest the first day at sea, he had decided that he'd rather bed a pantheress.

"What have you seen, Bryax?"

He handed her the telescope and pointed. "Over there, Jeiss. Two ships. They're riding awfully high in the water, moving awfully fast, and I'm worried about those blocky shapes under the canvas tarps."

Jeiss considered. "You've got something, Blondie. When Bolla swung us out away from the Archipelago of Truth, that brought us into some interesting waters."

"Interesting?"

Jeiss lowered the telescope. "Pirates, Blondie. They're not flying any colors, but I've seen those lines in my

nightmares. Be a good lad and climb down and tell Captain
Bolla that there may be Black Racers closing—fast. Then get
the noncombatants off the deck.''

''Aye!''

Bryax delivered his message and was immediately set to
work. The *Bolla Fifteen*, unsurprisingly, was well armed.
Arbalests and ballistae were clamped into place and buckets
of sea-water drawn in anticipation of fire.

All of the Company—except for Rabble—volunteered
their services. Rylus and Tambor were given a ballista to
crew. Angie readied her medical kit and Bryax assured
Captain Bolla that he remembered how to repel boarders.
Even Hulhc took responsibility for one of the fire control
gangs. In this air of martial cooperation, Rabble's absence
was noticeable.

While the *Bolla Fifteen* readied for battle, scouts in the
crow's nest tracked the presumed Black Racers. At one
point, their tack seemed to carry them away, but soon there
was no way to deny that the ships were heading for them.

''They flank us, Captain,'' Jeiss reported tersely. ''And
lookouts say that they may be equipped with liquid fire.''

''Oh, for a charm against fire!'' the Captain groaned.
''But, lacking that, hold to your posts, friends. There aren't
any of us who can hope for ransom!''

He lowered his voice in explanation to those of the
Company within hearing. ''Bolla Shiplines established as
policy that there will be no ransom of ships or people. Keeps
us mean. If any of you care to surrender, we will not hold it
against you.''

Rylus shrugged. ''No one to ransom Tambor nor me. All
that we have is on this boat.''

Hulhc smiled thinly. ''I do not believe my farms could
raise anything. Our wealth is the land.''

Angie did not speak but wordlessly dipped her hand into a
water bucket and washed the paint from her cheeks. The
dripping smears eloquently announced that she had no plan
to claim the immunity traditionally granted to a Far Shore's
Healer.

The novices to battle rapidly learned that, unlike what history books would have one believe, there is nothing orderly about a battle. Everything happens at once, especially when, as in this fight, the battle is fought simultaneously on two fronts.

For Rylus and Tambor, poised by their weapon on the starboard side, the battle began when they could fire their ballista. For Bryax, it was the mad turmoil of furling the sheets, ever conscious that he wore but the lightest armor and of the unfamiliar weight of a hatchet nestled at the small of his back. For Hulhc, it was the sting of sweat in blistered hands as he hauled aboard bucket after bucket of water to soak deck and sheets in the forlorn hope that the enemy's fires would be slowed. For Angie it was a cool assessing of her kit and heated conferences with the *Bolla Fifteen's* resident chirurgeon.

Only for Rabble, still singing loudly and off-key, was the battle of no concern. Scrapper and Gimp, however, seemed to know what was offing and set themselves by her cabin, the dog on the lintel before the door and the cat, with impossible lithe dexterity, above the door.

The pirate raiders glided into place, port and starboard, one slightly fore, the other slightly aft. While crossbow-wielding sailors aboard each vessel made raising one's head worth one's life, the pirates flung grapples at the *Bolla Fifteen*. Bryax and the others chopped through line after line, but more always came. Eventually, the pirates were able to swarm aboard.

Bryax was ready for the first pirate who topped the rail, spitting the man through the throat as he swung over. Bryax's kill cost him a furrow in his thigh from the pirate's cover fire, slowing him long enough for more pirates to pile aboard. The same thing was happening all around the *Bolla Fifteen* although the flights of arrows grew more sparse as the pirates and the *Fifteen's* sailors joined in hand-to-hand combat.

Nor did the combat spare those who were not warriors. Hulhc slung a bucket of water directly into the face of the pirate advancing upon him. The pirate stumbled back, temporarily blinded. More in terror than from tactical sense, Hulhc swung the bucket around and released it into the pirate's belly. This time, the man went down. Encouraged by Hulhc's example, others in the fire brigade brought water, buckets, even coils of rope into play.

For Rylus and Tambor, the battle was going less well. The chubby beastmaster had been felled by a sword cut to the face. Wild-eyed, his partner stood over him, a hatchet in one hand, an unloaded crossbow in the other. His determination was so evident, his expression so grim, that the pirates shunned him in a way that they did not the trained warriors in Bolla's crew.

Despite the muddle, despite the fact that they were flanked by two ships, the crew of the *Bolla Fifteen* held its own. On board the starboard Black Racer's vessel, the wild-eyed commander lifted a curved horn to his lips and winded a braying cry. Immediately, the pirates began to retreat. Bolla's crew was not willing to let them depart unblooded, however, until Captain Bolla clambered aloft.

"Let the rats go!" he bellowed. "They're beaten and not worth the wounds to you."

"Beaten?" Insane laughter from the starboard pirate ship interrupted Captain Bolla. "We may be, but you will never live to slander the terror of the Sea of Truth!"

"Captain!" Jeiss screamed from the rigging. "They're readying the fire!"

Hulhc, his left arm in a sling torn from his tunic, immediately started his team hauling more water aboard. Most of the pirates still aboard the *Fifteen* were either wounded or dead. Hearing Jeiss' shout, these crawled for the side, obviously preferring to drown than to burn alive.

"War and Chance!" Bryax cursed, tightening a makeshift bandage about his thigh. "Captain Bolla, I don't think they're bluffing!"

The first blob of fire hit squarely on a shrouded sail. Despite the water Hulhc's crew had lavished on it, it went up like a spilled oil lantern. The next shot hit the deck. The third charred the sailor at the wheel. Screams of fear and horror arose from the same crew that had been triumphantly celebrating the pirate's retreat moments before.

"Jeiss!" Captain Bolla gestured for her to come to him and spoke softly. "Guard the lifeboats. Don't let anyone use them yet. The pirates will sink them or sell them to slavers."

More loudly, he called, "The rest of you! Back to your ballistae and arbalests! Any without a weapon, help with fire control. Our only hope is to sink them and recover after!"

Rylus reluctantly left Tambor to Angie's intent care and went to man his post with two members of Bolla's crew. The dark-skinned healer had lost her omnipresent smile and labored over her friend's still form with swift but steady hands.

Bryax wiped his streaming, smoke-burnt eyes across his torn and blood-stained sleeve. Incongruously, beneath the clamor of the fire brigade, the groaning of the weaponry, the rattling of the ratchets, the shouts as Captain Bolla and Jeiss tried desperately to save their ship and crew, beneath this he could hear Rabble drunkenly warble the chorus of an old marching song.

Anger flared in him. Sloshing a bucket of water over a smoldering heap of sail-cloth, he stalked to Rabble's cabin.

Scrapper growled at him, but he pushed the bitch back with one hand. Ignoring Gimp's hisses, he kicked open Rabble's door. Rabble looked up, bright-eyed and smiling, from her bunk. The room reeked of mint and she held a partial bottle of *pfneur breit* in one hand. The cabin was littered with empty bottles, a cask of brandy, soiled cups, and a stale hunk of bread.

Scrapper dashed into the cabin and set herself between Rabble and Bryax while Gimp beat at the top of the man's head with a solid paw.

"Have a drink, Shield Brother?" Rabble said, extending the bottle.

"War and Chance shame you, Rabble!" Bryax swore, pushing the brandy aside. "The ship is under attack, we may go under, we may burn to death, and you offer me a drink?"

"Go under?" she repeated, blanching. "Fire?"

She staggered to her feet, bent with effort to pat the still growling bitch.

"Quiet, Scrapper. Gimp, leave Bryax alone."

Amazingly, the cat did as it was told. Rabble threw back her head and breathed in the smoky air.

"Fire," she said wonderingly. "Fire?"

"Pirates," Bryax growled, spinning on his heel, "and we're in big trouble. Sister."

He was halfway to the amidships zone where most of the fires were when he heard Scrapper's nails on the deck and realized that Rabble was following him. Her gait was still unsteady and she viewed the water with loathing.

Those oversized brown eyes took in the carnage, the blood-stained deck, lingered on the fires. Then she straightened as if a decision had been reached.

"Where's the pirate's commander?" she snapped, sounding completely sober, though she still held her bottle in one hand.

"On the starboard vessel," Bryax answered. "Looks like they're trying to clear off before we can sink them, but they've got to cut their own grapples."

"Starboard?" Rabble said confusedly.

"Right side," Bryax answered. "Rabble, what in the name of the Four Elements are you doing?"

The slender redhead had begun to climb the nearest rigging, Gimp alongside her. She paused when she reached a solidly anchored bit of line. She tested it, nodded, and poised to swing outward, over the water between the *Bolla Fifteen* and the retreating pirate vessel.

"Rabble, what are you doing?"

"Making a call, Sword Brother," she dropped her bottle, scooped up Gimp, and swung out over the water.

Bryax could have sworn he saw her shudder, could have sworn that the jump was impossible, but as he raced to the rail, groping for a line to throw her when she hit the water, he saw her land solidly on the pirate ship's raised stern deck.

Gimp leapt to freedom, but did not flee. Instead, the

scrawny grey-striped tabby bristled, spitting feline threats at the first pirate who took an uncertain step in their direction. Rabble dipped a contemptuous bow to the pirate captain, then lashed out with her right fist and knocked him to the deck with a single blow.

Grasping the rail, she vaulted down to the main deck, Gimp a limping grey streak next to her. She came to a stop where the pirates had been readying their next catapult load of liquid fire. With an almost loving smile, she grasped the sides of the cauldron and, before the shocked pirates could realize what she intended to do, she spilled the contents onto the deck.

One of the catapult's operators, a thick-set woman with tattooed forearms, moved to intercept Rabble. When her head parted from her fountaining neck and landed in the puddle of liquid fire, the rest of the pirate crew ran screaming.

On the *Bolla Fifteen*, Bryax swore softly. "War and Chance . . ."

Behind him, a call from Jeiss announced that the port-side Black Racer had ceased attacking and was fleeing.

"If they catch the wind, they'll get away, Captain Bolla," she added.

Betram, his sapphire-set teeth very visible as he gaped at the sight of Rabble on the starboard ship, waved a limp dismissal of the other vessel.

"Let them go, Jeiss. They'll tell others to dread Bolla Ships." He turned to Rylus. "Rylus, what does your drunken redhead?"

"My redhead?" Rylus asked, turning away from his ballista with a worried glance towards Tambor. "Rabble?"

He looked to where Bryax had raised an arm in mute indication. The sea beyond the starboard side was at first glance a tower of flame. The true picture, when all fell into perspective, was hardly more reassuring. The pirate ship was in flames. Fire raced up the masts and jumped along the lines and rails between decks.

Many of the crew had leapt overboard and Rabble darted

among the flames, harrying and slaying those who remained with equal facility. From somewhere she had acquired a sword and in the lurid red light it was wavy and copper-colored. Gimp bounded alongside her, a demon-cat framed in fire, standing bipedal to swat with his one front paw at the fear-maddened pirates. Those who chose to flee Rabble found that their choices were limited to the friendless waters or the burning vessel. Those who turned to fight found death.

"War and Chance!" Bryax swore, suddenly shaking himself from almost hypnotic fascination with the scene. "That ship is nearly engulfed. How's she planning to get back to us?"

"She doesn't plan," Angie said. "Not her. If we do not rescue her, the water will claim her."

"I've a boat ready!" Jeiss called. "Bryax, come with. I'm not sure she will listen to me."

"What makes you believe that she will listen to me?" he muttered, but he got into the boat.

Jeiss took the oars, rowing them steadily toward the burning ship. Catching sight of the dinghy, many of the pirates who had made the desperate leap into the sea began swimming toward them. Jeiss never paused in her oar strokes, but indicated the boat-hook resting on the bottom of the dinghy.

"Hit 'em if they get too near, Bryax," she ordered.

As Bryax hefted the boat-hook, Captain Bolla bellowed down. "Keep going, Jeiss. I'm sending out other boats to pick up those who want to surrender and we'll plug any who get too near to you."

"Like fish in a barrel," Jeiss laughed viciously.

Bryax cringed a bit from the anger in the First Mate's voice and turned his attention back to the burning pirate ship. Rabble continued her solitary battle. She neither laughed nor screamed nor shouted battle oaths but stalked her prey in a joyful silence that was somehow more terrifying than any sound could be. Gimp stayed with her, making leaps with an uncanny three-legged grace. More

than one of the pirates now splashing in the waves bore the
four long slashes of his single forepaw.

"Rabble!" Bryax hollered when they got close enough
that she could be expected to hear over the crackle of the fire
and the screams of the dying. "Rabble! The ship is going
down! It's burning to pieces!"

She appeared not to hear, bending to rip a gold- and gem-
encrusted necklace from the pirate captain's neck. Apparently she had paused for other looting as well because her
hands and wrists glittered in the firelight.

"Rabble!"

She continued unhearing. He stood in the bobbing dinghy, holding the boat-hook as a balancing pole.

"Chance take you, Rabble! The boat is sinking!"

She stopped in mid-stride, orienting for the first time on
his voice.

"Come to take me back to the *Fifteen*?" she grinned, but
he could see that she had paled beneath her freckles when
she looked at the water.

Jeiss bumped the dinghy against the burning hulk. It was
now most definitely listing in the water. Gimp's triangular
face appeared at the rail first, the cat accepting Bryax's hand
down as if it was his due. Rabble came a moment later. She
clutched a bunched cloak, bulging with something heavy and
her eyes were scrunched shut. She fumbled at the rail.

"Rabble," Bryax coaxed, "give me the cloak. Then give
me your hand."

She obeyed with a childlike stiffness that did not conceal
her dread. The cloak clanked metallically on the dinghy's
wooden bottom. Rabble held out her hands like a little girl
waiting to be picked up, making no effort to step over the
side of the boat. As frustrated as he was, Bryax was touched
by her trust.

"Hey, Rab," he said, more softly. "Hang on, I've got to
bust out the rail here."

The dinghy's rocking made the task more difficult, but a
couple of slams with the boat-hook broke the polished
mahogany rail. Rabble flinched, but she held out her arms.

Bryax lifted her, stumbled as the boat rocked, and the two of them fell into the bottom. Jeiss started rowing at once, the boat riding at an odd angle until Bryax set Rabble in the bow and then stepped over Jeiss into the stern.

Around them three other boats collected dripping and dejected pirates, most of whom eyed Rabble fearfully. Rabble for her part did not seem like an object of fear. She huddled in the bow of the dinghy, Gimp clasped to her chest, flinching back from every wavelet that splashed into the boat. Once aboard the *Bolla Fifteen*, Rabble recovered somewhat, hugging Scrapper and accepting the dog's jubilant welcome.

"What will you do with the pirates?" Bryax asked, once he had helped Jeiss winch the dinghy into its cradle.

Captain Bolla frowned thoughtfully. "There will be bounties for these in the Domain of Dragons. After I collect them, I will reserve a portion for repairs to the *Fifteen* and share the rest out to the crew—and you folks—for a battle won."

Kimit, the *Fifteen*'s chirurgeon, came above deck then. He had scrubbed his hands clean up to the forearms, but his linen tunic was spotted with blood and his eyes were shadowed with purple. He gave the captain a tired salute.

"Kimit, what's the count?"

"We lost three, Captain—Mayi, Wildee, and Teramana. Nat may lose a leg and Tambor hasn't yet come around from that blow he took to the head. We've cuts, slashes, and bruises nearly more than I can count." He paused. "We would have lost more but for Angie, Captain. She's sitting with the wounded now. We'll spell each other right into port."

Captain Bolla found a smile of congratulations for the chirurgeon. "I hate losing anyone, Kimit, but you've done well. I'll give their families a share of the bounty but that won't soften what I have to tell them."

Rabble stirred from where she sat on the deck. From around her neck she lifted the gold and diamond chain she had stripped from a pirate's corpse. Tossing it to Betram, she unwrapped the bundled cloak she had carried away from the wreck. Tangled together within was a profusion of rings, bracelets, necklaces, daggers, and other small trinkets. Most bore jewels or were made of precious metals and tossed back the sun. Rabble tore a few more rings from her fingers and added them to the heap.

"There," she said, pushing the lot towards Betram. "Take it, Captain, for your ship and crew and the families."

"Rabble, I . . ."

"No, take it! If I hadn't been such a coward the fight might not have been so ugly."

She got to her feet. The others stared at her.

"Coward?" Captain Bolla said hesitantly. "You took out that ship all by yourself. You weren't crew. You made no secret that you hate sailing. You a coward?"

"She was a coward," Bryax said flatly. "Let her give you the stuff."

"Rabble, thank you." Captain Bolla looked after the soot-smeared redhead as she retreated to her cabin, then at the members of the Company.

"Choose something, if you wish, for you and for the rest of your Company. I will sell the rest for cash and divide it that way—fewer hard feelings when the shares are clearly even."

Rylus nodded and fished an arm-band set with a scrim-shaw bear from the pile.

"For Tambor," he said, his voice breaking. "It's gold and ivory, rich enough for both our shares."

Hulhc shifted through until he came up with a modest pair of amethyst earrings. "I wonder if I can arrange with you to have your shipline get these to my wife? We live in the Downs, not far from the Dark Opal Lake."

Betram nodded. "We have arranged such things in the past. Bryax, aren't you going to take anything?"

"I don't know if I want any of Rabble's spoils," the blond warrior growled. "She . . ."

"Disappointed you?" Jeiss said, bending and sorting

through the loot. "She's only human, man. Wind and Water! You expect too much of her. Why not take these two boot daggers?"

She held up a set, well-made, workable weapons, beautiful for their craftsmanship rather than from decorations. Bryax took them without comment, tucked them into a pocket, and stalked off, muttering about needing to change the dressing on his wounded leg.

During the rest of the voyage to the Domain of Dragons, Rabble did not stir again from her cabin.

11

And so I wrought them in magic and art, their form, their image; however, I could not capture but the merest fragment of their glory and power.

From the writings of Y'teera, Mage

THE TRAVELLING Spectacular was not three full days in Bookhome before they received summons from Elejinor, the Duke of Dragons, to give a command performance at his capital city of Dragon's Spire.

Rylus summoned all the company to the pavilion near the menagerie wagon in which Tambor was slowly recuperating from the wounds he had taken in the sea battle. With the share of the bounty Captain Bolla had paid them, there had been no great need to put on a Spectacular and with Tambor so sorely injured Rylus had no heart to do so.

Knowing that the journey must be halted if Tambor was to heal, Hulhc had taken the delay graciously. He had holed up in the public sections of the library, emerging so grey-skinned with fatigue at night that Rabble and Bryax would march him to a late open tavern and threaten him until he ate a meat pie or a bowl of stew.

Angie collected exotics for her plant collection and most evenings permitted Betram Bolla to escort her to a variety of night spots. They made a good match, the ship's captain and the Far Shore's Healer but to Hulhc's immense relief, Angie gave no indication of leaving the Spectacular for a life before the mast.

Rabble and Bryax had made up—though Bryax was inclined to study her when he thought she wasn't looking. A handful of mercenary warriors with whom Bryax had once served were now posted in the local garrison. Ferman's Oath had long ago quelled a budding romance with one young woman and Bryax lost no time in seeing if she was still interested now that the terms of their oath had lapsed.

"Did you ever notice," Bryax said to Angie one morning over gossip and hangover remedy, "that Rabble never meets up with any old friends? I have at a couple of ports. If you spend any time doing mercenary soldiering you almost got to—but she never has."

"Maybe no one survives too long in her company," Angie offered. "Our Rabble's deadly when she gets going and I'm not certain she always knows who's friend and who's foe when her blood is up."

When Rylus summoned them to the Spectacular's camp, new romances and old puzzles alike were forgotten in the excitement of seeing the royal seal broken and the heavy parchment scroll unrolled.

Rylus sat on the campstool next to Tambor's sickbed and cleared his throat, reading with the same portentous cadence, if not the same volume, that he narrated the Spectacular:

To Rylus and Tambor of the Downs, Masters of the Travelling Spectacular—Word has reached our ears of the exotic wonders and sophisticated dramas presented by your wonderfully mobile productions company. We

hereby command you to attend our Court at our palace
at Dragon's Spire and there amuse us with a full
presentation of your art. A guide and escort will be
provided for your safety and you may be assured of a
tangible expression of our gratitude.

—*Elejinor, Most Honorable Duke of Dragons.*

There was a moment of respectful silence, then Tambor said, "I don't suppose we dare refuse."

"Refuse!" Hulhc stroked his beard in agitation. "You know that this Duke Elejinor claims to be a wizard! He may have knowledge that could help me to achieve my goal. Please! We must accept this invitation."

"Wizard or not, I don't see how we could do other than accept," Rylus said. "This is his domain and the armed and armored 'gentleman' who delivered this missive did not look as if he would accept a negative answer."

"Do you think this Duke has heard of the trouble we had in the Domain of Roses?" Bryax asked.

"I suspect so. The Domain is ruled by his brother," Rylus answered. "Just remember, there is no rule that says two brothers need be alike in any way."

"From what I have heard in the Library," Hulhc hastened to add, "they are nothing alike. Duke Elejinor is as capricious as his brother is legalistic. Whether they share the goal of dominating the Archipelago, I didn't really find out."

"Then we go." Rabble stopped pulling burrs from Scrapper's coat. "Do you want Axe and me to carry our acceptance to the escort, Rylus? I'd like a look at their gear. Bryax and I may be able to figure out if they mean us harm from that and from how much courtesy they offer a couple of mercenaries."

"You will be—prudent?" Rylus asked, concealing a smile in his hand.

"Promise," she rose, brushing dog hair from her legs. "You may think that I like people challenging me outside of the arena, but I assure you, I've had enough of that to last me for a good while. Coming with me, Axe?''

Bryax nodded, ''Let's leave most of our own gear here. Bookhome does have weapons codes. Rylus, where did they say to send your answer?''

Rylus finished trimming his quill before answering. ''The messenger said the Golden Bell. I suppose that's an estate here in the city. You can ask in the market.''

''Don't need to,'' Bryax said. ''We definitely leave our gear in camp. The Golden Bell is the fanciest inn in Bookhome. The little rooms cost the same as a suite almost anywhere else and don't bother asking for a common room. There aren't any.''

''Guess I'd better wash my hands and clean off the rest of the dog hair.'' Rabble grinned crookedly. ''I wouldn't want to make a bad impression.''

The Golden Bell was as impressive as anyone could wish, a towering structure in polished basalt, fronted by dozens of green glass windows, each one an oval taller than Bryax. Flowering fruit trees were set in squat terra-cotta pots on the wide, shallow steps. Two pages clad in purple tunics trimmed in gold with gold braided fillets around their blunt cut hair stood like well-bred statuettes on either side of the door.

When Bryax and Rabble marched up the stairs, the two pages turned as one and pulled open the doors. The warriors passed through and reconnoitered.

''Shall we ask the clerk?'' Rabble asked, indicating a counter where a haughty woman sat, glowering her assurance that Rabble and Bryax were most certainly where they should not be.

''Seems like our best course,'' Bryax agreed. ''What was the name on that parchment Rylus read to us?''

''Cenai a'tal,'' Rabble said in a mellifluous, lilting accent.

The woman at the desk turned, trying to conceal her interest as to why such riffraff would have business with the

Duke's representative. Equally swiftly, she decided that this was none of her business. When Bryax and Rabble came up to her, she gave them a smile that was chilly but courteous.

"How may I assist you?"

"We are seeking Cenai a'tal," Rabble said, flirting the syllables in the same curious fashion, "or her representative."

"May I say who is asking for her?" the woman said, pulling parchment and pen to her.

"Representatives of the Travelling Spectacular," Bryax said.

The woman wrote out a message in a scrolling hand and then tugged a braided silver cord. There was a soft jingling and a girl of about nine dressed in a golden tunic trotted up, accepted the parchment, and scampered off.

"Your answer will come momentarily," the woman said. "Please wait over by the fire."

They were not kept for long. Flanked by two female guards in red livery trimmed with gold piping and bearing on each shoulder an elaborate device of a red dragon rampant, Cenai a'tal herself descended the main stair.

She was a fair-skinned, petite woman of indeterminate age. The low-cut bodice of her grey satin gown drew attention to the pearl choker about her neck from which depended a gold dragon crafted so that a single large ruby made up the body. Her curly blonde hair was drawn up and back from an unremarkable face, but her green eyes were clear and her expression was that of a person who expected to be obeyed.

She gestured toward a side parlor. Rabble and Bryax followed her in, waiting until Cenai a'tal had seated herself in a padded armchair before taking seats in two less commanding chairs. Her guards posted themselves one inside and one outside the door.

Rabble and Bryax shared impressed glances. Cenai a'tal was an unknown quantity, but her guards wore tailored chain mail. The mail's fine links did not conceal that this was armor made for battle, not for show. Each of the guards also carried an elegant hand crossbow—fully functional for all the delicacy of the mechanisms.

"I believe you have a message for me from your masters?" Cenai a'tal's voice was high without being shrill and her accent carried the same lilting note that Rabble had given her name.

"Yes, ma'am." Bryax's Downs accent sounded even more blunt and countrified in contrast. "We have this."

He handed her Rylus' letter. Cenai a'tal dipped her fingers into the cleft between her breasts and pulled out a nearly flat, embroidered suede case. From this she pulled out a construction of wire set with polished glass and placed it on her nose. Peering through the lenses, she read the note while Bryax stared at her in frank surprise.

"They're called spectacles," Rabble said softly. "They help you to see more clearly. Before the Loss, magic would have been used. They are very inventive devices."

Cenai a'tal waited for Rabble to finish speaking, then favored her with a brief smile.

"From the contents of Master Rylus' note, I can deduce that you are Rabble and Bryax. Well met."

The warriors nodded and Cenai continued, "We hope to leave tomorrow after breakfast. The trip will take about three days at wagon pace. We will provide lodging and food for the road."

She pulled a small drawstring bag from the recesses of her capacious bosom. "Please deliver this to Beastmaster Tambor and tell him to use it to get several days' provisions for his animals. Dragon's Spire is somewhat isolated and it would not do for him to run short of fodder."

Bryax accepted the purse with an embarrassed nod. Nothing Cenai a'tal had done or said had been less than proper, but she radiated sensuality like a hunting tiger does menace. Moreover, she was plainly aware of the effect she had, and her proper manners only accentuated the result.

Rabble spoke, her accent perfectly mimicking Cenai

a'tal's, "Will we need to make any other preparations, ma'am? Bryax and I usually guard the caravan. May we speak with your entourage about road conditions?"

"No further preparations should be necessary," Cenai replied, "and my escort will handle any guard duties. We expect no trouble as we are travelling under the Duke's banner."

"He is well-loved, then," Rabble said.

"He is the Duke," Cenai a'tal replied and then dismissed them.

The road to Dragon's Spire was strenuous, but not unrealistically demanding. Their escort set a pace that was steady but leisurely and each night Cenai a'tal arranged for accommodations in the finest hostelry that the area could supply. The guard was competent if disinclined to socialize while on duty and so the Company was left largely to itself.

Hulhc joined Angie atop the menagerie wagon, cross-legged on a cushion, poring over notes he had taken in Bookhome. Images from lovingly illuminated manuscripts haunted his dreams and shaped the knowledge that he was painfully committing to memory.

His father's notes had contained nothing of the structure by which the wizards had ruled themselves—perhaps because he had taken it for granted. Now Hulhc learned that there had been no universal code—rather there had been many individual groups, rather like craft guilds. Each of these guilds had sent representatives to attend councils on a regular basis and to staff teaching institutions. Thus, there had been a certain universality of goals and ideals, even if no strict code.

He wondered where his father had fit into this structure. Back at Grey Hills Farm, he had found it easy to believe that the Wizard of Grey Hills had been a powerful fellow. From all that he had learned in Bookhome, he suspected that his father had been a fairly small player—a specialist in domestic magics—lights, wards, charms, philters, and the like.

Oddly, this thought didn't dishearten him in the least. The

forces the greater wizards were told of as commanding seemed like powers that should be reserved for deities.

Despite the philosophical skepticism that he had expressed when Rabble and Bryax had sworn their Oath at the Temple of War and Chance, Hulhc was troubled by this thought. Could it be that the Deities were never more than human wizards of enormous power? If that was the case, did it change anything? The effects would be the same, but the world might not be.

Such thoughts bothered him and often he would find himself staring unseeing at a page, his eyes blank, his troubled soul only vaguely comforted by Angie's humming as she combined her herbs and powders in ancient rites of the Far Shore's healing tradition.

For those not distracted by existential musing, Cenai a'tal herself proved to be the greatest diversion of the trip. The woman was clearly suited for her position as the Duke's representative. She was intelligent, firm with her underlings, yet creative when a thrown horseshoe or a wobbly wagon wheel threatened to slow their progress.

Her aura of sensuality was clearly apparent to others than Bryax, yet her escort was entirely female, robbing her of what should have been an opportunity to be served by a loyal and adoring troop. However, she was not above using her charms to manipulate. Indeed, when Tambor was able to resist her wheedling "request" to give her one of his silky, golden monkeys, she retired in a sulky pout.

"I don't like her," Angie commented, after Cenai had stormed away. "She's too fond of herself."

"You're not jealous, are you?" Rylus commented.

"Of that?" Angie snorted. "She can't touch what I got. Makes me mad to see all you fellows dressing up like you're going courting."

Bryax stopped in the middle of combing out his beard. "Hey, I don't meet a Duke every day, Angie. I'm just trying to keep from embarrassing the company."

Rabble chuckled sleepily from where she lounged in Dog Meat's saddle and Bryax blushed down to his collar.

Two days' travel took them out of the more fertile lowlands and into steeper, rockier terrain. Rabble hitched Dog
Meat in front of the lead wagon's four horses and, surprisingly, the war horse threw himself into the pulling. Hulhc
and Bryax's horses were less cooperative, but Tambor
persuaded them to pull with the menagerie wagon's horses.

The fields they passed between were far too rocky for
crops and the occasional vine-terraced slope did not look
thriving. Despite this, they passed farm-holds that looked
much more prosperous than The Grand's windblown but
hard-worked farm.

"What do they grow out here?" Hulhc asked, during a
pause to rest the horses.

"Grow?" Cenai answered. "Not much grows here. The
soil is too much rock and clay. The farms around here raise
goats, mountain sheep, and slaves."

"Slaves?" Hulhc's voice dropped to a growl he didn't
bother to conceal.

"Oh, yes," Cenai apparently didn't hear his anger.
"Since the Loss, the need for cheap labor has increased.
Slaves take time to mature to a useful age, but the return is
very good. We hope to start exporting soon."

"How very nice," Hulhc said. "For you."

On the third day, Cenai a'tal ordered the caravan to stop
in a walled market town. She pointed to where a winding
road vanished into low clouds.

"Dragon's Spire is up there," she said, pride visible in
the set of her round shoulders. "We should be there by mid-
morning tomorrow."

"We could finish the trip today," Tambor said. "The
horses are in fine fettle."

"They may be, but the road won't be good in that fog. My
guard advises that we wait until morning when the weather
may have cleared." Cenai smiled too politely. "Of course, I
have already arranged for accommodations for you and your
animals."

"Of course," Rylus shrugged. "Rabble, get Dog Meat's

team over to the livery stable. We'll follow, but warn the proprietor about the bears. The last fellow nearly had a heart attack when we asked for a box stall for them."

"Got it," Rabble said. "C'mon, Dog Meat."

The inn where Cenai a'tal had taken accommodations for them was called The Flower of the Mountains. The wooden sign over the door was carved in the shape of a five-petaled lily with a woman's face nestled in the center. Heading in from settling the horses—and the owner of the livery stable—Rabble punched Bryax gently on the shoulder and pointed to the sign.

"What do you think, Sword Brother? Does that face look at all familiar?"

A slow grin spread over Bryax's features. "Why, that looks just like Cenai! Do you think she's from here? Do you think that's why we're stopping?"

Rabble shrugged. "I don't know, but she certainly is popular."

Cenai hosted them to a grand banquet in a dining area that was opulently decorated with portraits of the dukes of the Domain.

"Guests for Dragon's Spire often stay here," she explained, as she carved portions from a raisin- and apple-stuffed boar. "I will command the owner to treat you well if you are looking for entertainment."

"Thank you, lady," Rylus said, "but Tambor is yet weak from his wounds. I believe we will retire early."

Tambor, who had grown rather grey under his golden tan, nodded agreement.

Angie declined as well. "I'm for helping settle Tambor in and then finish wrapping some samples I collected along the road. I've never been this far north and, ah, have I found treasures!"

"And I also will retire early," Hulhc apologized stiffly. "At my age, I cannot travel all day as well as some."

"Don't worry about me and Rabble, m'lady," Bryax said. "We can find the bar on our own."

After Cenai a'tal had retired, Kazu, the captain of her guard, joined the two mercenaries in the inn's dark, wood paneled bar. She was a small brunette, too muscular to ever be called petite. Her skin was weathered and her brown eyes had a slanting tilt that recalled Tambor's.

"Mind if a friend and I join you?" Kazu said. "We don't get out often."

"Not at all, Kazu," Rabble said, gesturing for the striking brunette to take a seat across the polished pine table she and Bryax had taken.

"Let me get Vieth," Kazu grinned, eyes sparkling. "She's not as chatty as me—the only reason she's not Captain of the Guard. She's far better with spear or sword."

Vieth, a slim grey-eyed woman with close-cropped pale blonde hair, came in a moment later. She smiled and ordered a round for the table. Without Cenai a'tal's somewhat intimidating presence, the mood relaxed, helped along by several tankards of dark ale.

"So," Rabble said, sipping from a golden brandy made by local vintners, "tell us what we should do to stay out of trouble in Dragon's Spire. I'm getting a . . . reputation for it finding me."

Kazu laughed. "Dueling is strictly forbidden among all branches of the Guard, so if you stay clear of any visitors the Duke has, you should be safe there. The Duke doesn't mix much with commoners—sorry about that—so you shouldn't be troubled there."

"What's he like?" Bryax asked. "I've never dealt with a ruler, except for a few military commanders."

"You'll see him for yourself," Kazu said. "He's quite handsome, with the most compelling eyes. They make you shiver."

"Dragon's Spire—the castle—is haunted," Vieth added, her tone, hushed, almost afraid.

"It is," Kazu agreed. "Even since the Loss. We've all heard the sounds and even seen things at night when we've been standing watch. Everyone says that the hauntings are because Duke Elejinor still has magic and things awaken in his presence.''

"Must be quite a place," Rabble said, swirling the liquor in her brandy snifter. "I can hardly wait to get there. Cenai a'tal could, I noticed."

Kazu and Vieth traded glances, then Vieth sighed.

"Cenai a'tal is probably the second most powerful person in the Domain," she said in her soft voice.

Kazu was more blunt. "The Duke wants her to wed him, but she has never agreed to do more than grant him an occasional night. Some say she has magic, too, and that's how she stays so captivating, despite being less beautiful than many women who have tried to win him."

Vieth snorted, "I've seen her perfumes, jewelry, and wardrobe. If she has magic as well, she's wasting a great deal of effort on mundane charms."

"The Duke, though, he's the real thing," Kazu said. "I've heard spirits talk with him, seen him move things without touching them, all sorts of wonders."

"Why does he have magic when no one else does?" Rabble asked, her tone carrying just a shade of doubt.

Vieth frowned. "It's in his blood, they say."

"That's true," Kazu said. "The Domain of Dragons bore wizards each generation. Also, the Domain of Dragons contains the finest magical library in the region. The Duke moved many of the best books to Dragon's Spire when he was a young man."

"When you see what he can do," Vieth said, her voice dropping, "you will believe."

Rabble snorted. Fearing conflict, Bryax interrupted.

"Tell me, ladies. Cenai a'tal hinted that this place had attractions other than good service and a picture of her on the sign. Can you show us around?"

Kazu's gratitude was evident in her soft, dark eyes. "There is something very special, Bryax, some famous mosaics. Let me get the key to the grand baths from the innkeeper."

"I'll get a couple of towels," Vieth said, "and meet you by the front desk."

The two guards departed, swaying slightly.

"Baths?" Rabble trembled. "Not for me, Axe. I'll just snag a bottle and take it to my room. Tambor will have me up early to get the horses ready for the road."

"That's fine, Rab," Bryax said. "You do that. I'll let the lovely ladies take me on the tour."

As Bryax waited for Kazu and Vieth to return, Rabble headed up the stair to her room, Scrapper at her heels, Gimp dangling sleepily from her free hand. Halfway up the flight, she paused to give Bryax a wink so lascivious that the blood rose to his cheeks. Then she vanished, her chuckle trailing behind.

"Where's Rabble?" Kazu asked when she returned, an enormous brass key slung from her index finger.

"She's gone to bed," Bryax explained. "She has a thing about water—she hates it like fire."

"A shame I didn't think of showing you this earlier, when Farmer Hulhc was awake," Kazu said, after they had remet Vieth and headed down a short flight of stairs that ended in a pair of brass bound oak doors. "These mosaics were done to celebrate the Elements—some say that they were portraits done from life."

"Even if they weren't," Vieth added as Kazu worked the lock, "the baths themselves are magic relics. The wizards could fill them with hot, scented water on command. The Duke has learned the charm and often does it for his guests. Most of the time, the innkeeper just fills it with stream water and calls that a good deal."

"With two bathing companions such as yourselves, I wouldn't care how cold the water was," Bryax began, but his teasing proposition trailed off as Kazu opened the doors and held a taper to the nearest lamp.

The flame travelled down the lamp-wick and caught the oil, illuminating first the lamp itself—a small basin held in two sculpted hands—and then the nearest mosaic. Moving in opposite directions, Kazu and Vieth lit the rest of the lamps and soon the mosaic was revealed in its entirety.

"War and Chance!" Bryax swore respectfully. "Home and Hearth! Peace and Prosperity! Your Duke keeps these locked in a bath? These belong in a temple."

Kazu frowned slightly. "Grandfolks say that this Inn stands where once there was an exclusive college for the more esoteric forms of sorcery. Long ago, maybe fifty years before the Loss, the Elements granted the wizards' request to give them audience and this chamber was chosen. It's a natural cavern and even before the mosaics were done it was considered a place of inhuman beauty. One of the wizards, Y'teera, was an artist and turned her art to capturing the likeness of the divine presence. So, everyone agrees that the mosaics shouldn't be moved. If the tale is true, within this past century, the Elements themselves manifested within this cavern."

Unlike Hulhc, Bryax wasn't one to pepper his hosts with questions, nor to poke about in corners to see how the mosaic was set as would Rylus. His appreciation was of a simpler, more direct sort. Even before Kazu had finished telling of the cavern's history, he began to walk slowly about the room, studying the mosaics with respectful awe.

Thousands upon thousands of tiny pieces of glass, marble, gemstone, and gleaming metal had been set flush in the wall and polished to a glow. The artist had not disdained the natural rise and fall of the subterranean chamber's walls, but had incorporated them into the design so that the figures appeared to have depth and shape.

"Lovely," Bryax breathed. "Perfect."

The mosaic was dominated by four large figures, each on a heroic scale. All were vaguely human in shape, all were androgynous, but not the poor androgyne that humans sometimes manage—the weak compromise of male and female that robs the male of potency, the female of grace and beauty. These androgynous figures were strong yet supple, broad and powerful without being blocky or clumsy.

Moreover, despite the complete absence of any external genital organs, the figures exuded creative fertility. If ever there were images of the Elements from which all matter, all endeavor, all emotion sprung, these figures were the truest representations that a human hand could shape.

The first form that Bryax bent knee before was that of Earth. Gems had been used to build this portrait and their multifaceted shapes digested the lamplight and gave it back as a rich-hued rainbow. Like all of the figures, Earth bore what might be a weapon, might be a tool. The shaft was a glowing beam of purest gold, the head's broad shape something that might be a shovel, might be a warrior's spearhead.

The next figure was that of Air. Here, Y'teera had broken shards of glass to outline a figure that was less a presence than an effect. The colors of the ''body'' were pale blues and icy whites. Air bent an ivory bow more solid than itself and fired from a quiver of glassy arrows that faded into invisibility as they flew away from the archer. The streaming force emanating from Air bent the trees and flowers near to it, set ripples in the water that stretched between Air and the figure that next confronted Bryax's pilgrimage.

Water was sculpted on one of the roughest sections of the cavern wall. Jewels in all shades of blue—a type for each of the seven lakes and some of which Bryax had never dreamed—offset with emeralds, jade, and shining onyx, poured and frothed into the vaguely human shape. The tool that Water bore was a fountaining of silver and tarnished bronze that might have been a trident.

Fire could have been anticlimactic after the other three Elements, but there was such raw power in the figure that Bryax again sank to his knees. Red and glowing, the figure rose from embers of chalcedony, sandstone, and other opaque gems in hues of red and orange. The body was a blaze of rubies, topaz, and opals with a scattering of diamonds for burning sparks. From the flare of Fire's body rose a wavy bladed sword, apparently forged from its own fiery mass. Whereas the implements wielded by the other Elements had both domestic and martial uses, what Fire bore was clearly a weapon. Bryax found himself obscurely pleased to see the patron of War and Chance manifested in its martial aspect.

Realizing that he had remained on his knees, Bryax rose, turning cautiously, fully expecting to find Kazu and Vieth amused at his expense. The two guards' faces bore almost identical gentle smiles, not mocking, more shared appreciation for a glory that familiarity had not made any less wonderful.

"Beautiful, isn't it?" Vieth said softly.

"He must think so," Kazu added. "He hasn't even looked at the pool yet. Still game for a swim? The place isn't a temple, even if it feels like one."

She was loosening the laces at her jerkin's neck as she spoke, releasing round, firm breasts. Bryax forgot dignity in a more earthly awe. Vieth bent to unlace her soft leather boots, sitting cross-legged to pull them off. Her calves were muscular but slender. She seemed shyer than Kazu and Bryax turned his gaze away.

"Coming?" Kazu called. Somehow she was already nude and in the water. "The water's only chilly for a moment."

Bryax fumbled with his clothes, still respecting Vieth's privacy. Kazu was distraction enough, gliding through the water like an otter, teasing him with glimpses of shapely buttocks, each adorned with a saucy tattoo.

The water, when he dove into the bath's blue-green depths, was cold. Kazu, however, was very warm, and Vieth proved much less shy than he had imagined.

12

DRAGON: *a large, mystically-inclined reptilian creature known to possess great cunning and greed.*

Standard Bestiary (15th edition)

ZEBRA: *a mythical creature resembling a small black and white horse. Some reports indicate that zebras more closely resemble mules rather than horses.*

Standard Bestiary (16th edition)

"CAN YOU stay on a horse this morning?" Rabble teasingly asked Bryax as she led his horse over to the inn. "Kazu said that we wouldn't need the riding horses for draft duty today."

"I can ride," Bryax said, swinging into the saddle to prove it. "Kazu say anything else?"

Rabble just chucked and groomed a tangle out of Dog Meat's mane.

"You knew," Bryax said fondly. "You knew that they weren't girls' girls, didn't you?"

"Of course. Wasn't it obvious? If they were girls' girls then they wouldn't be of any use for Cenai's bodyguard, not if our guess as to why the Duke wants her guard to be female is correct." Rabble set Gimp in his saddlebag. "You're looking good these days, with the longer hair and the fuller beard you started growing on shipboard. I didn't think that the ladies would resist."

Bryax grinned, then grew more serious. "Wish you'd stayed long enough to see the mosaics in there, Rabble.

Beautiful things, made of a dragon's hoard of gemstones, but only a soulless one would value them only for the stones. They're eerie—powerful. Looking at them I could believe the story that the Elements themselves came to pose for the wizard artist.''

"I think I've seen those mosaics." Rabble's brown eyes were puzzled. "Or at least heard of them."

The subject of the mosaics was abandoned as the rest of the Company and their escort poured out of The Flower of the Mountains. The Guard was in full uniform, their tabbards in perfect order, their weapons and tack polished to a gleaming finish.

Gowned in a pinkish dress of shimmering satin, white roses in her hair and tucked into her plunging neckline, Cenai a'tal rode her palfrey in the middle of her guard. The Duke's occasional leman easily outshone the women of her guard, but she kept fussing with the tiny white baby's breath she had tucked into her hair and plunging neckline.

Riding in front of the first wagon, Rabble and Bryax emulated the Guard's formality, if not its spit and polish. As they progressed up the road that snaked up to the Dragon's Spire from the inn, the two mercenaries inspected it critically.

The road was well maintained, with stone posts at the half-mile points and heavy wooden rails to protect places where the road curved or a cliff dropped away.

"Didn't Cenai say that the road was dangerous?" Bryax asked. "I can't think when I've seen a better kept highway, even if it is steep."

"Well, yesterday afternoon was foggy," Rabble said, but her tone belayed her belief in her own words.

With less confidence than the warriors, the remainder of the Travelling Spectacular prepared to meet the Duke.

Tambor inspected his travel-worn breeches and tunic. "These are fine enough for the show-ring, but to meet a Duke?"

Rylus was busy straightening his own cloak and adjusting

his belt over the bulge of his belly, but he spared a smile for his partner.

"He won't be looking at how we're dressed, I'll wager, and we have saved our best for the performance."

Hulhc grunted agreement. He had already donned the finest in his collection of grey robes. For once, his books could not hold his attention. Angie glowered at Cenai a'tal and shook out the folds of her russet Far Shore's Healer's robe and daubed delicate blue forget-me-nots on her cheeks.

The journey's end was signalled by rough, rocky walls that framed the approach to the city of Dragon's Spire. The castle itself was hidden by the wall, but its shadow darkened the road. Kazu motioned for Bryax to come to her.

"When we get to the castle," Kazu said, "leave your weapons in the side court. Would you tell Tambor that his beasties must be left there as well? We'll quarter them after the Duke has greeted you."

The blond warrior nodded. "Should we leave all of our mounts there as well?"

Kazu considered. "Yes, that's a good thought. Do you think Rabble's pets will stay?"

Bryax shrugged. "I can only ask."

They rode through the city, directly to the Castle. After depositing the bulk of their gear in the side court, the Company followed Cenai a'tal into a central courtyard. Here they got their first clear look at the castle of Dragon's Spire.

From the road, it had been a looming presence; within the walls its artistry was evident. At first glance, it was a confusing mass of sharp-topped towers and metal steeples. The natural rock from which the castle was built was a dark, grey granite, flecked with mica. Arching windows and doors were trimmed with polished black onyx or white marble, veined with the lightest grey. The ornate balcony of black marble that commanded a view of the courtyard was decorated with ropes of flowers and satin bunting, the only bright thing in an expanse of black and grey.

Yet, despite the architect's attempt at sky-reaching attitude, Dragon's Spire could not escape the impression of brooding over the lands stretched out below its perch with a somber and pervasive melancholy.

"Not exactly homey," Rylus muttered, straightening his overtunic for the twentieth time. "Chill, even."

"Still, you must admire the architect's taste in rain gutters." Tambor indicated the wealth of long-necked dragons that drooped from every roof corner, crept up steeples, and postured on stairs and ledges.

"Hush, now," Hulhc scolded. "The Duke comes—there on the balcony above!"

Flanked by Cenai a'tal and an armored soldier, the Duke strode onto the balcony. He stood just slightly less than six feet tall, broad of chest and heavy of forearm. His hair was chestnut brown and fell to his shoulders in a blunt cut bound back from his noble brow with a band of supple snake-skin. He wore a forest green tunic bordered with curvetting dragonettes, embroidered in gold thread. As he raised his broad hands in benediction, the sunlight glittered from his emerald signet ring.

"Welcome Tambor, Rylus, and all the members of your Travelling Spectacular." The Duke's voice was deep and resonant, schooled like that of a professional orator. "We are pleased to have you here for our amusement. Our agent, Lady a'tal, made promises to you of rewards for your service. It is our pleasure now to offer you our first gifts."

At his signal, Kazu and Vieth entered out through a pointed arch. Kazu bore a silver platter heaped with silk bags. Vieth grasped a green satin lead rope attached to the halter of a bristle maned, black-and-white striped pony.

"A zebra!" Tambor crowed, forgetting himself. "Woods and Water! Is that really a zebra?"

The Duke of Dragons smiled. "Indeed, it is, Master Tambor. Many curious creatures have come my way. When I heard of your Spectacular, I reserved this one for you. Master Rylus, one of those sacks contains coins. One, labeled for your Healer, contains seeds and leaf for an exotic spice once imported from the most tropical reaches of the world. Another contains a painting on ivory of the Wizard of Grey Hills—I believe Farmer Hulhc will treasure this."

Hulhc gaped, tripped on the hem of his robe, and then
bowed clumsily. He slid the ivory oval from its pouch and
cradled the scrimshaw portrait in his hands. It showed a
beardless young man who rather resembled his grandson,
Rue.

"Papa!" Hulhc whispered, so softly that the sound could
have been mistaken for the snuffling of Tambor's newest pet.

"I hope these tokens compensate you some for the
inconvenience of your journey," Duke Elejinor continued,
then he made an outward sweeping gesture with both hands.
"Welcome!"

There was a roll of thunder so loud that the zebra reared
and kicked out with dainty hooves. Then twin rainbows
launched through the misty air to form a triumphal arch.
When the applause had died down, the Duke turned to
indicate the armored man at his side.

"By great good Chance, the third son of my brother, the
Duke of Roses, has arrived to visit me. You might say that I
have had your company brought here somewhat for his
amusement. May I present to you the Lord of Rosewood!"

The warrior tucked his helm under his arm and stepped
forward to accept their salutes.

Rabble's voice carried clearly through the formal silence.
"War and Chance, Bryax! The Duke's nephew looks just
like that kid I whipped way back in Falconersville!"

"Well, we aren't the only ones who know how to stage a
Spectacular," Rylus stated ruefully.

The members of the Travelling Spectacular were comfortably settled in a suite of rooms in one wing of Dragon's
Spire. The castle itself was cool and somewhat clammy; its
broad flagstone corridors that echoed back the sound of their
boots. The corridors were hung with various tapestries of
indifferent quality that did little to chase back either the chill
or the gloom. Widely spaced flambeaux gave light enough to
find one's way and not much more.

The suite itself was quite a bit more attractive—one
suspected Cenai a'tal's influence in the muted colors. The

stone floor in the central room was covered with heaps of soft, heavy rugs, most of which bore the dragon motif. Deep chairs and other furnishings were richly carved and upholstered in woven horse hair that prickled.

Kazu had escorted them to the suite and bid them to make their repast from the banquet of meats, cheeses, bread, and fruit spread on a large, oval table. They were to decide for themselves how to allocate the use of the private rooms that radiated from the central chamber.

"No, we're not the only ones who know how to stage a Spectacular," Tambor agreed, doling grapes out to his delighted monkeys. "But no one has done us any harm, yet. We're well-housed; we even have our own stair down to where the animals are stabled. We're hardly being threatened."

"There is the minor problem that Rabble has made an enemy of our host's nephew," Hulhc said in dry disapproval. "Well, Rabble?"

Rabble ignored Hulhc's question and sliced off a thin bit of smoked trout and dropped it to Gimp. Growling, the three-legged cat dragged his treat beneath Rabble's chair. Scrapper bolted a chunk of roast beef and wagged her tail expectantly. Then Rabble started building a pile of meats and cheeses on a thick slab of dark brown bread.

"Rabble?"

"What do you expect me to do, Hulhc?" she said, her brown eyes wide. "If a rematch is requested, I'll give it. I'll even try to leave the fool alive, though had I slain him the first time, we would not have this problem. I'd guess that Angie did well by his arm or they wouldn't be taunting me."

She chomped into her meal and chewed with innocent enthusiasm. Hulhc felt himself dismissed and sighed as he poured some wine. Rylus paused in dismembering a brace of stuffed pigeons.

"Hulhc, pour me some of the white, would you?" He spun the filled goblet in his fingers. "According to the briefing I received as you folks were putting up the beasties, we will be given the next few days to rest, adjust to the thinner air, and tend the critters. When we are ready, we're going to be putting on a full Spectacular.''

"Will we just be doing the Spectacular," Angie asked, "or will we be doing the fairground attractions as well?"

Rylus pushed a pot of plum jam over to Angie. "Save me from myself, please. I'm going to speak with Cenai a'tal about that. The Duke may be only interested in the Spectacular, but there is a city here—even the castle is a town in itself—and those folks would surely enjoy having their fortunes told or playing some games of Chance.''

"Before the game of War," Bryax grumbled, with a fond smile for Rabble.

Rabble leaned back in her overstuffed chair, balancing her plate on her belly. Only the slight grin tugging at the corners of her mouth showed that she was listening at all.

Hulhc studied her and sighed.

13

Gratitude, like miracles, should never be expected, only appreciated.

Mountain proverb

DECIDING THAT the Spectacular's visit was excuse enough for a holiday, the Duke rapidly agreed to Rylus' suggestion that the Travelling Spectacular's games and amusements be set up. In addition, the Duke requested that the menagerie be opened to the public without charge. Tambor, delighted with his zebra, overruled Rylus' grumbles and agreed.

In return for free run of the Dragon Spire's horticultural gardens, Angie agreed to give each resident of the castle a chit for a free fortune or medical consultation. Not everyone decided to take her up on this offer, but even so Angie found herself as busy as a cat with a dozen kittens.

In order to not disrupt the castle's routine overmuch, the Spectacular's attractions did not begin until mid-morning and were closed soon after dusk. Therefore, Rabble and Bryax had plenty of time for roistering with the Guard. Unlike Cenai a'tal's all-female guard, the Duke's soldiery was of both genders. The castle troops were well-trained and equipped, but Rabble and Bryax found themselves welcomed as kindred within the worship of War and Chance.

Only the mention of the Duke's nephew could strain their accord and, as Rabble did not care to learn anything more about her opponent and Bryax was learning diplomacy, the subject was neatly avoided.

The night before the Spectacular, the pair made their unsteady way up the outside stair, singing bass and alto parts on a Downs' drinking ditty.

"An she wiggle, diggle . . . wha, wha, what!" Bryax's deep voice trailed into silence.

"No, Axe, it's 'she wiggle, diggle, dip, and . . .'" Rabble broke off. "What in the name of Peace and Prosperity! Do y'see that?"

"Uh, huh . . ."

Pale, wraithlike figures drifted in the stairwell, accompanied by the sound of an unearthly harp. At first sight, they seemed a throng, then the throng thinned to a more substantial trio, two females with silvery hair spilling past where their feet should be, a third somewhat more masculine in the breadth of shoulder and trimness of hips.

"I'm not that drunk," Bryax stated.

"I'm not drunk at all," Rabble said, bending to snag her dog by the scruff of its bristling neck. "Scrapper, heel!"

The cur sank back, a warning growl still rumbling in her throat. Rabble patted her reassuringly.

"C'mon, Axe," Rabble said. "Let's go see."

"Hey, Rabble, do you believe in ghosts?" Bryax stalled.

She glanced back at him over her shoulder, the gold flecks

in her eyes glittering. Her sword was held loosely in her hand.

"Why not? C'mon!"

Side by side, they raced toward the spectral figures. Their boots rang dully against the flagstones as they leapt the stairs two at a time. Yet, before they could close, the ghosts shimmered and vanished up toward the vaulted stone ceiling, leaving behind only a final eerie chord and a scattering of whitish dust.

"Do you think they dissolved?" Bryax said, looking side to side then up. "They certainly didn't go up. Look at those spiderwebs!"

"I'd hate to meet what spun them," Rabble agreed. "Fine, they didn't go up—but did they need to? I don't think spirits would disturb webs. They're supposed to be incorporeal, remember?"

"I've heard something like that," Bryax replied, "but no one has seen a spirit since soon after the Loss. What are they doing in this castle?"

"Maybe the Duke *is* in touch with the lost powers," Rabble's tone was flat. "We are getting closer to the Storm Shroud Mountains and Hulhc did say that the Loss came latest here."

"Maybe." Bryax tapped the wall with his knife hilt, glanced nervously around. "Let's clear out of here before those specters come back."

"Done, Sword Brother," Rabble said, sheathing her sword. "Done."

When they entered the suite, the rest of the Company was already asleep, the doors to the bedrooms all closed. Camp beds had been made up and set to either side of the now cleared buffet. Their saddlebags were set one each at the foot of the beds.

"That's what we get for staying out late." Rabble yawned, dabbing her face with water from the ewer. "You going to be able to sleep?"

"You mean after seeing those things?" Bryax stretched. "I've slept after battles with the blood still on my hands and the screams of those I've killed still in my ears. A few pale creatures lurking in the stairwell aren't going to keep me from my sack time.''

''Sleep well, then.'' Rabble flung herself on her cot and wrapped her arms around Gimp. ''Sleep well.''

They had barely dropped off when a shrill ululating scream ripped through the air. The two warriors were on their feet and heading for the main door of the suite as it sounded again, a horrid thing that seemed to rise from a single, many-throated entity or a chorus of the cursed.

The bedchamber doors clattered open behind them.

''Where are you going?'' Rylus said, emerging from one room, a monkey-draped Tambor only a half-step behind him.

Rabble spun to answer as Bryax eased open the door and peered out into the dusky corridor. Her sword was in her hand; Gimp crouched between her ankles while Scrapper growled beside Bryax. The shrill wail sounded again.

''We're going to find out what's making that noise,'' she said matter-of-factly.

Angie leaned nude against her doorjamb and grinned cryptically at Rabble. ''Not scared of the night demon's wails, not our Rabble—eh?''

''Not me either,'' Bryax said, turning his head and keeping his voice low. ''Corridor seems clear, Rab. Ready?''

Her answer was to step after him out of the door, the three-legged cat bouncing at her side, her long-fingered hand reaching to pull the door closed after them.

As the door was shutting, she heard Hulhc grumble, ''They're either braver than I had guessed or crazy!''

Again the wail shrilled, longer this time, echoing from the stone alcoves, apparently directionless. The humans stood poised, uncertain where to start, but Scrapper's finer hearing was not fooled by echoes.

Growling, the scruffy bitch slunk up the corridor toward the center of the castle. Without a word, the warriors followed, treading lightly though the repeated wails might have drowned out even the tapping of nail-soled boots against the flagstone corridor.

They left the wing in which the Company had been housed without seeing any being—either human or supernatural. Scrapper led them on, pausing at each cross corridor to check her bearings, finally coming to a curtained arch. Here the halls were carpeted with richly colored runners that sank beneath their feet. The deep-set windows were enclosed with stained glass in elaborate patterns, many depicting various types of dragons. Bright, new tapestries covered the walls.

"We're out of the second-best wing," Bryax guessed.

Rabble nodded. "And the noise is louder. Scrapper is barely hesitating now. There's light over that way . . ."

They hurried, guided now as much by the light as by the sound. The way opened out into a wide gallery bordering the vaulted reception hall on the floor below. At one end, they could see a door that probably led to the balcony from which the Duke had greeted them on their arrival. Stone pillars topped with crouching brass dragons, their bodies bright, their wings greened with verdigris, marked three grand staircases down.

Scrapper hunkered down by the thick, curved stone railing that bordered the gallery at waist height. The humans and cat followed more slowly.

The wailing was punctuated by human voices reciting something in measured tones. With one accord, Bryax and Rabble peered over the rail and down, trusting the shadows to hide them from whatever lurked in the brighter lit regions below.

The reception hall was even more ornately decorated than the gallery above, but neither the opulent wall hangings, nor the inlaid gold and silver dragons that curved and twined in the green marble floor, nor even the blazing chandelier that depended from a chain of iron wrought in the form of interlocking dragonettes could distract attention from the bizarre and horrid scene below.

The Duke of Dragons stood at the base of the centermost of the three stairs. He was clad only in a shirt of fine white linen that reached to the middle of his bare calves and a longer robe of dark crimson velvet whose gold border brushed the floor. His sole ornament was a teardrop pendant of milky crystal that blazed with lambent light on his breast.

He was accompanied by several retainers, some fully clad, as if they had been standing late watch, others tousled as if roused from bed by the commotion. Rabble and Bryax barely spared these a glance, their startled gazes drawn inexorably to the creature that dominated the foyer's center.

A serpentine monster writhed on the smooth marble tiles, its brown and orange scales contrasting harshly with the green marble. The gigantic body split into not one but three necks, each only marginally more slender than the main trunk. Each neck ended in a terrible head, high-browed and horselike—if any horse could be scaled, fanged, and gifted with darting forked tongue. At this moment, its glittering sixfold gaze was focused on the Duke of Dragons, menace apparent in the arch of its necks and its whistling screech of rage.

To his credit, Duke Elejinor fell back only one pace, though his retainers scurried much farther, some retreating up the stairs toward the landing where Rabble and Bryax crouched behind the balustrade. Rabble's attention never wavered from the drama below, but Bryax shifted uncomfortably.

"Rabble," he whispered, his mouth just inches from her ear—though the din from the monster made such caution unnecessary—"we must be away before the rest of the Duke's people retreat up here and we are found!"

The golden flecks in Rabble's enormous brown eyes twinkled as she grinned wickedly at Bryax. She leapt to her feet, pulling him up with her.

"Retreat? Nay, Sword Brother, we should save the Duke, not flee like his craven retainers."

Scrapper barked anxiously, drawing the attention of a few

of the retainers. One pointed and yelled something. The Duke's attention strayed from the monster for a second, his aristocratic mouth rounded into an "O" of shock.

"Stop that crazy woman!" came the cry, but the warning was given too late.

Rabble leapt from the top of the stone bannister, down and across to the burning, many-candled chandelier. Almost as if she grasped the candlelight itself, she caught the wrought iron and swung there for a moment, rocking back and forth.

The monster angled back one of its heads and saw her hanging there. Venomous slime drooled from its gaping jaws to fall forth and steam as it contacted the floor. Duke Elejinor forgotten, it centered all of its attention on the morsel dangling over its jaws.

A shout of horror frozen in his throat, Bryax pounded down the nearest stair, the three-legged cat and one-eyed bitch right behind him. He was but halfway down when Rabble let go of the chandelier and plummeted downward. The contrast of agitated candlelight and monster smoke was such that she appeared to slide to the floor on a rope of light. As she dropped to the floor, rising from bent knees into a fighting crouch, her copper sword in her hands, the Duke spoke a single awful word.

Milky white light flared from the crystal at his breast and before Rabble could attack, the monster vanished in a cloud of foul smoke that drew racking coughs from all who breathed it. Then the Duke collapsed.

"The Tridrake is the family's curse," Duke Elejinor explained nearly an hour later, when all had assembled in a parlor off of the main foyer. "It has been tormenting the family since before the Refting—the Loss—and has recently reappeared. Some say it is a living embodiment of the family's heraldic beast, others a mockery created by a spiteful wizard; but whatever its source, it is very real and very dangerous."

Bryax nodded in rough courtesy. Rabble, sprawled in her chair, snorted something that might have been acknowledgment or perhaps something ruder. She was still resentful that her daring rescue had been interrupted by the Duke and that afterward Cenai had publicly rebuked her for forcing the Duke to endanger his life by invoking the powerful Word that had banished the monster.

The red-haired warrior's mood was hardly sweetened by the presence of Durez. The Falconersville cavalry officer had visibly gloated when Rabble had stood stupidly on the marble floor, sword poised to battle a vanished foe. Rabble had ignored his jibes, but her lazy-lidded gaze did not completely conceal a malicious glimmer. Gimp was less restrained and drooped across Rabble's lap, ears on side and icy-green gaze travelling with unmitigated disapproval between the Duke and his nephew.

Later still, Rabble and Bryax returned to the Company's suite. Bryax filled the others in on what had happened; Rabble sat pensively against a wall, sipping *pfneur breit* from a square glass bottle.

When Bryax had finished, Rylus commented, "Something smells and we're too far from the coast for it to be the Great Salt Sea."

Angie nodded thoughtfully. "Spirits in the stair, dragons in the foyer, no magic else in all the world. Stinky."

"Rylus, didn't you say that Brytti sort of warned you about this Duke?" Tambor said, combing the mane of one of his monkeys while another clung, chattering nervously, to his skin.

"Yeah, I can't quite remember what Brytti said though."

"Why do you doubt the presence of magic?" Hulhc interjected sourly. "We're here because all of my research pointed to the Storm Shrouds. Why shouldn't there be real magic here?"

"Why not indeed?" Rabble spoke for the first time.

Startled, Hulhc looked over at her. "I thought you were a doubter?"

"I am. There's too much going on here for coincidence. That dragon and Durez both just happening to be here. No, there's a plot of some sort."

She tilted back her bottle and drained enough to sprawl a strong man on the floor. All that happened was that the golden flecks in her eyes burned brighter.

"There was something," she continued, "something I can't quite remember. Something about what the Duke did. It had the taste of real magic, not show . . ."

"Ah, Rabble," Angie said, "but how would you know the taste of real magic? How would you know?"

Rabble frowned. "I have no idea, Angie, but I'm no less sure for all of that."

14

Eavesdroppers rarely like what they hear, but those overheard like the eavesdroppers even less.

Rylus

WITHOUT TELLING anyone but Tambor, Rylus set out to solve the mystery of the source of the Duke of Dragons' power. His choice to pursue the mystery alone was not because he didn't trust the other members of the Company—not precisely. Simply put, each of them had something that made them inappropriate to the task. To quell Tambor's protests he had explained.

"Hulhc is so excited that we may have at last found working magic that he actually blushes when the Duke deigns to pass through the fairground. Angie barely has time to eat or wash between the demands on her. Bryax is smarter than he sometimes seems, but he's Rabble's Sword Brother—not to mention that he's been tumbling a few of Cenai a'tal's guards.''

''And Rabble?'' Tambor asked with a teasing smile. ''Our Rabble? Surely you don't doubt her courage.''

''Courage, no. Common sense is another question.'' Rylus grew serious. ''But more than even that, I fear that the Duke has something in mind for her. While I don't have the faintest idea what that might be—he's not just interested in a tumble—I don't want him to get a shot at her.''

''You're protecting her?'' Tambor nodded approval. ''Good, I like her more and more with each day that passes. Don't ask me why. Maybe it's how she's so gentle with the beasties. Go, then. I'll cover for you.''

So late afternoon, when no one would expect Rylus to be anywhere but the fairground, found the fat showman climbing the very stair where Rabble and Bryax had confronted the spirits. His task so reminded him of the illicit errands of his childhood that he restrained an impulse to sneak, reminding himself that he had every right to be on this stair.

Reaching the vicinity where Rabble and Bryax had seen the spirits, he inspected the walls and floor. Alert for approaching footsteps, he probed the mortar seams with his fingertips and a slim, steel file. As he worked, he absently hummed along with a tune played by a small flute and drum ensemble in the courtyard below, but his attention was elsewhere. What he suspected he would find would not be obvious, but it should be findable by a trained hand.

Rylus paused as his fingertips brushed against mortar slightly less coarse in texture than that which surrounded it. Drawing back, he lit a candle and studied the seam. In color it was identical to the rest of the wall area. That in itself was suspicious. Had this been a patch, there would have been no need to take such care, especially in a wing of the castle where there was ample evidence that second best was good enough.

With a low grunt of satisfaction, he found the outlines of a

sliding panel about two palms in width. He left it undis-
turbed, his mind turning wheels and pulling ropes. Holding
his candle high, he studied the tangle of cobwebs.

Rylus had not been Tambor's partner for as long as he had
without learning something about natural science. In all the
wispy strands he found only one shrivelled spider and nary a
fly or moth. Cleverly done then, but human work, not
spider. Somewhere up there must be concealed the threads
that had raised and lowered the three specters Rabble and
Bryax had seen.

Having learned enough to confirm his suspicions, he blew
out his candle, tucked it in a belly pouch along with his file,
and trotted up the stair. He progressed in a leisurely fashion
through the galleries, nodding to servants and the occasional
resident.

The reception foyer, as Rylus had hoped, was empty, the
castle's residents either about their tasks or visiting the
fairground. Leisurely descending the same staircase by
which Bryax and Scrapper had charged to Rabble's aid, he
surveyed the area. To any but the most astute observer, he
might have seemed impressed, even awed, by the opulent
artwork, but nearly concealed within their fatty folds, his
eyes darted from point to point weighing and assessing.

A slight smile twitched across his thin lips as he surveyed
the marble-tiled floor and its inlaid silver and bronze
dragons. His step lightened as he trotted the rest of the way
down the stair. Withdrawing his file from his pouch, he
began selectively tapping against the stone, his head cocked
to catch the faintest difference between sounds.

Gradually, his investigation revealed the outline of a trap-
door in the floor. Pressing down with a delicacy surprising in
a man of his bulk, he listened until a faint click signalled the
release of a hidden latch. Grinning to himself, he slid back a
wide panel that disappeared on oiled runners beneath the
floor. In the chamber revealed below, he could make out the
outlines of a large, still figure with three heads.

Lighting a candle, Rylus lowered himself into the pit by

means of the knotted rope ladder that was already in place. The figure did not stir, even when he reached the floor of the pit.

Before venturing closer, Rylus found the lever that moved the floor above back into place. Then he stood stock-still, listening. The beast did not even breathe, but in the distance he heard the mutter of muffled conversation.

Shielding his candle flame, Rylus cat-footed over to the three-headed shape. He couldn't restrain the slight chuckle that bubbled from his lips when his light revealed a three-headed dragon standing on a platform tiled in a fashion identical to the floor above.

"Just as I thought," he mused silently. "The Duke of Dragons' 'family curse' is a mechanical fabrication. A lovely job, though. The Duke is wasted on rulership."

Lovingly, he ran his fingers over the creature. Its hide was the artfully tanned skin of some large reptile, touched up with dyes and gilt to give it a supernatural shimmer. He pried apart the hide along a side seam to inspect the inner workings, finding hook and eye fasteners already in place.

The Tridrake's skeleton was carefully articulated metal, threaded with cords that could be pulled from below to create lifelike motion. Each of the long necks contained a selection of whistles rigged so that when a bellows was pumped the air would shriek through.

"Yes, I think I see how you work, beauty," Rylus muttered, as he refastened the side. "They push you up through the floor and then someone below works your mechanisms. I wouldn't be surprised if there was a spotter or two who give the ones below a hint or two. Maybe they use mirrors."

Glancing around to see if his guess was right, he caught a glint of light, brighter than his candle. Moving toward it, he heard the mutter of voices. Curiosity overruled common sense and pinching out his candle flame, he moved closer.

With great reluctance he walked by shelves stacked with cogs, wheels, piping, and a wealth of wire. Until he came to a heavy wooden door that had been propped about a hand-breadth open, probably to create a breeze. Angling himself just right, Rylus found that he could peer into the room beyond without being seen himself. Therein he saw Duke Elejinor, Cenai a'tal, Durez, and a pair of figures so wrinkled and bent that Rylus was not certain whether they were male or female.

Not knowing whether to curse his luck or bless his fortune, Rylus hunkered down to listen.

". . . my honor demands satisfaction, I tell you!" Durez insisted sulkily. "I didn't pursue her here just for your sakes."

"Perhaps not," replied one of the ancients, sweeping cobwebs of grey hair back from the shoulders of a dark red robe, "but the one you wish to duel is far more dangerous than you realize."

"Perhaps even more than she realizes," the second added, fretting with a trailing sky-blue sleeve.

"My nephew deserves something for serving us so well," the Duke said, his tone less commanding than inquiring. "If he had not ridden ahead with news of this flame-haired warrior . . ."

"And if you, my lord, had not found the description significant," Cenai interjected.

"Then you would not even realize how close she—if it is indeed she—has come," the Duke concluded.

"Hmm," the red-robed ancient toyed with a pendant set with an intricate pattern in crystal. "What you say has merit . . ."

"And has had the last three times we've presented it," Durez growled sullenly.

"What I don't understand," the blue-robed ancient interrupted, "is why Your Grace felt the urge to draw out this creature with your mechanical toys."

The Duke winced at this description of his elaborate creation and Rylus felt an unwilling pang of sympathy.

"Y'teera, I wanted to test her," the Duke replied, his tone deferential, "to see if she showed any of the signs you had told me to watch for or if she was simply skilled with a sword. I certainly would not have wished to disturb your Ancient Wisdoms or to draw you from your essential tasks merely at a suspicion of my own."

"You think she suspected nothing?" Y'teera continued.

"I think not," the Duke replied with some of his usual haughtiness. "I will admit that I was somewhat startled when she jumped over the railing to assault the Tridrake. I had expected to see her come down the stairs. However, I used the smoke charm you had taught me to cover the removal of the mechanism."

"And did it work well?" the red-robed one asked eagerly.

"Why, yes, Weatus," the Duke said modestly. "Quite well."

"There were enormous, billowy clouds," Cenai added. "I've never seen it work so powerfully."

The ancients looked at each other, as if that last bit of information had answered some unspoken question for them.

"Well, Elejinor," Weatus said, "perhaps we can permit the duel. We may need to summon assistance and an affair of honor would keep the Travelling Spectacular here while we did so. Don't you agree, Y'teera?"

"Yes, that will do," Y'teera said. "Before we leave, Elejinor, I would like to see your mechanism. I may need to have you speak with some craftsmen I have working on temple adaptations."

The Duke rose. "My workshop is around you. I keep it a secret from most of my staff—frankly, I prefer to be thought a wizard. The Tridrake is through that door."

Rylus had begun retreating as soon as he realized where they were headed, but, because he did not dare relight his candle, his progress was slow. None of the alcoves he probed seemed likely to conceal his bulk and the only exit was apparently the one through which the Duke was even now leading his guests.

"Mind your step," the Duke said, holding his lantern aloft. "I fear it is rather cluttered. Now . . ."

His speech trailed off as the light illuminated where Rylus stood, lounging against the Tridrake's flank.

"Good day, Your Grace," Rylus said, managing a cocky smile. "Seems that you and I have a great deal in common."

Tambor received the Duke's message about an hour later. The heavy vellum scroll was etched with characters that glowed for a brief moment then faded as he read their message. The words remained seared on his mind as he gathered Bryax and Rabble to him.

"Rylus is in trouble of some sort," he told them, his hands twisting the vellum as if he could wring a fuller story from it. "He had his doubts about the Duke's claims to magical power. Rabble, you must do what they want and get him back!"

"Easy, Tambor," the redhead said soothingly. "Who is making demands?"

"And what demands?" Bryax added, taking the blank vellum and turning it to and fro.

Tambor lowered himself onto a bale of hay and mechanically started polishing a length of the zebra's halter.

"It said, 'Tambor, Rylus is resting well but, if you wish him to avoid being hanged as a spy, arrange for Rabble to meet Durez on the field of honor at the culmination of tomorrow evening's Spectacular. Durez must win said meeting or Rylus dies.'"

"Elements!" Rabble swore. "Of course, I'll throw the fight, Tambor."

"Thanks . . ." Tambor began, but Bryax interrupted.

"She may intend to, but can she?"

"And should she?" Angie cut in from where she had been standing in the doorway.

"Angie!" Tambor exploded. "How long have you been listening?"

"Long enough, worried man, long enough to learn," she waved her hands vaguely. "The fortunes all stopped happening—told me an old man would bear twins next Spring—that a three-legged fish would inherit a family's lost fortune. So I tossed the coins again—this time for me—and knew we had trouble. Not hard to tell where I might be listening best with Scrapper and Gimp outside of the wagon and Dog Meat staring this way and stamping his hooves."

"Angie, what did you mean when you said that you wondered if I should accept Durez' challenge?" Rabble asked. "If I don't, Rylus is in danger. He's a hostage against my behaving in the fashion the Duke wants."

"Would you do this—throw this fight—if they didn't have Rylus?" Angie asked.

"Of course not!"

"Then let's take Rylus away from the Duke," Angie challenged. "This Domain is not so large that we can't run and the Storm Shrouds belong to no one but the Elements."

"I'm tempted," Rabble said, "and not just because I've been insulted. We don't have any evidence that the Duke will free Rylus. In fact, we need to consider that he may not free him at all."

"Or any of us," Tambor added, tight-lipped. "Travelling shows are easy to make disappear."

"We would need to leave the wagons," Rabble said, "and most of the smaller animals and draft horses. Can you accept that, Tambor?"

Tambor frowned. "Those wagons have been my home for many years—but Rylus has been my dearest friend for even longer. I'm more worried about the menagerie, but . . ." He rubbed his jawline thoughtfully. "Give me a few hours and I'll find someone to care for them."

"Without giving anything away," Angie cautioned.

Tambor nodded stiffly. "Of course."

"Good," Rabble said. "Angie, you fill Hulhc in on what's been happening. Bryax, see if you can figure out where Rylus is being held."

"I've an idea how to go about that," he said. "I'll just take a wander and look for Kazu and Vieth. I happen to know they're out of the castle today, escorting a supply train, but while I'm asking around, I can see if the guard has been tightened anywhere.''

"Good," Rabble replied. "Take Scrapper with you. She may scent Rylus.''

"What are you going to do, Rabble?" Angie asked.

"After Tambor and I pen an acceptance to Durez' challenge, I'm going to smuggle some of our travelling gear outside of the castle's walls. I figure I'll load up Dog Meat and then use needing a private place to practice as an excuse to go out.''

"Be careful," Bryax hugged her. "They may have spies follow you.''

"I'll be careful," Rabble promised. "Let's meet back here at the dinner hour. That will give us ample excuse to talk.''

"Poor Rylus," Tambor said. "He's got to be worried.''

"Don't worry, beastmaster," Angie said, with a wicked smile. "If he knew what we are planning to do, he'd be more than just worried. He'd be scared!''

15

Knowing when you exceeded your welcome is the key to being a good guest.

The Tome of Social Graces

RYLUS WAS contemplating the little red bedbugs in the straw ticking and wondering how long it had been since they had eaten a good meal when one of Tambor's golden monkeys scolded him from the wrought-iron-barred window of his tower cell. Glancing anxiously over his shoulder to the heavy oak door and seeing no sign that the guard had heard anything, he hurried over to the window.

"Hush, you furry beggar," he snarled as loudly as he dared.

The monkey drew back, offended by Rylus' tone. Rylus immediately softened and took from his pocket a crust of the bread that had been part of the feeble excuse for luncheon that the Duke had sent to his "guest."

Accepting the crust, the monkey squeezed through the iron work on the window and jumped to cling onto Rylus' vest. With a chirp quite unlike its shrill scolding, the monkey plucked at a satin thong slung over one of its shoulders and under the opposite arm. A slim tube hung from it.

"What's this?" Rylus asked, lifting the thong free from the pleased monkey and uncapping the tube.

When he shook it gently, out slid a pair of his most delicate lock-picks and a rolled spill of parchment. Chortling, he hid the lock-picks in the hem of his vest and started to unroll the spill.

As if it understood that its task was completed, the monkey patted the side of Rylus' face with a smooth-skinned palm and then leapt to the window. Peering out through the bars, Rylus could see it picking its way to the garden below, using handholds of rough stone and, lower down, ivy that would never have borne even a child's weight. When he was certain that Tambor's messenger had safely escaped, he unrolled the parchment.

"Tonight there will be a diversion. Unlock your door— there is no bar—and leave by the *left* stairway. Tam."

Rylus smiled. He then tore the parchment into strips and chewed it up. It tasted at least as good as the Duke's bread.

"The llama and the zebra are ready," Tambor reported to the group huddled in his wagon. "Even the bears and monkeys are behaving—exceptionally well, I might add. It's almost as if they know exactly what I want and why."

"I've the less, um, exotic, gear ready, including horses big enough to carry Bryax and Rylus," Hulhc added. "We won't be as comfortable as with the wagons, but everyone will have dry clothes and food. We'll be able to move faster, too.''

''My coins led me to the owner of a livery stable who will take two of the remaining draft horses in trade for housing the rest and hiding the wagons,'' Angie said. ''She is here tonight with her two sons, one of whom has some skill with critters, and will care for the little menagerie.''

''Can they be trusted not to give us away?'' Hulhc asked.

''I think so,'' Angie said. ''My coins say they have no great love for the Duke. Besides, I gave the lady a liniment that will ease the achy joints of an old pet horse that she keeps. We're friends now.''

''And the diversion?'' Tambor said.

Bryax grinned. ''Ready. There are two stairs into the tower where Rylus is held. The left one goes directly outside, the right into the Duke's wing of the castle. Rabble and I have plans to draw the guard off of the outer stair. After we get Rylus, we'll go out over the wall.''

''As for your own cover for leaving Dragon's Spire,'' Rabble added, ''I talked with Angie and with her help I've put together some toys that should provide more than enough distraction—especially for these people who believe in magic.''

''I know what to do with them,'' Angie assured her, ''but will they work?''

''They will,'' Rabble promised. ''Now, don't wait for us—just head for the Storm Shrouds. Scrapper's nose will be enough guide for us to catch up with you.''

''Then all we have left to do, is wait,'' Hulhc said, scratching his nose, ''and worry.''

Angie put the canisters in the trash near the kitchen entrance to the castle and crept away. Across the walled compound, Hulhc had dropped his into the red-hot coals that still smoldered from a pig roast earlier in the day. Tambor had risked the cleverest of his monkeys to deliver small paper packets into the torch sconces by the main gate. Now, they nervously waited to see what exactly Rabble's promised distraction would do.

Bouncing from wall to wall in his tower cell, Rylus also waited. The lock-picks were in his hand and he strained his ears for the faintest sound that could be the sign that rescue was imminent.

Outside the prison tower, her hand on Scrapper's head, Rabble knelt beside Bryax in the garden. Both wore tunics with the Duke's crest over their armor and could, if one did not look too closely, pass for members of the Guard.

"How long will it be?" Bryax whispered hoarsely.

"Soon," Rabble answered. "If everything doesn't just . . ."

She was interrupted by a terrific boom followed by a series of shrill whistles from over by the former barbecue pit. Angry shouts came from the guards posted at the main gate. The replies from their fellows in the castle were drowned out by a second series of explosions from the kitchen yard. Bright yellow flame blossomed moments later.

Rabble's eyes shone as she poked Bryax. The blond warrior was poised, one hand on his sword, the other cupped over a ringing ear. Scrapper looked even less happy, but remained determinedly crouched by her mistress' feet.

"We give Rylus a moment to open his door," Rabble reminded Bryax. "Then we clear the stairs for him."

"Right," Bryax said, touching a bundle of pre-cut binding cords at his side. "Remember, we take prisoners."

Rabble nodded impatiently. "Let's go!"

At the base of the stair, they met with a burly member of the Duke's own guard. He was peering upwards to where irregular trails of green and gold stars had left a smoky after-image against the dark sky.

Striding forward as if bearing a message, Bryax barked, "Report to the main gate at once! We're to relieve you here!"

Startled, the guardsman began trotting away and even as he

turned, his lips shaping a question, Rabble had neatly knocked him cold. She rolled him under a nearby shrub and followed Bryax into the tower's stair.

Torches set in iron sconces shaped like fire-breathing dragons with wings outstretched illuminated the wide, curving stair. Bryax started up. Rabble paused and knelt beside Scrapper.

"Stay here, girl, and bark us warning."

The bitch growled once and then sat on a camp chair still warm from the now unconscious guard.

Rabble sped to join Bryax, who had paused a few steps shy of the middle landing—one flight short of the floor on which Rylus was being held—and was tracking the guards above by their restless shadows. A new barrage of explosions from outside and a series of inarticulate commands made it impossible to overhear what was being said.

Bryax tilted his head right. "I'll take that one."

Rabble's response was to shift her balance slightly left. At Bryax's signal, they bolted up and out.

The two on watch wore the uniforms of Cenai a'tal's elite guard and they proved their right to those uniforms by pivoting as one to confront the intruders. At the same moment, the four recognized each other.

"Bryax!" Vieth said. "What is going on here?"

He slowed. Rabble was less disconcerted. One kick spun Kazu's sword from her hand and a roll brought Rabble up to pin the other woman's sword-arm behind her back. Kazu's remaining hand was pinned with only a touch more effort.

"We've come for Rylus," Bryax said, "or don't you know who you're guarding?"

"Rylus? Rylus is the spy?" Vieth replied, her surprise evident, but her sword rising to guard position. "We rode back in today and Cenai told us we were to take a watch stand because a dangerous spy had been captured. But Rylus?"

Another explosion, accompanied by a shower of silver sparks just visible through the window, punctuated her words. Rabble shifted her grip on Kazu and glanced up the stair. No sign of Rylus.

"Is there another guard up there?"

"No, no real need, since there are guards on both lower landings," Kazu answered, "and a non-present guard can't be compromised or bribed."

Bryax and Vieth lowered their blades by mutual consent. Vieth frowned at Kazu.

"We were overpowered," Vieth said slowly. "Right, Kazu?"

Kazu hesitated and Rabble tightened her hold, pressing with her forearm across the guard's throat. When she released the pressure slightly Kazu nodded vigorously.

At the top of the stair, Rylus had worked open the heavy lock. Turning left, he heard what sounded like conversation from beyond the curve of the thick-walled stone stair. Wondering if the voices belonged to friend or foe, he paused. The rapid tread of feet ascending the right-hand stair broke him from his contemplation.

The Duke of Dragons, two guards behind him, rushed onto the landing. Rylus bowed.

"Good evening, Your Grace," he said, backing toward the left-hand stair. "I have enjoyed your hospitality, but I fear I must be going now."

The Duke lurched toward him. "Seize him, guards!"

Rylus laughed mockingly and fled down the stairs. "Why not use your magic to stop me?"

He nearly collided with Rabble ascending, but she waved him past. There were two thuds behind and then she tore down the stair after him.

Below, Scrapper was barking wildly. Behind, the Duke was shouting orders. Without, yet another series of explosions echoed above the panicked screams of the castle's inhabitants and the shouts of the hastily organized fire brigade in the kitchen yard.

At the base of the stair, Bryax and Scrapper were holding their own against three guards. A sword slice beading blood coursed Bryax's cheekbone just below the eye and a hank of his hair lay by his feet.

"We're here, Sword Brother," Rabble yelled with inhuman glee, bounding to his side.

The guards took one look at her bright eyes and another at her copper-bladed sword and perhaps recalled that this was a woman who made her living winning sword battles. Prudence won out over duty and they all broke and ran. The three companions ran to where a ladder was concealed behind some late flowering peonies.

"You first, Rylus," Bryax ordered. "We'll hand you Scrapper."

"Joy," the fat man muttered, but he topped the wall in record time.

The others followed rapidly, Bryax pulling the ladder up after. As Rabble thumped to the dirt, she whistled. Almost immediately, Dog Meat trotted up, herding Bryax's dun and one of the draft horses for Rylus. Rabble impatiently shouldered Rylus into his saddle.

"We're lucky that they were too shaken to remember bows," she said, swinging into her own saddle. "We won't stay that lucky."

"Do you know which way to go?" Rylus asked, nudging his horse into line behind Dog Meat. "It's awfully dark out here."

"We head into the Storm Shrouds," Rabble said. "We're to meet the others out there."

The game trail they followed away from the castle barely permitted them to ride in single file. Several times, Rabble dismounted, chopping through the tangled brush while Bryax and Rylus kept a wary guard. Eventually, they left the noise and smell of Dragon's Spire behind them. Later still, their game trail crossed a marginally wider venue that might be called a road.

"Do we take it?" Bryax asked.

"It goes the right direction," Rabble said. "Damn the night for being so cloudy! I could use a bit of moonlight."

As if in answer to her words, a gust of wind parted the clouds, revealing a fat waning gibbous moon. Shrugging a trifle uneasily, Rabble dismounted and inspected the road.

"Looks as if the others have been through here," Rabble straightened. "I see bear prints and that little hoof is the zebra's. There doesn't seem to be enough horses."

"You think someone didn't get away?" Bryax asked.

"Could be," Rabble remounted. "What it does mean is that we're still ahead of the Duke's forces. There would definitely be more marks on the trail. Let's move so we can catch the others before the Duke's people catch us."

Following the road through a wary darkness became more exhausting as the adrenaline faded from their veins but they continued into the mountains. Intermittent glimpses of the stars gave them a sense of time passing, but only when Rylus' horse—by far the heaviest burdened—began to stumble did they call a rest.

After they had fed and watered the animals, Bryax handed out small sacks of roasted oats sweetened with honey and mixed with walnuts and dried apples. Rabble dug a flask of *pfneur breit* from her saddlebag. Somewhat cheered, they hunkered down over their cold fare.

"Think the Duke will really send people after us?" Bryax asked.

"Don't know," Rabble replied. "Depends on how badly they want Rylus and how much Durez wants a fight."

"There may be more to it than that," Rylus said gruffly.

Briefly, he repeated the gist of the conference he had overheard in the Duke's subterranean workshop. When Rylus had finished, Bryax reached over and took a slug from Rabble's flask.

"So you *were* spying," he said, coughing slightly. "That changes things a little."

"Not much," Rabble said. "What he's learned is all a piece with the strangeness we've encountered since arriving at Dragon's Spire. I'm more interested in knowing who those ancients were and why they would be looking for me."

"I don't know," Rylus said, rubbing legs that were stiff from riding. "I had hoped that you knew something that you hadn't told us."

Rabble shook her head, her sincerity obvious even in the dim light. "I have no idea."

"What I do know," Bryax said, "is that we had better ride. They'll be certain to follow."

16

Even nothing may become something if you believe in it with sufficient force.

Engraved over the entry to the College of Magic, Bookhome

WHEN THEY caught up with the others a few hours after dawn, Tambor was riding the zebra, while Angie rode the llama. Hulhc was on his scrawny grey horse, Gimp riding pillion. The reunion was noisy and enthusiastic, but after assurances had been shared that no one was hurt, the reunited company rode on without further delay.

"I thought for sure that no sleep, little food, and too much strong drink had me hallucinating when we first saw you," Rylus commented.

"Ah, you mean Angie and my stylish mounts?" Tambor chuckled, giving the zebra an affectionate rub on its bristly mane. "When time came for leaving, we had the choice to go without mounts or without supplies. We grabbed the supplies and ran like water downhill. When we had a chance to regroup, I thought that some of the beasties might do mount duty and to the surprise of my life found them agreeable. Those pirates did me a favor unknowing. If I hadn't lost so much weight when I was ill, Z'ripes never would have been able to carry me.''

"The bears are doing flank guard," Hulhc said, his voice not hiding his wonder. "They're out there, just beyond sight, so hold your arrows."

"Say, Hulhc," Rabble said, "now that we're out here, where are we going?"

"The Storm Shroud Mountains," the farmer answered.

"But aren't we there—or at least nearly there?" Rabble asked. "The maps say that they begin beyond the Domain of Dragons."

Hulhc frowned. "I had planned to hire a local guide in one of the towns and maybe get more sense of the magic's ebb from local tales. Our hasty departure rather changed my plans."

"In other words," Rabble said, "once we reach the mountains, you don't really know where we should go."

With remarkable patience, Hulhc pulled a map-case from his saddlebag. "This indicates a town ahead of us along this road. Why don't we go there and ask my questions?"

Rylus frowned. "What if the Duke's people go there also?"

"No matter," Hulhc said firmly. "I believe we will be outside of his Domain. No one claims more of the Storm Shrouds than what they can patrol for themselves."

"That doesn't mean they won't follow us," Rylus said.

"True," Bryax cut in, "but it does mean that we'll be as much the law as they are. I say we go on—at least we can get a hot meal and a bed by the fire."

Unhappily, the town on Hulhc's map wasn't there—or rather it was, but no one was using it. In fact, from all appearances, no one had used it for a long time. A few stone walls marked where buildings had once stood. Vines entwined shapes by the riverbanks that might once have been end points for a bridge. The less permanent building materials had long ago been returned by water, wind, and fire to the earth.

The Company, astride their varied mounts, stared down the gentle slope into the fertile vale, nearly identical expressions of dismay on their tired faces.

"This is the place," Hulhc said unhappily comparing the landmarks to his map. "That is a branch of the Gramblin River down there and . . ."

"Hulhc," Rylus said, "where did you get that map?"

"From my library, my father's library," the bony old farmer straightened in remembered pride. "He was a great traveller, he was."

"I'd guess the map didn't know to update itself," Bryax said dryly. "Lots have changed since your father's day. What do we do now?"

"We could still camp there," Tambor suggested. "There's fresh water and a stone wall is a better wind break than none."

"I don't know," Bryax said. "We'd be better able to keep watch up here."

"Quiet!" Rabble interrupted. "I thought that I saw movement down there. Something white, over where those two walls rise."

The others stopped quarrelling and stared where she was pointing. In the silence, the only sound was the horses shrugging against their tack and sleepy birdcalls.

"There might have been something white down there," Angie said after a moment, "but I'm not sure it wasn't just the bouncing of a cottontail's rump."

"The beasts don't seem edgy," Tambor offered. "I think they might be if it were strangers or a dangerous predator. Angie is probably right. You saw a rabbit or a deer."

Rabble didn't look convinced, but she didn't argue either.

"Let's camp below," Rylus said. "I feel exposed up here. The vale isn't steep enough to block our escape if the Duke's people catch up with us. I'd feel better with a wall or two to shield our firelight. I don't know about the rest of you, but I've been dreaming of a hot meal since noon. A cup of tea and a hot pack for my aches wouldn't be amiss either. If we camp up here, we'd have to do without all of that."

"The night will be cooler still," Angie added. "We've climbed a fair amount during the day's ride and, at these heights, even a summer night chills the bones."

"I surrender," Bryax said. "Let's find our camp spot before we lose what's left of the light."

Camp was set in a cozy angle between two intact stone walls. Rabble knelt to build a fire in what may have been the house's original hearth while Bryax assisted Tambor in grooming the animals. Tambor's shivering monkeys hung around Rylus' neck as he readied a kettle for water and set out supplies for supper.

"When you've done with the animals, Bryax," Angie called, "I want a pat and a glimpse at the slice on your face. Earlier, I saw it was starting to pucker and yellow."

"Just a few more minutes," the blond warrior promised. "Rabble, you're going to have to look to Dog Meat. The nag's in one of his moods."

"He's just making up for being cooperative earlier," Rabble said. "I'll take care of him and then fetch some more wood for the fire. There's a good deadfall just over the way."

She was bringing back her second armload when the corner of her vision was teased by a shape of glimmering white. Dropping the wood, she wheeled but saw nothing other than Scrapper staring up at her in confusion. Gathering the wood again and doubting her own sanity, Rabble rejoined the others.

"I'll take first watch tonight," she offered. "Even with Tambor's bears lurking out there, we'd best have a human awake."

"Fine," Bryax said, from where Angie was inspecting his face. "Wake me after."

"Give me dawn watch," Tambor said. "I'll use it to feed and ready the beasties. I can even poke Rylus a bit early so he can cook breakfast."

"Thanks, partner," Rylus said dryly.

Angie leaned back and looked critically at Bryax's wound. "I should have stitched that earlier. Let me see what I can do now to keep it from infecting. Hulhc, pass me a cup of hot water.''

"Hulhc is asleep," Rylus said, his tone far gentler than was his wont. "Dropped right off, sitting against a tree."

Tambor passed Angie the cup of warm water. "I keep wondering why an old farmer would be so keen on searching for lost magic. That was a fine daughter we met and a handsome grandson. He speaks well of his wife, too."

"His wife isn't well," Angie said, dabbing a warm, damp square of linen at the crusty scab along Bryax's cheekbone. "He near begged me to send her medicines several times before we left the Lakes. I did, of course, for what good they'll do."

Without taking her gaze from the gathering shadows outside of the fire circle, Rabble added, "At least Hulhc knows what he's searching for and maybe even why. How many people can say that?" She paused and then said more softly, "I know that I can't. I only wonder why it's taken me so long to even wonder."

"Rabble, what do you mean?" Bryax asked, wincing slightly as Angie slapped a hot compress onto his face and motioned for him to hold it there.

"I've been listening to all of you during the time we've been travelling," Rabble said hesitantly. "I'm starting to believe there are—holes—in me."

"Holes?" Angie said, a mite too casually, her fingers dexterously mixing powdered herbs into a thick paste.

"I know all sorts of things—but I don't remember learning them. I don't seem to have any memories of a family or a childhood, but I've all this other stuff I must have done to know it so well." Rabble didn't turn to face them, drawing instead in on herself, wrapping her arms around her bent knees until she was another shape at the edge of the firelight. "But I don't remember when I did it. My clearest memories start with the day that Tambor found me."

"On Old Shrine Highway," Tambor recalled, "back in early spring. We'd just started the season's tour. Elements!

It seems so much longer. I don't know what the Spectacular would be like without you in it, Rabble.''

"Thanks. I know I've caused you trouble."

Angie glanced worriedly at her. "Ease up on that cloth now, Bryax. I've the poultice ready."

"Is it hot?" Bryax said.

"Don't be such a child," she scolded, "or shall I have Rabble come hold your hand?"

Bryax looked at the incongruously fragile warrior huddled onto herself, at the worried dog and cat leaning against her. He bit back his initial, indignant reply.

"Yes, Angie, I think I need someone to hold my hand. Rabble?" He raised his voice slightly. "Could you do your Sword Brother a favor?"

She turned then, her large eyes red-rimmed but dry. "Sure I can, Brother. You need a hand to hold?"

She came and sat beside him and took his broad, scarred hand into her own more slender and surprisingly unmarred one. The gesture was neither motherly nor romantic, but somehow born of the same dependable mien that she had shown toward him ever since they had sworn Ferman's Oath back in the Downs. Giving Rabble a warning nod, Angie peeled back the bandage, exposing the wound.

Cleaned, it was evidently on the verge of serious infection. The edges were raw and rumpled looking and the interior was coated with a film of pus over angry red skin. Bryax didn't wince as Angie began treating it with her poultice, but the hand that held Rabble's clamped down. The redhead blinked, but did not draw away.

"Nasty, nasty," Angie muttered. "That soldier didn't clean his sword too well, did he? No poison, but enough filth that just a rinsing didn't clean it enough. I don't dare stitch it—I'm not certain that the edges will heal. We'll just have to treat it and hope that the scar isn't too ugly."

"Whatever you say," Bryax said, his voice strained. "I didn't want to say how much it was hurting, but I thought something was wrong."

Angie shook her head. "I'll bandage it with herbs and an old song my grandfather taught me that's supposed to help the wound remember how to heal."

Bryax nodded, accepted the catnip and lemon balm tea she gave him to sip while she worked, and was nodding off almost before she had finished.

"I'll take his watch," Angie said firmly. "He needs the rest in order to heal."

"Then he'll rest," Rabble said. "I'll wake you."

The company rapidly followed Hulhc and Bryax into sleep. After a while, the only sounds were soft snores, the crackle and spit of the fire, or a horse shifting from foot to foot. Rabble watched through the first hours of the night as the last bit of the summer evening yielded to twilight and then to stars.

Once, out in the darkness that filled the ruined town like its remaining inhabitant, she thought she saw something large and white, standing as if watching her. When she moved to get a clearer look, there was nothing. Noting that the animals seemed unalarmed, she did not pursue.

The next morning brought a light rain, an uncomfortable foreshadowing of the coming autumn, doubly unpleasant after the warm summer weather in the lower regions. Huddled in Dog Meat's saddle within her encompassing oilskin, Rabble forgot the night watch in her concentration on staying as dry as possible.

Even the knowledge that any pursuit would be slowed by the rain couldn't overcome the company's pervasive mood of weariness. The conversation over the breakfast fire that morning had not done much to alleviate the gloomy mood. Growling with—and at—Hulhc over old Wizard Grey Hills' map, Rylus had reluctantly concluded that their best course of action was to continue deeper into the mountains, seeking another large town.

The suspicion that this town, like its predecessor, no longer existed sank into the Company with the rain. Yet, each knew that they did not dare return to the lowlands until the Duke of Dragons and his mysterious allies would have lost their interest in Rylus and Rabble—and in those who had made possible their escape.

So they rode on in the rain and by mid-day the drizzle had been burnt away by the rising sun. Tambor's bears found an enormous honeycomb within a split tree trunk. When the Company had outdistanced the bees, they stopped for a meal of pancakes, honey, and late up-country blueberries.

Licking her fingers clean, Angie critically studied Bryax's bandaged cheekbone.

"The rain wasn't kind to my work," she said. "Let me scrub it off and redo it before we ride."

"It doesn't hurt as much," Bryax volunteered.

"All the more reason for keeping the dressings fresh," Angie replied. "Rylus, is there any more hot water in the kettle?"

"A cup or two," he said, carrying the pot to her. "Help yourself."

Pale blue powder, a pinch of witch hazel, and another of ground willow bark went into the hot water, followed with a touch of pressed rose petal "for the spirit." Angie stirred the mixture until it thickened, humming a repetitive tune. Setting it aside, she softened Bryax's dressing with the remnants of the hot water and peeled it back. Using a cloth dampened with her potion, she cleaned the wound. Her gentle pats increased in frequency and intensity.

"Angie? Don't take off the skin!" Bryax cautioned.

"The wound!" she cried. "This is impossible! All I can find is a pale pink line. Somehow it has gone from raw infection to all but healed in the span of a day and a night!"

"You did say that sleep heals," Rabble offered.

"Not like this!" Angie protested.

"Far Shore's Healers have a reputation for being the best," Hulhc began.

"Not like this!" she repeated. "Not since before my parents' time. Not since . . ."

"The Loss?" Rylus interrupted. "Hulhc, is this a clue?"

"It very well could be," the farmer said, nearly tripping over his robe in his hurry to inspect Bryax's face, "but the map says we're a full day yet from the next town where I may be able to learn more."

"If the town is still there," Rabble muttered.

"We can certainly cover more ground before camping tonight," Rylus assured Hulhc.

"But I'm not letting the beasties get exhausted," Tambor interrupted. "Neither Z'ripes or Llorn are accustomed to carrying riders. They've been very helpful, but I won't have their joints strained."

"I never asked you to do such a thing," Hulhc assured him. "Are the bears still with us?"

"Sodded with honey," Tambor said, "but eager to see what's over the mountain."

"How do you know?" Angie asked, her hands stopping in mid-motion as she repacked her bag.

"I just do," Tambor said, with a puzzled frown. "Don't you?"

"No," she said, and all but Rabble echoed her head shake.

"I do," Rabble said. "Somewhat. I can—follow—what Dog Meat, Scrapper, or Gimp want, but not the rest of the beasties, not the way Tambor does."

"We can talk while we travel," Rylus said with a worried glance back down the road. "Daylight won't wait on us."

"And we don't want to wait on the Duke's troops," Angie added.

The Storm Shrouds unrolled on all sides of them now, a lush green that expanded rather like an eighth Lake around them. These were not the sky-reaching mountains that legends from before the Loss said towered across the Great Salt Sea. These were gentler slopes, like a slumbering beast, hiding mystery in every misted valley or clouded peak.

The road they followed now was little more than a game trail. Only the occasional mile-post buried in the weeds made them at all certain that they had not gone completely astray. More heartening was that there was no trace of Duke Elejinor's forces. As evening drew close, they made camp in a grove off of the trail.

"I fear," Rylus said as he brought Rabble wood for the fire that was springing to life under her skillful ministrations, "that this next town will be as vacant as the last. We have yet to see any sign of human habitation at all."

"At least any sign that is not at least a generation old," the red-haired warrior agreed. "Hulhc's disappointment will be difficult to contain."

"Where is he now?" Rylus asked.

"With Tambor's bears, fishing in the stream over the rise. Bryax and Angie are taking a turn bedding down the mounts." Rabble's expression turned serious. "Rylus, how much further will you go on this mad journey?"

Rylus sighed. "The Dragon's Spire is off limits to us now. We would be wisest to avoid both the Domain of Dragons and the Domain of Roses. Currently, our trail is taking us north and roughly west. When we are far enough west that heading south again would put us at the fringes of the Domain of Dragons, then we will discuss this. For now, we've come a long way. Summer is not yet over. Hulhc deserves time for his quest."

"You're a noble man, Rylus," Rabble said, her smile lit by the tongues of new fire. "Thank you."

Later, when they were all dining on river trout stuffed with 'cress and wild garlic, Rabble saw something white in the woods that was there and then gone. No one else, not even Bryax who was sitting beside her, seemed to see anything.

An after-dinner stroll, however, revealed not even a bent leaf where she could have sworn that she had seen the figure of a man on a horse.

17

I walked out in the dead of night
And there I saw a pale wight
His shape was dim in the firelight
And he looked at me and smiled.

The Ballad of the Ghost Prince

BY THE end of the next day, the company reached the town on Hulhc's map. As they had dreaded, it was deserted. A herd of deer flashed white rumps and bounded away from a meadow that must have once been a market square. The buildings that remained standing were covered in vines; saplings split once-solid stone.

"It may rain again tonight," Bryax said. "I'd sure like to find something with a solid roof."

"Or even one not so solid," Angie agreed.

"Let's scout ahead, Axe," Rabble suggested with a glance at the threatening sky. "Scrapper! Point girl!"

Hidden beneath grass and weeds a road curved into the town. The horse's shoes struck off buried cobblestones, echoing the thunder's distant rumbles. Gimp leaned from his saddlebag, swatting the purplish heads on the tall grass and eyeing butterflies with undisguised malice.

"That tall building—over to the left—looks most promising," Bryax said when they had come to level ground.

"Slate roofing," Rabble said, "and in a nice pattern. You don't see work like that in the Downs these days."

"Not often," Bryax agreed, reining in and dismounting. "This door looks clearest. I'll just cut these creepers at the base."

"Good. Scrapper, mind the horses."

The bitch wagged her tail once and Dog Meat stomped indignantly.

"With me, Rab?" Bryax asked. "I think I've guessed what this building was."

"The temple?" she nodded. "Yeah, it has that feel. I bet it's mostly pre-Loss construction—you just don't get colors like that without a magical touch."

Working together, they pushed until one of the great oak doors swung inward. The iron lock was too rusted to be any real trouble, but the seasons of wet weather had swollen the wood into place.

"Roof's solid here," Bryax said, his voice sounding hollow beneath the vaulted ceiling, "and most of the windows, too. Still, I feel . . ."

"Strange about camping in a temple?" Rabble's chuckle was a bit forced. "Well, neither the deities nor the worshippers seem to be using it."

Further inspection of the town showed that none of the other buildings were in anything close to usable condition. The storm front was building and the promise of sleeping warm and dry quelled even Bryax's superstitious concern. The mounts were quartered in a lean-to rigged between two extravagant flying buttresses, their rations augmented with several armloads of wild hay, fresh-cut from the surrounding area. Tambor sent the bears off to find their own shelter, but kept the monkeys in near the fire.

They made camp in a large entry foyer. When the day's foraging was set to cooking and bedrolls were flattened out so that the damp could dry from their folds, the company relaxed around the fire.

"Feels good to have a roof between us and the rain," Rabble said. "Somehow, I doubt the Deities mind. They might even like to have human visitors."

"You talk as if you think they live in these places," Angie said.

"I know. It's just a fancy." Rabble dug a watch candle

from her pack. "I'm going to take a look around before it's too dark and I'm too tired. I want to know what's behind us."

She lit the wick with a bit of kindling and it flared as if eager to join the venture. Hulhc rose stiffly to his feet, dusting off his increasingly battered robe.

"I'll walk with you, if you don't mind," he said somewhat gruffly. "I'd like to see how the mountain folk honored the Deities."

They walked into the main building. Rabble's candle revealed only hints of the building's construction, but a half-dozen paces from the entry, Hulhc found wall sconces, some of which still held lamps with oil.

"The people didn't leave right after the Loss," he said, inspecting the brackets. "When the magic lights failed, they hung these from the walls. The oil is probably too rancid to do us any good, but . . ."

"Let me see if I can light it," Rabble said. "I would certainly like to see more than what one candle can show."

"I never fancied you as caring about architecture, Rabble," Hulhc said, "or is this solely a military impulse?"

"Neither," she said, trimming a lamp-wick so it burnt clearly, "I . . . I have a feeling about this place. I just want to look more."

Something in her tone kept Hulhc from pressing.

The sanctuary they had entered was roughly oval. In the center, unravaged by any hand but Time's, were the four shrines to the Elements. They were built so that they backed against each other, no one given precedence over the others.

Lamplight revealed that the shrines were made of wood, elegantly carved and then painted to highlight details of the carving. Shrines to different aspects of the Elements radiated out from this central focus. Many portions had been dismantled and carried away, their locations marked only by a bolt hole or the remnant of a pedestal on the floor.

Hulhc dusted a detail of Earth's shrine with his sleeve. The deity was represented as a range of mountains that was also a recumbent human figure. Trees, flowers, and fields alike were depicted in minute detail. Rivers and streams twisted their courses and then flowed to join the great Element, who was celebrated in the next panel.

Water appeared as a figure who both embraced and caressed Earth and was in turn embraced and caressed. From the tiny raindrops, to the village well, to the distant dark lines of the Seven Lakes and the Great Salt Sea, Water's omnipresent omnipotence was represented with almost finicky fidelity. The heavy clouds that hovered in the mountain peaks were blown by Wind, that most mobile aspect of Air.

Air is always the most difficult of the Elements for a human artist to depict, but those who had designed this relief had clearly been inspired. The scene was the same mountain region as in the other two shrines, but here the emphasis was on the presence of the Invisible One. Tree branches were ruffled, hair was tossed and tousled, wavelets danced on ponds and streams. Children puffed out bladders, musicians blew on pipes or reeds, an infant drew its first breath dangling from a rosy-cheeked midwife's hand while its panting mama looked on with pride. Candle flames fluttered and bonfires roared so that the worshipper's attention was carried around to the shrine of Fire, the most unpredictable and yet the most generous of the Elements.

Fire, like Air, is not easily shown as a place. So, on Fire's shrine, the deity was depicted in all its myriad domestic uses, not just candle flame and lantern light, but hearth fire, forge coals, bonfire, and smokehouse. Travellers sat in snug safety around their campfires and festivals were celebrated with torchlight parades. Fire's dangerous side was shown as well, for any worshipper needs reminding that—unlike Earth or Air—this is a most capricious deity. A thatched roof was shown engulfed in flames, a forest fire raged up a mountainside, lightning crackled in the skies, and a ship burned, even though at sea.

"These are wonderful!" Hulhc exclaimed. "Wonderful! Each one brings you to the next and around again so that the celebration of one Element becomes a celebration of all Four in all their aspects. This must have been a vibrant worship center before the Loss."

"I agree," Rabble said softly. "I wonder how they could bear to leave it?"

"Maybe they didn't have much choice," Angie said.

She stood in the entryway from the foyer, a candle in her hand, which she lowered slightly, then blew out as she realized that the sanctuary was awash in lantern light.

"We heard you talking," Tambor said, following her in, "and got curious about what had you so interested. It *is* a beautiful temple, isn't it?"

"Almost seems impious to be camping in the foyer, after all," Angie added.

A jagged flash of lightning followed by a loud crackle of thunder punctuated her statement. Rain began drumming harder on the roof. They laughed nervously, and returned to the warm safety of the fire in the foyer.

"The Elements seem to be telling us to stay inside," Rylus said from where he was tending the supper pot. "The rain is a solid curtain and the lightning is so bright that you can see across the square."

"I'm not going out again without a direct order from the Elements," Bryax added, coming in from outside. His hair and beard were streaming and he pulled off a sodden tunic as he spoke. "I just made the mistake of going out to check on the mounts. They're fine. I glimpsed the bears; they're holed up in a collapsed building across the way."

"Are they dry?" Tambor asked.

"Dry enough," Bryax replied. "The cinnamon one raised her head to look at the crazy human, but the other wasn't budging."

"Speaking of warm and dry," Rylus said, "the kettle has boiled and I've made tea. The stew should be just about heated as well."

"I'll be there as soon as I've put out the lanterns," Rabble said, gesturing for the others to precede her. "After everything this temple has survived, we don't need to give it over to Fire.''

Many hours later, while the Company slept and the storm's intensity had given way to a simple patter against the leaves, Rabble bundled herself in her oilskin and hat and reluctantly took a turn outside. Strolling around the side of the temple toward the mounts' shelter, she came to a sudden, startled halt. There, on the pathway that their mounts had broken through the weeds, stood a charger as white as milk even to its eyes and the linings of its ears and nostrils. Astride this white horse sat a man just as devoid of color. His trim hair and forked beard, styled in a cut fashionable some generations before, were deep, solid ivory. His limbs and clothing were shaped of lighter shades of pale. Even his lively and laughing eyes were pearl touched with cream and snow. Removing his hat from his head, he bowed deeply, saluting Rabble with the fluttering plume before returning the hat to its jaunty perch atop his head.

''My lady,'' he said, ''a pleasant, if somewhat damp evening, is it not?''

Shifting her flopping hat further back on her head was the only sign of apprehension that Rabble permitted herself. Her copper sword hung at her side, her allies were near, and, admittedly, she was very curious about what this pale rider wanted.

''It is wet,'' she replied carefully, ''though not as wet as earlier. In any case, the rain seems to have little effect on you.''

''No,'' the rider stroked his horse along the curve of its elegant neck. ''We are rather beyond wet—though Blizzard here still does not care for lightning.''

''Oh, why not?'' Rabble heard herself ask with inane calm.

''Was lightning that did this to us,'' the rider replied, ''not natural lightning, but it hardly matters, I suppose, in the end. By the way, I have been remiss in introducing myself. I am Zane, late of the Light Horse of the Wizard Marr.''

"Wizard Marr?" Rabble said. "No wizard has fielded troops since the Loss."

"I know," Zane replied, "but then, I've been this way since the Loss."

"This way—you mean all white?" Rabble asked.

"This way," Zane replied. "Dead."

18

"Where went your color, oh pale wight?
"Why do you fade in the firelight?"
Said he, "I lost it in a sword fight.
Lost my color and my life."

The Ballad of the Ghost Prince

RABBLE STARED. "Dead? But . . . But that would make you a ghost and there aren't any ghosts, not anymore, not since the Loss."

"The Loss," Zane considered. "My ghostliness is rather connected with all of that, but surely your ladyship does not wish to stand out in the rain just to hear my story."

"Stand in the rain? No." Rabble gestured towards the lean-to. "I was going to check the mounts. It will be dry there. Will you—can you?—come with me and tell me your story there?"

Zane nodded. "As you wish, m'lady. I must compliment you on your composure. Of course, I expected nothing less of you. You don't seem at all discomforted by my deadness."

Rabble grinned. "No, I guess that's what a warrior does—live with deadness—your own or someone else's.

You, at least, are more cordial and conversational than most of the dead I've encountered. Come along."

"Please, precede us into the shelter," Zane said. "We will not take up much room."

In the lean-to, Rabble vaulted astride Dog Meat and slouched forward against the war horse's warm neck. Scrapper reclined on the dirt near Z'ripes, who viewed the cur with an aristocratic mixture of disdain and trepidation. When Zane and Blizzard joined them, the ghost horse and rider should have crowded the makeshift shelter, but though they neither grew nor diminished in size, they occupied space without overlapping any of the other creatures in the lean-to. Rabble contemplated the mystery and then dismissed it when her head began to ache.

"So, how does it happen that you and your steed are ghosts?" she asked, smiling quickly in case the question was rude.

"Well, it had to do with the Wizard Marr and the events of the Refting," Zane said. "There was much fighting then—as you might imagine—and I was away from my troop, doing a bit of scouting. Blizzard and I were unwise enough to silhouette ourselves on an overlook and an enterprising weather-worker hit us squarely with a lightning bolt."

Rabble nodded encouragement when Zane slowed, apparently uncomfortable. He resumed after a thoughtful moment.

"I—we—neither of us—well—neither of us noticed. What I mean to say is, there was this flash and then this incredible burning tingle and then we went right back to our scouting. It was only after I went back and tried to report and no one would pay me any heed that I began to think that something was wrong. At first, I thought we'd been charmed invisible, but later—when one of the wounded at the hospital started having hysterics about a ghost roaming about—I went back to the overlook and considered that the charred up mess on the look-out point could just be me and

Blizzard. By then it was too late to change. We'd been tricked into being ghosts.''

"How can someone be tricked into becoming a ghost?" Rabble frowned. "I don't understand."

Zane sighed. " 'Tricked' might not be quite fair as a way to put it, but what I mean is that by the time we knew we were dead we had already kept living—after a fashion. Now, I don't feel any great desire to finish dying, but I'll admit that only having Blizzard for company does get a bit lonely. That's why I was so glad to find you, m'lady.''

Rabble sat and listened to the drumming of the rain on the planks of the lean-to's roof. The ghost seemed quite content to wait with her. He hummed softly a tune she almost remembered and toyed with a lock of Blizzard's mane. The ghost horse stood with equal patience, lipping at a bit of hay and not seeming to mind that the hay remained untouched in Dog Meat's manger.

After several minutes, Rabble was able to put words to something that had been niggling at her since Zane had first confronted her.

"Zane," she said, "the animals can't see you, can they?"

"No, m'lady, they cannot."

Rabble considered further. "Will the rest of the company be able to see and hear you?"

Zane paused. "Maybe, m'lady, if you can convince them that I'm here. There's power in some of them."

Rabble dismissed this last, a more pressing concern taking shape. "Then why can I see you, Zane? Why don't I have any trouble?"

"Because you are who you are, m'lady," he said, sounding very surprised. "How could it be otherwise, what with who you are, and what you've done, and what you've lost to be here? I knew from the moment that I heard what happened that you'd be coming back and that you'd be able to see me and Blizzard and I've been waiting. It just took me a while to get the courage to speak with you—you being who you are and all. You've been very kind, though, and not nearly as frightening as I had thought."

"Slow! Slow!" Rabble exclaimed. "You're talking non-sense, Zane. What do you mean? I've never been here, so how could I come back? You must have me confused with someone else."

The ghost stared at her. "Maybe so. Maybe. Why don't you tell me why you've come to this deserted town?"

Rabble shrugged. "Hulhc and, I guess, Rylus. Hulhc is . . . wants to find out where the magic went after the Loss. He'd looked at books and listened to legends and set us off this way. Then Rylus . . . had a difference of opinion with the Duke of Dragons and we left rather more quickly than we'd intended without a chance to hire a local guide or search up more legends like Hulhc had planned. Thought we'd be able to talk with the locals, though, but you're the closest to a local we've seen."

"This region has been mostly deserted since some ten years after the Refting," Zane said. "These mountains have never been too easy for living in and without the magic, they got less so. I'd say that magic had made the townsfolk soft, not as if I didn't know there were forces making it hard to boot."

Rabble shook her head in confusion. "So everyone left?"

"Pretty much," Zane replied. "There are scattered fami-lies making a pretty good living, but the towns are gone— except for the Holdfast, of course."

"The Holdfast?" Rabble said. "Where's that? Do they know anything about the Loss?"

Zane slipped his hand slowly up under his hat and scratched his head. "You really don't know? Well, like I told you, I was a cavalry rider in the forces of the Wizard Marr. You never did ask why."

Rabble forbore from saying that she hadn't had a chance. "Why, Zane?"

"It had to do with the Refting."

"You mean the Loss?"

"No, the *Refting*. Downlanders have this peculiar notion that the magic was lost. It wasn't lost, it was . . ."

"Rabble? What in the Elements are you doing out here talking to yourself?"

Bryax stepped into the lean-to and through Zane. He paused within Blizzard's forequarters, the horse's elegant neck curving over him like a mist.

"It's dry enough in here," Rabble replied. "I just came out to check the mounts."

Bryax studied her. "I heard you talking, Rab, and it wasn't to Dog Meat. Is there someone actually living in this ruin?"

Zane chuckled. "Not exactly living, m'lady. Tell him."

"Hush," she said to the ghost.

"I swear to obey, m'lady. I will be as silent as—the tomb." Zane sniggered, but fell silent.

Bryax looked at her as if wondering what game she was playing. Leaning flat on Dog Meat's back, Rabble stared up at the mismatched boards, branches, and thatching that they had combined to form the roof. She heard Bryax shift patiently from foot to foot, pull a hunk of hay and feed it to his horse, felt Dog Meat stretch to cadge a share.

"Sword Brother," she said finally, "can you believe something impossible if I ask you to?"

"I'd try," he said, "though I'd prefer if you'd look me in the eyes while telling me."

She sat up and jumped from Dog Meat's back to stand in front of the big, blond warrior. Zane, still astride Blizzard, had moved so that he no longer occupied the same space as Bryax. She was relieved. The effect had been unsettling.

"You asked who I was talking with," she began, then stopped, wishing this was a problem her sword edge could solve. "His name is Zane. He's a cavalry scout."

"For Dragon's Spire?" Bryax said, dagger suddenly in his hand in a throwing grip.

"No, for the Wizard Marr."

"Wizard? There are no wizards since the Loss. Does one still claim the title? He must be wizened indeed or a trickster like Duke Elejinor."

"I don't know, Axe," Rabble said softly. "I was just talking with Zane when you came out. I hadn't had a chance to get him to answer all my questions."

"Where did he flee to? I must be getting as old as this 'Wizard Marr' to not have heard a man depart."

"He didn't. He's still here."

"Where?"

Rabble indicated the spot from which Zane and Blizzard had been following the conversation with interest. The ghost's broad, cheerful smile said he appreciated the humor of the situation, but true to his promise to Rabble he had not spoken another word. His smile had dimmed somewhat when Bryax had scoffed at the possibility of wizards.

"Bryax, I asked you to believe in something impossible. Can you believe in a ghost?"

"But . . ." Bryax began, then he stopped. "All right, Rabble, if you ask me, I'll believe in a ghost, but I don't see anything in here."

"Look in that back corner, just to the right of the llama. Tell me what you see."

Bryax stared, a hand on his sword, his blue eyes narrowing with the effort.

"Rab, I don't see any . . ." He stopped in mid-sentence. "Wait, I . . . Just for a moment, from the corner of my eye . . . I could have sworn there was someone in the corner."

Rabble nodded encouragement, wondering if Bryax could hear Zane's delighted chuckle. Scrapper raised her head from her paws, glancing sleepily about as if wondering what had so excited the humans. Bryax pivoted slowly on one boot heel, his gaze wide and unfocused, his broad-palmed, calloused hands spread, the tips of the fingers moving like the questing antennae of a moth.

For all the gentleness of his motion, he exuded an aura of tension and alertness. He wavered for a few passes, then snapped into position like a dog on point.

"There!" he said, putting out an index finger to pin the

apparition. "War and Chance, but you're hard to see! Faint and wispy like steam from a cook pot or a spent storm cloud, but I see you now, you and your horse. What'd you call it, Rabble?"

"Zane," she said, looking at the nearly solid—to her—figure on his horse. "His name is Zane."

"Zane," Bryax repeated, nodding cautiously at the ghost.

"I was thinking," Rabble went on hurriedly, "that—if Zane consents, of course—that he would be perfect as a guide. He knows this area and, unlike any local guide we might stumble across while wandering around out here, he also knows something about the Loss. From what he was saying, he was still—around—when it happened."

"Sounds interesting," Bryax said. "I have one worry. How good will a guide we can barely see be to us?"

"I can see him just fine," Rabble said heatedly. "Maybe it just comes with practice."

"Maybe," Bryax said doubtfully. "The animals don't seem to know that he's there."

"If I may interrupt," Zane said. "I would be honored to guide my lady and her companions wherever they wish to go—if I know the way. Where is it you wish to go?"

"Where the magic went," Rabble replied.

"Where it was put," Zane corrected firmly.

"Is this difference important?" Rabble asked, "because if it is then I think we should tell everyone at once."

Bryax nodded agreement. Now that he was trying, apparently, he could hear Zane more easily than he could see him.

"Oh, yes, it is important." Zane's figure dimmed slightly, as if his inner light had ceased to illuminate his form for a flicker of time. "It is very important. It may be the most important thing in all the world."

19

*Believe the impossible, count the distant stars, but don't forget to set
the kettle over the fire if you want to drink tea.*

Mountain proverb

INTRODUCING ZANE to the rest of the company was a
fascinating, if frustrating, project. Tambor, Angie, and
Hulhc all could see the ghost with a fair amount of ease,
although none as easily as Rabble.

Rylus, like Bryax, could just barely see a wispy image.
When difficulties were worked through, disbelief dealt with,
breakfast set to cook, the animals fed, and the day pronounced a wet continuation of the preceding one, the
company settled around the fire as the ghost spun the tale of
the Loss—or the Refting, as he insisted on terming it.

"All of you have heard tales of the days when magic was
as common in the world as butterflies in a flowery meadow
or water in the Seven Seas," began Zane. "And you have
heard that those days were wonderful, too, that one could
sail through the skies in ships woven of light and wind or
plumb the depths in vessels of shell and pearl. And this was
true. I was born in those days and lived then.

"The people with the greatest power and influence were
those who could work magic and these fell into two groups:
the wizards and the priesthood. The wizards—the most
powerful of them, at least—studied from childhood to learn
how to focus their internal powers. The members of the
priesthood studied less and their powers were more capricious, but the greatest miracles were theirs to command. The
reason, of course, was that the power they channeled was not
their own, but rather belonged to the deities that they served.

"Unsurprisingly, a rivalry grew up between the two traditions or, more precisely, between factions within the two traditions. The majority of those who worked in magic or interceded with the Deities were content to do well what they did and to bask in the wealth, respect, and, often, power that came with skill in the magical arts.

"However, a potent minority within each group contested the other tradition. Magic itself added a new complication into the conflict, for the most powerful of the wizards learned that they could employ magic to extend their lives. Thus, these lived as mature men and women long after the rest of their generation had passed into death. The Deities never granted this gift to their priesthoods—indeed, the stress of channeling miracles was often so great that it would burn out the channeler prematurely. At best, a servitor of a peaceful aspect of an Element could hope to live into old age, healthy in mind and body, but never with the artificial staving off of grey hairs and wrinkled skin enjoyed by the powerful wizards.

"And as the life-spans of some of the wizards extended to hundreds of years and their powers grew to rival the Deities, a curious, yet compelling theory evolved among some of the wizards. What if—they asked—what if the Deities are nothing more than powerful wizards who have learned to defy death even more skillfully than we have? What if their priesthoods are simply wizards who do not wish to face that their power has its heart in their own manipulation of the forces? We can end this ancient rivalry by revealing the truth, freeing humanity to blossom into its full potential. Without awe for divine forces to hold us back, we can become something far greater than we can even imagine now."

The company sat so enthralled by Zane's reshaping of history that only the hiss and splash of the kettle boiling over brought them back to the present. Rylus ladled out oatmeal with raisins, while Angie prepared tea. As bowls and cups were handed around, Rylus squinted apologetically at the ghost.

"Uh, can we offer you something for breakfast, Zane?" he said, speaking a bit too loudly.

"Thank you, no," Zane replied. "I'm afraid that eating is rather beyond me."

When everyone was settled and the kettle refilled from an ancient well, the ghost resumed his story.

"I have no idea how long the wizards took to prepare their plan. Please recall that I was just a cavalry scout, not an intimate of the wizards. In fact, much of what I'm telling you now, I gathered after events had been set in motion. I'm not certain that if I had known what the Wizard Marr and his allies were planning, I would have agreed to participate. I might have resigned my commission and gone home."

"Then you had associated with the Wizard Marr before this?" Hulhc asked.

"That's right. The most powerful wizards lived rather like Domain rulers do today, though the majority did not trouble themselves with petty details of land rulership. Usually a Domain ruler was quite happy to host a wizard in return for a few magical favors. But, I get away from my main tale."

Angie smiled, looking up from the herbs she had begun sorting as soon as she had finished her oatmeal. Except when they had been most pressed by the Duke of Dragons' forces, she had stopped to clip oddities and rarities along their route.

"Don't worry, Zane. What you're saying is all fine and fascinating," she said. "With the rain to fuddle pursuit we aren't hurrying off to muddle in the mud."

Zane flourished his feathered hat to her, then resumed.

"I don't know exactly what the wizards did, but they first built a crystal lattice imbued with power deep within a cavern in the mountain called Shadowridge. Then they summoned the essence of the Elements—not the elements, but the Elements. Do you understand me?"

"The archetypal force, the thing that they had ascertained was really a guise for ancient wizards of incredible power." Hulhc nodded.

"That's what they went after," Zane said, "and they had made the crystals in their fancy lattice resonate with the proper force to block magic going out and it set up something of a hum or a buzz so that even working magic would be messed up."

"A distortion field," Hulhc said. "I've read about such spells in my father's books. They were supposed to create this as a limited effect, but for what the wizards were planning, they would need something very potent and possibly permanent or wizards as potent as these 'Elements' might have been able to resist."

"Why not just kill them?" Tambor said with uncharacteristic fierceness. "I wouldn't want to be permanently imprisoned."

"Make that two of us," Rylus agreed. "My latest imprisonment renewed my dislike for that particular situation."

"Wait!" Zane said, raising one hand. "You're getting ahead of the story. You're right, but only to a point. I don't know how much power keeping the Elements entrapped would take. I don't know how long the wizards planned to keep them. I've learned a great deal in the years since, but mostly what I know is what I saw when I was there."

"Please forgive, Zane. We all can chatter like Tambor's golden furries," Angie said. "Tell on."

"More tea anyone?" Rylus asked.

"Here," Bryax said, extending his mug.

As Rylus poured, Zane resumed his story.

"Now, the wizards began their enchantment and they must have had some success, because the wards and watches they had set to check for reactions detected the approach of small forces with the stamp, to sorcerous eyes, of those who drew their power from their service of the Deities.

"That's where I came into the conflict. Wizard Marr sent a group of his household guard to track and confront the Deities' force. His logic was that any confrontation would involve praying for miracles and any miracle granted would weaken those who called themselves the Elements."

"Were you up against an army?" Bryax asked.

"No, a smaller, specialized force. We guessed that the Elements did not wish their vulnerability known—but the size of our opponents' force didn't make our task any easier. I don't know how you feel, Bryax, but I'd rather fight an army of press-ganged soldiers eked out with a few mercenaries than a small group of fanatics."

Bryax nodded seriously. "Nasty, especially if they had miracles to command."

"Miracles," Angie said. "That's so hard to believe."

"Is it?" Zane's expression was quizzical. "To conclude my tale, our group, along with teams from the other wizards, successfully fought back the Elements' forces. We had casualties—of which I may have been the most flamboyant—but none of those who sought to oppose the wizards on the physical plane succeeded. The wizards won their magical battle as well. The Elements were imprisoned within the crystal lattice and cut off from either drawing power or dispensing it. And then the wizards learned their terrible error."

Zane paused, not merely for effect, but as if he could hardly bring himself to tell this last bit. The company waited in uncharacteristic silence. Even the monkeys stopped chattering.

"What happened?" Rabble said softly, the first words she had spoken since Zane began his tale.

The ghost looked at her intently, as if searching for a hidden meaning in her words. Then, with a ragged sigh, he went on.

"The wizards learned that they had been wrong. They watched in horror as the magic drained away from the world and only the crystalline lattice and those in close contact with it retained any magical ability at all."

"Why?" Bryax said. "I'm missing something here."

"Why?" Zane replied. "Because the Elements were—are—what they are. They are the Deities who in many guises infuse all aspects of life. Magic is merely an outgrowth of

their by-play, of their energy—at least as I understand it—
and when the wizards used that very power to bind them
away from interaction with the world, the magic drained
away until it was gone.''

"Wait! Wait!" Hulhc grouched. "This doesn't make
sense. If the Elements were really deities, wouldn't locking
them away cause the world to crumble into nothing? It still
functions, creates, lives, shapes.''

"I eavesdropped as the remaining wizards debated this
very issue," Zane said. "I doubt you would be comforted to
know that they did worry that the world was endangered on a
structural level. They fully intended to release the Elements
at the first sign of reality crumbling.''

"How comforting," Angie said dryly.

Zane grinned at her. "That's about how I felt, but I
wasn't going to argue. I thought I might end up on the wrong
side of the lattice.''

"So why didn't everything just stop being?" Tambor
asked.

"Remember, I'm not an expert on this," Zane cautioned,
"but what I've gathered is that since the wizards went after
what they thought of as 'people'—humans, with human
intellect and motives—what they captured was the minds, in
a sense, of the Elements. It makes sense in an odd way. I
find it hard to believe that mortals—even nearly immortal
wizards—could capture deities.''

"Let me see if I have this straight," Rylus said. "These
wizards essentially trapped the minds of the Elements so the
body—the world—is continuing to function, the way going
to sleep doesn't mean that you die.''

"Or that you don't need to watch your breathing or keep
your heart beating," Bryax added. "We're living in a world
which is in a coma.''

"That about says it," Zane said, "at least as I have come
to understand it.''

"Oh, my!" Angie exclaimed. "So that's why you call
what happened a Refting, not a Loss. The magic was taken

away by the very people who had benefited the most from having the magic in the first place.''

''And the rest of us—or our ancestors—were left to suffer,'' Tambor's voice grew tight and angry. ''Left stranded away from their families and homelands, their . . .''

He broke down and, ignoring the wet, strode out into the courtyard in front of the temple. Those remaining inside could hear him weeping.

''His father committed suicide when he finally accepted that he couldn't go home,'' Rylus explained softly. ''Tambor was raised by relatives—the crew of an airship which had set up their own community in the Downs. Tambor's mother was a young woman in the crew—much younger than his father—and she idolized her husband and . . .''

Rylus shrugged, embarrassed that he had told even this much of Tambor's private history. Then he rose and went outside after his partner.

''Why didn't the wizards just release the Elements when they realized what they had done?'' Rabble asked, poking the fire beneath the kettle back to life.

Hulhc laughed dryly. ''I suppose that they were terrified. To have set out to trap ersatz deities, to uncover wizards masquerading as something more, and then to realize that they were wrong. I don't suppose that they would have expected much mercy.''

''Yep,'' Zane said. ''That's what I've gathered, but there's more. Some things that happened later, fairly recently as such things go.''

''Spill it,'' Angie said, repackaging her herbs. ''You don't need to be scared. We're not wizards or deities.''

Zane hesitated, then he said softly. ''Well, it has to do with Fire.''

He was interrupted by Rylus bursting through the doorway. ''Grab the gear and hurry, folks. Tambor's getting the mounts ready.''

''What's the rush?'' Bryax said, his hands busy gathering up the mess kit and stowed the parts.

"The troops from Dragon's Spire," Rylus replied. "The bears came up to Tambor all frantic, practically led us to where we could take a look at our back trail. The Duke's people are coming for us."

20

Those who play with Fire are likely to get burnt.

Proverb

ZANE MANIFESTED outside of the temple astride Blizzard. Ghost horse and rider watched incredulously as the company mounted their motley steeds and fell into travelling order, Tambor's bears restlessly bumbling at the flanks.

"Bears?" he said. "Striped horses? Giant woolly deer-goats? What games have you been playing with me? Are you renegade wizards?"

Angie studied him. "If you lived before the Loss, surely you must have seen odder creatures than these. Perhaps it is you who are toying with us, eh?"

"No, Healer, not at all." Zane gestured at the llama who was happily mincing his way up the rocky trail, Angie on his back. "As a member of a wizard's guard I saw imps and sprites aplenty. One wondrous day I even glimpsed a unicorn in a sunflower-filled meadow. Beasties like the one you ride are rare now, though, and never then or now have I seen such strange mounts bear their riders so docilely nor have I seen carnivores welcomed by herbivores—not, I should say, without magic's aid."

"Omnivores," Tambor said, trotting up on Z'ripes. "Bears are omnivores and these two prefer honey and fruit and fish to horseflesh. Perhaps the others can smell it."

"Perhaps," Zane said and he and Blizzard vanished to reappear where Rabble and Dog Meat were riding point just behind Scrapper. Gimp hissed as the ghost took form, but no one other than Rabble seemed to notice his arrival.

"Where is your company headed?" he asked her.

"Away from those who pursue us," she said curtly. "After that, well, we all signed on for Hulhc's quest. Now you've told us more than we imagined was possible. I guess it will be up to him to call our next move. He may decide this is too big a problem for him."

"He'll go on," Zane said firmly.

"How can you be so certain?"

"He's on a larger mission than merely satisfying his curiosity about the fate of magic," Zane said. "I can see it in his eyes."

They had rounded a rise from which they could look down and along the back trail. Motion from the greenery along the trail and occasional glimpses of a horse or uniformed figure was not heartening.

"We have the distance on them, for now," Rabble said, "but we won't keep that advantage. The trail gets rougher ahead. They have bows and when we need to slow down . . ."

Zane nodded. "That seems a reasonable concern."

Rabble scowled. "Why are you staying with us, anyhow, ghost?"

"Would you believe that in the days before the Refting but after my 'ghosting' I went to a card reader who told me that my fate was tied to that of a red-haired warrior, a woman who wasn't what she believed she was, and who would attract me to her by virtue of what she was missing?"

"No." Rabble slapped Dog Meat's shoulder. "The others have almost caught up, nag. Let's see some action."

Zane and Blizzard paced the steel-dust grey, passing through the trees and shrubs at the trail's edge.

"Why don't you believe me, Rabble?"

"Oh, I believe that you went to a card reader, but I don't believe that people can foretell the future."

"Not even Angie?"

"Angie's pretty good," Rabble admitted, "but I don't know if what she does is magic. For all her flower faces and herbs, she's a sensible, sensitive soul. She's just good at knowing people."

"Would it bother you if I stay with the company?" Zane asked.

"Not if it doesn't bother the others," Rabble's gaze grew quizzical, "and not if you'll make yourself useful."

"You only need to ask, m'lady."

"You were a scout when you were alive, right?" When Zane nodded she continued, "I want you to go down and get me a full report on the group on our tail—weapons, armor, mounts, any weaknesses. You can keep yourself from being detected, can't you?"

"Yes, m'lady."

"Rabble."

"Yes, Rabble. I can get your report and no one will ever see me." He started to mist away.

"Thank you, Zane."

"Ever, m'lady."

"Rabble," she growled, but he was gone.

She pulled Dog Meat off to the side when the trail widened. The heavy growth of the lower altitude was giving way to scrub pine, cedar, rock, and wiry saw grass.

"Bryax!" she called as the tail of the column came abreast of her. "Hold a moment. The rest of you go on—we'll catch up easily."

Bryax's voice was low and hoarse. "We're in trouble, Rab. There's no way we'll avoid them out here and there's not enough cover for you and me to double back."

"I know." She pushed her hair back from her eyes. "I've sent Zane to get us a report on what we're up against."

"Good." Bryax glanced sidelong at her. "Rab, what is he doing, following us? I thought he belonged to the ruined town back there."

"No," Rabble said, and Zane's return saved her from saying more.

"M'—Rabble," the ghost said with a flourish of his plumed hat. "I have done as you requested. Those who pursue are all mounted on the sturdy mountain ponies that are specially bred in these regions."

"War and Chance!" Bryax swore. "I remember those from a campaign when I was hardly more than a lad. They're sturdy all right. They'll go all the day and half the night."

"They're not very strong, though," Rabble said. "Elejinor's soldiers won't be able to carry much in the way of armor and weapons or supplies."

"They do have a pack horse," Zane said.

"Let's step back," Rabble said. "How large a company is it?"

"Thirteen, of which a dozen are soldiers," Zane replied. "The one in charge is being addressed with a great deal of respect by the others. His name is Durez."

"Durez!" Bryax said. "No surprise. Another must be Iron. Durez probably convinced the Duke to give him others."

"From what Rylus said—what he overheard—the Duke might not have taken much convincing," Rabble said slowly. "Those two old robed people had some influence over him."

"Wizards?" Zane said. "If so, that explains the odd man."

"Odd?" Bryax said. "One of the dozen?"

"No, a thirteenth," Zane answered. "No armor—by the way, they're all wearing heavy leather. Everyone but this man has a personal hand weapon and everyone has a long-bow and lots of arrows. He's just riding along with them, looking vaguely miserable."

"If they have bows, we had better take them out now," Rabble said briskly. "Zane, ride ahead and find a place where our noncombatants can be sheltered. Keep an eye open for a good spot to set up an ambush."

"I am yours to command, m'lady." The ghost vanished. Bryax shook his head. "Weird. Useful, but weird. I'll ride ahead and fill the rest in, Rab. When Zane reports to you, whistle and I'll rejoin you.''

''Very good. Scrapper, you go ahead and take point.''

The bitch and Bryax trotted away, leaving Rabble with her thoughts. She abandoned them gladly enough when Zane and Blizzard ghosted into form alongside her.

''I've found a perfect spot!'' Zane crowed so enthusiastically that Rabble nearly cautioned him to be quiet. ''A short distance ahead, the scrub gets heavy and the trail pretty much vanishes.''

''It isn't exactly clear now,'' Rabble growled, ''but once we take all the horses along it, it will be.''

''True, but that means we can pick the route our pursuers will likely follow. Now, the scrub forest continues into an area filled with boulders and stress-fractured rock. In the midst of this, there is a fairly deep cave . . .''

''Wait, let me signal Bryax,'' Rabble said. ''He needs to hear this before we make our plans.''

By an hour before sunset, their plans were set. The company set up a campsite in front of Zane's cave. The cave itself was completely hidden by pliant scrub growth—so well hidden that Angie commented that only a ghost could have found it.

''Well, I guess we've covered everything,'' Rabble said, rubbing the last of the rabbit stew from her bowl with ash cake.

''We don't want them dead,'' Bryax reminded the company, with a significant glance at his red-haired sword sister. ''Not if we can help it. A Domain ruler's nephew's blood is not blood I want to answer for.''

''Speak for yourself,'' Rabble said softly, but when Bryax glared at her, she nodded. ''We don't want them dead—I know.''

Zane grinned. ''Yeah, there are worse things we can do than killing them. Right, m'lady?''

No one else appeared to hear him and Rabble ignored the words.

"Is the false trail in place?" Bryax asked Tambor, more to break the tense mood than because he needed to know.

Tambor nodded. "And the mounts are penned up outside of easy arrow shot."

"Then all we need to do is wait," Bryax said with brusque confidence, "and hope that they'll live up to our worst expectations and attack without warning and after dark. Zane?"

Bryax spoke a touch too loudly, as if his own difficulty in seeing and hearing the ghost was reciprocal. The pale horseman sighed and broadly flourished his plumed hat in acknowledgment.

"Yes, Commander? Shall I take my watch stand?"

At Bryax's nod, he vanished.

"I sure hope he's on our side," Hulhc grumped. "Relying on a dead man who knows too much and persists in a magical existence when by his own account there is no magic seems a might chancy to me."

"Each of us will watch as usual," Bryax reminded him. "Zane is just our cock's crow against the dawn."

Angie stood from where she had arranged false bedrolls around their fire circle.

"Tea kettle's hissing with spicy brew and I for one am going to take my cup to bed in the cave."

"I'm with you," Rylus said, scraping the last of the meat from the stew pot. "Tambor?"

"Right after I check on the bears a last time."

Soon the campsite was empty of all except Bryax, Rabble, Scrapper, and Gimp. Bryax banked the fire and poured himself some tea. Rabble sat hunched forward, staring into the coals. All were aware that evening had vanished into night and that the enemy from whom they had been fleeing for days was now closing the gap.

"Think they'll come tonight?" Bryax said, his voice hoarse and soft.

"Yep," Rabble said. "Angie's coins do, too. They'll spot our trail, then our fire, guess we're stopped, scout our position while we 'sleep.'"

Rabble spoke slowly, the cadence of her voice granting the mundane words a strange poetry. She looked away from the fire then and grinned. "If you believe Angie's stick tossing, of course."

"Why not?" Bryax stretched, his joints popping in an erratic symphony. "I've got a ghost who looks like the last remnant of imagination after a three-day binge as an advance scout. I can take a stick tosser, coin spinner, card reader as a tactical advisor."

"I wonder why you have so much trouble seeing Zane?" Rabble asked, half to herself.

"Don't know, but nobody else sees him as clearly as you do, Rabble, and I'd swear that most of the beasties don't see him at all." Bryax drew a coin from his pocket. "Want to toss me for who takes first watch?"

Rabble laughed. "With your coin, Sword Brother? Do you want to stand now or later?"

"Now, I think, I'd like a last chance to review our gimmick before I need to worry about enemy scouts."

"Good." Rabble rose and gathered her cat, who dangled his three legs limply from her hold. "I'll rest now. Scrapper, watch with Bryax and make certain that no one harms him."

The mutt gave a low sweep of her tail and padded to Bryax's side. With a final nod, Rabble, too, vanished into the cave. Bryax stood a long moment listening to the snap of the fire coals, the soft shifting of the mounts in their pen, and the almost familiar sounds of the mountain insects and night creatures. Then he turned and began his inspection rounds.

As Angie had predicted, the attack came after mid-watch and was as subtle and stealthy as a commander could wish. Ten armed and armored soldiers left their mounts a safe distance down the trail and stole forward. Their light armor made no more threatening sound than the chirp of the crickets and for greater stealth any bright metal was masked with mud or wax or wrapped against the light.

They stole forward from three sides using the cover offered by scattered boulders and dense scrub. The fourth side was a gentle rise, alongside which the Company's mounts were penned. Two archers, the best in the elite group Durez had been assigned by his uncle, were given the dangerous task of climbing this rise and setting a second ambush to support those on the lower ground.

All perfect, all neat, all elegantly controlled. Durez resisted the impulse to sing, contenting himself with rehearsing the words he would say to the red-haired bitch as he spitted her on his sword. All his uncle and his uncle's aged advisors had asked of him was her copper sword as proof of her death. He planned to give them her arrogant head as well.

Iron, his forward scout, crept to his side.

"All asleep around their fire, Lord." He bared his crooked smile. "The redhead is on watch, drowsing though. Even her dog is asleep at her feet."

"Too easy," Durez replied, pleased. "The archers should be in place now. Touch the signal. We advance as one on a slow count of ten."

The command rippled by hand sign, swift and silent as thought. Durez rose from his crouch, drew his blade, and strode into the enemy camp, his soldiers the fingers on a hand moving with him. Rabble rose and he was irked when he saw that arrogant grin shape her lips instead of the fear and surprise he craved.

Her copper sword was in her hand and her bitch growled at her side. Durez had committed himself to action before he thought to wonder why none of the people in the bedrolls were stirring. By then, he realized that he had been tricked and bitter despair made his sword leap in his hand. With a feral snarl, he leapt at the woman.

A thin grey streak leapt out of the shadows to one side of him and four sharp points of pain sunk into the soft, unarmored space behind his right knee. He howled, overreaching his lunge and stumbled toward the fire. It flared,

apparently fanned by his approach, catching the silk lining of
his cloak. Tearing the clasp free and leaving the expensive
garment to burn, he turned on Rabble.

She stood watching him, poised but unharried. Iron lay—
dead or unconscious—off to one side, her dog growling over
his prone form. Durez raised his blade in a defensive guard
and continued his advance. Rabble raised her own blade to
counter. Then a deep male voice—that of Bryax, Rabble's
beefy blond brother, broke the stand-off.

"Hold, your lordship, and look about. Your soldiers are
surrendered. Your cause is lost."

Rabble shrugged as if saying "Take a look" and Durez
darted a glance away.

On one side of the camp, Tambor stood, hung with his
rudely chattering, near omnipresent monkeys. Two towering
furred shapes flanked him—brown bears on their hind legs,
but not dancing as they did in the Spectacular, prepared
instead to attack. Rylus and skinny, grey-bearded Hulhc
covered the next side. The old farmer held a crossbow as he
might a leveled pitchfork, but was no less deadly for his
unfamiliarity with the weapon that Rylus held with ease.
Bryax, a longbow over his shoulder, a sword in his hand,
covered the remaining flank, Rabble's moth-eaten, flea-
bitten war horse pawing the ground beside him as if promising to avenge his mistress should she be hurt.

Durez hardly dared to bring his gaze up to the rise where
he had set Kazu and Vieth, the best of his archers. Sure
enough, that infernally perky Angie stood silhouetted
against the night. Two lumps that must be the archers were
on the ground beside her.

His soldiers had indeed surrendered or, like Iron, had
been subdued with remarkable speed. One lay near Rylus,
another near Bryax, a third just past Iron beneath a scrub
oak. A slim grey cat sat licking the white mitten of his lone
front paw and with swift enlightenment Durez realized who
he had to thank for the wounds that still leaked blood down
the back of his leg.

"You must kill me before I will surrender!" he said with more courage than he felt.

"That's fine by me, you charred popinjay," Rabble snarled.

Her sword twisted his guard away in a single motion.

"Rabble, no!" Durez heard Bryax shout. Then red and black exploded in his head and he knew no more.

21

"Stranger, stranger, what do you fear?"
"I sense the will o' wham is lurking near"
"Foolish stranger, there is no such thing!"
"Then I fear what the nameless darkness brings."

Darkness Has a Name (Traditional)

RABBLE AND Bryax weren't speaking to each other when they rode back to collect Durez' last soldier—the odd man, the observer sent by the Duke. Scrapper trotted along on Rabble's right side; Zane took rear-guard.

"You didn't need to hit him so hard," Bryax broke the nerve-twisting silence.

"I let him live," Rabble replied. "Again. And that's more than he'd do for me. He wants my blood, if you'd recall."

"I do." Bryax sighed. "I had hoped we could mediate a truce once we had proof for the Duke that we'd dealt with his nephew and soldiers mercifully. That's going to be hard with Durez missing an ear and trussed up with a shattered collarbone."

"The ear's a pity," Rabble admitted. "He dodged

poorly. The collarbone will keep him out of further mischief.''

"Pardon, m'lady and Commander," Zane interrupted, "but we're near their encampment. It is just over the next rise."

"Now, Rabble, let me handle this," Bryax said, spurring his horse to point.

Dog Meat snapped at the other horse's haunches as it went by, but Rabble merely nodded.

"Ho, the camp!" Bryax called as soon as they were within sight of the makeshift pen that held the expected horses and pack animals. The only other feature was a small fire pit. Apparently, Durez had planned on moving in to the company's camp once they had been subdued.

No one came forth at first, then from where he had been sitting, leaning against a rounded boulder, a weedy man jumped to his feet. His worn and travel-stained robe still showed something of its original sun-bleached beige, but the details of the embroidery that was worked from neck to hem were lost beneath mud. The man swept lank, yellow hair from his forehead and peered into the darkness.

"Who's there?" he called, his hand white-knuckled on his walking staff.

"We've come to bring you to join Durez and the rest," Bryax evaded.

"You're not one of his soldiers," the man replied.

"No," Bryax said, moving his steed into the firelight. "You might say that he has joined our company."

Gaping, the weedy man looked Bryax up and down, registering the sword in hand, the well-oiled armor, the wry grin. The tip of his nose quivered as he registered that his side had lost, but his look of fear became panic as Rabble, followed by Zane, rode into the light.

"Now, will you help us gather your comrades' gear and ponies," Bryax said, "or do we need to add you to the gear?"

The man's mouth snapped open and shut, but no words

came forth. He raised a trembling hand and indicated Rabble, then Zane.

"You? You?" He fell to his knees, then his hand dipped to where a silvery knife with a crescent blade dangled from his waist-band.

Rabble and Bryax raised their own blades in reflexive parry. Scrapper, more clearly divining the man's intention, growled once, deep in her throat, and leapt forward. Her teeth closed around the man's wrist, stopping him not two fingers' breadth away from slicing his own throat. He tumbled onto his belly, whimpering, and neither of the humans needed the dog's keen nose to smell his terror.

"War and Chance!" Bryax swore as he disarmed the man. "What ails you? We have your comrades prisoner with barely a score of bruises between them. What makes you think that we would slay a horse boy like you?"

The prisoner's trembling ceased instantly and he drew himself up somewhat haughtily as Bryax bound his wrists behind him. Momentarily, something deadly glimmered in his eyes.

"I am no 'horse boy,' warrior. I am Gersam'tris, observer of these fools."

"Observer?" Rabble said. "For whom?"

Gersam'tris looked at her, his pose of contempt not completely hiding his earlier terror. "For the keepers of Shadowridge, the dwellers in Holdfast, for those that you should have the wisdom to fear."

"Shadowridge?" Rabble repeated. "Zane mentioned it earlier . . ."

"A mountain in the Storm Shroud range," Zane said, and curiously enough Gersam'tris appeared to hear him speak. "The one I told you about earlier, the one that the wizards used for the Refting."

Gersam'tris eyed Rabble, a low wail of renewed terror trembling from his throat, but Rabble only shrugged.

"So his masters are the surviving wizards or perhaps their descendants. That fits with what Rylus overheard, with what we've been expecting. Let's sling him on a pony and get back to the others.''

"You're taking all of this very calmly," Bryax said when they were stringing the ponies into a line out of hearing of Gersam'tris, who now trembled under Zane's guard.

"Shouldn't I be?" Rabble said, genuine puzzlement in her brown eyes. "Isn't this what we signed on to find for Hulhc?"

"Well, yes," Bryax agreed. "But wizards, Reftings, imprisoned deities—I don't mind telling you, Shield Sister, that if Hulhc called this all off I'd be gone as fast as my horse could carry me and deal with Duke Elejinor as I must."

Rabble grew thoughtful. "I'm not scared at all—just tingling with anticipation. It's like this is what I've been intending to do from the start."

"Now, that," Bryax said with an unconvincing smile, "really frightens me."

They returned to the camp with their prisoner and prizes to find a heated debate already in progress. After Gersam'tris had been imprisoned in the cave with the rest of Durez' soldiers, Rabble and Bryax joined the others around the cook pot.

"Killing them is out of the question," Tambor said for what was clearly not the first time, "but so is taking them with us if we continue on."

"And I, at least, will go on," Hulhc said. "Whether or not the tale that Zane told us is true, my resolve is unchecked. I will not turn around so close to success."

"Parole them," Bryax suggested somewhat indistinctly around a mouth full of venison stew. "If Kazu and Vieth would give me their Oath, we can send them all home, lives and honor intact."

"The other soldiers might follow Kazu and Vieth's example willingly," Rabble added. "Their loyalty is to the Domain of Dragons, not to Durez or the Domain of Roses. Durez and Iron may not be from Dragons, but they still should abide by a warrior's oath."

"And with that broken shoulder," Rylus added, "even Durez may see the wisdom in living to fight another day."

"It's nearly daylight now," Angie said. "Waiting to present our offer seems like piddling acid into their stomachs—they don't know we won't slay them outright. I'll go and get Kazu and Vieth."

The two elite guards listened carefully as Bryax outlined the terms for their parole.

"You want our oath that we will not pursue you further," Kazu said, "and that we will prevent the others from doing so until we have returned to Dragon's Spire."

"That's right," Bryax said. "In turn, we will get as many as possible to swear Oath to obey you and Vieth as their new commanders."

Vieth snorted softly. "Our soldiers will, but Durez will not like obeying common soldiers. Iron will follow his lead."

"If they refuse," Rabble interjected, "they die. They alone are not innocent in this matter."

Kazu frowned, but nodded her agreement. "Bryax, come and bear witness, then. Rabble—no offense intended—you will just be a goad to what Durez perceives as his honor."

With little reluctance, the matter was settled, parole was given, and all the prisoners but Gersam'tris were released, their gear intact, to ride with first light down into the lowlands.

"I still don't trust Durez," Rabble said, slouched in her saddle, her hand caressing the pommel of her coppery sword.

"Why?" Angie said. "You've defeated him how many times—two? three? Maybe he's getting sorry about bruised limbs and broken bones. Maybe he sees how scared this Gersam'tris is of you and decides that wisdom says go back to uncle and papa and tell lies about how well he fought."

"Maybe," Rabble said, "but I think I'll ask Zane to keep watch on them for the first day or so—until the distance between us is safely grown."

"Wait!" Hulhc said. "If you let him go, who will be our guide?"

"That's easy," Rabble replied, her grin wicked. "We couldn't release Gersam'tris on a warrior's parole. I think I can convince him to guide us."

Zane protested at leaving and Gersam'tris turned white beneath his travel grime—apparently the choice between betraying his masters and challenging Rabble was horrifying—but in the end, Rabble had her way.

The Company rode further into the mountains. Gersam'tris was permitted to ride in the center of the group when it became clear that his terror of Rabble would not permit him to ride with her on point.

Once underway, Rylus brought lumbering Bet into line beside Gersam'tris' more agile mountain pony and studied the man. He rode well, with a studied sense of balance that seemed to anticipate every shock. Angie had insisted that he wash and now that his blond hair was bound back from his face and the grime gone, he was less a comic figure. Still, his gaze rarely left Rabble and if she chanced to look at him he tensed.

"How long until we reach this Shadowridge?" Rylus asked.

"Two days, maybe three," Gersam'tris replied. "I've never come from this direction. It could take longer if we come across some chasm or ravine I'm not aware of."

Rylus nodded. "And I don't expect that we would be wise to ride right in and offer to put on the Spectacular, would we?"

Gersam'tris almost smiled. "No, I don't expect so."

"Rabble is mean," Rylus continued conversationally, "but I don't think I've ever seen her be unfair—at least by her lights. Why are you so scared? You don't even know her."

"If you don't know, then all the better for you," Gersam'tris said with a shudder he didn't bother to conceal. "I am certainly not going to disturb your rest."

"Peace and Prosperity!" Rylus swore. "You're a hard

man to like. You could be kinder to people who have just spared your life.''

"I am being kind," Gersam'tris assured him, "as you will know, soon enough.''

22

"Does anyone ever tell the whole truth?"
                                        Hulhc

THE RIDGELINE that they followed for most of the day was exposed and hot beneath the sun. However, the same elements that had worn the ridge bare had also made a fairly smooth trail for them to follow. A stream flowed in a cut along their way so, despite frequent stops to water the animals and splash sweaty faces, necks, and arms, they made a good distance before evening.

Zane arrived as they were finishing the last of the fat river chubs that Rylus, with the help of the bears, had netted from a deep pool cut by the water in the blue-grey rock.

"Darkness falls earlier lower down," the ghost said, "where the mountains cut off the sun. I waited until the dozen made camp and then until Durez and Iron slipped off. Then I returned."

"Slipped away!" Bryax said. "Then they are foresworn!"

"As I heard his lordship explain to Iron," Zane said, "his prior oath of vengeance outweighs all other oaths."

"Still, we have two days of travel on them," Rylus said. "They are not likely to catch up to us."

"They don't plan to," Zane said apologetically. "They ride directly for Shadowridge. Durez knows the lower roads. They may even arrive at Holdfast before we do."

"War and Chance!" Bryax swore. "That filthy oath twister!"

Rabble's eyes burned in the firelight. "Now do you believe that he cannot be reasoned with? Next time we meet with Durez—I swear—he will die!"

Night passed too slowly for them, but they did not dare risk the mounts on dark travel. Restless dreams pressed them from all sides and by morning they rose with eyes ringed with shadows.

Breakfast was gulped down between packing and saddling and they were on the trail before the dawn's pink had faded from the sky.

Rylus shifted his bulk in the saddle uncomfortably. Tambor, much slimmer than when they had begun, grinned sympathetically.

"I miss the city, partner," Rylus said. "Hot baths, warm beer, and my bed in the wagon. I foreswore a life of adventure when I was a boy and saw what real work it was."

Tambor twinkled. "I remember the stories you've told. Easier to build a wheel than to pick a lock or pocket. We'll be back to the Spectacular soon enough with stories to tell around the fire."

"I hope," Rylus said, looking ahead to the looming mountains. "I hope."

The day warmed to mirror the one before and, but for a brief stop for lunch, they rode steadily. At the end of the line, Angie brought her llama up alongside Hulhc's dour grey. Softly, so that Bryax riding tail guard would not overhear, she spoke teasingly to the farmer.

"So, Farmer Grey Hills, now we know—if the ghost's story is true—where the magic went and who makes it and who takes it. When we get there do we just peek in and say we've seen it or do you mean to go and seek it out?"

"Why not toss your coins or read your cards or mash tea and tell me?" Hulhc growled, his beard and hair, beneath his wide-brimmed soft hat, soaked with sweat.

Angie chose not to take offense at his grumbling. "I have—all three—and the answers all say that a piece is missing so I can't know. Thought you might have that piece and so came asking.''

"You asked what question?'' Hulhc said, scratching his beard.

"If we stop and look or if we go in.''

"And you didn't know enough to know?'' he said. "What kind of fortune-telling is that?''

"The best I can do,'' Angie frowned. "I never claimed real lore—not in anything but healing. My mother taught me to see what is there and to give good advice. She also taught me that there are those who take advice better if it comes from diviner's art or a puff of smoke rather than from common sense or an observing eye. Maybe in the days before the Loss things were different—I only know my now.''

"And I did, too.'' Hulhc wiped sweat from his forehead and sighed. "I've been unfair. You asked a reasonable question. I guess I hoped that you would have the answer as well.''

"What is it you want, Farmer Grey Hills?'' she said, tossing an imaginary hand of coins into the air and pretending to study their pattern.

"Flying ships, unicorns and dragons, clean clear lights.'' His voice dropped and became husky. "Miracle cures.''

"I thought so,'' her tone was compassionate. "Your wife.''

"Yes,'' he answered as if embarrassed.

"Tell the others,'' Angie urged him. "They'll help you still.''

"Aren't they anyhow?'' Hulhc replied. "I'm not certain that they'll think one old woman's life is worth challenging wizards. Let them feel free to turn around without guilt when they want.''

Angie shook her head and smiled. "Stubborn kindness, but as you say. Your wish is safe with me.''

That evening they made camp beneath the remnants of an old apple orchard whose trees still bore sweet if irregularly shaped fruit. Both Zane and Gersam'tris agreed that they had come within a day and a half's travel of territory that the wizards still claimed as their own.

"Then this may be our last really restful camp," Rylus said, readying his cookware around the fire that Rabble was stoking. "I'm pleased to announce that the bears have brought us the centerpiece for a truly marvelous meal."

With a flourish he brought out the carcass of a half-grown piglet.

"Apple-fed pork," he continued happily. "Tambor, if you'll get me a dozen or so good apples and if Hulhc will cut me supports for a spit, I'll butcher and scald this lovely creature and give you a meal you'll never forget."

"Let me get the apples," Angie volunteered, "and find what else there might be for sharp eyes to see and nimble fingers to carry away. If people once lived here, there may be fresh garden herbs and vegetables not too far gone into the wild."

She proved a prophet and when her cullings were brought back to Rylus he crafted a meal that not only included pork and baked apples, but also peppers, squash, and a tart garnish of late raspberries. They ate until the pork was reduced to bones for the dog and the vegetables to rinds for the bears and monkeys.

"Eat more," said Rylus, pressing Tambor to take the last bit of meat from the tray. "Once you were a strapping lad, now you're near skin and bones."

Tambor grinned in rueful acknowledgment. "I fear you're right, Ry. Amid pirate arrows, illness, and all this running and riding about I have lost some girth. Z'ripes might prefer carrying me this way, though. I promise when we're settled around a winter fire I'll do my best to emulate the bears and do naught but eat and sleep."

"Where's Zane?" Bryax asked, squinting off into the darkness. "Or is he here somewhere? I thought I'd finally gotten the knack for catching sight of him."

"He's been around," Rabble said, flipping a bone to Scrapper.

"He has indeed," Angie added. "Flickering in and out

like the last firefly of the season. Call him, Rabble. Perhaps he's lonely.''

Rabble shrugged and cupped her hands around her mouth. ''Hey, Zane! C'mon back!''

For a moment the only response to Rabble's call was a baleful glare from Gimp, who had been draped in drowsy elegance across her lap. Then Zane and Blizzard appeared, somehow encompassed without loss of size or girth in the arm's length between Rabble and Bryax.

''You called, m'lady?'' He bowed and swept the ground with his plume. ''Rabble?''

''Yeah, we wondered where you had gotten to.''

''Elsewhere. Resting, I suppose. Being, even when one is dead, is rather strenuous. Since I could not join in your repast, I went with Blizzard and,'' he paused, hunting for a precise word, ''coasted for a bit.''

''Thanks for coming back.'' Rabble smoothed her hair back from her widow's peak with a greasy hand. ''Did you 'coast' most of the time—I mean, since you died?''

Zane nodded. ''After the Refting, yes. I got rather lonely being the only ghost and I didn't trust the wizards. I couldn't go away from the mountains—they seemed to be my limit. So Blizzard and I rode with Time until the recent troubles awoke me.''

''Troubles?'' Hulhc asked. ''That's right, you were starting to tell us about them when we were interrupted the other day—the day you were telling us about the Loss.''

''Refting,'' Zane corrected. ''That's right. Shall I tell the rest?''

Gersam'tris emitted a panicked squeal of protest.

''Yes, I think so,'' Bryax said, with a suspicious glare at the wizard's man. ''If he doesn't want us to know, then I think I do.''

Mutters of agreement came from the rest of the company. Angie leaned to check that the tea kettle over the fire was full.

''A story would help to settle dinner,'' Rylus urged. ''Tell away, Zane.''

"I'm not so certain that this is a settling story," Zane replied. "Now, I recall that I told you about the Refting and how the Elements were imprisoned in a crystal lattice by the wizards. The magic drained from the world, but that didn't mean that all knowledge of the conflict between the wizards and the champions of the Elements vanished with it. A few remaining stalwarts desired to free the Elements from their prison, but they were hampered by several things.

"What magic that could be tapped remained in the wizards' hands since they had proximity to the Elements. Therefore, any who wished to oppose the wizards would be without miracles. Another problem was more political. Several of the temples had discovered that they could do quite well with ersatz miracles and without wizards to compete with them or to prove them charlatans; they were even profiting. In some cases, they were doing better than before the Refting, since they had no need to rely on capricious Deities."

"I can see that," Rylus interjected, "rather like Duke Elejinor is doing in his Domain."

Zane nodded. "So even those who survived and knew the true state of affairs were hard put to find support. Time passed and—as I came to learn later—the truth was lost in musty records and rediscovered by a temple scholar up near Lake Torenia."

"That's a rather isolated area," Hulhc said. "Some call that the Sea of Strangeness. It's a good region to lose something or to find something that others have tried to make lost."

Zane smiled. "I see you understand the complexity. The woman who made this discovery belonged to a large, devout family. She bypassed the temple hierarchy completely and enlisted her siblings and cousins. Together, they devised an audacious plan. One group would travel into the Storm Shrouds and attempt to distract or otherwise weaken the wizards' control of the lattice. The second—smaller—group would travel to an ancient, reportedly potent shrine and incant old rituals to evoke one of the Deities. They hoped that this coordinated effort would free one or more of the imprisoned powers and then the fight would be up to the divine.''

"Coordinated?" Bryax asked. "I'm no great tactician but how could they coordinate two such different groups at such a distance?"

"The date that they picked was especially sacred to the Deity they hoped to free," Zane replied, "and one easy enough to chart—the summer solstice."

"Then the Deity they hoped to free," Hulhc said quickly, "was Fire!"

"War and Chance!" Bryax swore. "That's a dangerous game."

"Exactly," Zane said, "but they needed Fire's power if they hoped to win."

"But it didn't work," Tambor said. "Did it?"

"Well," Zane flickered, "not exactly as they planned. The wizards were more paranoid than their opponents expected. They, too, remembered the consecrated days and felt that if any of the Elements would be strong enough to break the crystal lattice, it would be on its own Day. Forces readied to deal with an outbreaking Element could easily be turned against human opponents.

"In the Downs, a small group began its incantation, not suspecting that their counterparts were already foredoomed to failure and that the wizards had magically discovered the entire plan. Even as the rote to summon Fire was being chanted around an altar piled with scented woods, rare oils, and expensive incense, the wizards were reaching out to crush the singers as their allies had already been crushed."

"Oh," Angie whispered. "The poor dears . . ."

"The wizards didn't know everything," Zane continued. "The most important thing that they didn't know was that before the wizards' defense had driven them back, one woman—the very one who had first found the old records— had penetrated into Holdfast and had made a tiny break in the crystal lattice. This was enough to allow imprisoned Fire to connect with the prayers of those gathered about the ancient shrine in the Downs.

"Now, Fire has many aspects—cooking hearth, warmth in winter, smithy forge, and even more symbolic aspects like temper, passion, and love. But since it was for its martial aspects that these people had chosen Fire as the Element to release, when a portion of the Element fought free of the lattice and answered their call it was the Fire of War who came—the Fire they call War and Chance. As they were destroyed by the wizards' magic and their call fell silent forever, a small portion of the Element took form."

"War and Chance!" Bryax swore. "Do you mean to say that we have the martial embodiment of Fire wandering around out there?"

"Not precisely," Zane said, looking at Rabble. "I mean to say that she is here with us."

Rabble raised her head then and looked at each one of them from dark brown eyes that burned.

23

"The whole truth is rarely as wonderful in reality as it is in dreams."

Weatus, Mage

THE LONG silence that followed Zane's revelation was broken by Angie.

"Well, can I say that I am surprised?" she said with a nervous laugh. "Our Rabble has always been a trifle intense."

" 'Our Rabble,' " the flame-haired warrior repeated

slowly. "Am I still that, Angie? Still just one of the Travelling Spectacular or am I suddenly something to fear? Gersam'tris certainly thinks that I am."

"Did you know, Rabble, all along, who you are?" Bryax asked.

She looked steadily at him. "Would you believe me if I said 'no'? That I only started to feel there was more within my memory as we drew closer to the Storm Shrouds?"

"Of course," Bryax answered firmly. He paused. "Sword Sister still?"

"Would I break an oath sworn somehow on myself?" Rabble touched his hand. "Sword Brother."

Angie shook dried camomile and peppermint to steep in hot water and began lining up mugs.

"Soothing," she said. "Like we all need."

Rabble declined her portion and pulled out her flask of *pfneur breit*, lighting the rim of her cup before drinking.

"More to my taste," she said. She took a long pull of the fiery stuff and then continued thoughtfully. "There have always been memories, memories of too many battles, of conflicts and tactics known as thoroughly as if I'd been there. I guess I was, in a sense. Lately, I've been—not dreaming—but remembering more and more until I can concentrate and see this orchard with harvest bonfires burning or spring smudge fires or even further back to when this area was cleared with axe and flame. Wherever flames have burned, I have been there and yet that is not me—this mind is incomplete, unable to grasp as an Element must grasp, so I am just Rabble."

"The wizards all want to cork you back into their bottle," Rylus said hesitantly, "and I guess that you want to break this crystal lattice Zane has been telling us about and free the others and the rest of yourself."

"I guess," Rabble said. "I guess."

"Of course you do! You must!" Hulhc exclaimed. "Then the magic will return to the world and things will be back to normal."

"And people will start relying on miracles and tricks again," Gersam'tris burst in, "and will be little more than puppets and serfs to those who have power."

"Not to mention what will happen to your little coterie," Tambor snarled. "They won't fare too well when the Elements are free, nor when the rest of us can tell the truth about the Refting."

"I do find it rather ironic," Hulhc added, "that those who deny magic to the rest of us are those who are benefiting most from what little remains. Some of those wizards must be something like two hundred years old now."

"Older," Rylus corrected. "You forget that many were ancient before the Loss."

In the general wave of anger and indignation that had swept the camp, Rabble and Bryax sat silent. Bryax looked confused, his gaze continually straying to Rabble as if unwilling to accept that his drinking and fighting buddy was truly the avatar of one of the four Elements. Rabble stroked Scrapper and Gimp, her long fingers restless, her expression brooding.

"Axe," she said beneath the hubbub of the ongoing argument. "Come for a walk with me. I can't think with all of this noise."

He rose, reached for his sword-belt, then hesitated. "I guess there's not much use in my taking that, is there? You can beat anything."

"Don't count on it," she said with a shadow of her grin. "I'm not sure what would happen if there were more than a couple and I'm very certain that I'm as vulnerable to arrows as anyone."

Bryax took the sword-belt.

"Axe," she said when they were out in the darkness, "I don't know what to do. If I free—or at least try to—whatever is imprisoned in that lattice I would be doing what I once would have wanted and I'd be doing what Hulhc wants, too. But Gersam'tris does have a point, much as I hate admitting it. Magic does make things easier—not just little things like lights, but the big things like conquest. Would the rebels in the Archipelago of Truth welcome the return of flying ships? Would all the little farmers and crafters welcome magical goods that would take away the value of their labors? Would Alba and Betram Bolla welcome seeing their shipping line wiped out when magical means can send people and goods faster?''

"I don't think I've ever heard you talk so much at one time, Rabble," Bryax said. "And I'm not suddenly any wiser than I've been, but I keep thinking of that farm we stayed at before we crossed from Saltport. The Grand sure would have welcomed magic. I don't think having to compete in the marketplace would have mattered to her—I know it didn't bother my grandfather.''

"And I did promise myself then that I'd learn what I could do to help her,'' Rabble said softly. "War and Chance! Why isn't this easy? Heroes in legends never have to worry. Evil is there and needs to be gotten rid of and everyone is better off in the end. We don't even have a princess for you to rescue and set you up with a kingdom for life.''

"Or a prince for you,'' Bryax grinned.

"I don't think I'm eligible," Rabble said stiffly. "I'm not even a person. I'm just a spark of Fire. I wonder if I go up in a puff of smoke when we're all done?''

"I didn't even think of that!" Bryax said, horrified. "We can't risk that. We'll have to turn around—learn more. Those Elements have waited this long. They can wait a bit more.''

"Maybe,'' Rabble said, "but none of our lives will be worth fish scales if the wizards' agents find us—and we know that the Duke of Dragons is one. Who else might be? I think we had best go on, if go on is what the rest decide to do.''

"Will you really, Rabble?'' Bryax asked.

"Yes, now that I know what type of creature I am, I don't feel I have any choice. Like Zane, I'm a victim of the act of my creation,'' her smile glittered crookedly in the moonlight, ''but that doesn't mean I go in careless or hot-headed. I value what I am for as long as I'm me.''

''Then I'm with you, whether or not the others go.'' Bryax took her hand. ''I can't say that I don't feel strange about it—but Sword Sister, still!''

Rabble glowed. ''Good. No—great! We'll need to consult with the others on a plan. They're not warriors, but they're sharp.''

''We'll talk with them,'' Bryax agreed. ''And Gersam'tris. And Zane.''

''I wonder what we're unleashing,'' Rabble said as they returned to the camp. ''I really wonder.''

''Take the warrior's escape,'' Bryax advised her. ''Act. Don't think—at least not too much.''

The old orchard became base camp while they made their plans. Gersam'tris was restricted to a small area beneath a gnarled apple tree—left comfortable but unable to either escape or overhear their planning. If he tried to wander, Gimp wailed from his perch on one of the branches and Scrapper or the bears herded him back. After a few such go-rounds, the wizards' man stayed in his place.

Zane brought back details that they used to build exterior maps, but even the ghost did not dare penetrate too deeply for fear that one of the magically adept would have the eyes to see him.

''I've been wondering about that,'' Angie said as she looked over the charcoal sketch that Rylus had made from Zane's dictation. ''Why can some of us see you more easily than the others? Rylus and Bryax go all glassy-eyed with staring until they have you firmed up just right and yet I don't have much trouble unless you're standing by something that's so light that your white just mixes right in.''

''Well, I'm not much of an expert on this stuff,'' Zane replied, ''being the only ghost I know, but I do recall that in the days before the Refting most folks couldn't see me real well and not at all if I phased so I was mostly somewhere else. The ones who could see me easily were those who did magical workings—like the old card reader who gave me hope for Rabble's coming. I always figured that because they worked with magic, they knew how to see the supernatural working.''

''That doesn't answer for us,'' Angie said. ''None of us but Hulhc had even been born when the Refting happened and he was just a laddy.''

''But maybe,'' Hulhc said excitedly, ''Zane has given us the answer, just inside out. It's not that those who worked with magic could see Zane because their workings had made them sensitive—they were able to work magic because they were sensitive to it.''

''Are you saying then,'' Tambor stopped currying Z'ripes in mid-stroke. ''Are you saying that some of us are magically sensitive?''

''I am,'' Hulhc affirmed. ''Think—is the rapport you have with your beasts any less than miraculous? Remember how quickly Angie healed Bryax's wounds after we escaped from Dragon's Spire? The Far Shore's Healers were said to enhance their herbs and potions with magic. I think that's exactly what she does. What other purpose would all that sing-song she does when packaging her ingredients serve?''

''To keep me from getting bored?'' Angie said, but her tone was uncertain.

''You forget one thing, Hulhc,'' Tambor said, almost reluctantly. ''There is no magic to be sensitive to, for us to use.''

''Isn't there?'' Hulhc crowed. ''Zane told us that the magic had its source in the Elements. We have one of them, or a part of one of them, at least, right here: Rabble! If you think about it she is the most amazing one of us all. She must exude magic. Her animals understand her every word, that odd sword appears in her hands, even when you'd swear she'd been empty-handed.''

''Remember how she fought on the pirate ship?'' Rylus added, intrigued by the puzzle. ''She was wreathed in flames, but came back aboard our ship unsinged. She may have magic enough and to spare, just the way the wizards near the lattice apparently tap what leaks through to serve their needs.''

"Why don't I feel happier about this?'' Bryax said dryly. "So now some of you might have the ability to pull off a magical stunt or two. Might!''

He waved his sword to emphasize his words. "Such a talent is random, untrained, and maybe useless. Tactically, it's unsound. I'd feel safer sword practicing blindfolded using an old stick while my opponent bore live steel. This is crazy talk and crazier thinking, Hulhc.''

"Is it?'' the old farmer challenged. "Is it? Remember that my father was the Wizard of Grey Hills. I've studied his books and learned his lore. I won't let some muscle-bound mercenary tell me what I can and cannot do!''

"Just remember what you hired this mercenary for, old man,'' Bryax shouted back. "I plan to do my job and keep you alive while you insist on ferreting out trouble. And keeping you alive means not basing tactics on unproven, unpredictable, and dangerous stuff.''

They glowered at each other, tension as thick as the increasingly warm air. Anger dwindled only slightly as each realized that he had overstepped himself. Yet each was too proud to admit it.

Near the map, Rabble and Zane waited impassively. Rylus and Tambor traded glances that made only too clear that both were regretting coming this far.

Hulhc cleared his throat. "I suppose that the solution is to let go . . .''

Angie interrupted. ". . . of this piddle paddle shouting pride and get back to working out how to squirm into Holdfast past the wizards and to get back out again alive when the job is done.''

"She does have a point,'' Rylus added quickly. "You both have raised—em—valid tactical considerations. Our next question is how to best implement Hulhc's insight without, as Bryax wisely said, over-relying on an unpredictable element, one that our opponents are certainly more skilled at employing than we are.''

Bryax and Hulhc nodded slowly and the planning session continued. By nightfall, they were as ready as they could be from a distance and agreed to add final touches once their goal was in sight.

The next day, Rabble and Zane rode out in advance of the Company in order to scout out the wizards.

"That's the place?" Rabble said, surprise causing her to rein in Dog Meat far more roughly than was her wont.

"That's it," Zane replied. "I wouldn't steer you wrong now, would I, m'lady?"

Rabble sighed. In the days since Zane had revealed who— or what—she was, she had tried to accept his homage as belonging to her source rather than to herself. Something about the sparkle in his pearly eyes made her wonder if she wasn't being stubborn, but at least this solution gave her a reasonable excuse not to correct him every sentence or so.

"I know that you described it, Zane," she said softly, "but you hardly prepared me for this!"

Shadowridge was not nearly the tallest mountain in her memory, nor was it the most foreboding. Still, there was an ominous quality about it that made her shudder as if she had been dunked in a lake.

Tucked in a vale between two more conventional mountains, each with their slopes well-covered with greenery just beginning to show autumn colors, Shadowridge had a patchy, leprous appearance. Some of this came from logging along its slopes, but even those plants that remained were sparse, sickly yellow or faded green. The bare rock that showed through this poor covering was mostly blue-grey granite seamed here and there with schist heavy in mica fragments that gave back a poor parody of the sunlight.

At the mountain's base coursed a rocky, white-foamed river. Periodically, its course ran adjacent to powerful sulphur springs and the river mist and steam combined to create dense fog which shrouded the mountain's lower reaches. Against this grim and unwholesome backdrop, the wizards had created their stronghold.

Towering prisms of cut crystal supported a ledge that

jutted out over the foaming river. On this ledge a village from a child's play-set had been built. No two structures were the same; each was inspired by different, far-flung cultures, cultures that had been lost to each other since the Refting. A miniature palace of white marble filigreed in silver sat beside a quaint mud house with gently curving sides and arches and support beams of chiseled amber.

Nearby was a perfect replica of a Downs farmer's house—perfect if any farmer could thatch in straw of gold and find cobbles in polished opals. A many-windowed structure with domes peaking to saucy curves sat beside the cottage and a log house of ebony and mahogany beside that. Erratic rainbows arched over these buildings and others, replacing the birds and bees that the steam, mist, and sulphur had banished.

"Why select such a foul setting for artistry like this?" Rabble said.

"Maybe they wanted to distract themselves from what they had come for," Zane offered. "Or maybe it didn't matter. Perhaps they figured that when they had defeated the Elements they could redo the landscape. Remember, no one knew that they would suddenly be limited in what magic they could perform. However, that toy village is not really Holdfast. The real stronghold is within the mountain behind."

Rabble let the ghost direct her gaze to two arched entryways level with the village, set flush in the sheer rock wall.

"So those are the entries into the mountain that you mentioned during the briefing. I see two below, but where are the rest?"

"Above, concealed by those junipers on that ledge," Zane pointed. "Wizard Marr told us that they were intended to be accessible only from the air. In an emergency, the bottom could be sealed, and the wizards would still be able to leave."

"By those flying ships that Tambor is always mentioning?"

"Right," Zane said. "Or by giant eagle, flying fish, dragonette, or any of a double dozen of other ways that wizards travelled. There is a stair inside, but I can't think of any way we could get to the entry to use it—at least not without being seen."

"Rapelling seems our only option," Rabble agreed, "and I don't fancy climbing up—hoping to remain undetected—just to climb down again. I guess we'll just have to fight our way in."

"Wonderful!" Zane said sarcastically. "M'lady, if you try, you'll all end up like *me* and that's if you're lucky."

"We shall see what . . ." Rabble's retort trailed off. "Look down there, coming out of the 'farmhouse.' "

"Durez and Iron," Zane said softly. "So they did come here. Durez is no longer favoring that shoulder. I wonder if he has Angie to thank for that. M'lady, they're waiting for you."

"Good. I'm not terribly worried." Rabble's expression shifted from grim to shocked. "Zane, look way down that road, the one that snakes up here. I thought I saw two riders! Familiar ones."

Zane squinted. "They're beyond the bend. Wait."

He flickered out and then in. "It's Kazu and Vieth, Rabble, and they're talking blood—Durez' blood, with Iron's as baste."

"We've got to intercept them," Rabble said. "Not only will they get killed, they may give us away! Get me to them and never mind the trail. Dog Meat is up to it."

Zane took her at her word. Following the ghost horse and rider, Rabble guided Dog Meat over a treacherous course. About halfway down the slope, the steel-dust grey snorted in astonishment, braced himself stiff-legged, tossed his mane and gave a whicker of colt-like delight. Shaking his head in a wide arc, he hurried to catch up with Blizzard.

"Ah, you can see him now, you shaggy scoundrel," Rabble said, giving the horse an affectionate slap on the shoulder. "Good, make things easier for me."

They intercepted the two elite guards in a sheltered hollow along the deer trail which was all that remained of the road to Holdfast. Both women were begrimed, their torn tunics and cloaks giving ample evidence of a punishing ride. The mountain ponies, bred though they were for this terrain, looked little better. They hung their heads, blowing out through dilated nostrils.

Holding up empty hands, Rabble boldly rode Dog Meat out to block the trail.

"Am I right in guessing that you're after those two traitors?" she said bluntly.

"Guessing," Zane muttered. "I told you what they were saying."

The ghost's words went unheard by the two women.

"Traitors? Maybe." Kazu spat from a dry mouth. "Oath-breakers at least. They may be following some secret instructions from Duke Elejinor, but they broke the oath they swore to us. Vieth and I put the senior swordsman in charge when our group was safely within range of the Spire and headed back. Durez and Iron left a trail like a plough horse's. Not hard to follow."

"Running to their bolt-hole," Vieth added bitterly. "You aren't planning on trying to stop us from going after them, are you?"

"Never," Rabble said sincerely. "I respect honor and despise Durez. I saw you while I . . ."

"We," Zane cut in.

". . . was scouting the very place they've gone. I think you had better take a look before chasing them further. Let me take you up a side trail."

"Very well," Vieth agreed.

Kazu nodded. Then they brought their ponies in line behind Rabble—and Zane, had they known. Despite the exhausted ponies, Rabble brought them directly up the steep trail to the nearest vantage point.

"War and Chance!" Kazu swore softly, staring at Shad-owridge from the hidden overlook. "Wizard built or I'm an islander."

"That's right," Rabble said, "and there are still wizards there. My company plans to go in for our own purposes. Would you care to join us? In return for your help, I'll even leave Durez to you."

"Done," Vieth said.

Kazu—seeming slightly surprised by Vieth's relative talkativeness—nodded. "Where are the others?"

"They're setting up camp in a glen a distance back along this ridge line," Rabble added. "We can be with them fairly quickly."

Rabble explained what the two elite guards intended— and that she fully supported their initiative.

"But you'll be killed!" Bryax said, releasing Kazu and Vieth from the double-armed bear hug with which he had greeted them. "Not only is Durez a skilled duelist, but sure as water is wet he's got wizards down there!"

"Better dead than dishonored," Vieth said darkly.

"She's right," Kazu added, "and not just on the level of ideals. We hold our positions in Cenai a'tal's guard by virtue of our honor and prowess. If we let the word get out that some royal-blooded, bloody-minded scrap of a man could shame an oath given to us and walk away after, we would be out of a post within a year. Who would take our orders? Therefore, my brawny, blond-blade master, we've got to go after them and take them—or their heads—back to Dragon's Spire."

"Or die trying," Vieth muttered.

"War and Chance!" Bryax swore, but he didn't protest further.

Later, when dinner was over but for mint tea and honeycomb, Rabble upgraded their tactical map with Zane offering corrections and encouragement over her shoulder.

"Looks bad and worse," Angie offered. "The best door in is high and out of reach. If we go in the ground way, we'll never make it past the first hall. I don't need cards or coins or magical second sight to tell me that."

"Magic!" Hulhc scowled, staring into the fire. "I keep thinking that magic holds our answer. We've got it—at least

Rabble does—and the wizards have no reason to suspect that we do. You're certain that there is no way to that upper opening?''

"None unless you can fly," Rabble said. "Climbing is out—too visible and too slow even if the climber wouldn't be a gift target to a novice archer. And don't even ask about making the climb by night. Even I'm not that crazy."

"She'll attack flaming pirate ships and three-headed dragons," Rylus said with a dry laugh, "but climbing sheer rock walls of crumbling stone by night is out. Peace and Prosperity! Still, I don't fancy the odds if we go in the front door."

"Nor I," Tambor added, "and I won't send the beasties in as a diversion. This isn't their quarrel."

"Flaming pirate ships," Hulhc said, a mad light in his grey eyes. "Diversions. Home and Hearth! I think I have a plan!"

Rapidly, he outlined an idea. Despite the brief explanations about Rabble's true nature, the ghost scout, and the like that they had already received, Kazu and Vieth glanced from person to person as if trying to decide who was craziest. After some debate, the Company came to accord.

"We'll need a trial first," Bryax said with a sigh, "to see if your theories are right, Hulhc. Are you game, Rab?"

"Sure," she shrugged casually, but interest lit gold sparks in her brown eyes. "There's a smallish ravine off to the east, back the way we came. Let's go there."

"I've some spare rope," Tambor said, pulling himself to his feet. "Haven't needed it for the bears. I'll get it."

Mountain-bred Kazu climbed down the side of the ravine and carried the rope up the other side. Once there, she stretched it taut like an acrobat's tightrope and tied it to a tree. She signalled that it was secure.

"Now we set it on fire . . ." Hulhc said, setting actions to words.

As soon as the rope was ablaze, Rabble winked at Bryax and walked out onto the flame. She had to hop and jump a bit, for the rope did not burn evenly, but once she began her stroll, the fire seemed to grow stronger and more steady. To the observers, it was quite evident that Rabble ran on the fire, not on the charred and breaking rope.

Moments later, Rabble stood beside Kazu across the rocky chasm. She waved back then yelled.

"Scrapper! Stay! Stay you dumb dog! I'll be right back!"

Scrapper stayed, but she whined nervously.

Rylus patted the bitch and shook his head as if he hardly believed what they were planning.

"This chasm could be spanned by Kazu climbing," he said, "and we'll need a heavier rope and a slower burn, but by Luck and Craft we'll do it! I'll need to work out a way to get that heavier line across first."

"Let me work on that," Tambor said. "Hulhc's convinced me that there is something to this magic. If I really do have a way with the beasties . . ."

"You do," Hulhc assured him gruffly.

"Then I could have a go at convincing one of these mountain eagles or hawks to help. A big enough raptor could carry a rope across, no problem, and sort of snarl it in that bit of a tree near the opening. It doesn't need to be that well anchored, not for what Rabble is going to do."

"I still worry about those wizards taking a shot or two at Rabble," Bryax said. "What if they do something like the lightning bolt that turned Zane from a man into a wisp of ghost stuff?"

"I assure you," Zane said. "Blizzard and my fate was not typical. Most victims ended up very dead."

"I believe I can keep Rabble safe," Hulhc said. "Watch."

He extended his arms so that bony wrists poked out past stained sleeves. Closing his eyes, he began to gesture lightly with his fingertips. At first, nothing happened. Then a pale mist began to rise from the bottom of the ravine.

Sweat dotted Hulhc's forehead and ran into his beard. When the screen of mist became thick enough to occlude their view of Rabble, he let his arms drop with a theatrical outrush of breath.

"There," he said proudly. "I can make a mist to cover her. It should even be easier to do by Shadowridge, if the fog and mist is as thick as Rabble and Zane have reported."

Rylus nodded, wonder making his round face gleam. "That was incredible, Hulhc. How did you know that you could do that?"

"I *am* the son of the Wizard of Grey Hills," Hulhc said pride melting into a shy smile, "and I've been practicing everything I could remember since before we started the journey. Now I have magical energy to manipulate rather than empty rotes to practice."

"Let's get Rabble back here," Bryax said, readying the gear. "Tambor's finding a bird is the only thing that delays us."

"I believe that I can help him," Zane said.

"Good." Bryax shook his head in mild disbelief. "The rest of us will finish rehearsing details. Then . . ."

"Then, when morning raises the mist and muddles the waking minds," Angie said, tossing a fortune coin in the air and watching it sparkle as it fell, "we go in after the wizards!"

24

War and Chance dance Death with the off-shoot of Fire. What is she then, that she can dance death with herself?

Angie

MORNING CAME misty and damp and even Rabble didn't complain. The company broke camp with the thoughtful thoroughness of people who know quite well that they might never return.

The young male peregrine falcon that Tambor had found the day before barely tolerated the presence of the rest of the company, but its golden gaze darted after Tambor's every move as he loaded gear onto the horses. When Rylus came over to help, the bird shrilled warning.

"Easy, Windraider," Tambor soothed. "About ready, Ry?"

The fat man hung a heavy coil of sulphur-scented rope from Z'ripe's saddle.

"Yes. Gersam'tris is gone?"

Tambor nodded. "I made certain he 'overheard' me telling the bears to leave Vieth and Kazu's mounts alone. Then Rabble and Bryax had a rather fiery 'argument' about who would accompany the women on the preliminary strike and who would stay as reserve. He's not stupid. He'll hurry to report."

"If he hasn't already," Rylus said. "Hulhc says that communication magic isn't easy, but Gersam'tris is probably schooled in it since he was sent as an escort for Durex's troop."

"I'm not so certain. He may not realize that Rabble sheds magic and believes that he needs to go closer. Certainly any reserve he carried is exhausted by now," Tambor replied.

"Whatever, we had better stop talking and get moving," Rylus said.

Tambor smiled at his partner. "One of the bears is going with you as a back-guard, but they're afraid of Shadowridge. Don't count on it overmuch and be careful."

"You be careful," Rylus admonished. "I don't feel right about sending you with just Hulhc and Rabble."

"Don't worry. Our part will be done quickly and we'll be with you for whatever comes after."

Neither said "with luck" but both knew that luck alone could bring this wild plan off successfully.

In another part of the camp, Rabble was taking her leave of Bryax.

"Don't do anything foolish, Sword Brother." She whistled and Scrapper bounded up. "I'm sending Scrapper and

Dog Meat with your group. They won't be able to get in my way.''

"Right." Bryax hesitated, then he took her hand. "Be careful, Rab.''

She shook her fiery head. "That's not my nature. I can't start now. Just trust me to make it in and we'll go from there.''

Rabble strode to where Kazu and Vieth were checking their weapons and armor.

"War and Chance be with you both," she said.

"Thank you, Rabble," Kazu said, slightly awed as she realized the source of that blessing. "And thank you for giving us the opportunity to redeem our honor.''

Rabble nodded and turned away, nearly crashing into Angie. The Far Shore's Healer had her medical kit to hand and broad-petaled yellow lilies painted on her cheeks.

"Cards say War and Chance dance Death with you, Rabble," Angie said worriedly. "You walk into an ending and it isn't only for the wizards.''

"I guessed that," Rabble replied. "Can I refuse this challenge because it might end me? Whatever else I am, I've been a warrior. Death is part of the trade. I'm going to accept that.''

Rabble's brown eyes narrowed and she motioned Angie to a more private area. "What really scares me is whether I *am* a person, Angie. I've said that I'm 'just Rabble' but what if I'm not even that? What if when I go to free the Elements, I just stop being me and get absorbed into Fire?''

"I see," Angie said. "I had better come with you. Maybe I'll have the eyes to see the portents for you.''

Rabble gaped disbelievingly. "No, Angie. The others will need their healer.''

Angie's expression clearly showed her conflicting responsibilities. At last, she sighed.

"You're right, fire light," Angie said. "I'll go tell that grouchy grey-beard to go with you. You need a backup if . . . if what you say is the way of the day.''

She scurried off before Rabble could argue and the

pressure of time fitly ended all further discussion of the issue.

The company split into two parties. The smaller—Rabble, Tambor, Hulhc, Zane, and several of the beasties—began a slow trek up to an overgrown slope roughly across from the hidden entry to Shadowridge. The remainder, along with Kazu, Vieth, and the majority of the animals, took the easier trail into the valley from which rose Shadowridge.

During their descent, Bryax's company reached an area from which they could see the wondrous structures of the wizard's village. They also saw that there was a great deal of activity in those cobbled streets. A small throng of robed men and women—most with hair of white or grey and walking assisted by staves or canes—gathered by the cottage with the golden thatch.

As they watched, Gersam'tris was escorted out between two figures—one bent and clad in robes of sky blue, the other straight as a stalk of corn, clad in wheaten gold over a rounded pattern of soft purple.

"Luck and Craft!" Rylus hissed. "The one in the blue is Y'teera, the wizard who spoke with Duke Elejinor back at Dragon's Spire. Pity Zane isn't here. He might be able to name the other for us."

"Rabble will need Zane," Bryax said, "and I don't think even she could convince him to be elsewhere. Let's ride. Kazu and Vieth, take point. You're going in first."

"We remember," Kazu said, touching her spear shaft, "but having seen that place, I can't say that I'm unhappy for the cover you'll be providing."

A short stretch of perfect cobbles made up what must once have been planned as a great road into the village. The unfinished approach to the road was muddy and full of ruts. It was also heavily overgrown and Bryax *tsked* cheerfully as he and Rylus found ambush spots within bow range.

Angie dropped further back with the animals and an anxious expression. She kept tossing her fortune-telling coins into the air and studying the patterns as it fell.

Kazu and Vieth rode boldly up the road and between the marble gargoyles that flanked the entry into the village. The people who drifted out of the various structures wore expressions of carefully schooled disinterest, but nonetheless a tingle of anticipation permeated the air.

Trotting her pony down the middle of the street, Kazu stopped at the statue that dominated the crossroads and rapped her spear against the base. The ring of wood against stone seemed a cue for response from the gathering crowd. Y'teera of the sky-blue robes stepped forward.

"What brings you here, strangers?"

"Blood," Vieth said.

"Blood and honor," Kazu added. "We have tracked two men who broke oath with us. The trail ends here. If you do not hand them over to us, we will still hunt them out."

"And slay them," Vieth continued, "if they refuse to submit to the judgment of our lord."

Many hundreds of feet above, Tambor looked across at the nubby green mass of juniper that masked the upper entryway.

"I'm going to send Windraider across a few times to make sure that he has the target set."

"Good," Rabble said, uncoiling the rope.

Gimp stood on his back legs enthusiastically batting the rope with his one front paw. He snarled, flashing his white needle fangs, but forbore from biting the chemical-soaked line.

Arms outspread, Hulhc stood on a rock that jutted out over the ravine. Errant breezes fluttered his sleeves, tousled his grey hair and long beard. He looked powerful—even mysterious—but the lines of his face were grooved deep with the strain. He breathed steadily and slowly. The mist in the ravine thickened with elemental patience.

In the village, no one was paying any attention to the gradual shifting of the weather patterns, for Kazu had continued haranguing the "villagers" to turn Durez and Iron over to her.

Vieth had fallen silent, content to glower, her spear stuck into the dirt by her horse's side, her sword in her hand while she worked the blade over with whetstone and oiled cloth. The rasp of stone against metal was an irregular, gratingly persistent demonstration of their determination.

After some formal debate, a contingent of the wizards went into a house built entirely of doors of myriad shapes and styles. From this, after a brief time, emerged Durez, Iron at his heels.

"By what right do you presume to challenge me, guard?" he drawled, obviously enjoying goading Kazu.

"By Honor and Oath, boy," Kazu replied, biting the last word so that she seemed to doubt his right to even that appellation.

The color rose in Durez' cheeks. From where he waited with strung bow, Bryax chuckled appreciatively. Rylus hushed him, but his own grin made apples of his cheeks.

"Any oath sworn in your presence cannot bind me," Durez sneered. "I did not acknowledge your authority over me—only did not argue over your usurping command."

"Oath was not sworn to me, but before War and Chance who all warriors honor, boy," Kazu replied. "My companion and I seek to amend the slight to the Deity. We will accept your surrender to judgment at the court of our lord, your death, or your surrender to judgment on an immediate field of honor. What is your decision?"

"I await the coming of one with whom I have a true matter of honor to settle," Durez replied. "I will not depart from here until she comes. If you and your companion wish to die, I will duel with you. Name which of you will fight and which will serve as second. Iron will second me."

"Our quarrel extends to Iron as well," Kazu said. "We offer him the same terms of surrender."

"I stand by my lord," Iron said.

Kazu studied him briefly. "Then we will begin with him and deal with you thereafter."

She and Vieth drew back and matched hands in a fluttering of fingers. The lot for battle was chosen and silent

Vieth patted Kazu on the arm. Kazu looked as if she would argue, then glanced at the thickening clouds above.

"Vieth will fight for us," she announced. "I will serve as her second. Boy, will you name your weapon?"

"There is little room for jousting here," Durez said, "so let us begin—and end—with sword and shield."

Vieth nodded and dismounted, unstrapping her shield from over the mountain pony's pack. Her device was Cenai a'tal's Flower of the Mountain done in pink and gold. As Durez' shield bore a cluster of roses for his territory within his father's Domain, the shields were ironically springlike.

When the wizards directed lackeys to quickly chalk an arena of sorts in the central square directly before the house of domes, Kazu permitted herself a brief smile. This was the very spot they had surmised would be chosen based on their observations. Fair play seemed a bit more possible with Bryax and Rylus lurking above with bows ready.

A woman with the light step of a girl, for all her hair fell silver to her feet, clad in a many-layered robe of cloudy gauze, stepped into the arena and raised a long-necked trumpet to her lips. Her face puffed red as she blew the call for all to assemble.

Faint but clear, the single trumpet call filtered through the heavy cloud cover that Hulhc had assembled. Windraider had successfully anchored the cord in the juniper across the ravine between the two mountains. Rising from beside the small fire pit that she had kindled, Rabble gave Tambor a strong, unprecedented embrace.

"Thank you, Tambor, for everything you've done for me," she said, so softly that had her lips not been near touching his ear he might not have heard, "and good luck."

"War and Chance be with you, Rabble," he said in surprise.

"They can't help but be now, can they?" she replied dryly. "Ready, Zane?"

"Ever, m'lady."

"Ready, Hulhc?"

"I wish you wouldn't insist on carrying me," the farmer said. "It's undignified."

"But certain," she said, holding her arms out and crouching so she could hold him piggyback. "You did a fine job bringing us the cloud cover, but you're near worn out. If you're to be more than a hindrance when we reach the other side, you must have some strength left and this road is not one you could walk without magic."

Hulhc sighed agreement, but his blush was as deep as a late summer tomato as he took his place. Gimp, who rode his lady's armored left shoulder, looked back at him and hissed, green-gold eyes narrow and speculative.

"Light it, Tambor," Rabble ordered, her breathing as even as if she did not carry the weight of armor, weapons, and grown man.

Tambor knelt and set a hot coal to the end of the rope that Rylus had impregnated with oil, sulphur, and Elements alone knew what other inflammables. It caught, burning slowly but steadily across its length. A slim wire buried within kept it from dropping away entirely and when several yards were ablaze, Rabble stepped onto the fire and over the ravine, walking the substanceless bridge.

Tambor felt his pulse leap and he soothed the agitated hawk on his arm, but Rabble was tranquil. A wind fanned the flames and Rabble ran with them. Hulhc scrunched his eyes shut and muttered prayers he would have sworn forgotten since childhood.

Zane and Blizzard tread the mist to the left of the burning rope. The ghost rider's expression was as anxious as Rabble's was calm. When at last they bridged the gap and stood safely on a ledge, Zane cheered.

"Hush," Rabble cautioned him as she helped Hulhc to a spot against the rock-face where he could collapse. "There may be those here who have the skill to hear a ghost's voice."

"Sorry," Zane said with an unapologetic grin. "I haven't seen anything like that since the Refting. It seemed like a good omen for setting things straight."

"Maybe. Hulhc, your mist is holding nicely," Rabble observed as she broke the wire and waved for Tambor to reel in the ashy remnants of their bridge. "No one should have seen us and—unless Durez is far more skillful than I recall—we should have a diversion below us. Are you strong enough to venture on?"

"No," Hulhc pulled himself to his feet, "but I must be or all of this will be wasted effort."

"Well spoken," Rabble turned to Zane. "Scout ahead. If you have any way of being less visible now is the time to use it."

"As you wish, m'lady." He dismounted. "I will leave Blizzard with you."

The pale horse turned its head as if disapproving, but remained when Zane misted from sight. Rabble lifted Gimp from his perch.

"You first, cat, then me, and Hulhc follow close behind. We'll start now and let Zane find us."

Dry leaves and other bits of wind-blown matter told that the passage had been unused for many years. Still, the occasional sconce held a flickering globe of eldritch fire— enough to guide them toward the greater brightness that was the heart of Shadowridge. With the three-legged cat bouncing on point, they crept into the dim-lit tunnel.

Following the trumpet call, Vieth and Durez had entered the makeshift arena. The spectators were strangely silent— no one took bids or called out encouragement to a favorite. Yet, excitement did ripple through the gathered wizards. Some of the aura of surprised tension and fatalism that most had worn like an extra garment fell away.

In his hiding place, Rylus shifted uneasily. "The mood is all wrong. Can they suspect us?"

"Maybe," Bryax whispered in return, "but we are too far committed to turn back. We're going to have to hope that Rabble pulls off her part."

The clashing of swords against each other, the duller thud of shield blows returned their attention to the arena. Durez bettered Vieth in both height and muscle, but she was the swifter. Moreover, Cenai a'tal's elite guard trained daily, a strenuous routine meant to prepare the women to deal with larger opponents.

For the first several rounds of circle and feint, parry and dodge, they seemed so evenly matched that Chance would elect the winner. Then Vieth's strategy became apparent.

Taking advantage of her lighter armor and greater mobility, she danced back and forth within the arena raining light blows on Durez and then dodging his return. Durez' heavier gear offered better protection, but hauling it back and forth wore into his strength. His face flushed ruddy and his breath came hard.

"She's got him!" Bryax grinned. "He can't keep that up for much longer and she's mountain born and mountain trained while he's only been living here some weeks. The thin air will get him as easily as her sword."

"This is where we watch for treachery," Rylus cautioned. "Durez has allies here."

Letting his crossbow rest, he angled a spy-glass he had purchased in Bookhome and scanned the clustered watchers. Most were intent on the duel. Iron's face was frozen in a neutral expression that told clearly that he, too, had seen Durez' danger. Rylus noted this, but passed on quickly, seeking the sky-blue and red robes of Y'teera and Weatus, the two wizards he had seen in the Duke of Dragon's private rooms.

Weatus was intent on the fight, but in her partner's shadow Y'teera bent over a sigil etched on a large, flat cobblestone at her feet. She made odd, looping passes with the heel of her staff and a faint pinkish glow—invisible to any without Rylus' enhanced vision—glimmered from the sign. Her lips moved to shape unfamiliar syllables. In the arena, Durez' movements strengthened.

"There's our treachery," Rylus said, handing Bryax the spy-glass and directing him where to look. "She's using magic to fortify him."

"Magic. War and Chance! What can the two of us do against that?" Bryax growled. "Y'teera is well-covered down there, but I could take a shot at her."

"That might do it," Rylus agreed, "but could get a whole mess of magic after us—especially if you kill her."

"You don't mean to let them cheat?"

"No, but can you hit the sigil she's made there?" Rylus asked.

"That's a harder shot," Bryax said. "If I missed I might hit her."

"Well," Rylus said, "that will solve our problem, too. Give it a try."

Bryax selected an arrow from his quiver, gauged the wind. Below, Durez was obviously gaining strength. He had drawn first blood with a lucky slash that caught Vieth along an exposed section of her forearm. Kazu paced the chalked line shouting encouragement, her voice the only contrast to the clatter of weapons.

"Sovereign Air, guide my shaft," Bryax prayed, then loosed his arrow.

All attention was riveted on the combat, so no one seemed to notice as the arrow sliced the wind. Not until it shattered into splinters of wood and flint on the cobblestone was there any reaction, but that reaction was far greater than Bryax and Rylus had expected.

The sigil burst into a brilliant flare of blood-hued light that sent Y'teera reeling back, her gnarled fists buried in her eyes. Durez stumbled, sweat streaking his face as if all the penalties for his exertions came home at once. Vieth came in for the kill, screaming with rage.

The crowd that had gathered to watch the duel reacted strangely to this culmination. A ripple like heat over a cook-stove passed across the audience. Then, all but Iron, Kazu, and bent Y'teera vanished.

"Trickery!" Bryax gasped. "They were never there at all!"

"If they weren't," Rylus said, grabbing his gear and running heavily down the slope, "where are they?"

Hulhc straightened as soon as their group moved toward the heart of the mountain. Turning his head from side to side in the manner of a dog questing after an elusive scent, he grunted in satisfaction.

Moving up, he whispered in Rabble's ear. "This place is rife with magic, much more so than outside. I feel ever much stronger. Do you want me to turn up the lights?"

"No," she hissed. "Don't act like a wine-drunk fool. We don't want to be detected. This has been too easy."

Hulhc stared at her as if she were insane. "Walking across a burning rope is not my idea of easy, but you will have your own way."

"I will," she said and a slight glimmer of light off of her sword blade punctuated her words.

Zane reappeared in Blizzard's saddle, leaning a bit as if welcoming the support. The trio paused to hear the ghost's report.

"This tunnel empties into a demi-cavern—not a natural one, I think. There are stairs carved from the living rock two flights up and two down with catwalks at each level. I could only inspect briefly, but most of the levels appear to be given over to storage and living quarters."

His pearly gaze locked with Rabble's warm brown. "On the second level there is a great stone door, twice or thrice my height and the power that emanates from behind it is the strongest that I felt anywhere in this place."

"That must be where the crystal lattice is," Hulhc said, unnecessarily.

"So it seems," Rabble replied, "and so that is where we will go. What did you see in the way of guards, Zane?"

"Nothing," he said, "and I cannot believe that there are none. Perhaps they all wait behind the Stone Door."

"Perhaps," Rabble said, "but I doubt it."

*　*　*

Angie, astride Bryax's dun, was the first one into the now near deserted village. Vieth had knocked Durez' feet out from under him and stood with one foot on his chest and her sword point at his throat. Kazu held a drawn sword on the sobbing Y'teera.

Angie drew rein by Iron. "You keeping your place, solemn man?"

"I see no need to interfere," he said. "Vieth has not acted out of order."

The stress on "Vieth" was slight but noticeable and Durez, who had not shown any fear to that point, craned his neck so that he could fix his friend with a suddenly panicked gaze. Any further interplay was quelled by Bryax and Rylus pounding into the square.

Bryax cast around, looking for something to fight in the suspiciously deserted square. He settled for joining Kazu. Y'teera, hands still over her flash-blinded eyes, was working her way to her feet.

"Hold," Kazu commanded in a voice as chill as death. "The duel is not yet resolved and I have no desire to have you interfere again."

Y'teera lowered herself to the ground. "I will not interfere in any way, Kazu. I could not, even if I were so inclined. The backlash from my broken spell has crippled me—for now."

Durez had not yet stirred, pinned as much by Vieth's unforgiving gaze as by her boot on his chest. Vieth glanced at Kazu who nodded agreement to her unspoken question.

"We offered you the opportunity to surrender for judgment or to die here," Vieth said, the words coming slowly. "Again, we offer you the same choice out of respect for your uncle who is our Domain Lord. If you surrender, you will go to judgment, stripped of weapons and armor and bound onto your pony. We know now that your oath is less than nothing to you, so we cannot offer you parole."

Durez' voice squeaked as he replied. "I see. And Iron?"

"He will be given the opportunity to make his choice

himself," Vieth said. "Think only of yourself. You're good at that."

"Slay me then," he said boldly, "and deal with the consequences when report of your perfidious act reaches my father and my uncle!"

"There is nothing 'perfidious' about a warrior defending her oath," Kazu spat. "Without faith in our word, we would be nothing."

Iron nodded slowly. "I agree."

Durez began to kick then, bucking so that the tip of Vieth's sword pricked a bloody welt along his throat. Vieth grimaced at this final descent into cowardice. Then she pulled back her sword arm and brought it forward in a clean cut that spilled Durez' life into the glittering cobbles.

"Stairs look clear," Rabble whispered as she and Gimp peered out of the tunnel. "Step lively, Hulhc."

"It's awfully open," he said doubtfully. "We're certain to be seen."

"More certain if you drag your heels," Rabble said. "Zane, that door you saw. It's on the second level. Can we reach it from here?"

"I've been checking," he replied, "and the only stair to that area is on the ground level. The catwalks don't go all the way around."

"Lowering ourselves from this level would be chancy," Rabble decided. "Very well—we go down, across, and up again. So few options has the taste of a trap. Stay alert."

The stone stairs gave back little sound as they stole stealthily downwards. The second level—except for the Door across the cavern—proved to be little more than stone benches rimming the cavern with a catwalk in front and a narrow walkway behind.

The catwalk's outer edge was fenced by stonework, intricately carved with images of the Four Elements and their major secondary manifestations. Rabble paused to caress a representation of Fire's martial aspect.

"Looks more like a temple than a wizard's auditorium," she mused softly.

"This must be where it was done," Hulhc added excitedly. "Where the wizards gathered to unmask pretenders and instead refted magic from the world."

Rabble's slight shiver was invisible to the others. "This place reeks of sorrow and old sins."

Then without further comment, she continued their descent. Zane and Blizzard were waiting for them when they reached the ground floor. He gestured toward a broad archway through which fresh air and muffled crashing sounds came.

"That's the way to the village. Sounds as if the duel hasn't been resolved."

"No time to check," Rabble said, trotting toward the stair that led to the great Door. "Wherever the wizards are, they won't stay away long. I . . ."

Her words were cut off by a grating clash, stone against stone with a scream of steel.

The base of each stairway vanished in a geyser of white, foaming water. Stone panels slid to seal the doors out of the ground level. Even the archway to the village was filled to three-quarters of its height with a bulkhead of satiny granite.

"Water!" Rabble yelled. "Water!"

Gimp leapt from where the floor was becoming slick and wet up onto Rabble's armored shoulder. He hissed anxiously. Zane rode Blizzard directly into the water.

"Come on ahead, Rabble. You can't stay there—you'll drown!"

"I can't!" she said, backing away from an advancing trickle. "It's water!"

"And she is Fire," came a disembodied male voice, "and soon she will be weak enough to be extinguished."

"Marr," Zane muttered. "Still here. They must have prepared for this."

"Ever since they knew she escaped and would one day find her way back," Hulhc agreed. "And I won't be their tool, no matter how innocently. There must be something . . ."

His dour expression brightened. "Hold tight, Rabble. Don't let them stop me . . ."

"I'll do what I can," she said unsteadily. "But hurry!"

Durez' blood snaked in red rivulets. Vieth withdrew her foot from his chest, wiped her sword clean on a trailing length of her opponent's cloak, and turned to face Iron.

"Your turn now. Same choices as him."

"Judgment," Iron said promptly, unbuckling his sword belt. "I surrender myself to your custody."

"Keep your weapon," Vieth said brusquely. "These mountains hold dangers."

"Durez thought that you would rescue him," Kazu said, her gaze never leaving the trembling wizard at her feet. "Didn't he?"

"Yes, but he had abused my honor once too often," Iron said. "I was the son of a poor family. My entry into the Guard of Roses was the highest position anyone in my family had ever achieved. When the Duke's own son made me a boon companion, I was so honored that I overlooked the type of man he was. However, as I watched him go mad with a desire for revenge on your red-haired companion-in-arms, I realized that he truly thought that birth-rank and privilege equalled quality."

"And that you were just a prop for that image," Kazu finished.

Overhearing them, Y'teera began to titter insanely, though her eyes remained shut and her body crumpled into itself.

"Playlets! Playlets! Yet within the great drama at last unfolds. Fools, fools, what matters these little playlets?"

"What do you mean?" Bryax said apprehensively. "What game do you play?"

Y'teera refused to reply, rocking back and forth, her shriveled arms wrapped around her knees.

"Iron," Angie asked. "Where are the rest of the wizards?"

"I'm not sure," Iron said. "I was as fooled by that creature's art as you were. I do know that the opening over there leads into a complex at the mountain's heart. We were never permitted farther than a great central cavern, but the interior felt vast."

Tambor came skidding in as Iron finished, his animals milling around him.

"Has some charm been cast on all of you?" the beast-master shouted. "The beasties tell of people who were there and then vanished, of flashes of light that blind. Those banished illusions are surely a sign that some trap is being prepared for Rabble! We must go after her!"

Purpose returned with a jolt. Humans and animals alike tore for the opening into the mountainside.

Behind them Y'teera sat, abandoned, muttering, "Playlets! Playlets! The great drama unfolds."

25

Light buried beneath Earth,
Oceans where there are none,
Fire standing firmly upon Water,
Crystal broken by a name.

"Endings" by Rue Napen

HULHC KNELT, ignoring the cold water that sopped into his wool robe. Spreading his fingers into broad fans, he touched the pooling water with the pads of his fingers.

The crashing of the geysers muffled most of what he said, but a snarled, "Freeze, would you! Ice!" rose above the tumult. A frosty light gathered around him and then frost spread from his fingers.

"Nice idea," Zane said, "but you can't hope to freeze it all. It's already knee-deep."

"I don't," Hulhc said, the sweat from his eyebrows becoming icicles before it could fall free. "Only a raft."

Understanding him despite her terror, Rabble slogged through the water, freeing a chunk of the strongest ice from the slush around it with her sword. Hulhc lifted his hands, tracing them around the edges to shape the floe. When the water had risen to waist height, he had completed a craft that was not quite a boat but more graceful than a raft, with a handspan of freeboard and a stabilizing centerboard.

After placing Gimp in the icy bow, Rabble scrabbled up, dragging Hulhc in after.

"Ice for Fire," came Marr's disembodied voice. "Clever, farmer. Do you think we were unprepared for such?"

In the dark alcove off behind one of the stairways, there was a loud splash. The boat bobbed, but nothing untoward happened.

"Find a way to move that hulk toward the stair," Zane urged. "They'll use archers if they don't have any other tricks. I'll go and see what that splash was."

He and Blizzard tore off above the rising waters. Rabble removed her unstrung bow from her shoulder and spun a hole in the ice boat's bottom a handspan or so back from the bow.

"The ice is firm but I can anchor this," she said. "It won't be the straightest mast ever, but we can sling my cloak as a sail. While I work it out, Hulhc, you find us wind. I suspect that it will be easy enough to raise here and somehow I feel that the wizards will be reluctant to call on an Element in such a pure form."

Hulhc nodded, though he was pale from his previous exertions.

"Take my staff to use as a crossbar for your sail," he said, then he closed his eyes and began puffing his breath experimentally.

A faint but steady breeze arose in response to his promptings, growing strong enough that as Rabble held the sail they began to move across the flooded cavern, toward the Stone Door.

"We've done it!" Hulhc crowed, "and at the rate that the water is rising, we should be able to forego the stair and sail right to the threshold."

Rabble didn't appear to hear him, her attention riveted on a ripple of motion beneath the cold, dark water. She gestured with a toss of her red hair.

"Something is in the water, Hulhc. Come, hold the sail." She drew her sword and glanced about. "I'm prickling all over. Where in Fire's name is Zane?"

Her concern for the ghost vanished as she caught sight of the large, grey-white fins that emerged to cut the water around the ice boat. The sharks' bodies were solid shadows beneath.

In the bow, Gimp ceased shivering to watch the lazy arch of the shark's approach, his curiosity tinged with menace. Rabble waited as well and when the first shark passed near enough for her to reach, she tentatively stabbed at it with her blade. Her reach proved far too short.

The shark submerged and moments later the cumbersome vessel was rocked from below, splashing the sailors with icy wetness.

"Rabble, do something!" Hulhc pleaded.

The red-haired warrior was white beneath her freckles, her customary arrogant fire for battle gone in sick dread of the water and of the sleek monstrosities gliding about them.

"Rabble!" Hulhc repeated.

Rabble moaned. "Y'don't expect me to swim after them, do you? I don't have the reach to hit them and my bow's all tangled up with the sail."

Hulhc tore his attention from blowing wind into the makeshift sail. One hand pulled at his beard as if pain could force an errant idea into the fore.

"Rabble, that sword of yours. It's puzzled me for weeks.

You're never without it—even when I could swear you weren't carrying it. Could it be an extension of your power?''

A shark jostled the raft, sloshing water aboard. Gimp hissed and swatted after the fin as the shark slunk by, its wide, tooth-filled mouth a mocking grin.

Rabble snagged the dripping cat by the scruff of its neck before it could tempt the shark further.

Gimp growled protest. ''My fight, too,'' his slanted green eyes seemed to say. ''Someone needs to protect us.''

Setting the cat down, Rabble hefted her sword. ''You have a point, cat. You and Hulhc both do.''

The golden flecks in her eyes brightened as she glowered at the wavery copper blade. The raft steamed beneath her boots and heat radiated from her as from a winter stove. The sword became molten and in response to her need reshaped into a wickedly barbed harpoon the pink shade of freshly polished copper.

''Elements!'' Rabble said gleefully. ''Now that's more like it! Come and show me your fishy smile again, darlings.''

Hulhc glanced from his work and noticed that the boat was turning into slush where Rabble stood. He bit his lip and blew harder, wishing he didn't feel so much like they were toys floating in a malevolent child's bath.

Behind the steps, Zane saw the conjuring chamber that still bore the shapes of the sharks which had been released into the water. Burnt black crystals showed how much power had been stored here to make the feat possible. A cowled figure stepped from the shadows.

''Hold, eldritch creature,'' it said, and he knew the voice.

''Marr,'' Zane replied. ''You and I both live after all this time. Why am I not happier at our meeting?''

''Do I know you?'' the wizard said.

''I was in your service when I died,'' Zane said bitterly, ''but I suppose it is too much to hope that you would remember me.''

Marr touched a crystal whose facets still held a few

glimmers of light. Before Zane realized what the wizard intended, a net spun of strands of light as pale as himself burst into being, tangling his limbs.

Marr raised his staff and began incanting. "Begone. Beyond. To the death that has claimed thee . . ."

Zane felt himself sliding into the coasting realms. He struggled, ignoring the wizard's words, working his dagger free.

"War and Chance!" he shouted. "Don't forget your servant now!"

His ghost blade brightened, becoming steel, then red as if the metal was just shy of molten. The net wisped to nothing at its touch.

Marr's words ebbed to silence and he fled past Zane into the flooded cavern. The ghost turned to follow, but whatever Marr had done to him had made him sluggish and when he emerged the wizard was gone.

Rabble, he saw, was struggling with sharks that were lazily circling the boat. Zane watched for a moment, then decided that his best part would be to find help for her.

"Come on, Blizzard," he said, wondering if the horse was as weary as he. "We've got to find the others."

Blizzard heeded him, the great heart and spirit that had survived after death giving the ghost horse strength. They phased out and reappeared in the tunnel down which the rest of the company was running.

"This way! This way!" Zane cried, waving them past deceptive side corridors. "Hurry! M'lady and Hulhc and the cat are near drowning with sharks awaiting to scour their bones. You must help them!"

No one wasted breath to question the impossibility of this statement. Even Scrapper and Dog Meat appeared to understand. The heavy war horse bolted ahead and bugled furiously when the stone bulkhead halted him. Scrapper barked loudly as if to say, "We're here! We're here!"

On the other side of the bulkhead, Rabble had harpooned her first shark. The monster was half again the size of the clumsy ice boat and fought her with calculated ferocity. Its two comrades refused, in a very unsharklike fashion, to turn on their wounded fellow, but persisted in jostling the unbalanced and steadily melting boat.

Almost without thought, as if her muscles recalled a reflex long unused, Rabble sent a jolt of fire down her harpoon. The shark thrashed as its living flesh cooked from within. Rabble jabbed again and again, working the red-hot harpoon barbs through flesh, sinew, and rubbery cartilage.

When the shark's thrashing slowed, she hauled the barbed head free. Sliding on the melting deck, she made her way to the bow where, with foolish bravery, Gimp was battering a second shark on the crest of its cruising fin.

"Idiot cat," she swore affectionately. "Move it!"

Now that she had a feel for her weapon's abilities, slaying the second shark was almost easy. The third appeared to have developed some intelligence and largely remained submerged, rocking the rapidly melting ice boat.

Hulhc's magic had brought them three-quarters of the way to the Stone Door, but only the most optimistic estimate would say that they would reach their destination before the boat disintegrated.

Then they heard a steady thumping from behind the bulkhead between the cavern and the outer corridor. Bryax's voice rose over the din of wind and sharks, calling counterpoint orders between the blunt thuds.

Watching the remaining shark's shadowy form glide beneath the thin hull of the boat, Rabble swore from frustration and hoped that the company would reach them before the shark.

Thud!

"Pull her back again!" Bryax bellowed, shrugging sweat from his forehead with his shoulder. "I felt a crack this time."

The others adjusted their grips on the roof timber that they had wrenched free and turned into a makeshift battering ram.

When they had arrived at the bulkhead, the blockade had

seemed impassable. Bryax had leapt at the opening along the top, determined to get in. When he got a handhold he had discovered that the rock was merely an inch thick. Encouraged, they had set about breaking it down.

"Heave!" Bryax called. "Heave!"

This time there was a definite, solid crack. A jagged line appeared in the featureless stone, water leaking at its edges.

"Give it another solid one!" Bryax cried. "And stand ready to leap out of the way when the water bursts free."

The last hard ramming blow hit home with frustration and fear to power it. The stone shrieked as the wood hit it from one side and the water pressed it on the other.

Rabble heard that shriek with a dull certainty that help had come too late. Her burning harpoon had hastened the melting of their boat, disintegrating it into chunks of ice. Hulhc clung to one, his robes trailing in the water, his face pale and greasy with fatigue. She knelt on a smaller piece, Gimp perched on her shoulders, his claws anchored in her armor.

The shark glided in a lazy figure eight around them, apparently satisfied waiting for them to fall to him rather than risk Rabble's harpoon.

When the bulkhead finally broke, the water rushed from the gap with tremendous speed. The ice chunks rocked, tossing their unsteady passengers into the cold water. Gleefully, the shark tore into Rabble's leg, ripping a gash through her leather greave before realizing that the sudden change in environment applied to it as well.

Hulhc found the strength to keep his head above water, but Rabble and Gimp were pulled under and tossed out into the corridor, draped limply across the carcass of a harpoon-slain shark.

The last living shark smashed into the fragments of the bulkhead, jagged rock tearing open its underbelly. It contorted, tearing at its own vitals until it died, the last shudders of its fading life passing unnoticed.

The initial gush over, the water's flow was reduced to a

trickle fed by the much-reduced geysers. Dog Meat and Scrapper rushed to their mistress. The war horse gave ground only reluctantly when Angie sloshed up.

Scrapper gently picked Gimp's limp body from the ground much as she might have a newborn puppy. The cat dangled limply as the bitch shook him, then began coughing up quantities of viscous fluid. He staggered to his feet when Scrapper set him down, hissing weakly between gagging fits. Unimpressed, the bitch began a sloppy tongue bath that served both to force out more water and to infuriate the cat.

Angie worked over Rabble in a fashion that was nearly as direct, but the red-haired warrior remained unmoving. Hulhc tottered through the break in the bulkhead, leaning heavily on Rylus' arm. He watched Angie blow air into Rabble's mouth and pump out the water.

Then he creaked in a voice so tortured that it was hardly his own, "Not air—fire."

Angie didn't stop her efforts, but snapped at Bryax, "You hear him—make fire!"

Bryax looked at the sodden corridor, then, without hesitation, stripped off his cloak, the upper parts of which were dry. Kneeling beside Rabble, he struck sparks against the fabric. Tambor dropped his own cloak and then bolted outdoors, trailed by Kazu.

They returned as Bryax had gotten the first weak sparks to catch on some frayed threads. Kazu bore an armload of twigs and bracken, Tambor a saddlebag containing watch-candles and a flask of cooking fat.

Carefully nurtured, the fire grew. Tambor pulled another flask from Dog Meat's saddlebag.

"Pfneur breit," he said, kneeling to force the liqueur into Rabble's mouth. "It's as close to fire as anything liquid can be."

Without prompting, those who were not working on the wounded had taken up guard posts. An eerie feeling had descended over them all. The bulking carcasses of the sharks, the flinders of stone, the looming cavern just beyond

the bulkhead lent an unreal air to the situation. Hulhc looked
from side to side as he donned dry clothing brought from his
horse's pack.

"What are you looking for?" Iron asked.

"A voice addressed us, just before the water erupted and
again when we'd constructed our boat. I keep worrying
where the speaker is."

"I wish that I could help you," Iron said, "but we rarely
saw anyone other than Y'teera and Weatus. The voice wasn't
his, was it?"

"It was Marr," Zane growled from where he knelt in
anxious vigil by Rabble. "I know that voice, even after all
these years. Marr who was one of the leaders of the cabal.
Marr who tried to banish me lest I aid you. Fire burn him
and all his allies."

"She might, she might," Angie said softly. "Farmer
Hulhc's fire light is working. I feel breathing and a weak
pulse."

The cavern mouth was far too grim a place for anything as
hearty as a cheer, but thin smiles touched watchful faces.
Angie handed Bryax a lit candle.

"Hold this to your Sword Sister's lips. I'll clean, poultice, and patch that leg. Move horse!" She swatted Dog
Meat on one feathered fetlock. "She'll need you sooner if
you let me help her now."

The war horse lumbered back a few steps, remaining
protectively close. His ear twitched as if bitten by a fly, then
he snapped, catching something between square, white
teeth. It shrilled in a voice like a human's.

Before Dog Meat could crush his catch further, Hulhc
darted over. Not challenging Dog Meat's right of possession,
he peered at the little figure. It wore red trimmed with gold;
its form was that of dragonfly with a human's face—Weatus'
face. It was also clearly dying.

"What do you want?" Hulhc asked angrily.

"Why tell you?" Weatus' voice asked mockingly. "You
will know soon enough and regret soon enough. You most of
all, Farmer Grey Hills."

It died then and the dragonfly sparkled into dust.

"They watch us then," Bryax said grimly. "Can we take them before they do more than watch?"

"We must," Rylus said. "They will benefit more from a rest than we will. Can Rabble be moved?"

"I don't know," Angie said. "My patients usually need to breathe air, not fire. Her leg is bad, though. She'll need to be carried."

Dog Meat stomped, his iron-shod hoof striking sparks from the stone.

"We have a volunteer," Tambor smiled. "Do what you can for Rabble, Angie. I'll reset her stirrup so the injured leg can stay straight."

"And don't forget, Angie," Hulhc said softly, "that the magic to heal is here for you—even if Rabble is too weak to radiate any."

Angie nodded, but her discomfort with the concept of replacing her skill with tricksy magic was evident in the set of her shoulders. She worked on her bandaging with anxious energy and by the time Tambor had redone Dog Meat's stirrups and Hulhc had packed his sodden clothing away, Rabble was stirring.

Bryax held her so that she could lean back against his chest as he spooned *pfneur breit* into her as a more conventional invalid might be fed soup. Zane watched a bit jealously, but his envy faded when Rabble smiled at him. She picked up a candle and breathed liquorish air over the flame. It flared and her eyes sparkled brighter gold.

"I feel like a squashed fish," she said. "A very unpleasant sensation. But I feel much better than I did before. I didn't feel anything at all and that feels worse than you could imagine."

Bryax patted her. "Drink up, Sword Sister. We've still got trouble."

"And I'm good at that," Rabble said firmly. "Haul me up and give me a lean over to Dog Meat, Axe. Let's end this. Let's end these wizards' tyranny."

Her voice dropped. "Let's end . . ."

26

Every warrior knows that, no matter how well-spent, the life of a single friend is a high price to pay for victory—two friends is a price behind estimate.

Vieth

THEY STRODE into the still-damp cavern. The shark carcasses were naught but shriveled reeking skins that had melded with the stone. The spell that had generated them ended, geysers had once again been sealed beneath granite slabs.

The cavern itself was lit with many yellow-white globes, but though their light was such that the colors that veined the stone walls were easily discernable, they were not bright enough to reveal the faces of the four cowled figures who stood in a curved line before the Stone Door, a dozen or so of their followers ranked below them in double line before the stair.

Rabble, astride Dog Meat, led the Company. Scrapper on the horse's left flank, Gimp riding pillion. The rest of the defiant group ranged themselves in a double fan behind. The four warriors took the edges, the others in between.

Rylus held a cocked crossbow. Tambor leaned a hand on the shoulder of one of his bears, the golden monkeys hanging as still and silent from his shoulders as the gold earring in his ear.

Angie and even Hulhc wore indecision, wondering if their newfound magic had potency against masters of the art.

Zane and Blizzard defied the pull of Earth and balanced above and slightly behind Rabble, a storm cloud, brooding and potent.

A low hum rose from the inner line of followers, a tense sound that vibrated as if each throat produced a note flat of the one produced by its neighbor. Ruddy light followed the sound, trembling with its shifts in pitch and spreading to curtain the cowled four off from the rest. The front line extended arms forward, palms down, fingers flat. Eldritch sparks, equal parts green and gold and blue jumped from finger to finger.

Now one of the four spoke. The voice was female but not that of Y'teera. This voice was as cool and distant as an eagle amidst white clouds, its timbre the coaxing of flutes.

"If you lay down your weapons now, we shall go easier on you. Refuse and some—if not all—of you may die."

"What can we expect otherwise?" Bryax said sternly.

"What right have you to question?" the lady rejoined. "You are trespassers and effectively our prisoners here. Submit or not. I care little."

The decorous exchange continued ineffectively for several moments. The wizard giving nothing, even as Bryax framed more and more direct questions and accusations.

Under her breath, Angie muttered to Hulhc. "Something is wrong. I think she is stalling, but why? Everything she says is true—with them so arrayed against us, we will suffer if we attack. Even I can feel that this time neither their numbers nor their magic is illusion."

Hulhc frowned. "Bryax won't surrender—so he is the one who is actually stalling. I wonder if she realizes that?"

"I offer you another proposal," the sweet voice was just a touch exasperated, "since you persist in being difficult. Name a champion from your numbers to combat a champion from ours, in accord with the ancient tradition of these lands. If your champion wins, we will permit you to depart, but we will place a binding on you so that you cannot tell what you have learned about the Refting."

Rabble straightened in her saddle, ready to accept despite a wounded leg. Bryax shot her a warning look.

"Your offer is interesting, but what is the nature of this combat?" He paused. "Y'teera magically assisted Durez in his battle—this is hardly in accord with the traditional forms as we know them.''

One of the cowled figures shook with mirth and Y'teera's voice creaked from the darkened folds, ''Lots of good my help did him!''

Bryax shrugged. ''It would have done more if we hadn't been suspicious. What of it? Will magic be permitted?''

''Would you prefer that?''

''No,'' he said bluntly. ''We have some small talents among us, but the advantage would be all yours.''

''Very well, but then the one you call Rabble cannot fight for you. She is naught but a magical construct.''

Rabble flared, but Bryax raised a hand and she fell to fuming. Bryax waited to make certain that Rabble was under control, then continued. ''I can't decide issues of memory and battle without conferring with my company.''

''We will wait,'' the mellifluous voice agreed.

''What do you say, folks?'' he said, when all but Iron, who had insisted on standing watch, were gathered.

''Do it,'' Rylus said. ''I'm not sure if I want to remember any of this so win or lose, we win something.''

''Fine,'' Tambor said, ''if they keep their word, but what happens if we lose?''

''The same as if we don't try,'' Angie said. ''Do it, but watch, sharply.''

The others reluctantly agreed. By common consent, Bryax was named champion. Rabble leaned from her saddle to give him a tight embrace.

''For Luck, Sword Brother. We'll keep an eye out for treachery.'' She smiled with a touch of her usual wicked humor. ''Make certain that you know who takes your oath so that we know who to take vengeance on if they fail.''

He nodded stiffly and stepped forward.

''Before we agree,'' he called to the cowled watchers, ''with whom do I make this bargain? What is your name, lady?''

"Name?" her voice broke shrill. "That is mine to know, but you may call me Licia."

"And is that binding?" Hulhc shouted from where he stood.

"For this," Licia agreed. "I so swear, by my power as a wizard."

"I guess that's all we can do," Bryax muttered.

As Bryax strode away from the company towards the designated area, Licia gestured to one of the acolytes in the front row. His robe dropped away, revealing skillfully crafted black leather armor of a slightly old-fashioned style.

The overlapping plates were cut to give ample coverage of joints; shoulders and knees were set with curving spikes of yellow-white bone. The helm he lifted from a niche in the cavern wall was open with nose, cheek, and chin guards. It protected without concealing his face or the familiar sneer of contempt on his lips.

"Gersam'tris!" Kazu gasped. "I never would have known him for a warrior."

"Not just a warrior," Rylus said harshly. "An assassin. I recognize those blades he bears. They were used by the hired killers of Tunisha, a nation beyond the Great Salt Sea. If he follows in their traditions, then Bryax is doomed."

Bryax hefted his graceful long sword of tried steel and his battered shield. He bowed to Gersam'tris and without further formalities, the combat began.

Within a few passes, the observers could see that Bryax's shield, rather than his sword, was serving him best. Gersam'tris darted in and out with his paired blades. One was longer, meant more for stabbing than cutting. The shorter blade was broader, keen-edged. Both were equipped with wide flanges to catch and break an opponent's weapon. Only the fine quality of Bryax's gear, hand-picked booty from the fields of winning campaigns, saved him from that trick.

From Dog Meat's saddle, Rabble watched anxiously, dodging and feinting along with Bryax. To those watching, it was painfully evident that she felt that she should be in his place and every cut and bruise that Bryax took Rabble felt as if it were her own.

The wizards' party was a mirror of indifference. The five remaining in the front ranks continued to toss sparks between their fingertips. The second rank hummed tunelessly, their red haze a palpable force around them.

Of the four senior wizards, only Y'teera appeared to notice the fight at all, an occasional cackle or "Well done!" rising from her hooded form. The others stood straight and indifferent as if the resolution of the combat was already known to them.

Then Gersam'tris' blade penetrated a weakened spot in Bryax's shield, badly lacerating the Downs warrior's arm just below the arm guard. Bryax stumbled, arm limp, shield falling, blood fountaining forth.

However, Gersam'tris had put himself into unwitting difficulty for his longer blade was lodged in the shield's layered metal and wood. As he struggled to free it, his shorter blade's parry was marginally slower than it should have been. Bryax's wild sword stroke caught him a glancing blow alongside his head, sending him reeling back with a cut below his eye and without his primary weapon.

Cheers rose from every throat but Rabble's. Turning to see why she did not share their excitement, Angie saw that the red-haired warrior sat bolt upright and unmoving on her equally still horse's back. Even Gimp and Scrapper were frozen in place.

On the field, Bryax had taken advantage of Gersam'tris' fall to rip and tie a crude bandage around his arm wound, but he was unsteady on his feet. Gersam'tris advanced on him with his remaining blade, all black humor and mockery gone, replaced by lust for the kill.

Fearful of the effect a general alarm might have, Angie touched Hulhc lightly.

"Sneak a peek at our Rabble," she whispered, "and tell me what they've done to her."

Hulhc glanced over, cursed venomously. "I don't know the technique, but it's a binding of sorts—perhaps a version of the same ritual by which they entrapped the Elements. The debate, the armed contest, all must have been meant to give them time to set this up.''

"The silent ones, the wizards who have said nothing since our coming,'' Angie said. "They might be the center of the charm. Problem. We know which Licia is and which Y'teera. One of the others is probably Zane's Marr, could the other be Weatus?''

"While we whisper,'' Hulhc growled. "Bryax dies.''

The grey-bearded farmer's face wrinkled in concentration. Then a gleaming line of golden shafts, each rather like a shaft of wheat, sprang into being and separated the combatants. Angie ran to Bryax, her healer's bag thudding at her side.

"This combat is null and forfeit,'' Hulhc declaimed, "and Licia, you stand foresworn.''

There was a ripple of shock as the rest of the company heard this announcement, saw Rabble unmoving, guessed something of what had been done. Bows and arrows suddenly were held ready in several hands, the dry rachetting of Rylus' crossbow underscoring Hulhc's challenge.

"Foresworn?'' the mellifluous voice said. "I suppose, had I sworn by aught that bound me, but though the name Licia has been used for me, I am no wizard, nor am I bound by any threat to wizard's power.''

She tossed back her cowl, revealing the silver-haired beauty who had signalled the start of Vieth and Durez' duel.

"War and Chance!'' Kazu swore. "Doesn't anyone here value honor?''

She loosed an arrow from her bow. It flew toward its target, crackling into flames when it hit the red haze, but maintaining enough form and momentum to continue, true to course, and bury itself in the hollow of Licia's throat. The silver-haired woman managed one astonished wail of pain, then fell backward.

"No one,'' Hulhc answered Kazu's question, "not even among themselves. That foolish woman believed herself as well protected as those she served. Am I right?''

"She should not have unmasked," the voice they knew as Marr's said, his tone labored. Although he did not lower his cowl, he "faced" Kazu. "We have honor, but it is not as you know it. Ones like Ourselves cannot be bound by the same restraints as lesser mortals. With great age and greater wisdom comes rules to fit our greater vision."

Kazu spat. "Wise? Wisdom? Is it wise to toy with Deities? You'll get yours—that is evident enough to *my* small wisdom."

"Fool!"

Marr swept his hands outward, his sleeves flapped, the humming rose. Then sparks jetted from the fingers of the front row of acolytes. Buzzing like angry bees enveloped Kazu. She screamed, her body jerking uncontrollably. When the sparks swarmed back to their source, she was dead.

"You motherless atrocity!" Vieth howled, loosing two arrows in rapid succession before Tambor grabbed her.

The arrows flew no less true than Kazu's had, but when they reached the red haze, they vanished in a cloud of dust and foul-smelling gas. For the first time, there was rolling belly laughter in the cavern. It came from Gersam'tris.

"You think that you are something—you mortal fools. I overheard your whispered plotting, your delight in your petty magics. I suffered the indignity of my 'captivity,' playing the coward, waiting for this moment. How does it feel?"

Rylus raised his crossbow to waist level and pulled the trigger. The quarrel shot out, impacting with a dull thud on the abdominal plates of Gersam'tris' black armor. A long bow arrow might have broken, but the quarrel plowed through, only stopping when it broke rib and hit the armor's back plate.

"That's how it feels," Rylus snarled.

Gersam'tris stared down in disbelief, blood flecked his lips. He brought his own sharp-edged blade up and slashed his wrist below the gauntlet.

"Poison," he gasped. "My honor. You were very lucky, Bryax."

"War and Chance!" Bryax swore. "They're all mad!"

Angie's hands were busy with flint and steel behind the shelter of her medical bag.

"Could be, Big and Blond, but if we don't rouse Rabble, they have the power to slay us all. Might, even if we do rouse her."

Bryax leaned as if accepting further treatment for his wound. "My arm feels much better. Thanks."

"Magic." Angie breathed onto the glowing embers. "Fast but not thoughtful. Cover for me now."

Gersam'tris' death had distracted attention from more personal issues only momentarily. Kazu's corpse remained huddled where it had fallen. Tambor released Vieth with a muttered warning.

"Wait! Do you want to avenge her or end up like her?"

Vieth snarled something wordless, but she didn't attack. The remaining silent wizard faced them. He neither raised his arms nor gestured, but the power cycling around him licked whitecaps in the magic that eddied through the cavern.

"Enough," he said in a deep, commanding voice. "Fire's off-shoot struggles against the binding even as we fence. Be held, all of you. Your fates are lesser things."

When he said "Be held" each of the company's remaining members discovered that they could not speak nor move any more than to blink or to swallow. Helplessly, they could only watch as the wizard continued.

"Marr, your ghost troubles me by its petty attempts to free the offshoot. Deal with it."

"It's not my ghost, Urik," Marr said. "Nor did I have any part in its becoming what it is, but I understand."

Zane dodged the first strands that Marr cast at him, still trying to urge Rabble to alertness.

When Marr flung a comet of eldritch energies at him, Zane spurred Blizzard nearly clear of the web-work of energy that it trailed. The strands that touched either ghost scored sickly yellowish whiplash marks which sealed quickly but took some of the ghost's substance with them.

"M'lady, forgive me!" he implored as a second comet bore down on him. "Away, Blizzard!"

Ghost horse and rider leapt, but whether soon enough or not, no one could say. All that was certain was that when the comet's yellow glow faded Zane and Blizzard were there no more.

Ignoring his fellow wizard's workings, Urik turned toward Dog Meat. "Horse, come free. Then move only at my will's bidding. Apprentices, part and then seal again as they pass."

Dog Meat stirred at Urik's command and moved, but stiffly, a hobby-horse granted motion but not volition. Rabble and Gimp sat motionless on his back.

Scrapper shook as if coming abruptly awake. Seeing Rabble being carried away from her, the bitch slunk close to the war horse's flank, her good eye daring anyone to try and take her away from Rabble.

Urik did not appear to care, the tips of his fingers just visible within the sleeves of his robe as he coaxed Dog Meat up the stairs and to the Stone Door. The acolytes at the first rank built an arch of sparks for horse and rider to travel under to the second rank which parted the red haze like a curtain of insubstantial velvet and let it fall when the prisoner was through.

Then the steel-dust grey war horse stood before the great Stone Door, his rider captive in the saddle. Urik's voice held a note of surprisingly human relief when he spoke.

"Almost done. Y'teera, Marr, open the doors. You others, hold fast."

The Stone Door opened inward, pivoting with a gristmill grind of stone on stone to reveal the Crystal Lattice. Neither Zane's account nor their own imaginations had prepared any in the company for the marvel of impossible engineering that floated in the dark heart of Shadowridge Mountain.

Unsupported by chains or columns or any mundane means, the lattice spun in the air. It was widest at the center, tapering to a point at both ends, making a ten-faceted diamond shape. Each facet was outlined with braided silver and gold cables, set with long clear crystals that breathed a gleam that united the whole. Precious gems captured and mirrored the light, weaving the whole into a dazzling spectacle of concentrated magical energy.

"Stand ready," Urik said to Y'teera and Marr. "I'll need to break the binding just before we open the Lattice. If she gets free before the Lattice can claim her . . ."

A dreadful scream of pain and terror interrupted his instructions. In the cavern below, Angie was aflame. The tiny fire she had been tending when Urik had cast his hold on them had caught her long overtunic and was spreading through her clothing and up her hair.

Whether in compassion or merely in shock, Urik let his lesser binding spell cease. Bryax ran to the burning woman and enveloped her in his arms, smothering the flames as best he could. Tambor tore open a water bottle as he ran to join them, his monkeys screeching at the reek of burnt flesh and hair.

Vieth and Iron, with Rylus only a moment behind, loosed arrows into the first rank of apprentices. Two fell. One, only wounded, ran up to the safety of his fellows. The red haze clung to him and sent him to his death in a flare of blood-red light. The last apprentice threw herself down on the cavern floor, hysterically begging for someone to take her surrender.

Above, in the chamber of the Crystal Lattice, Rabble stirred. The gold flecks in her eyes overwhelmed the brown and her hair tossed as if a hot wind blew it back from her widow's peak to snap red-gold around her shoulders. The coppery sword was in her hand and no longer was it merely flame-shaped, it was aflame.

"In ancient days, on battlefields and in plundered cities burnt offerings have been made to me, but never have I tasted the flesh of one who called me Friend."

Her voice was terrible, hardly human, and the Company struggled not to fall to their knees in awe.

The red haze failed and fell as the apprentices trembled and crouched in wordless supplication. Even the wizards were shaken.

Only Rabble's three animals seemed unaffected. Dog Meat stomped a proud hoof. Gimp affectionately bumped Rabble with his head and Scrapper wagged a cautious tail, never forgetting to keep a wary eye on her enemies.

From nowhere, Zane reappeared. He thumbed his nose at Marr and then took up a guard post to one side of Rabble.

"Sword Brother," Rabble called. "Will Angie live?"

"I think so—Rab," Bryax replied, "but she's badly hurt. Can you do anything?"

"I am the fire of War," she said sadly. "I harm. I cannot heal. Which of you grovelling on the stair would earn my favor and help my friend?"

The slim hand of the woman who had surrendered rose trembling over her bent head, though her body remained prone on the floor.

"My name is Nin'chee. I have some training in healing."

"Go, Nin'chee," Rabble returned her attention to the three wizards.

The chamber filled with the sound of crackling flames. One did not need to have travelled with her from the Downs, across several seas, and through the mountain reaches to know that Rabble was very angry. Oddly, though, none of the three wizards so much as trembled. Urik raised his head and laughed mockingly.

"I suppose that you believe that we are at your mercy," he said, his voice as strong as before.

"Your retainers have surrendered or died," Rabble replied. "Your traps are sprung. Your safe-hold is breached. Yes, I believe that we have you."

The sword in her hand flashed and became a lance tipped with fire. She raised it so that the point was even with the cowled robe's hood.

"I offer you two choices," she continued, her voice even and pitiless. "Ask and I will slay you. Or you may enter into the Crystal Lattice and let those powers you have offended judge and punish you."

She raised a remnant of the cord on whose burning length she had crossed into Shadowridge. "I give you the length of this rope's burning to decide, but each must decide for him—or her—self alone. I will permit no conversation.''

With a snap of her fingers she ignited the cord. The three wizards stood, heads slightly bowed within their cowls, presumably meditating over the advantages of immediate over certain death. In the silence, Hulhc came pelting up the stairs.

Zane's whisper broke into Rabble's watchful thoughts. ''M'lady, we're being played with—I'm sure they have some trick yet.''

''I agree,'' Hulhc said between wheezes. ''There is a glow about each of them—an odd light. I don't know how to say it better, but I would guess from my readings in my father's old books that they have warded themselves in some potent and subtle fashion.''

Rabble nodded. ''Then step to where I can protect you both, but not too far. I may need your counsel.''

In the cavern below, Nin'chee continued to work over Angie, Vieth watching her with poisonous attentiveness. Iron stood where he could guard the entryway. Bryax, Rylus, and Tambor mounted the stair to the chamber, drawn despite a fear nearly primal to be at the end of what they had helped to begin.

The rope burnt to ashes. Rabble shrugged ever so slightly then addressed the wizards.

''Have you made your choice?''

''We have,'' Urik said, and with no further warning he raised cupped hands. Water fountained forth, cold and rimed with ice.

Rabble dodged, her lance hissing steam where it met the water, but not extinguishing. She drove it toward Urik's head, but when it should have penetrated the cowl a swarm of sparks barred entry, bursting forth to burn her face and hands with miniature lightning.

''Ward!'' Zane cried, his hand going through Rabble's arm as he sought to pull her back. ''I've seen the type. It's a personal protection shaped by the hidden birth name of the caster. They're unbreakable unless you know the caster's name.''

Rabble cursed, but did not follow the ghost's urging to retreat. Dog Meat was far too blocky to easily avoid the mists and water spouts that Urik and Marr kept directing her way. She was repeatedly drenched, but the aura of ambient Fire that emanated from her had protected her so far.

Her own attacks were equally ineffective. Urik's confidence was apparently not merely heroics.

Y'teera's ability to manipulate the powers had evidently been weakened by Bryax's attack in the village, but she had ability enough to summon a breeze that played havoc with archery. She cackled insanely, crowing in infantile delight when the arrows grazed her ward and crumpled into ash. Amid this exchange of blows, Hulhc spoke from the shadowed culvert in which he had taken refuge.

"I know who you are, Wizard Urik." The old farmer's voice broke. "Rue, son of Hulhc, father of Hulhc, grandfather of Adona, great-grandfather of Rue, farmer of Grey Hills."

He stepped forward and cast a large stone he held in his hand. The toss was underhand and awkward, but it struck Urik squarely in the chest.

The wizard's hood fell back revealing features not unlike Hulhc's but weirdly younger though his hair was snow white and his skin pale, blue-veined, and translucent. Urik's eyes, however, were not framed with furrows from years with only candle or lantern light. His teeth were unbroken and unstained. Age he bore, but not the harsh ravages of time. These his magical art had spared him.

Father stared at son with fear and surprise and son at father with pain and disillusionment. All other action in the chamber ceased, as if Hulhc's words had immobilized everyone present along with destroying his father's ward.

"Boy? Is that you, son?" Urik/Rue said and the similarity of his voice to Hulhc's was apparent in a way it had not been before. "Why are you here? Why are you with these people—with *her*?"

"I came to look for the magic," Hulhc said, his face flushed with anger or embarrassment. "These people are with me—Rabble is on my payroll. Father! Why did you vanish? Why did you do this to me?"

"To you? To me, you mean! My great plan a catastrophe, myself forced into an exile that I never deserved, doomed to a life-long guardianship of immense powers whose fury, if released, would certainly destroy me." The ancient eyes glittered with unshed tears. "Then in the end, to have my vigil betrayed by my own son! 'Why did you do this to me?' you ask. How could you do this to *me*?"

Hulhc reeled back. "I . . . I didn't come to betray you, Father. You *died*, remember? I came because my wife is dying and magic seemed her only hope for a cure. I came because I idolized your memory, you . . . you—liar!"

The last word bore all the hurt and anger of a child whose dreams have been scattered to dust and ashes. Urik did not notice. Mad, senile tears coursed down his pale face and he backhanded Hulhc across one grey-bearded cheek.

"Impudent whelp!" he snarled. "How dare you speak to your father in such a fashion! I'll show you what it means to cross the master of Shadowridge Mountain!"

He drew back his hand, pinching the fingertips as if eating air through them. Hulhc stood frozen, his hand pressed to the purpling mark on his face, his eyes wide with horror.

"No, Urik!" Marr shouted. "This is madness!"

"So you betray me at the last, Marr!" Urik shrieked, reangling his cast. The blot of power sped toward the other wizard. "Rorque, you forget that I know you!"

Marr raised bent arms to shield his face, but the flash of silver-grey surrounded him nonetheless and Marr fell, crisped to a shadow.

Urik spun to strike at Hulhc, a new globe of power forming in his hands, but Rabble had forced Hulhc behind her.

"War and Chance!" she roared. "This is my task, farmer! What did you hire me for if you're going to fight your own battles?"

She impaled Urik's cast on the point of her fiery lance. The energy fizzled.

"Last chance, Rue," Rabble said. "Me or the Elements!"

Urik's response was to fling himself toward her, his eyes

insane with feral hate. He died on her lance tip. Then, like Marr, his ancient body burnt to dust.

Hulhc's choked sob was the only sound in the chamber. Rabble looked down at him, pity in her brown eyes.

"I'm sorry, Hulhc. I had hoped he would choose a more honorable option. The Elements might have been kinder than he would have believed."

Nearly forgotten, Y'teera's cracked voice cackled. "You'll know soon enough. Urik alone remained of those who held the master spell that bound the lattice. It breaks apart even now! Don't run!"

Her words stopped Rylus and Tambor, who had begun leading a swift but orderly retreat.

"Immortal things have trouble seeing mortals, just as mortals have trouble seeing ghosts," Y'teera said. "Hold still and they may pass us by without notice."

So all remained as still as possible, though every nerve screamed for them to run and hide. Even Tambor's monkeys clung to him in frozen terror. And the Crystal Lattice began to shatter.

Rods encrusted with gems flew from their places on the rhomboid torus. Gems smashed into powder against floor and ceiling and walls. Precious metals ran into molten pools that were absorbed by the suddenly porous stone of the chamber. The urge to run, to hide, was overwhelming, but a new terror kept them locked in place.

Into their minds flowed a cacophony of thoughts and images, a wild inhuman debate that each perceived without understanding more than a fragment. The cacophony grew in complexity as the lattice shattered, increasing in force until all but Rabble and Zane were cringing on bent knees, hands clamped over ears or eyes as if such poor barriers could halt the invasion.

Then the Crystal Lattice was naught but a memory and the full force of each of the Elements was felt within the chamber. Earth asserted itself—male/female, growing/dying, desolate/fecund—a dichotomous mass that vibrated into the stone heart of the mountain and then vanished.

Water was a dampness that stifled breathing even as it rejuvenated parched tissues. It was the very pulse in the bloodstream and the sap in the trees; it was the Seven Lakes, the Great Salt Sea and then it, too, was gone.

Air was an insubstantial caress, a brisk bite on a winter morn, a push behind a sail. Omnipresent, yet rarely noticed, it laughed, twisted, and fled into the world.

Fire alone remained. Hot as anger, warm as a mother's hug, burning glow of sunrise, red-gold molten metal, Home and Hearth, Forge and Firmament, it hunted and touched upon Rabble. Knowing her as War and Chance, it claimed her in a burst of flame that took horse, dog, cat as well and left nothing but Zane's anguished, panicked cry, "My lady!"

27

> *Eater of Air,*
> *Devourer of Earth,*
> *Boiler of Water,*
> *Fire, hear our plea!*
>
> The Invocation of Fire

THEY KNELT there, in a chamber bereft of light, for light had fled with Fire and the wizard's globes had died with them. Slowly the members of the company came back to themselves, remembering who and what they were, rather than remaining caught in the torrent of the Elements' release.

Rylus, ever practical, was the first to find a voice. "Does anyone have a lamp or torch? I have a tinderbox."

There was a long, long pause, rustling motion, then Bryax

spoke, his voice rusty with unshed tears, "I have a candle-stub. Make a spark and I'll find you."

The remaining four clustered to the candle's pale pool of light. Wordlessly, they sought Y'teera and found her tossed and broken against one wall, impaled by a silver rod that had once been part of the Crystal Lattice. All looked at the grisly sight, but none dared comment.

Nor did anyone ask where Rabble was, for though eyes had been shut or covered with screwed fists, all had seen Fire claim her into itself and all had seen the look of regret with which she had faced her reunion with her greater self.

"Hey!" Bryax yelled, defying black silence and red-gold memory. "Vieth! Iron! Angie! Anybody down there?"

"I'm here," Vieth called back.

"Iron here."

"Angie hasn't woken," came Nin'chee's thready so-prano, "but I'm with her."

"Stay there, folks," Bryax ordered, "and we'll come to you. Link hands, now, and tap each step real careful. I want to get down before the candle gutters."

They made their way down the stair and before they reached bottom Iron and Vieth had kindled a second light from the remnants of the fire that had nearly killed Angie.

Their blaze revealed the remaining apprentices, all dead, all with an expression of stark terror on their faces. Of those who had imprisoned the Elements or sought to keep them within the Crystal Lattice, only Nin'chee remained.

Bryax glanced at Nin'chee as he gathered Angie in his arms. "Rabble kept her word. Angie looks stronger, so I guess you did, too. Come with us, away from this place."

The last wizard of Shadowridge meekly smiled and walked alongside her patient.

Rylus cursed as he barked his shin against a rock. "Has anyone—like you, Hulhc—tried magic since . . ."

"I . . . yes," Hulhc said. "There is nothing. I can feel the power—stronger than ever—but it eddies around me, not through me as before."

"So it is with me," Nin'chee whispered hesitantly.

"Let me lead," Tambor offered. "One of the bears has stayed with us through all of this and he seems to know his way."

They followed Tambor and the bear, cautiously at first, then more rapidly as earsplitting rumbles and crashes began behind them. The dark breeze brought the gritty taste of crushed stone and the smell of water.

"We must hurry," Nin'chee said. "Earth reclaims for its own the prison house. Soon nothing will remain."

The elegant village on the ledge was twisted and torn when they emerged, but in the market square where Durez had died, their mounts waited untouched, watched over by Zane and a misty rider with high cheekbones, mounted on a battered war horse, a three-legged cat riding behind, and a one-eyed dog alongside.

"Rabble!" Bryax yelled. "How?"

"Hurry!" she urged. "Mount and ride. This plateau exists on sufferance alone and that for not much longer."

They obeyed, Nin'chee taking Durez' pony and Angie in Bryax's arms. No sooner had the last hoof left the ledge than the crystal pillars that held it over the river burst into slivers of light.

Momentarily, the air was suffused with rainbows, then the ledge broke clean away and the lot vanished into a wash of clear water and howling wind.

"Some day," Rabble said, when the living had ridden as far as panic could take their exhausted bodies, "that will be a beautiful place. The Elements will reclaim it for themselves."

"But Rabble," Bryax said. "Aren't you . . ."

"Dead?" she replied. "I don't know, because I don't know if I was ever alive in the way that you are. There will be time to speak of this later. Over that hill you'll find a glen that was the site of a farm before the Refting. There's fruit on the trees, fish in the pond, and plenty of brush for the fire. Angie will come around soon and she'll need some coddling."

Later, after night had fallen and humans and animals had

been fed, Zane and Rabble rejoined the company around the campfire. In the darkness, she was less obviously changed, but to those who had her immolation seared on their memories, she was an eerie presence—far more so than Zane, who they had never known any other way.

"How much do you remember after Urik—Rue—died?" Rabble asked.

"Enough," Hulhc said, his face gaunt and despairing. "My father's death broke the last hold on the Elements. They are free, but the magic is still gone."

"Is it?" Tambor said. "I still feel this—rapport—with my beasties, as solid as before."

"Wizard's magic has indeed been blocked," Rabble said, "but traces of natural magic remain, just as the Elements themselves do. These may even become stronger with time."

"But Rabble," Bryax said, "I don't care about any of this. What happened to you?"

"Well, Sword Brother, I'm what's left over," she answered with a wry grin. "Zane is a ghost because some of his spirit persisted when his body was slain. I'm what's left after Fire reabsorbed War and Chance. I guess that through the experiences and thoughts of my brief 'life' I became more than just a fragment of an Element.

"My life, as it were, remained after Fire incinerated the body and took War's fire into itself. Now, I'm really 'just Rabble.' Zane found me and brought me around—me and my beasties. Had he not, no doubt we would have dissipated after a little while. Now we can keep Zane and Blizzard company. They've had a lonely time since the Refting."

"And us?" Angie said. "Will the Elements let us go?"

"I can't see why not," Rabble said. "They don't exactly feel gratitude, but they don't feel that you are any danger to them either—even with what you know. I expect that you'll find the world will change, but magic will never be what it was before the Refting."

She knelt before the brooding Hulhc. "You didn't fail, Farmer Grey Hills. Nor did you betray your father. Go home to your family and see to the harvest."

"But my wife," Hulhc said. "I failed her. I wanted magic to cure her. Why does she deserve less than those who lived before the Refting?"

"Death still came then," Zane said. "Only the wizards believed that it could be put off indefinitely and they paid the price when they believed, too, that they had become more than human."

"But, to address your immediate concern," Rabble said cheerfully. "You saved your wife before you ever left the Downs. Those herbal remedies that you asked Angie to compile for her provided the cure. She's been on the mend and her only remaining illness is anxiety as to whether you will ever come home."

"I will!" Hulhc said, dour features brightening. "Home and Hearth, I will! Have you known this long?"

"Only since this." She gestured over her ghost form. "Zane showed me how to travel and I left long enough to find some answers for you all."

The smile Rabble turned on her friends was warm and oddly loving.

"Rylus, Elejinor is dead. Cenai a'tal reigns in the Domain of Dragons with the full support of the people. You and Tambor should have no trouble regaining your wagons and the other trims of the Spectacular. Iron, you should find a receptive court to hear the charges that Vieth must still bring before you. Be true to your honor and I suspect all will go well."

"I will remember your words," Iron said steadily. "Thank you, lady."

"Just Rabble," Rabble said gently. "Ever and now . . . just Rabble."

"You don't plan to come with us, Sword Sister?" Bryax asked anxiously.

"No, Axe." Rabble actually seemed cheerful. "If Hulhc will forgive me my contract, I will move on. The world will be awakening to its new magic. Ghosts would hinder, not help you. Perhaps someday you will find me again."

"Go, Rabble, I release you," Hulhc said, his voice choked, "and be happy being 'just Rabble.'"

"I hope to be." She smiled at them all.

Rabble swung onto Dog Meat's saddle and set Gimp on her lap. Scrapper wagged a fond tail. Zane swept off his hat and bowed.

Then they vanished.

28

That we found a welcome in the Domain of Dragons—the same place from which your mother and her soldiers had chased us away—proves something, but I am not clever enough to say what.

Bryax

WHEN THE Travelling Spectacular headed back into the lowlands, Bryax stayed in the Domain of Dragons with Vieth, who understood him far better than he knew. Iron, too, remained, having concluded that his welcome in the Domain of Roses would be more forgiving after some time had passed.

In Bookhome, the Travelling Spectacular again took passage on the *Bolla Fifteen*. Captain Betram Bolla was delighted to see them all—but especially to see Angie. In his company, she lost the somber air that had clung to her since her burning. At the end of the voyage, he had little trouble convincing her to remain with him and satisfy her wandering spirit before the mast.

Nin'chee agreed to take Angie's place with the Travelling Spectacular and, though she was not a Far Shore's Healer, she had a certain insight into healing that some claimed was near magical.

In the company of the reduced Travelling Spectacular, Hulhc went home to Grey Hills Farm. He never told the complete story of his summer wanderings to any but his wife. All his family and friends agreed that he was a changed man, with his hopes now set on the future rather than trapped by visions of the past.

Rylus and Tambor took to wintering at Grey Hills Farm, delighting young and old alike with the Spectacular's tricks and trappings. However, when spring sent the farmers into the fields, they harnessed up their wagons. In later years, young Rue went with them as they began their leisurely journey north. Along the way, they took passage on various Bolla ships, visiting with Angie, and ending always in the Domain of Dragons.

There, looking from Dragon's Spire into the wild mountain lands, they would tell Bryax, Vieth, and Iron how the world was changing as magic crept back into people's lives and belief in the Elements and all their deific forms took on new firmness.

Balancing one or more of his children on his knees, Bryax, in turn, would tell variations of a local legend, a legend of two ghost riders, accompanied by a cat and a dog. Seeing them, the wise folk said, was a guarantee of perfect weather the next day, for the sky behind the riders would be red, as if Fire burned in the mountains.

About the Author

Jane Lindskold is the author of four previous novels published by AvoNova. She is also the author of a scholarly biography of Roger Zelazny, and is completing two novels begun by Zelazny before his death in June 1995. Dr. Lindskold currently lives in Albuquerque, New Mexico, where she writes, gardens, bead weaves, and collects reproductions of carousel animals.